A WANTON
MURDER... A
MALICIOUS KGB
MOLE... AN
ANGRY
DANGEROUS
AMERICAN
PRIMED FOR
VIOLENCE AND
REVENGE!

J. C. POLLOCK
Author of *MISSION M.I.A.*

PAYBACK

PRAISE FOR THE NOVELS OF J. C. POLLOCK

MISSION M.I.A.

"Vivid and believable . . . taut adventure."

—*Publishers Weekly*

CENTRIFUGE

"Pure combat adventure coupled with permanent attitudes of the Vietnam experience . . . [to satisfy] a desire for an almost effortless adventure with lots of combat action."

—UPI

CROSSFIRE

"First-rate . . . the accuracy of this book in terms of special-warfare techniques and mechanics is so good it could be used as a training manual."

—G. Gordon Liddy, *U.S. News & World Report*

Also by J. C. Pollock

THE DENNECKER CODE

MISSION M.I.A.

CENTRIFUGE

CROSSFIRE

J. C. Pollock

PAYBACK

A DELL BOOK

Published by
Dell Publishing
a division of
Bantam Doubleday Dell Publishing Group, Inc.
666 Fifth Avenue
New York, New York 10103

ISBN: 0-440-20518-2

Reprinted by arrangement with Delacorte Press

Printed in the United States of America

Published simultaneously in Canada

July 1990

10 9 8 7 6 5 4 3 2 1

RAD

ACKNOWLEDGMENTS

A special note of thanks to Susan Olsen for her patience and kindness in sharing her rather extensive, in-depth knowledge with me.

Also, an apology is in order for causing her to take a wrong turn and lose her way, missing an important appointment while answering some of my inquiries on her mobile telephone. For that I am truly sorry. For all of her accurate, detailed, and invaluable information, I am profoundly grateful.

For Tom and Odette Worrell—Pass it on.

PROLOGUE

Nordhausen, East Germany
December 1988

The wind buffeted and tore at the parachute canopy, tossing it erratically about the night sky. Captain Larry Manes swung wildly in his harness, a pendulum gone mad. His hands held the steering toggles in a death grip, fighting for control as gusts up to fifty miles an hour drove him toward the swift-flowing river five hundred feet below.

Stealing a frantic glance over his shoulder, he searched the sky for the rest of the team. Two of his men were a few hundred feet above him, locked in the same deadly struggle. The fourth man was nowhere in sight, having plummeted past moments before, his parachute hopelessly tangled. Manes had watched anxiously as the young Special Forces sergeant, with only seconds to spare, cut away the main chute and deployed his reserve; still out of control, he was swept downwind toward a distant ridgeline.

The tightly knit operation plan was coming apart at the seams. It was Murphy's Law at its worst, starting shortly after takeoff from the mission's launch site in West Germany. An electronics malfunction aboard the aircraft had gone undetected, causing a navigation error that resulted in the jump master releasing the infiltration team off course, miles from the intended drop zone. Manes realized it upon exiting the aircraft. The rolling countryside passing beneath him did not match the terrain features of the satellite photographs he had studied. Deteriorating weather was further complicating matters: the winds at the lower elevations were much stronger than the mission planners had predicted, and a snow squall had developed during the team's descent from thirty thousand feet.

Manes's goggles began to fog, and his vision was blurred by the driven snow. As the ground rushed toward him he fought to maintain the delicate balance between panic and the positive force of the adrenaline surging through his body.

A crescent moon filtered through a thin layer of clouds, casting a pale, eerie glow over a dense pine forest that ran to the river's edge. His eyes strained as he scanned the snowy terrain for an opening. Any opening. Just large enough to squeeze his stocky frame into and avoid being blown into the trees or the dark, icy water. He saw the lights of a village off to the north, and in his peripheral vision he spotted open fields, upwind and hopelessly out of reach.

Three hundred feet from the ground he got a brief reprieve. A lull in the wind provided a few precious seconds to gain a semblance of control before another powerful gust rocked him in the direction of the river. At two hundred feet a low, rounded hill to his left broke the force of the wind, and then he saw it: a small clearing, no more than thirty feet square, just short of the river. Calling on all of the experience and technique gained in over seven hundred jumps, he steered for it.

Pulling down hard on his left toggle, he descended in a tight spiral. He was late in flaring his canopy to decrease his rate of descent and landed with a bone-jarring jolt that sent him tumbling across the clearing into the base of a tree at the water's edge. Momentarily stunned, he quickly regained his composure and got to his feet. Shrugging off his harness and pack tray, he glanced up and watched helplessly as a horrible drama unfolded before him.

Despite a frenzied attempt to stay aloft for the few additional seconds it would have taken to reach solid ground, the first man landed in the middle of the river. He bobbed to the surface only to disappear again as the swift, treacherous current caught his parachute and pulled him under, carrying him to his death beneath an ice ledge extending out from shore.

The second man landed in the water but closer to the bank. He managed to unfasten the chest strap and pull the quick-release devices that allowed him to shed his parachute and harness. Swimming with short, powerful strokes, he angled for shore.

Manes plowed through the knee-deep snow, barely maintaining his balance as he ran along the bank. He shouted against the wind, trying desperately to throw his teammate a rope. But the dark swirling water pulled the hapless soldier out of reach and into the main channel, sweeping him farther downstream, beneath the same ledge that had claimed the first man.

Manes stopped running and dropped to his knees, cursing as he stared at the point in the river where his friends had disappeared, the anger and frustration raging inside him. He forced these crippling emotions to the back of his mind as he focused his thoughts on the mission and the fourth member of the team—and the top-secret equipment the man carried with him. Finally he shouldered his rucksack, took his bearings, and headed toward the distant ridgeline where he had last seen the young sergeant.

The cold wind stung his face as he emerged from the dark recesses of the forest and trudged through the deepening snow. He skirted a field near the base of a hill, paused to check his position, then moved on. He carefully searched the heavily wooded hillside where he had seen his teammate descend, crisscrossing the ground and scanning the thick evergreen canopy above. As he neared the top of the ridge a flash of light drew his attention back down to the field he had skirted; another light winked in the darkness, and another. Someone was tracking him.

Faint voices carried on the wind drifted through the forest

as the East German Army patrol spread out and moved slowly up the side of the hill, their flashlights probing the deep shadows. Manes unslung his weapon and glanced about for a place to hide, immediately dismissing the gut instinct upon realizing that his footprints, clearly visible in the mantle of snow now covering the ground beneath the trees, would lead the patrol directly to him. Glancing in the direction of the voices, he considered the bleak possibility that his remaining teammate had already fallen into the hands of the men following him and that continuing his search could result in his own capture.

He crossed swiftly over the ridgeline to the far side of the hill and stopped beneath a towering spruce to choose a line of march through the valley below. Forty feet above him, concealed from Manes's view in the upper branches, the young Green Beret sergeant dangled in his harness, his neck snapped by the impact of his uncontrolled descent into the trees. Still attached to the sergeant's load-bearing equipment by a twenty-foot lowering line was a forty-pound canister in a specially padded pack tray and carry bag. It was lodged in a crotch of the tree. Thick intertwining limbs below made it all but invisible from the ground.

Manes moved down the hillside and distanced himself from the approaching patrol. With the team radio at the bottom of the river, his only hope of reporting the details of the failed mission was to evade and escape back to the mission support site in West Germany. He could well imagine the mounting tension in the operations center at the MSS when the initial entry report failed to come in. Keeping to the edge of the forest, he jogged at a steady pace until he reached a rail line he knew led to the border. While he stopped to rest near a trestle spanning a deep ravine, he heard the sound of a train before it rounded a curve a few hundred yards farther up the tracks.

He let the engine pass before he broke cover and ran alongside the slow-moving freight, keeping pace with an open boxcar as it reached the trestle. He grabbed a handhold on the side of the car and tried to swing his body up and through the open door. His gloves, frozen and stiff, caused him to lose his grip—first one hand, then the other as he fought to stay on his feet, finally stumbling and falling, his upper body landing beneath the wheels of the train.

His chest was crushed and he was dragged to his death before his boot snagged on a crosstie, tossing him out from under the train, where he bounced off the side of the trestle. He fell silently. The force of the wind, in a powerful updraft, momentarily suspended him in midair; then floating slowly downward in an almost graceful spread eagle, he disappeared into the depths of the ravine.

1

New York City
Ten Months Later

Manhattan's Upper East Side, with some of the most desirable and expensive real estate in the world, is a glamorous and exclusive enclave for the wealthy, influential, and celebrated. Luxuriously housed in security high rises and fortified town houses, they are, for the most part, insulated from and impervious to the harsh realities surrounding them.

Nipper Denton's niche in this chic and fashionable neighborhood, his home for the night, was a bird-shit-stained bench along the stone wall bordering Central Park. Bundled inside a damp, grimy furniture blanket stolen off a moving van that morning, he was barely recognizable as a human form. A light drizzle that had started around midnight, then changed to a fine mist, had mercifully stopped. Nipper was chilled to the bone, shivering uncontrollably as he tugged at the collar of one of the three tattered coats that helped insulate his scrawny body. A gnawing hunger had kept him awake most of the night despite the pint of Mad Dog 20/20 he had sipped slowly to get numb and warm while carefully avoiding getting drunk and senseless and unable to react to the ever-present dangers of living in the street.

Outside his foul-smelling cocoon, the raw October night held the threat of the coming winter, a harbinger not lost on Nipper or the other bench dwellers and homeless wretches scattered along the tree-lined sidewalk and throughout the park. The time was fast approaching when their miserable nights would be spent on steam grates or in subway tunnels, anywhere warmth was to be found. And there were always the shelters, but Nipper hated them. Hated the rules, and the stink, and the fact that when the lights went out it was everyone for himself. He had even stopped going there for meals, preferring to panhandle, believing that if he hung around with the crazies who gathered there he would end up just like them. The street wasn't any day at the beach, but at least he had a measure of independence and could pick and choose the company he kept.

It was just past four o'clock in the morning when he pulled back a corner of his blanket and peeked out at Fifth Avenue's glistening, rain-slicked pavement. He glanced up at the trees, their autumn color lost in the darkness, or anemic under the harsh, sterile light from the streetlamps. A car streamed by and out of sight, and Nipper cast another, wistful glance that lingered on the soft warm glow of an eighth-story window in an apartment building across the street. Probably some rich pervert insomniac, Nipper thought. Got a telescope trained on the park . . . hoping for a rape or a mugging . . . wouldn't think of helping or dropping a dime to the cops. Fuckin' creeps!

Clutching the blanket at his throat, he sat up and looked over his shoulder, beyond the wall to the wooded knolls just inside the park, where he knew others were having an equally fitful sleep, their senses half alert for the predators who roamed the shadows. The sick ones were the most dangerous; the psychos, motherfuckers, beat the shit out of you, torched you for the fun of it. It was relatively safe on the benches, though; the bright streetlights discouraged all but the complete wackos. But you could never feel too safe, that was when they got you. Like they got him three nights ago, beating him senseless and robbing him of the fourteen dollars it had taken him a week to save. The constant violence was bad enough, but when it happened to you, when it was all over, there was no one to tell about the pain, no one to listen, no one who cared. He winced as he gingerly touched the long, half-healed scab across the bridge of his nose.

A liquid cough rattled deep in his chest as he felt under the bench for his sign—a square of cardboard hand-lettered in crayon that read "Even as you did it to the least of them my brothers so did you do it to me—Donations accepted." The sign was wet, but still serviceable, and he shoved it back under the bench, reminded that it had earned him a grand total of three dollars and twenty cents the previous day. He decided he'd put a new message on the unused side in the morning, knowing he hadn't gotten it quite right anyway, and besides, the guilt trip wasn't working, they weren't going for the human-bond bit. He needed something upbeat, promising, more appealing to the affluent passersby, who studiously averted his best pathetic gaze. It seemed the more humbly he solicited, the more invisible he became. He needed to make them think their money might make a difference—maybe a con like that slimy bastard down near the bookstand with the dog, a sign around the mangy mutt's neck, lying that he needed to go to the vet, even taught the son of a bitch to limp on command. Good scam, though.

But Nipper knew there was a fine line when working this neighborhood, an unwritten, though well-defined, code of behavior. You didn't make trouble, you stayed out of everybody's way, you shuffled, made yourself as unobtrusive as possible while still bumming enough to stay alive. Up here only so much was tolerated before the cops found an excuse to scoop you up and put you in Bellevue's nut ward. The more bizarre and deranged of the street people, the screamers and mumblers, those who talked aloud to no one in particular in words that were incomprehensible, knew enough to avoid the Upper East Side if they valued their freedom. And despite his appearance, Nipper wasn't crazy, and he wasn't stupid—having had a good job before the booze got him. He wanted no trouble with the cops and was careful to stay on the acceptable side of the line, not wanting to be locked up or banished to the less lucrative and even more dangerous parts of the city.

He wrapped the blanket tighter around his neck and tried to come up with a new message. He rummaged around in his outer coat, sorting through his pocket litter: a cigarette butt, a sliver of soap wrapped in a soiled handkerchief that served as a washcloth, part of a day-old pastrami sandwich and a piece of an onion bagel found in a garbage can behind a deli. He searched for his crayon, feeling secure only after finding it. Then, fishing out the half-smoked cigarette, he lit it, drawing the stale smoke deep into his lungs. Another cough shook him violently.

One block east and three blocks south of Nipper's bench, a New York City police car moved slowly along Madison Avenue. Officers Mike Concannon and Betty Fauzio were halfway through an unusually slow night of assisting medical emergencies and responding to calls from citizens who seemed more than a little lonely and suspiciously vague when questioned about their assailants. Fauzio chalked it up to a full moon. Concannon, with twelve years on the job, suggested a reason was superfluous, all things considered. Fauzio was thankful it wasn't like the previous night—vividly recalling the greasy, gray-green shapeless lump that used to be a human being she had helped fish out of the East River. It had been her first "floater." She shuttered involuntarily at the memory of pieces of rotted flesh that had fallen away as they pulled it into shore with grappling hooks.

But compared to her previous assignments, working the Nineteenth Precinct was preferable. The diversity of calls could range from a dead bag lady under the Fifty-ninth Street bridge to a burglary at some movie star's luxury apartment to dealing with demonstrations at foreign consulates. And the added stress of being responsible for protecting this elite neighborhood, with the potential for messing up a delicate situation involving a bigwig, had its pluses. There was always the possibility of busting a professional

burglar breaking into a multimillionaire's town house. A
collar like that, if it helped clear up other unsolved burglaries in the area, and with letters of gratitude from influential
neighbors, could do a lot for an officer's career. Her partner,
Concannon, saw it differently. Having run afoul of a few
wealthy, arrogant residents and scofflaw diplomats who had
caused him problems, he was hoping for a transfer to a
precinct with a lower profile.

Concannon shifted his huge frame behind the wheel and
glanced laconically about as they cruised the nearly deserted
street. Madison Avenue was as unique for what it lacked
when compared to other parts of the city as for what it had.
No spray-painted street-gang graffiti defaced the storefronts;
none of the "riot Renaissance" look of less affluent neighborhoods. The display windows of the outrageously expensive shops and exclusive galleries were not obscured by steel
gratings or chain link. The local residents enjoyed window-
shopping during the evening hours, and the shopkeepers
were not about to deny them a pleasure that invariably resulted in sales the following day.

The fact that most of what Officer Fauzio saw in the passing windows was well beyond her means—though she
would have done far more justice to the designer clothes
than most of the women who bought them—did not diminish her enjoyment in imagining what it would be like to own
them. She smiled inwardly, admiring a particularly attractive leather coat, then tucked an errant strand of dark auburn hair back under her cap as her trained eyes again
moved slowly along the sidewalk. Concannon slouched
deeper behind the wheel, sipping coffee from a Styrofoam
cup as they continued up the avenue.

Nipper Denton was drifting into a half-sleep when the
approach of a speeding car snapped him awake. Momentarily blinded by a flash of headlights, he averted his eyes
and blinked, then looked back to see a gray limousine with
darkened windows hiss by on the wet pavement. It

screeched to an abrupt halt and skidded into the curb not fifty feet from where he sat. The rear door facing the park flew open and a woman tumbled out, landing with a dull thud on the cobbled sidewalk at the base of a tree.

Nipper squinted into the shadows beneath the tree. The woman's skirt was bunched up high on her thighs; her legs, from the knees down, dangled over the shallow curb into the gutter. And they were nice legs, Nipper couldn't help noticing as he continued staring. And they weren't moving.

The limousine stopped for only a few seconds, then roared off, heading south, not about to honor the red light at the intersection of Sixty-ninth Street less than a block away. Nipper saw the white Porsche pull out from the cross street and slam on its brakes. He saw the limousine swerve defensively just as the small sports car broadsided it, sending it up onto the sidewalk. The crumpling of fenders and the tearing of metal echoed off the buildings and out into the park. The unrelenting blare of a car horn tore through the night as the driver of the Porsche slumped over the steering wheel.

At the intersection of Sixty-ninth Street and Madison Avenue, Officers Concannon and Fauzio heard the crash and caught a glimpse of the accident. Concannon came alive. He hit the sound and light switches under the dash, stomped the accelerator, and spun the wheel of the blue-and-white hard as he sped west on Sixty-ninth Street toward the park. The siren whooped and wailed and the red roof light flashed as Fauzio radioed Central and concentrated on her responsibility as the nondriver—her eyes expertly sweeping the sidewalks, alert for unwary pedestrians who might step into the path of the car.

Still deep in the shadows of the park bench, Nipper Denton surveyed the accident scene. The nose of the Porsche was embedded in the front end of the limousine, which had slammed into a tree. He saw the driver of the limousine force open his dented door and get out, apparently uninjured. A tall, blond-haired man in a black raincoat threw open the rear door facing the sidewalk. He climbed out and, closing the door behind him, cast a quick glance in the direction of the patrol car fast approaching the intersection. He paused to say something to the driver of the limousine, pointing an admonishing finger at him as he spoke. Then, crouching low, he ran across the sidewalk, vaulted the stone wall with the grace and ease of an athlete, and disappeared into the park.

Concannon cut the strident cacophony of the siren as he pulled to a stop behind the tangled vehicles. Nipper Denton got to his feet and, taking his blanket and cardboard sign, moved farther down the sidewalk for an unobstructed view. He stopped in the shadows and watched the two cops get out of the car, their hips laden with the hardware of their profession.

Nipper stared at the woman's body near the gutter, then back to the cops. "Fuck this shit," he mumbled, and slid over the wall, taking cover in a thicket of brush behind a fallen snow fence just inside the park.

Concannon looked into the Porsche's open window. The driver was groaning, only half conscious.

"You hurt bad?" Concannon asked, the scent of fine leather reaching him as his eyes searched the interior of the car.

"My head . . ." the driver whispered.

Concannon carefully moved the dazed man off the steering wheel, quieting the car horn, and rested him gently against the back of the seat.

"My neck . . . I think I hurt my neck too."

"There'll be plenty of time to build your case later, sport," Concannon said. "Just stay quiet for now, we'll get you some help." Turning to Fauzio, he said, "Call an ambulance for this guy. I'll check out the limo."

Viktor Kirilenko, uninjured and only slightly shaken from the collision, leaned against the rear fender of the limousine. He looked toward the park, then quickly back as Concannon reached his side.

"You okay?" Concannon asked, his wary cop eyes assessing the squat, solidly built man.

"I am not injured," Kirilenko answered stiffly, with more than a trace of a Russian accent.

"What's your name?"

Kirilenko made no response.

"Your name, pal. I need your name, driver's license, and registration for the vehicle."

Again, Kirilenko remained silent.

"What's your problem?" Concannon asked, tensing slightly at the man's behavior. He was clear-eyed and had no visible injuries, but something about him wasn't right. Behind the calm, collected facade he seemed unusually nervous and frightened.

"The ambulance is on the way," Fauzio said as she approached from the rear of the limousine. "But I think we have a situation here."

She motioned with her head and Concannon followed her to the back of the car, keeping one eye on Kirilenko.

"Diplomatic plates," Fauzio said, gesturing to the license plates.

"Shit!" Concannon said, staring at Kirilenko, who stared silently back.

"Get the sergeant over here while I try to talk to this guy . . . and run a make on the plates," he added, wanting to know to whom the limousine was registered and if it had been reported stolen.

Concannon returned to confront the Russian while Fauzio made the radio call and checked on the driver of the Porsche. The sound of an ambulance could be heard in the distance, no more than a few blocks away.

"Are you a diplomat?" Concannon asked Kirilenko, only to face more stoic silence. "Look, you already blew any chance at a deaf-and-dumb act, so how about a little cooperation?"

"Sergeant's on his way," Fauzio said as she walked slowly

around the wrecked cars. "Central's checking out the plates."

She leaned into the open front door of the limousine and checked behind the sun visors and inside the glove compartment for any personal or vehicle identification.

"No ID or registration papers," she called out to Concannon.

From the front seat Fauzio shone her flashlight into the back. There was a woman's taupe leather shoulder bag in one corner. She continued playing the light over the rest of the rear compartment, then suddenly stopped and held the beam steady. On the plush carpeted floor near the rear door were a woman's shoe and a pair of panties. An acrid coppery scent came from a dark, wet smear on the beige leather door panel. She backed out of the car.

"Mike, I think we might have more than a run-of-the-mill fender bender." She opened the rear door and, shining the light in, let her partner see for himself.

Concannon turned back to Kirilenko, whose eyes again belied his calm demeanor.

"Hey, pal," Concannon said. "I need some answers here. You talk to me now, show me some ID, or things are going to get a little unpleasant."

Fauzio left the limousine, her flashlight probing the shadows as she moved slowly along the sidewalk.

"Oh, Christ!" she said, stopping abruptly at the sight of the woman's body a short distance away.

One of the woman's shoes was missing, and her skirt, hiked up around her thighs, showed she wasn't wearing any underwear. "Mike," Fauzio called out, "you'd better read him his rights."

Moments later Fauzio's radio came to life and told her something she did not want to hear. The limousine was registered in the name of the Soviet Mission to the United Nations, and it was not reported as stolen.

She knew chapter and verse of the "Patrol Guide" procedures involving diplomats. Properly identified, they were not to be detained and were to be extended every courtesy and consideration. But the driver of the limousine had not properly identified himself and she had found no State Department "Blue Book" inside the car. Until there was some confirmation that he indeed had diplomatic immunity, Officer Betty Fauzio fully intended to treat the man now stonewalling her partner as a principal suspect in what appeared to be a homicide.

A few hundred yards from the accident scene, inside the wooded confines of Central Park, three young Puerto Ricans huddled at the entrance to a pedestrian tunnel beneath an overpass where East Drive ran through the middle of the park. Their minds on other matters, they had paid little attention to the sounds of the collision and the police siren on Fifth Avenue.

Hector held the remnant of a joint between the nails of his thumb and forefinger and pulled the last of the sweet-smelling smoke into his lungs.

"Come on, man," he said to his friend Jesus. "It's four in the fuckin' morning. We're not gonna get no more action."

Miguel nodded in agreement, though a sharp look from Jesus quickly changed his vote.

Jesus was a legend in his East Harlem neighborhood. Handsome, with dark wavy hair and a smile that sparkled, he was tough and street smart, a born leader. He sometimes worked the singles bars just below Ninety-sixth Street—the DMZ, as it was called by the Yuppies who lived on its border. He dressed well and was charming enough not to be spotted for what he was while sizing up his mugging victims, always waiting for the right prospects, then following them when they left. But he had gotten greedy and sensed that some of the bartenders were getting wise to him. So he had switched tactics, gone back to basics until things cooled down. And despite the anxiety and reluctance of his two friends, he had led them on their first foray to the Upper East Side.

"You wanna stay low-life spics forever?" he had chided them. "You wanna live with rats and roaches, beat people over the head who ain't got nothin'? We got abilities, man, talents, and down there's where the money is. And they don't put up no fight. They know better, no percentages. They're rich, they got insurance, so they just hand it over and hope you don't cut 'em up."

And so Hector and Miguel bought into Jesus's dream. And the night had gotten off to a promising enough start with Jesus snatching an elderly woman's purse just off Central Park West that netted them eighty-five dollars. But it had deteriorated rapidly into the rolling of three bums for a total of a little over eight dollars, taking some of the glow off the great adventure.

"Nobody worth a shit's walkin' through the park this time of night," Hector said.

"We give it another hour," Jesus snapped. "Some guy who lives on the West Side could be screwin' somebody's old lady who lives on the East Side and be headin' home through the park before the neighbors see him."

Hector accepted the logic and nodded in agreement. "Okay. Another hour."

Jesus and Miguel moved back through the tunnel, taking their positions at the far end, twenty yards from where Hector climbed a boulder to sit astride a large bronze statue of a sled dog overlooking the path to the tunnel.

Nikolai Malik stood in the darkness on a wooded rise inside the park, watching the proceedings at the accident scene. He got the sense of what was happening and smiled smugly, secure in the knowledge that Kirilenko was following orders. A few bums who had been sleeping nearby were awakened by the commotion and moved to the wall to watch, but none were aware of Malik's presence.

His pulse had quickened when the lady cop shone the light on the body of the woman he had shoved out of the limousine; he still felt some of the excitement at the thought of how easy it had been to simply pull up to the curb, grab her, and shove her into the backseat. She had tried to fight, until he hurt her. After that, with a few more timely applications of pain, it had been easy. He relished his time with this one and wished he could have prolonged it. She was beautiful, with an excellent figure, still firm, and it had gone well. She had done everything he told her to do, exactly the way he told her to do it. She even made the right sounds, just as he instructed. His thoughts returned to the accident, and he silently cursed Kirilenko for his stupidity and lack of composure in speeding away from the scene—an entirely unnecessary response. He failed to understand how Alipov could have assigned such an incompetent to him—an insidious voyeur who stole glances through the rearview mirror from beginning to end.

When the ambulance and another patrol car arrived Malik left his place of concealment and followed a path to the west side of the park. He felt a lump rising on his forehead where he had struck it on the divider partition in the limousine. He took out his handkerchief and dabbed at it. It was not bleeding, but he kept pressure on it in hopes of containing the swelling. He continued along the path, admiring the beauty of his surroundings—the glow of the lamplights on the wooded walks and the glittering display of lights from the towering skyscrapers bordering Central Park South in the distance. How different it was from Moscow. How much more free and diverse, and uninhibited.

From the sled-dog statue Hector watched the paths that converged in front of him. He was tired, cold, and hungry, and eager to get back to the familiar sights and sounds of his own neighborhood. Everybody spoke English down here, and they all dressed like the dummies in those fancy store windows. He just wanted to get back to Theresa; today was his nineteenth birthday and she was giving him a party this coming evening.

The echo of distant footsteps snapped him out of his reverie and he shifted his position for a better view in the direc-

tion of the sound. His eyes locked onto a tall blond man in a
dark raincoat rounding a bend in the path and heading toward him. Surrounded by darkness and having knocked out
the light in the lamppost near the statue earlier, Hector felt
secure and in control as he carefully sized the man up.

He was tall, bigger than him and Miguel, and Jesus. But
he was holding a handkerchief to his head. A drunk, maybe,
who had fallen. But he seemed steady on his feet and moved
like he was in shape. And he didn't look over his shoulder
nervously, as though he was uncomfortable walking in the
park at night, a sign of weakness that would have marked
him as an easy target. Maybe he was just a dumb hick tourist who didn't know no better, but Hector didn't think so as
he continued watching. On any other night a predator's instincts would have cautioned him to wait for another victim,
one smaller, older . . . but Jesus wanted one more score,
and Hector wanted to get out of this foreign land.

Malik and Hector had seen each other at the same moment, though the Russian, having caught the flicker of
movement atop the statue despite the deep shadows, gave no
indication, never broke stride. Putting his handkerchief back
in his pocket, he casually unbuttoned his raincoat, letting it
hang open as he walked. His senses heightened as the adrenaline began to flow, and his eyes scanned the area, looking
for the most likely ambush site. He guessed the tunnel just
past the statue, and headed for it with no discernible ac-
knowledgment of the man he was keeping within his field of
vision.

Hector sat motionless and, he thought, undetected as
Malik passed beneath him and continued down the path.
When his quarry was partway into the tunnel Hector dis-
mounted the statue in a fluid catlike movement and fell in
behind him—the signal to his friends that would trigger the
mugging. His sinewy body was coiled and ready as he took a
switchblade from his jacket pocket and flicked it open.

The unmistakable sound caused Malik to smile—the urban Cossack had committed to his course of action; his com-

rades would show themselves at any moment if they were good at what they did. His attention was now on the opposite end of the tunnel, thirty feet away, as he walked casually toward it in an unsuspecting manner.

Jesus and Miguel appeared suddenly out of the darkness, their slender frames silhouetted by a lamplight a short distance behind them. They moved forward with a slow, cocky swagger, and the sound of two more switchblades, opened almost in unison, resounded off the brick interior.

Malik stopped midway through the tunnel and moved off to the side, placing his back against the wall as the three young men converged on his position.

Hector stopped short of him, a few yards to his left, and Miguel an equal distance on his right. Jesus stood directly in front of him, only a few feet away, and raised his deadly stiletto, pointing it at Malik's face.

"Hand it over, man, or I'll cut you open," Jesus said. "Everything you got—money, watch, rings. I want it all."

Malik stood with his hands in the pockets of his raincoat, his face an emotionless mask in the dim light that reached them from the tunnel exit.

"I don't think so," he said, with no hint of an accent flawing his perfect English.

"Don't fool with us, man," Jesus said, his tone more ominous. "Hand it over, *now,* or you'll take one of your eyes home in a piece of cotton." A threatening motion with the switchblade added further emphasis.

Malik shrugged a cooperative gesture. He took his hands from his raincoat and slipped the right one inside the tweed sport coat, as though reaching for his billfold in the chest pocket. With lightning-quick reflexes he withdrew the .22-caliber automatic pistol from his shoulder holster. Before Jesus could react the tip of the silencer screwed onto the end of the barrel was only inches from his head.

"Hey, man, I was only—" was all Jesus got out before two sound-suppressed rounds tore into his left eye socket, dropping him to the ground in an instant. A split second later two more rounds, placed with equal accuracy, penetrated one of Miguel's eyes with the same deadly result.

"No, man. No!" Hector pleaded. "Don't shoot." He dropped his knife and tried to turn and run, but his muscles, rigid with fear, wouldn't respond. He simply stood there, frozen in place, transfixed by the weapon pointed at his head.

"Please! I'll never do it again. I won't say nothin' to nobody. I swear on my mother, man." He was crying now. "Hey, come on, man. Today's my birthday. I'm only nineteen years old."

His wide, expressive eyes continued to plead as he swore a silent oath that if only somehow he could get out of this alive, he would never leave East Harlem again. But it was not to be. The man before him was unmoved, his face devoid of compassion. Hector and Miguel and the mighty Jesus were not only out of their territory, they were, in the case of Nikolai Malik, completely out of their league.

"Happy birthday," Malik said softly, squeezing the trigger two more times.

The last thing Hector saw before the rounds ripped into his head and felled him like a young sapling before an ax was the small, cruel smile on the face of the man standing before him.

Calmly putting the pistol back in his shoulder holster, Malik exited the tunnel and followed a path in the direction of Central Park West, again admiring the beauty around him and enjoying the scent of the crisp fall air.

With the increase in activity on Fifth Avenue, Nipper Denton had moved even farther into the park, finding some high ground where he could not be seen and still watch most of what was happening.

What had started as a police car and an ambulance responding to a minor traffic accident had now become a three-ring circus. The first ambulance had taken the driver of the Porsche to the hospital, and another ambulance pulled up; the Emergency Medical technicians, in their white smocks and green pants, carrying black satchels, conducted a second cursory examination of the woman lying in the gutter, reconfirming what the cops already knew. She was dead.

Three more squad cars had arrived, and traffic was detoured around the crime scene. A twenty-man task force of detectives was brought in from Borough Command to canvass the area. One detective copied down the license numbers of the vehicles parked along the avenue in the immediate vicinity while another questioned the cop stationed in a "box" down the street, outside the residence of the Yugoslavian Mission, but he was too far away to have seen anything. Other detectives conducted a door-to-door inquiry of the high-rise apartments with a view of the crime scene, hoping to find someone who had been awake at the time of the accident.

A sense of morbid curiosity fixed Nipper's gaze on a member of the Crime Scene Unit, who, in the process of gathering forensic evidence, took a slide smear from the dead woman's vaginal area and placed plastic bags on her hands to preserve any microscopic bits of hair or flesh under her fingernails. Another man took photographs from all angles, and another meticulously drew a chalk outline around the body.

Moments later the green windowless van, known as the "meat wagon," arrived from the Mortuary Division. Two attendants dressed in green coveralls put the corpse in a body bag, loaded it in the van, then left as quickly as they had arrived.

A well-dressed middle-aged man, who, Nipper judged by the deference paid him, was in charge, moved away from the growing throng of reporters and mobile television news crews contained behind a hastily erected barricade.

Captain Ed Maguire was not in the best of humor. Not only had he been awakened from a much-needed sound sleep, he could see the handwriting on the wall with this case. He stopped to say something to a young uniformed officer, who immediately put strips of tape on the diplomatic license plates to keep the press from seeing them.

Officers Concannon and Fauzio stood by their patrol car as Maguire approached. Kirilenko was sitting in the rear seat, his hands cuffed behind his back.

"Did the driver of the Porsche shed any light on this mess before they took him to the hospital?" Maguire asked, stopping in front of the two uniformed officers.

"No, sir," Concannon said. "He was pretty much out of it from the knock he took on the head."

The captain gestured toward Kirilenko. "Has he said anything yet?"

"Nothing, sir," Fauzio replied.

"Did you toss him?"

"The patrol sergeant did a body search, sir," Fauzio said. "No identification of any kind on his person or in the limousine."

Maguire leaned in the open window of the blue-and-white and stared at Kirilenko. The captain's bent nose and lopsided face suggested a demeanor that was contrary to his even-tempered personality. The tough-guy appearance came from a lack of a defense against a left hook during a stint on the Marine Corps boxing team in his youth and later to a collision with a windshield during a high-speed chase.

Kirilenko stared blankly at the man looking in the window.

"One more time," Maguire said calmly. "Are you a member or employee of the Soviet Mission to the United Nations or a relative of anyone assigned there?"

Kirilenko's only response was to look away from the captain's steady gaze.

"Do you have diplomatic immunity?"

Kirilenko continued to look away in silence.

Maguire straightened up to face Concannon and Fauzio. "Take him back to the station house and put him in the cage. As far as I'm concerned, he's a John Doe, and I don't want him sent down to Central Booking until the DA gets a chance to try to talk to him. Understood?"

"Yes, sir," Concannon and Fauzio answered to Maguire's back as he marched off in another direction.

Nipper Denton continued watching until the Emergency Services trucks drove onto the scene. The highly specialized unit began to set up floodlights and comb the area, searching for any physical evidence the Crime Scene Unit may have overlooked. Nothing escaped their scrutiny—sewers, garbage cans, every nook and cranny within reasonable distance. It was when they trained their bright lights on the park and began moving in Nipper's direction that he silently left his vantage point and disappeared into the night.

2

Lieutenant Bill Rafferty was a tough, hard-charging old-school cop who evoked images of stakeouts, coffee in Styrofoam cups, and unfiltered Camel cigarettes. His hairstyle, with the exception of the length of his sideburns, hadn't changed in twenty years, but like most of the Nineteenth Precinct's detectives, he dressed better than average owing to the class of people with whom the job brought him in contact—garish triple-polyester sport coats with hang-glider lapels were too conspicuous in the land of Gucci loafers and Armani suits.

He had opted for the middle-aged preppy look this morning, choosing his blue blazer and gray slacks, his daughter's favorite. His borderline good mood vanished at the sight of Deputy Chief Polikovic waiting in his office. He glanced at his watch; it was seven-thirty. He was a half hour early and now regretted not having gone for his morning run, a routine that not only kept him in acceptable physical condition but helped prepare him for the tension and stress that went with the job. And having a deputy chief from Borough Command, with whom you had locked horns on more than one occasion, waiting to greet you first thing Monday morning, fell under the category of stress and tension.

Polikovic sat in the glass-partitioned office skimming over a handful of reports. He spotted Rafferty in the squad room, got up and poured two cups of coffee from a coffee maker perched on top of a filing cabinet; he handed one to Rafferty as he reached the door. An appraising glance at the blazer and slacks, with a questioning pause at the choice of an orange- and green-striped tie, brought a conditional nod of approval from the deputy chief.

He pointed at the small sign prominently displayed on Rafferty's cluttered, messy desk, which read, "A Tidy Desk Is the Sign of a Sick Mind."

"If there's any truth in that," the deputy chief said, "you've got to be the most mentally stable man I know."

"I have my moments," Rafferty said.

With his idea of perfunctory social amenities over, Polikovic immediately launched into the details of the homicide investigation that he was now dropping in Rafferty's lap. Rafferty listened with a growing distaste for what he was hearing.

"The assistant district attorney just left. He didn't get anything more than the uniforms who were first on the scene." He jerked a thumb toward Kirilenko, who was sitting on a bench in the detention cage at the far end of the room, and added, "We still have no idea who he is."

"Has anybody called the Soviet Mission?" Rafferty asked.

"They've been informed that one of their cars was involved in an accident, that we have the driver in custody, that he's refused to identify himself and is at least a material witness to a homicide, if not the principal suspect. The guy that answered the phone just listened and said they'd get back to us."

"He couldn't ID the driver?"

"He didn't ask for a description, or even acknowledge that the limo was signed out. It was five-thirty in the morning when we called. My guess is he doesn't know. Probably some low-level staffer with the weekend graveyard shift stalling until he can check with the general," Polikovic said, referring to the senior KGB officer with the Soviet Mission.

"That's not like those bastards," Rafferty said. "They usually have someone here ten minutes after we call."

"It's possible the driver wasn't alone. My guess is he's protecting someone, and the Russians want to talk to that someone first, before they get their boy out of here. Anyway, it's your baby now. That's the victim's shoulder bag on your desk with the preliminary reports."

Polikovic turned to leave, adding, "Proceed with caution, Bill. If you don't get any feedback from Intelligence or the Russians within the next few hours, then send him downtown and book him as a John Doe."

The deputy chief paused at the door and again gestured toward the wire-mesh detention cage. "You believe the balls on that bastard, dumps the body right on Fifth Avenue, didn't even bother to use an alley." He marched out, casting one last baleful glance at Kirilenko.

Rafferty looked out into the squad room and caught the eye of one of his sergeants pecking away at a battered manual typewriter. He motioned for him to come in.

"Take a Polaroid shot of the guy in the cage and have a uniform run it over to Intelligence, see if they can come up with a match," Rafferty told the sergeant, making a note to call them.

The Police Intelligence Unit, through liaisons with the CIA and FBI local offices and the State Department, kept extensive files on all persons with diplomatic immunity in the city. All sixteen thousand of them, Rafferty thought bitterly. Thirty-eight foreign mission residences in the Nineteenth Precinct alone. The largest diplomatic community in the world—foreign officials, their families and staffs—immune from every criminal and civil law. In his twenty-two years on the job he had seen those crimes run the gamut from acts of terrorism, rape, child molesting, murder, drug smuggling, spying, to the more mundane acts of shoplifting and parking in tow-away zones. They committed at least one felony a week in the city, and the cops were powerless to do anything about it. Their arrest records disappeared at the

request of the State Department, and the guilty walked, seldom if ever punished by their own government officials.

Rafferty recalled one case in particular—the son of a minor official with the Bolivian Mission to the United Nations.
A rapist who had left eleven victims in his wake. It had
taken almost a year of intensive investigation to find him,
and he was cut loose, walked out of the station house a free
man minutes after six of the women he had raped positively
identified him. Rafferty had made a point to be at the airport
the day he was being sent back to his own country—the
only concession his government had made. The young man
had spotted him and flashed an arrogant smile as he
boarded the plane. Two months later he was back in the
city, living in the same neighborhood where he had raped at
will.

Rafferty's stomach soured at the thought of what they got
away with, a reaction not uncommon to any cop who had to
deal with them. The State Department, to avoid inviting
reprisals on our own diplomats in the offender's country,
exempted what amounted to the population of a small town
from the rules of civilized behavior.

He had the sinking feeling that the man in the cage, murderer or not, would be back on the street before the day was
out. From the victim's leather shoulder bag on his desk he
removed a wallet and an address book. A laminated United
States Army dependent's ID card in the wallet identified her
as Katherine Simpson Gannon, married to retired U.S.
Army Lieutenant Colonel John Edward Gannon and resid-
ing in Fayetteville, North Carolina. The card gave her address and birth date—she was thirty-eight years old.

His gaze lingered on a snapshot of her, and a man he
assumed to be her husband, on a deserted beach. She was a
strikingly beautiful woman, what Rafferty considered aristocratic good looks. There was another photograph, a wallet-
sized print from a posed studio portrait of a ruggedly handsome man in an army class "A" uniform—the same man in
the beach photo. A green beret sat at a jaunty angle on his

head and his chest was adorned with five rows of colorful
ribbons. A Combat Infantryman's Badge was pinned above
the decorations and master jump wings below them.

Rafferty put on his glasses and examined the small photo
closely. He recognized the Vietnam campaign ribbon, one,
among others, he himself had been awarded for his two
years in-country during the early years of the war. The Purple Heart the man wore had three oak-leaf clusters, indicating he had been wounded four times. A Silver Star and a
Bronze Star for Valor with two oak-leaf clusters stood out,
but one of the ribbons, more than all the others, held his
attention, as much from respect as from professional interest. It was an award few men had received, and of those who
had, fewer still lived to wear it. The small white stars on a
field of light blue told all anyone needed to know about a
man's character. It was the Medal of Honor, the nation's
highest military award for valor.

He next paged through the well-worn address book, skimming over the entries written in a small, neat script. An
underlined number caught his attention: "Jack's number at
'the Ranch'—919-555-2436." An older number with the
same designation had been scratched out above it. Rafferty
leaned back in the rickety wooden desk chair, rubbing his
eyes and pinching the bridge of his nose in an attempt to
relieve the tension that was building. He hated this part of
the job, the calls to the victim's family. But who knew, the
husband could be the perp, although he seriously doubted it.

Under normal circumstances he would have had the department's Communications Division send a teletype to the
local police, who would then locate and advise the family of
the death, telling them to call the investigating officer for
further information. But after looking again at the photograph of the victim's husband, he dialed information in Fayetteville, getting the telephone number of the Gannon residence. He let the phone ring for a long time before hanging
up.

When he dialed the number for "the Ranch" the telephone was answered at once by a man who simply repeated the number in a no-nonsense tone. Gannon was not there; could he take a message? Rafferty left his name and number. The clipped, brusque voice on the other end said, "Yes, sir, I'll have him call you," and hung up.

Rafferty picked up the preliminary reports on his desk and began reading and making notes, his thoughts interrupted by the recurring image of the man in the photograph. "Shit," he muttered under his breath, and stared out across the room at the man in the cage.

3

Fort Bragg, situated in the heart of North Carolina, is the largest army installation in the world. It covers 135,000 acres and has over four hundred miles of roads, twenty-eight miles of railroad, numerous ranges and impact areas, and seven drop zones, which see an average of 146,000 parachute jumps a year. It has a post population of 124,000 personnel and is home to the XVIII Airborne Corps, the Special Operations Command, and the headquarters and training schools of the Army's famed Special Forces. Its annual operating budget, including military pay, exceeds one billion dollars.

Tucked away in a remote corner of the sprawling base, with extensive security measures protecting its perimeter, is a highly classified 550-acre compound that officially does not exist. The large, low-slung modernistic building that dominates the compound is the new headquarters, operations center, and training facility for Delta Force, the nation's elite counterterrorist unit.

Completed little more than a year ago, it is a far cry from the unit's former make-do quarters in the old Fort Bragg stockade. Referred to as "the Ranch" by Delta personnel, it is uniquely suited for their specialized brand of training, which includes free-fall parachute jumps of pinpoint accuracy from thirty thousand feet, storming buildings and mock-up aircraft with live ammunition and live "hostages," the use of high-tech optics and highly sophisticated man-portable satellite communications equipment, special-purpose demolitions, seemingly endless hours of combat and sniper shooting, assault tactics, high-speed and specialized driving, small-boat and SCUBA insertions, hand-to-hand combat, free-climbing techniques on buildings and rock faces, and any other skill—from driving trains and heavy equipment to refueling aircraft—deemed necessary for a given mission. It is a constant, rigorous, and demanding training schedule that prepares the highly dedicated troops for operations that include deep-penetration raids, intelligence gathering, hostage-rescue missions, and VIP protection.

Jack Gannon had been with Delta from its inception in November of 1977. Although he had retired a year ago on his fortieth birthday, with twenty-two years of army service, he had come back to work for the unit in an advisory capacity as a civilian with the title of Operations and Intelligence Specialist. As he sat in the mess hall eating his usual breakfast of chipped beef on toast—the infamous "shit on a shingle"—he watched the troops arrive. They had changed from civilian clothes—their "uniforms" when not at the Ranch—and now had on the olive drab one-piece jump suits they wore during their daily training. Civilian-style haircuts and a casual dress code were all part of a deliberate design to make them blend in with the population at large, particularly in the event of clandestine deployment to a hot spot where their special skills were needed.

A small smile creased the corners of Gannon's mouth as he studied the way they, to a man, carried themselves. Even, he noted, the two members of the Australian SAS temporarily assigned there as part of an international cross-training program that incorporated most of the world's counterterrorist units. He thought of it as an air of supreme self-confidence bordering on the constructive side of arrogance, a mind-set necessary for the harrowing work they did, and an

attitude that went with living on the cutting edge, where you
could expect to be under fire on any given day. They were
men of above-average intelligence, emotionally stable, all
possessing the almost inhuman physical stamina needed to
make it through a recruitment, selection, and training process with physical and psychological demands so punishing
and grueling that it wore down all but the very best. It was
not unusual for only two to four men out of a class of fifty to
finish. More times than Gannon cared to remember, an entire class had washed out of the program.

Despite its current efforts to add another squadron of
troops to the unit, Delta had not, and would not, lower its
standards one iota. Consequently, the self-esteem and enormous sense of accomplishment that came with the end of a
man's probationary period, following his initial training,
when he was finally accepted into the unit, was something
that would stay with him for the rest of his life.

Few people understood how effective and professional
Delta was. Out of an absolute necessity for secrecy, not one
of its many successes had seen the light of day. Only its rare
failures had received any publicity. And when the blame for
those failures was wrongly attributed to the troops instead
of where it belonged—with bureaucratic ineptitude and
planning doomed to disaster by interservice rivalry among
turf-conscious generals and admirals, each wanting a piece
of the glory, the integrity of the mission be damned—Delta
took the blows in silence.

Gannon, as a member of the assault team tasked with
taking the embassy and freeing the hostages on Rice Bowl,
the code name for the raid on Iran that resulted in the trag-
edy at Desert One, was painfully aware of where the finger
of blame should be pointed. The only positive result of that
hastily organized and improvised mission, he felt, was the
subsequent formation of a fully integrated and coordinated
counterterrorist capability to make certain it never happened again.

Gannon's pride in the unit, and his respect for the men

with whom he served, was what brought him back to work as a civilian. The 150 "shooters," as the assault teams and snipers were called, along with an equal number of support personnel, were among the finest troops in the world. A caliber of men who, if Delta were disbanded, their mission and exotic weapons taken away, could say with complete honesty, "Give us a week, sir, and we'll be the best artillery unit in the world." Or anything else they set their minds to, Gannon believed, for at the core they were the most outstanding group of NCOs with whom he had ever had the privilege of serving.

The faces were mostly young now; in their twenties, Gannon never failed to notice. In the beginning most of the men had a common background: multiple combat tours in Vietnam with Special Forces and the Special Operations Group. But the war had been over for thirteen years and most of the original members had retired or left the Army. And the torch had been passed.

Gannon washed down the last of his breakfast with coffee and walked out of the mess hall, nodding to a few of the men in response to the familiar "Morning, Boss" greeting they still gave him despite his now-civilian status. Descending the stairwell to the lower level, he tapped out some numbers on the cipher-locked door to the operations center.

"You got a message, Jack," Tom Halstead said as Gannon was about to enter his office. Halstead, a young-looking lieutenant colonel with a tough, angular face, was the current operations officer, one of the few remaining "old-timers." He had succeeded to this position when Gannon retired. "The call came in about twenty minutes ago," he said, handing him the memo.

Gannon glanced at the name and number on the slip of paper. "You know this guy?"

"Never heard of him."

"Wonder how he knew to call me here?"

A photograph of Gannon's wife brought a smile to his face as he waited for someone to answer the number he had dialed. Kate had only been gone three days, but he missed her, and always did whenever they were apart, which was a lot less now that he was no longer on active duty. And she was due home this evening, he reminded himself, scribbling a note to make sure he wasn't late for her flight.

"Lieutenant Rafferty here."

"Jack Gannon returning your call, Lieutenant."

There was a brief silence, then: "Mr. Gannon, I'm sorry to have to inform you that your wife was the victim of a homicide in the city last night. It would be best if you came to New York immediately."

Gannon sat stunned in disbelief. He continued staring at the photograph on his desk, unable to speak.

"Mr. Gannon?" Rafferty said.

"Yeah. Are you sure there hasn't been some mistake?"

"I'm afraid not," Rafferty replied. "How soon can you come into the city?"

Again Gannon hesitated, still not accepting what he was hearing. "Homicide? You mean she was murdered?"

"Yes."

"Why would . . . who'd murder Kate? How did it happen?"

"We're not sure. We can discuss that when you get here," Rafferty said. "Do you have any idea when that will be, Mr. Gannon? We need you to identify the . . . to identify your wife."

"You mean it might not be Kate?"

"We have every reason to believe it is. But we do need positive identification."

The finality of the man's tone told Gannon he was grasping at straws. "I'll be there as soon as I can. Today." He hung up the telephone, his gaze still fixed on the photograph as it began to blur from the tears welling in his eyes.

Halstead stuck his head in the door. "You want to take a look at this satellite photo from . . . What's wrong, Jack?"

Gannon looked up and simply shook his head.

Halstead entered the office and stood beside him. "Hey, buddy, what is it?"

"Kate," Gannon said, his voice just above a whisper.

"She have an accident?"

"She's dead."

"Ah, Jesus, Mary, and Joseph," Halstead said, his empathy for his friend sincere and heartfelt. "What happened?"

"She was murdered," he said, barely getting the words out. "I got to go to New York. Right away."

"I'll line up one of our aircraft. You'll be there in a couple of hours." Halstead placed a consoling hand on Gannon's shoulder. "Jesus, Jack. I'm sorry. I'm really sorry."

For the first time in his life Gannon felt incapable of making a decision, even unable to move from where he sat, feeling numb, as though his own life was being drained from him.

"I guess I can leave my car at the . . . or I could just . . ." His voice was weak and distant. His thoughts disoriented. "I need some clothes . . ."

Halstead had known Gannon for twenty years, fought beside him in Vietnam on numerous suicidal reconnaissance missions behind enemy lines where every moment could have been their last, and had never seen him lose his composure under any circumstances. He brought Gannon a cup of coffee and sat in the chair opposite him.

"I'll take you by the house on the way to the airstrip," he said, and dialed the number for Delta's aviation element at nearby Pope Air Force Base.

Gannon nodded and continued staring at Kate's photograph, completely unaware of Halstead's conversation until his friend pulled him to his feet and ushered him out of the office to the questioning looks of the other men in the operations center.

4

If Tom Driscoll's instincts were right, the seemingly unrelated message from the CIA's New York City office was the first break he had had in four months of overseeing the most extensive manhunt in the history of the Central Intelligence Agency. The report was a tenuous connection at best, the information from the police and coroner's office was preliminary, sketchy, but it was Malik. He could feel it. The psychotic son of a bitch had finally surfaced.

Driscoll reread the report as Nancy Edwards, the analyst who had brought it to his attention, looked on.

"It was on my desk with the overnight cables when I came in this morning," Edwards said. "A rape/murder isn't the usual diplomatic incident, and it fits the 'possible sex offender' flag on Malik's behavioral profile. But there's no mention of anyone else being with the driver, Viktor Kirilenko."

"What do we have on him?" Driscoll asked.

"Nothing that indicates he's in any position to sign out one of their cars for his own personal use," she said, scanning a computer printout she had run on Kirilenko. "He's on the staff at their UN mission, entry-level KGB, been there a few weeks. Has a wife and two children back in Moscow. Too new to the game for us to have anything in depth. But he does have diplomatic immunity."

Driscoll glanced at the police report, then at his watch. It was 8:20 A.M. "The Soviet Mission was informed of his arrest at five thirty-five and they still haven't picked him up?"

"As of fifteen minutes ago he's still in custody. But he hasn't been booked."

"No way in hell that driver was out by himself at that hour of the morning," Driscoll said as he stared across the room, his agile mind sorting through possible scenarios. "Their staff drivers are virtually sequestered in the mission or at Glen Cove when they're not working.

"Follow up with the coroner's office and the cops, get me everything they have," he told Edwards. "And see if State and the FBI have anything more on Kirilenko."

"What about the victim . . . Katherine Gannon?"

"Complete background check—family history, political affiliations, any connections to known terrorist organizations, no matter how remote. You know the drill. I doubt you'll find anything questionable about her, but I want it all laid out before I take it to the DDO."

Edwards hesitated as she turned to leave. "Am I missing something here? We've been spending an inordinate amount of time and manpower looking for this guy. The effort's out of all proportion, considering we have nothing that links him to any current KGB operations."

"You know what I know. The DDO wants to be kept abreast of his activities," Driscoll lied, remembering the Deputy Director for Operations' exact words to him: "Find the bastard, fast, or we'll both be working as gate guards."

The DDO and Driscoll were the only two people outside the National Security Council who knew the impetus behind the urgent search for Malik. The operation had a classification higher than top secret, carrying an SCI designation—Sensitive Compartmented Information—Code Word "Viper." The bigot list was more restrictive than any in the history of the Agency and specific code-word access was even limited within the NSC.

"Come on, Tom. Why the full-court press?" Edwards

probed again. "Before this incident cropped up I honestly believed Malik had been taken out of circulation and recalled to Moscow. And that look on your face says there's a lot more going on than you're telling me."

Driscoll shrugged. "I don't know any more than I've already told you. Now get on it and keep me posted."

He feigned further interest in the report until she left the office. He knew that his denial hadn't fooled her for a second. She was the best analyst on his staff and too intelligent and intuitive to believe that the massive effort to find Malik was powered by nothing more than the DDO's need to satisfy his curiosity about one KGB officer's whereabouts.

Out of his desk safe he pulled a thick file folder and removed an eight-by-ten blowup of a photo taken of Malik three years ago in Teheran—the most recent photo the Agency had of him. A hard Slavic face stared back. The eyes were riveting, dark brown, almost black, with diamond points at the back. A thin, cruel mouth turned up at one corner in an ironic half-smile. The sight of him made Driscoll's skin crawl. He had spent months compiling the information in the file and knew as much about Malik as anyone outside of the KGB, probably more than anyone other than his direct superiors. And what he knew evoked a conflict of emotions—as a fellow professional there was a genuine, albeit grudging, admiration for the man's mastery of the craft of intelligence.

Though there had never been any direct contact when Driscoll was in the field—sometimes missing him by days, sometimes only by hours, but always finding himself picking up the pieces following one of Malik's missions directed against Agency operations and assets—Driscoll considered him the most resourceful, cunning, and dangerous KGB officer he had encountered in his eighteen years with the Agency. Elusive, instinctive, moving with swift precision, he left behind a stunning list of bloody successes, with no one who could positively identify him as having been involved or even say with any degree of certainty that they had seen

him. He had constructed such an intricate labyrinth of cut-
outs that there were those who believed he was more than
one person or someone who existed only in theory.

Few men possessed his skills or used them as boldly, Driscoll had to admit, and yet he could feel only disgust and
contempt for Malik's complete lack of moral fiber, his cold-
blooded, ruthless indifference in carrying out his assignments, and his sociopathic tendencies, which Driscoll believed led him to brutally murder at least three women in
the past two years—four if the woman in New York proved
to be his work. His background left no doubt about the
genesis of his unusual abilities. If the Soviets had a social
register for KGB aristocracy, Nikolai Petrovich Malik
would head the list. His grandfather had been a deputy in
the Extraordinary Commission to Combat Counterrevolu-
tion, Speculation, and Sabotage, a mouthful in any language, which became known by its acronym, CHEKA, the
forerunner of the KGB. Its first chief, Felix Dzerzhinsky,
invented mass arrests and mass executions, enforced the
Great Famine and collectivism, set up the forced-labor-
camp system, had Leon Trotsky assassinated, and facilitated
Stalin's rise to power. Malik's grandfather had been his
right-hand man. His father had had an equally distinguished, if somewhat less grizzly, intelligence career, rising
to the position of Chief of the Operations Department of the
First Chief Directorate of the KGB before dying of a heart
attack in 1972.

Malik proved a worthy successor. He entered the KGB
training school at the age of fourteen and was soon singled
out as an exceptionally gifted student. He excelled in
tradecraft and became fluent in German, English, French,
Italian, Spanish, and Farsi. Pulled from the school shortly
after his eighteenth birthday, he resumed his training and
education on a one-to-one basis under the auspices of Directorate "S" of the First Chief Directorate—the KGB's elite
"Illegals" directorate.

Directorate "S" functioned independently of the other directorates and conducted the most secret and sensitive of the KGB's operations. Its officers knew no territorial boundaries, and though supported and controlled by an "S" Directorate officer—known as a Line "N" man—in Soviet missions and embassies around the world, they held no diplomatic immunity and had no discernible Soviet ties. They were deadly chameleons, their training and ear for languages enabling them to switch nationalities at will. With multiple sets of stolen or forged non-Soviet passports and documents, they changed identities and disappeared into the very fabric of a chosen society. Given elaborate cover stories thoroughly prepared over a period of years and backstopped to infinity, they were virtually indistinguishable from any citizen of the country they infiltrated. No mission was beyond their purview, whether a one-time assassination or a long-term infiltration involving the organization and control of a parallel network of local agents to carry out Moscow's instructions.

Malik, at the age of thirty-eight, was already a legend among his peers. Illegals' identities were unknown to each other and to all other KGB departments. Still, rumors of Malik's shadowy presence and daring exploits circulated throughout the intelligence community. Only a month ago Driscoll, in an attempt to pick up his trail, had taken part in the debriefing of a KGB defector who, even after being securely tucked away in an Agency safe house in Virginia, refused to acknowledge Malik's existence, let alone discuss what little he knew of him. It was the first time Driscoll had ever heard one KGB officer express such abject fear of another who was not his immediate superior. Such was Malik's reputation.

His specific area of expertise was exploiting international terrorist organizations for the purposes of the Soviet Union. His most recent known accomplishment was a well-conceived and planned operation that delivered fissionable nuclear material, stolen from a research center in Belgium, to Libya for use in their fledgling program to build nuclear

bombs. There was "soft intelligence" information of his involvement in a series of terrorist bombings throughout
Western Europe aimed at civilian targets, and conclusive
proof, as far as Driscoll was concerned, that he had ferreted
out and killed an extremely productive, highly placed CIA
asset within the PLO. Other recurrent rumors linked him to
various terrorist activities funded with drug money and
weapons smuggling in Central America and Mexico. Then,
six months ago, they suddenly stopped, along with all sighting reports. He had vanished, pulled back and gone under
deep cover for reasons that, once discovered by the Agency,
had touched off the current manhunt for him.

As the Agency's expert on Malik and head of its
Counterterrorist Group, the task of finding and stopping the
Soviet agent-assassin fell to Driscoll. CTG, as the group was
called, was formed after the failed Iran rescue mission, its
purpose to provide the assault forces of Delta and SEAL
Team Six with intelligence information on terrorist activities. With a comprehensive computer data bank on terrorists, a staff of highly skilled analysts, and access to the
CIA's thousands of intelligence assets, it virtually assured
that no mission would fail for lack of local agents to provide
timely and accurate on-the-scene intelligence anywhere in
the world. As the CTG's mission expanded into organizing,
training, and advising counterterrorist forces for friendly
Third World governments, this work was carried out by former SEAL and Delta Force personnel under contract to the
CIA. Later, an action arm, a small unit of "trigger pullers,"
was added for highly sensitive "surgical" raids, giving the
group a limited paramilitary capability.

Driscoll had spent five years with the action arm before
his promotion and transfer to Langley. His new position was
a step up the ladder, a career move, but boring by compari-
son. The assignment to conduct the urgent search for Malik
made him feel alive and vital again. He threw himself into it
in his usual manner—with a vengeance that grew more intense with each new revelation of the man's background.

The photograph on the desk reminded him that it was the first time in his career he had let it become personal, something the DDO had noticed and warned him against. People like Malik had that effect on him, on anyone with a shred of decency in them, he thought as he closed the file and put it back in the desk safe just as Nancy Edwards appeared in the doorway.

"I've got some background on Katherine Gannon," she said. "More to the point, on her husband. We have a rather extensive in-house file on him."

"And . . . ?" Driscoll prompted impatiently.

"And you're not going to like it; it raises a lot more questions than it answers."

5

Sergei Alipov blended in perfectly with the Monday-morning crowd jostling and weaving its way along East Sixty-seventh Street. From his manner and dress it would have been easy to mistake him for a typical New Yorker on his way to work. But if anyone were to ask, he could properly identify himself with diplomatic credentials as the Soviet Union's deputy permanent representative to the United Nations. He was, in fact, the highest-ranking member of the KGB in New York City. A major general, known as the *rezident,* he controlled over three hundred KGB officers operating under diplomatic cover out of the Soviet Mission and the United Nations in what was their most important and productive intelligence-gathering and recruiting area in the United States.

Unlike his predecessor, Alipov did not confine himself like a hermit to his eighth-floor mission apartment or to the Soviet estate at Glen Cove, Long Island. He took an active part in as many operations as his duties allowed; his distinguished looks, surface charm, and warm demeanor contributed to his high rate of success in recruiting new agents and assets. Unknown even to his fellow KGB at the mission, he held an even more important and secret post—he was the Line "N" man for the "S" Directorate's Illegals.

As Alipov approached the mission he slowed his pace and

returned a nod of recognition from the uniformed New York City policeman stationed, for security purposes, in a booth on the sidewalk near the entrance to the compound. The Nineteenth Precinct station house, directly across the narrow street, was temporarily vacant due to extensive renovations—renovations that Alipov knew would include the installation of the latest in communications intercept equipment by the FBI's counterintelligence agents, who maintained an observation and listening post on the top floor. He cast an appraising glance at the progress on the building; the work seemed to go on forever with nothing being accomplished.

The Soviet Mission, originally built as an apartment house, was now a warren of offices and small private apartments for diplomatic personnel and staff. As a result the building was often heavy with the scent of cooking—borscht and cabbage being the most pervasive—and it was not uncommon to encounter diplomats' wives, laden with bags of dirty laundry, in the elevator on the way to the basement laundry room.

The two Soviet guards at the bulletproof glass door inside the mission stiffened to a more correct posture at Alipov's approach and quickly pressed a button to open the inner door. Alipov brushed past them, ignoring their greetings, preoccupied and still hung over from a weekend seminar at a lodge in the Adirondack Mountains where he had been invited to address the Soviet-American Friendship Society. Although he considered such idealistic groups as no more than the "useful idiots" that Lenin had branded them years ago, he found them fertile ground for recruitment. And despite having drunk too much (something he had promised himself he would not do) he had made significant inroads with a politically naive physicist from Princeton University targeted months before as a susceptible candidate. "Make them friends before you make them traitors" was the tradecraft dictum, and he was in the process of doing just that.

On the seventh floor Alipov went directly to the *referentura*—the code and communications room—to check on the weekend cable traffic. He pressed the button hidden behind the light fixture outside the unmarked outer door and tapped his foot impatiently until the buzzer allowed him access to a small anteroom, where he was identified through a peephole set in a steel door. An armed guard swung the heavy door open and Alipov entered the soundproofed suite of rooms, where a constant hum filled the air—one of the measures taken to prevent electronic eavesdropping. As he stood before a half-door resembling a teller's window, the cipher clerk retrieved his briefcase from one of the safes and handed it to him. The briefcase contained summaries of current operations, code names of agents, and other highly classified intelligence documents. Each night, when the briefcase was surrendered to the cipher clerk, it was affixed with a personalized wax seal, imprinted with a disk Alipov wore around his neck. The first thing he did each morning was check that the seal was still intact.

Alipov scanned the weekend cables flagged for him by the cipher clerk, and finding nothing of any immediacy, he left the *referentura* and took the stairwell to the eighth floor, where he was greeted by one of his subordinates, a KGB major.

"We have a problem that demands your immediate attention, Comrade General," the major said. He was a small, thin man with bright blue eyes that were constantly in motion, as though he were expecting imminent disaster.

"What is it?" Alipov asked, noticing that the major was unusually nervous this morning.

"I believe we should not discuss it here."

Alipov nodded, and the two men remained silent as they walked along the corridor running the length of what was clearly the KGB's domain. All of the doors lining the hall were blank and kept locked even during the day, and each office was equipped with sophisticated countermeasures to ensure that conversations could not be electronically monitored. Alipov's office, with its double walls, was the most secure of all. Music and background noise were continuously piped through the air space between the walls. The major began talking the moment Alipov closed the door behind them.

"One of our staff drivers, Viktor Kirilenko, has been arrested by the police," he said. "He is being detained at the Nineteenth Precinct station house, their temporary facility on East Ninety-fourth Street. He has been there since five o'clock this morning."

Alipov felt his pulse begin to race. He struggled to conceal the anxiety that was taking hold. "What is the reason for his arrest?" he asked with a calm belying his inner turmoil.

"There was a traffic accident, and the authorities are claiming that a woman was murdered while in the car prior to the accident." The major took a deep breath and glanced about the room in a conspiratorial manner.

"General, it was the under secretary general's car, and there is no record of any authorization for Kirilenko to have been driving it. I have no way of knowing if he was on official business, and if so, for whom. It was not for the under secretary general. As you know, he has been in Washington since Thursday. I was wondering if you authorized its use for a special operation."

Alipov turned away from the major's questioning gaze. The anxiety had given way to a rage he was having difficulty controlling.

"I know nothing about it," he said, slowly collecting himself. "Have you questioned Kirilenko?"

"No, General. Since informed of his circumstances, I have been waiting to confer with you before taking any direct action."

"Why wasn't he released upon identifying himself as a Soviet diplomat?"

"The police said he has refused to identify himself, indeed

to say anything at all. I determined it was Kirilenko by having all of our drivers accounted for."

"Was he alone?" Alipov asked, involuntarily holding his breath in anticipation of the answer.

"To the best of my knowledge. The police said nothing about anyone being with him."

Alipov breathed a silent sigh of relief, taking solace in the hope that so far the damage was being contained. If he acted quickly, perhaps he could control the situation before it got out of hand.

"Get him from the police and bring him directly to me. And do not question him," he instructed the major. "I will conduct the interrogation once he is back inside the mission."

"Yes, General," the major replied, going to the door. "The ambassador's car has been impounded; shall I have it picked up and brought back to the mission?"

"Yes," Alipov answered absently, his thoughts now focused on the potentially disastrous mess he had created.

With the major gone, he paced his office, silently cursing himself for the stupidity of his actions. How could he have agreed to such a flagrant violation of the most fundamental rules of tradecraft? Malik's argument had had its superficial logic: with his forged United Nations documents and an official car bearing diplomatic license plates, he could keep his rendezvous with the Nicaraguan diplomat without fear of being stopped or detained by the authorities. At first Alipov had sternly refused to accommodate him, but Malik had been persuasive and manipulative, exhibiting an insolence bordering on insubordination that would have resulted in quick and harsh retribution for anyone else. His eventual acquiescence to the demands for a car and driver was not from any personal fear of him, but he was intimidated by Malik's direct line of communication to the chairman of the KGB. The importance of Malik's assignment was such that its failure and exposure would cause heads to roll, starting with the chairman, who had personally sanctioned the mission and ordered the full support of all Line "N" officers.

"Fuck your mother!" Alipov muttered, gripped again by anger and frustration. A woman murdered, raising the specter of past allegations that had been ignored and hushed up for lack of hard evidence. How careless had Malik been? It was unlikely that Kirilenko had learned anything of his mission. Still, he could confirm Malik's presence in the city and, if questioned by the chairman's internal enemies, set off an investigation that could see them all end up in mental institutions or forced-labor camps—if they were lucky.

He tried to compose the cable he would send to the chairman, informing him of the incident, but was unable to concentrate and decided to wait until he had all of the information. He managed to calm himself enough to begin a plan of action, part of which meant arranging another clandestine meeting with Malik.

6

"That was the Intelligence Unit," Rafferty said, hanging up the telephone just as Captain John Hanratty entered the office. "They got an ID on the Polaroid of the guy in the cage. He's for real. Viktor Kirilenko, a staff driver for the Soviets."

"Yeah, I know. I just heard from his pals at the mission. They're on their way over. Accusing us of the usual bullshit—the 'alleged murder' is a CIA provocation to embarrass the Soviet Union."

"And I suppose the Quiet Man in the cage was on official business at four in the morning."

"On his way to pick up one of their diplomats for an early flight," Hanratty said.

"Right. How come I knew that?"

"I got no choice but to hand him over when they get here."

"How much further you want me to go with this?"

"Once they take their boy out of here, there's nowhere you can go. The answers we need go with him." There was an expression of disgust on Hanratty's broad Irish face. As the commanding officer of the Nineteenth Precinct, he had seen it happen all too often. "Talk to the victim's husband and complete the paperwork. Unless the driver defects and pleads to murder one before his buddies get here, which somehow I don't see happening, it's over."

As Hanratty left the office Rafferty looked out into the busy squad room, which had now reached its midmorning crescendo. Kirilenko still sat impassively on the bench in the cage while the detectives went about their work: some talked on the phone, others typed, hunting and pecking out overdue reports. A black teenager with a shaved head and wearing a leather suit and a Mr. T starter kit jangling around his neck grinned and postured as a heavyset sergeant questioned him, the veins in the sergeant's neck bulging in response to his growing ire at the kid's smart-ass attitude.

Out of the corner of his eye Rafferty saw someone enter the room and pause in the doorway; he was wearing jeans and a brown leather jacket and carrying a flight bag slung over his shoulder. After a moment Rafferty recognized him from the photographs in the victim's wallet. He wasn't as big as he thought he'd be, probably just under six feet tall, with a tapered athletic build that suggested upper-body strength. But there was a self-assurance and power emanating from him that was out of all proportion to his physical size. After studying him for only a few moments Rafferty knew his initial impression from the photographs was right —this man had no more killed his wife than he had. Twenty-two years as a cop told him things like that. They also told him that if Gannon knew that the Russian in the cage at the end of the room had been involved in his wife's death, he would kill him with his bare hands.

Rafferty got up from behind his desk and went out into the squad room. "Mr. Gannon?" he said, extending his hand.

Gannon shook the proffered hand.

"Bill Rafferty." Rafferty glanced at his watch—it was eleven o'clock. "You made good time, under three hours," he added, for lack of any other small talk that came to mind.

"I got a military hop," Gannon answered flatly. "What happened to my wife?"

"My office," Rafferty said, and led him through the noisy squad room into the cluttered cubicle, where he gestured for him to take the chair beside his desk.

"How did Kate die?" Gannon asked.

"I'll get to that in a minute, Mr. Gannon," he said evenly, noticing for the first time the thin jagged scar running vertically down the right side of Gannon's neck.

"It's Jack," Gannon said.

"Jack, then. First I have to ask you some questions you're going to find offensive, but they have to be answered."

Gannon nodded and shifted in his chair to face Rafferty.

"Were you in the city last night?"

"No."

"Where did you spend the last twenty-four hours?"

"In Fayetteville, North Carolina. Except for six hours of sleep, I was working."

"At your ranch?" Rafferty asked.

Gannon paused, then realized that Rafferty had come up with the colloquialism for the Delta Force compound from Kate's address book.

"I don't have a ranch. That's just what Kate calls it. I'm a civilian employee at the JFK Special Warfare Center at Fort Bragg," Gannon said, using the cover story provided to conceal his true place of employment.

"What kind of work?"

"Survival-training instructor with Special Forces schools," he said, adding the rest of his employment cover.

"You work on weekends?"

"Sometimes. Depending on the training schedule."

"Were you and your wife living together?"

"Yes."

"Any marital problems?"

"No."

"Did your wife have a history of drug or alcohol abuse?"

"No," Gannon said, his voice taking on an edge. The reference to Kate in the past tense disturbed him more than the questions.

"What was she doing in New York City?"

"Visiting her mother."

"Where?"

"At the Carlyle Hotel. She has an apartment there."

"Has she been informed of your wife's death?"

Gannon visibly flinched at the last word. "Yes, I stopped in to see her on the way here. She's old and her health isn't good, otherwise she'd be here with me."

"Does she know what your wife was doing last night, where she went, and with who?"

"Kate loves this city. She goes for a walk every night whenever she's here. That's what she did last night—went for a walk after a late dinner with her mother in the restaurant at the Carlyle."

"What time?"

"Around ten-thirty."

"Wasn't her mother concerned when she didn't come back?"

"She fell asleep. When she got up this morning she thought Kate had already gone out."

Rafferty hesitated, then asked, "Do you have any reason to think your wife might have been seeing another man?"

Gannon's eyes hardened, boring into Rafferty. He took a moment to answer, getting control of the anger that had surged to the surface. "My wife wouldn't cheat on me," he answered calmly. "We had a good marriage."

"Things change."

"You didn't know Kate. If she wasn't happy, she'd have told me and left, but she'd never cheat on me."

"Did your wife have any connection, professionally or otherwise, with the United Nations, or specifically the Soviet Mission to the United Nations?"

"No," Gannon said, taken aback by the question. "What do the Soviets or the United Nations have to do with this?"

Rafferty held Gannon's gaze for a long moment, then told him what he knew, with the exception of the significance of the man in the cage. As Rafferty spoke Gannon seemed resigned, in control of his emotions, but there was cold fire in the calm face and a hint of a dangerous volatility just beneath the surface. When Gannon asked how his wife had died, Rafferty left out the lurid details, simply stating that the cause of death was a blow to the head.

"And you're telling me there's nothing you can do; he gets away with killing my wife?"

"I'm sorry, but that's the way it is. We've got to live with it every day, and believe me, we hate it as much as you do."

"You said he was a chauffeur. How does a chauffeur qualify for diplomatic immunity?"

"When he's in the process of discharging his official duties. And they're going to say he was even if he wasn't."

"That's not right . . . it's insane, for Christ's sake."

"Tell me about it," Rafferty said. "Can you think of any reason your wife would have been in a limousine owned by the Soviet Mission?"

"I don't know . . . no. What are you asking me? Did she take rides from strangers? Kate knew the city, she went to school here. She knew where to go, where not to go."

"Did she work? Anything that brought her in contact with diplomats or politicians?"

"Some volunteer charity work at Fort Bragg. She didn't even know anybody at the UN. She came into New York four or five times a year, for a few days at a time, always to see her mother."

A commotion in the squad room drew Rafferty's attention. Captain Hanratty, accompanied by three men in business suits, had entered. Their loud, demanding voices drew everyone's attention and carried into the office. There was no mistaking the language the two men spoke when they went to the cage to talk with Kirilenko. Rafferty got up to close the door, but it was too late. Gannon had seen and heard them; he stood to watch through the half-glass partition separating the office from the outer room.

The third man with Hanratty spoke in slightly accented

English. "I have shown you the proper documentation, Captain. Release him."

Hanratty nodded to one of the detectives, who unlocked the cage. Kirilenko hesitated briefly, then stepped out into the room, seeming more afraid of his own people than he had been of the cops.

Gannon moved to the open office door. "They're Russians," he said to Rafferty. "Why are they here?"

Rafferty's only thoughts were of how to avoid a potentially explosive confrontation. He moved through the doorway past Gannon and placed himself in front of him. Gannon was so intent on the Russians that he didn't even notice.

"Come back in the office and sit down, Gannon," he said in a calm but firm voice. "You can't do yourself any good out here."

Gannon didn't budge. Rafferty doubted he had heard what he said.

One of the Russians took Kirilenko by the arm and edged him toward the door leading out into the hallway. Kirilenko reacted defensively and pulled away from the man. He stopped in front of Hanratty.

"I did not kill woman!" he said. "I am not murderer!"

"Be quiet!" the Russian at his side ordered. "You are to say nothing until we return to the mission." The words were in Russian, but the tone and sense of what was said transcended any language barriers.

Jack Gannon had heard and understood. He was across the room before Rafferty could stop him. He shoved aside two of the Russians, sending one sprawling on the floor and the other over a desktop. He grabbed Kirilenko's neck with one hand and began slowly squeezing his windpipe.

"Did you kill my wife?" His words were eerily calm and soft-spoken.

Kirilenko struggled to break free. Gannon only increased the pressure. He pinned him against the wall and slammed a fist into his stomach.

"Did you kill my wife?"

One of the men Gannon had shoved aside sprang to his feet and attempted to grab him from behind. With eyes trained to detect movement and intuit thought in an opponent, Gannon saw him approaching from an angle and reacted. He struck with his free arm just as the man reached for him and landed a perfectly timed blow with his elbow that shattered the Russian's nose, dropping him to the floor in excruciating pain.

"All right!" The Mr. T clone had jumped up from his chair across the room and was shouting encouragement. "Good fuckin' shot!"

Gannon saw the second Russian get up and start toward him. He released Kirilenko, who slid to the floor gasping for breath. Gannon turned to face his attacker. He blocked a clumsy roundhouse right and grasped the man's wrist. With precision control he spun him around and delivered a quick, powerful punch to the kidney that sent him to his knees and kept him there.

"Oh, shit! You a bad motherfucker," the black kid shouted enthusiastically, an expression of mock pain on his face. "I felt that over here." He bobbed and weaved in imaginary battle.

The sergeant who had been questioning the kid grabbed him by the scruff of his neck and forcibly sat him back down in the chair.

Gannon's eyes were attacking and counterattacking now, watching, as an experienced martial artist does, all movement and potential threats around him, the information being processed by his brain into simultaneous action in an acute focus of mind and body.

The third Russian, the one in charge, stood immobile beside Hanratty, having decided that discretion was the better part of valor.

"Stop him!" he shouted at Hanratty and the cops in the room.

Rafferty was astonished by Gannon's quickness. No more than ten seconds had elapsed since he had left the office doorway and charged across the room. Now three men lay on the squad-room floor, and Gannon was headed for the fourth. The lack of an immediate response by the cops, although somewhat due to the speed of the attack, had its deeper motivations and was not entirely unintentional. But it was about to go too far.

With the aid of a burly detective, Rafferty managed to grab Gannon and pull him away from the startled Russian, who was ready to bolt for the door.

"Jesus Christ, Gannon!" Rafferty said, keeping a firm grip on him until he calmed down. "That was stupid."

Gannon said nothing. His eyes were on Kirilenko, who was being helped to his feet by the Russian who had taken the blow to the kidney. None of the cops in the room moved to help the man with the broken nose. The Russian beside Hanratty, convinced that Gannon was under control, finally did. He handed him a handkerchief to stem the flow of blood.

"Do you want to press charges against this man?" Hanratty asked the Russian in charge, forcing the words out through clenched teeth.

The Russian stared at Gannon, then looked to Kirilenko and the two men who had accompanied him. "No. No charges."

With a quick move of his head toward the door, he ordered his men to escort Kirilenko out of the squad room.

"You lucked out, Gannon," Rafferty said, keeping a restraining grip on him until the Russians were out of sight. "If those pieces of shit had pressed charges, I'd of had no choice but to lock you up, and that would really have made my day."

"Is that the son of a bitch who killed Kate?" Gannon said.

"He was driving the limousine," Rafferty said. "That's the only thing I can prove. But it's all academic, Gannon, we can't touch him no matter what he did. It's going to stick in your craw for a long time, but you're gonna have to live with it." Rafferty felt the tension drain from him and released his grip.

"No. This isn't where it ends." The look in Gannon's eyes said the threat was not an idle one.

"Come on," Rafferty said. "This isn't going to be pleasant, but I've got to take you down to the morgue to identify your wife."

Gannon followed him out into the corridor, the thought of seeing Kate dead weighing heavily. He felt as though he was moving in slow motion, disconnected, and it was all he could do to keep from crying.

The entrance lobby to the station house was noisy and crowded. Lawyers looked for clients; a junkie, hands handcuffed behind his back, stood before the tall desk with the arresting officer, and two uniformed cops physically restrained a screaming woman from attacking a man hiding behind another cop. As Rafferty led Gannon down the hallway a young man in a tweed sport coat and jeans approached him.

"Hey, Lieutenant. Remember me? Bill Peters with the *Post*."

Rafferty ignored him and continued walking. The reporter followed alongside.

"What happened in there?"

"Three guys fell down."

"Three Russians from the Soviet Mission, right?" He stepped in front of Rafferty to slow his progress.

"Get out of my way."

"Rumor has it that the woman whose body was dumped on Fifth Avenue last night was thrown from a car with diplomatic plates."

"Just make up your own story," Rafferty said as he elbowed past him. "You fuckin' people are real good at that."

"How about you, Mac?" the reporter said to Gannon as he walked by. "Did the Russians kill that broad?"

Gannon lowered a shoulder and planted it in Peters's chest with enough force to send him flying backward into the wall. He continued following Rafferty out of the building as though nothing had happened.

"Did you see that!" Peters shouted to the sergeant at the tall desk.

"See what?" the desk sergeant yelled back, having clearly seen what had happened. "You slipped, you clumsy fuck. Must be the floors. Hey!" he called out to no one in particular. "Were these goddamn floors just waxed?"

"Yeah, Sarge. This morning." A uniformed cop in the corridor picked up on the ruse without missing a beat. "It's like a skating rink; people fallin' down all over the fuckin' place."

"There you have it, pal. Watch your step on the way out."

7

As Deputy Director for Operations, David Wilson was in charge of all CIA covert operations. He liked things carefully planned and well organized. He did not like surprises, especially not the kind that made the hair stand up on the back of his neck, as it was doing now.

"It's a coincidence," Tom Driscoll said. "Nothing more."

"I hope you're right," Wilson said as he looked up from the reports Driscoll had brought to his office. "Because on the surface, if your assumption about Malik is correct, it doesn't look all that encouraging. A Delta Force advisor, with a top-secret clearance and access to highly classified intelligence information the Russians would give their right arms for, and his wife was in the company of their most effective Illegal, who just so happens to be the catalyst for any number of terrorist incidents. Convince me that I shouldn't be worried, Tom."

"Not about that," Driscoll said with confidence. "Gannon's military record speaks for itself. He has more decorations than an Italian street festival. Joined the Army when he was nineteen, spent his entire career in Special Forces, direct commission from staff sergeant to captain when he was awarded the Medal of Honor. Five tours in Vietnam with the Special Operations Group running reconnaissance missions into Laos and North Vietnam. He's held a top-secret clearance damn near from the day he joined the service. There's absolutely no reason to question the man's honor or loyalty."

"That's him. What about his wife?"

"She's a victim. That's all. In Munich, London, and Rome, the three places we have reason to believe Malik did the same thing, all of the murdered women were chosen at random, just pulled off the streets. They had no previous connection to Malik, any terrorist group, or the Soviets. Granted, Gannon's wife ending up as one of his victims is a coincidence that makes you raise an eyebrow, but only when you isolate it out of context."

"What's her background?"

Driscoll read from an annotated biography he had culled from the in-depth background a research assistant had given him.

"Wealthy family, old money, only child. Graduate degree from Georgetown Foreign Service School. She worked at our embassy in Bangkok right after she finished school. That's where she met Gannon, in 1969. He was on an R and R leave after he got the Medal of Honor. Whirlwind courtship, they were married two weeks later. Believe me, Dave, she's not the problem; he is, but not the way you're suggesting."

"You care to expand on that?"

"The best analogy I can give you is that Gannon's a truck full of nitroglycerin on a steep mountain pass with faulty brakes. Everything about him says he'll go after the man who murdered his wife. He's got the training and the resources—access to Delta's data banks and his buddies to help him. If he gets to Malik before we do, he'll scatter our operation to the four winds."

"We haven't given anything on Malik to Delta, and Gannon's got nothing to tie him to the murder of his wife. As far as he knows, or for that matter, even the cops, the driver . . . Kirilenko is the only suspect."

"Right now. But we've got to consider the possibility that

Gannon will find some way to get to Kirilenko. Guys like him don't lie down and roll over for anybody."

"If the Soviets follow their usual pattern, they'll ship Kirilenko back to Moscow tomorrow. Even we'd have problems getting to him there."

"We can only hope they ship him back."

Wilson's eyes scanned Gannon's military service record. He was looking for something that had caught his attention earlier. He found it under the heading "Specialized Training." He underlined one of the entries and handed the file to Driscoll.

"Did you happen to notice this?" he asked pointedly.

Driscoll's brow knitted into a frown as he read. "Holy shit! I must have skimmed over it. Talk about coincidence."

"I think the Director's going to want the President briefed," Wilson said. "In the meantime, put surveillance on Gannon. If he gets onto Malik, I want someone there to yank him."

8

The New York City Medical Examiner's Office is in a squat, gray-green building at Thirtieth Street and First Avenue near the Bellevue Hospital complex. Its architecture, to say the least, is not pleasing to the eye, but neither is what goes on inside.

The moment Gannon swung open the glass door and started up the stairs the odor hit him. It was a smell that cannot be adequately described to another person—you have either experienced it or you haven't. And once having done so, it stays with you for the rest of your life. It was the faint sickening sweet smell of death, drifting up from the basement morgue and permeating the building. A rush of memories took Gannon back twenty years, to the jungles of Laos and a mission to recover the bodies of a reconnaissance team that had been lost for more than a week.

Rafferty glanced over his shoulder as Gannon paused on the steps, shaking off the disturbing flashback.

"You okay?"

"Yeah. Just some old memories."

Rafferty nodded knowingly. "I get the same feeling every time I come down here."

The two men entered the lobby and crossed to the security officer's desk, where Rafferty identified himself and led Gannon through a doorway to a narrow corridor painted in a drab institutional beige. The smell was stronger here, and Gannon forced another unwelcome vision from his mind's eye.

In a small office off the hallway Gannon stood before the desk of a large black woman with a kind face. She glanced at Rafferty's shield and turned her attention to Gannon.

"Are you here to make an identification?"

Gannon nodded. The horror of what he was required to do had reached its full impact. Until now Kate's death was not entirely real to him. Only something he had to accept and deal with mentally, not physically face as an undeniable reality.

"I have some questions to ask you for my records," the woman said. Her voice was unusually soothing and sympathetic for someone who had to repeat the process countless times a day.

Gannon gave her the required information, much of it a repetition of what he had told Rafferty. No, Kate had no history of psychiatric care or any significant medical history. No, she was not an alcohol or drug abuser. He answered most of the questions without remembering having done so. When the woman finished, Rafferty led him into a narrow and cramped room where they faced a large window with a stainless-steel partition behind it.

Rafferty pressed a button on the wall and Gannon heard the sound of an elevator rising. The stainless-steel partition receded and a gurney with a body on it appeared just beyond the glass window. Shrouded in sheets, only the face was visible.

Gannon stared in revulsion and disbelief. It was Kate, but her face was badly disfigured. "Oh, Christ," he said, turning away, no longer able to stem the flow of tears. He pounded his fist against the wall and breathed deeply, trying to regain control. He turned back to the window and placed the palm of his hand on a level with his wife's face.

"Oh, Kate," he cried out softly. "Oh, honey, I'm sorry. I should have been with you."

Rafferty, affected by Gannon's grief, said, "Come on, Gannon," as he pressed the button that took the elevator back down to the morgue. "Don't beat yourself up."

Transfixed, Gannon watched Kate's body slowly descend out of sight.

Gently placing a hand on his shoulder, Rafferty led him out of the viewing room and back over to the woman at the desk, where he signed the family identification form. He had regained sufficient composure to remember the name of the funeral home Kate's mother had given him and signed a permission slip to have the body released to them.

As they left the room a fellow cop in an office across the hall called out to Rafferty.

"Hey, Pete, how ya doin'?" Rafferty responded to the former squad-car partner from his uniformed days.

"Anything I can help you with?" Pete asked, stepping out into the hall.

"Just finished with a family identification," Rafferty said delicately.

"What the hell happened to her?" Gannon blurted out. "You said it was a blow to the head. It looked like a lot more than that."

An overweight morgue attendant with a half-eaten doughnut sticking out of his mouth stood just inside the office.

"What's the name?" he asked.

"Katherine Gannon," Gannon said.

Before Rafferty could shut the morgue attendant up, he had flipped through a clipboard of forms and found what he was looking for.

"Oh yeah," the attendant said, the doughnut clenched between his teeth. "Somebody did a real number on this one. Beat the shit out of her. Broken left and right wrists, broken nose, fractured cheekbones, broken jaw, broken neck. Bottom line is the guy probably beat her to death with his fists, then snapped her neck for good measure, but not before he raped her. Also looks like she—"

Noticing Gannon's expression, Rafferty's friend stopped the attendant's rapid-fire litany by slapping the doughnut out of his mouth.

"You fuck! You moron fuck!" he snapped at the startled attendant.

"The fuck's wrong with you? Guy asked me."

"He's the victim's family."

"I thought he was a cop," the attendant said, picking up his half-eaten doughnut and wiping it off on his smock.

"Don't think, jerk-off, just get the fuck outta my sight!" He turned to Rafferty and said, "Sorry, Bill. That's the kind of assholes they're hiring these days."

Gannon had left the building as quickly as he could. Rafferty found him leaning against the wall just outside the entrance.

"Did you know all that?" Gannon asked.

"Some of it."

"Kate was the best thing that ever happened to me . . . the most kind, decent person you'd ever want to meet." He paused to fight back the tears, then said, "What kind of an animal would do that to another human being?"

"Animals don't do things like that. Just people."

"I know what you're thinking," Rafferty said, breaking a long silence as he expertly steered his way through a traffic-snarled street. "But let it lie."

"That's what you'd do? Let it lie?"

Rafferty met Gannon's gaze. "If I was a civilian? No. I'd hunt the cocksucker down, rip out one of his eyes, and eat it in front of the good one. For starters. But I'm a cop, and I have to face scumbags like that all the time. If I let it get to me, I'd kill at least four or five psychotic creeps a month. All I can do is arrest them and hope the system works often enough to keep the worst of them off the streets."

"I'm not a cop," Gannon said.

"No. But you have to know the cold, hard facts of this case. It's going nowhere. We can't touch the guy. And just between you and me . . ." Rafferty hesitated. As a cop he knew he shouldn't say any more, but as a human being he felt a bond of shared experiences, of war and loss, with the man sitting beside him.

"What?" Gannon said. "You said 'just between you and me.' "

"I don't think the guy you decked in the squad room killed your wife."

"There was someone else in the car? Why didn't you tell me that?"

"Because I don't know it to be a fact. Nobody saw anyone else. Some of the bums in the park were questioned; they didn't see anything. It's just . . . the way he acted when he was busted, and the Russians took their good-natured time about getting him out. Nothing you can sink your teeth into, just inconsistencies."

"Is anyone trying to find him?"

"No. Find who?" Rafferty said as he honked the horn at a taxi that had cut him off. "Look, you've got to realize that if there was someone else in that car, and the driver clammed up to protect him, the guy is another diplomat, so we're back to square one. What's the point in finding him if we can't bust him? It's a descending spiral, Gannon. This case is fucked no matter what we do."

"For you," Gannon said.

"Nothing I can say is going to stop you. I know that. It wouldn't stop me. But you start fucking around with the Soviet Mission and the CIA's going to come down on you, and they can play rough."

"I know how to play games they never heard of," Gannon said quietly.

Rafferty turned off Madison Avenue onto Seventy-sixth Street and pulled up to the entrance to the Carlyle Hotel. He waved off the doorman and turned to face Gannon. "Pretty fancy place your mother-in-law lives in."

Gannon managed a semblance of a smile. "Yeah. When Kate married me her mother considered it the equivalent of

Tony the Pony breaking into the paddock with the thoroughbred mare. But she got over it."

Rafferty laughed and took one of his cards from his jacket pocket, scribbled his home number on the reverse side, and gave it to Gannon. "I'm sorry about your loss."

"I know you are."

"You take care. If there's anything I can do, call."

"Thanks," Gannon said. "For everything."

The two men shook hands and Gannon got out of the car. As he reached the revolving door Rafferty called out to him: "Keep your powder dry, huh?"

Gannon gave him a thumbs-up and disappeared into the hotel lobby.

Rafferty pulled out into the street feeling certain he was going to see Gannon again; he only hoped it wasn't with his hands cuffed behind his back.

9

Margaret Simpson sat in a pale-pink silk damask chair in the solarium of her twenty-fourth-floor apartment. She had an exaggerated sense of occasion and was exquisitely dressed in a designer suit adorned with expensive jewelry, but the toll the brutal murder of her only child was taking had begun to show. Her hands had a slight tremor, responsible for the smear of lipstick that had strayed wide of the mark and a small blotch of eyeliner on the bridge of her thin aristocratic nose. She looked frail and weak, as if she had aged ten years since Gannon had seen her that morning. Most of the dinner she had ordered for them from the hotel restaurant had gone uneaten, and she had hardly spoken to Gannon during the meal, her blank stare fixed on an antique credenza where an arrangement of photographs taken of Kate since early childhood was prominently displayed.

The glass-enclosed room offered a spectacular view of the Manhattan skyline and Central Park. She sat silently looking out over the terrace. An occasional wistful smile appeared at the corners of her mouth. A Puerto Rican maid in a black dress with a starched white apron had finished clearing the dining-room table and announced that she was leaving for the night. Margaret Simpson nodded a weak "Good night" and went back to staring out into the brilliantly lit night sky. Gannon sat opposite her, deep in his own thoughts. More than an hour passed without conversation.

"She was so proud of you," Margaret Simpson finally said, and turned to look at Gannon. "And she loved you very much."

"I know," Gannon said.

"I was against it at first, you know. Your marriage."

Gannon merely nodded. He remembered the terrible fight Kate had had with her mother, who when informed of their marriage argued vehemently for an annulment.

"You made her happy. That's all I ever wanted for her," she said, her voice growing weaker.

Gannon watched as her eyes closed and her head slumped to one side. At first he was worried and got up and went to her side and took her hand. She murmured softly, falling deeper into a much-needed sleep.

He placed an afghan over her and silently left the apartment. It was nearly midnight, and the city, its daytime sense of urgency gone, was relatively quiet. Gannon crossed Madison Avenue and followed Seventy-sixth Street over to Fifth Avenue and the sidewalk paralleling Central Park.

The crisp October air revived him somewhat. He was physically tired. He had been up since six o'clock, but he knew sleep would not come easy this night. He picked up his pace in the hope of wearing himself down to the point of exhaustion.

His mind was flooded with memories of Kate. She had loved the city; he had hated it and never understood its attraction for her. She had once told him that it renewed her in a way she couldn't explain, so he never argued whenever she wanted to spend a few days with her mother. He remembered that she went to some sort of finishing school nearby. Finch College, he recalled. He walked faster and tried to fight off the grisly images that began flashing before him. But they forced themselves on him. Tormenting him. He heard the morgue attendant's words over and over again, unable to drive them from his conscious thoughts. Oh God,

Kate! How he must have hurt you. How frightened you were by violence. He felt himself about to lose control and sat down on one of the benches along the park wall.

A car sped down the broad avenue, then another. Gannon stared after them. He forced himself to remember pleasant things, special moments: their wedding in Bangkok when his rowdy, irreverent Green Beret buddies had frightened most of Kate's embassy friends away from the reception at the Oriental Hotel with behavior that bordered on barbaric. But they had won her over when they stood on the terrace six floors beneath their honeymoon suite and serenaded them until two o'clock in the morning. The drunken, tuneless repertoire didn't matter, she had said later, it was the thought that counted.

His memories faded as he became aware of his surroundings. The area was brightly lit by vapor lamps spaced at intervals for as far as he could see, which was a considerable distance. He noticed that two benches down from where he sat there was a man sleeping. Gannon got up and continued along the sidewalk. He passed a few more of the homeless curled up on benches. And there were still more on the grass inside the park. He paused and looked around again. It was past midnight, yet the powerful streetlamps extended visibility for blocks in either direction. He hurried back to the hotel.

From a pay phone in the small lobby off the Café Carlyle, he called Bill Rafferty.

"This is Jack Gannon," he said to the groggy voice that answered. "Did I wake you?"

"Don't worry about it."

"Where exactly did the police find Kate's body?"

Rafferty thought for a moment as he cleared the sleep from his mind. "Fifth Avenue at Sixty-ninth Street, on the park side."

"Thanks."

"Gannon?"

He had hung up. Rafferty rolled over and propped his

head up with a pillow. His wife still slept soundly at his side. She had long ago learned to unconsciously screen out the late-night calls.

He thought of his day with Gannon. In a world where putting together a multimillion-dollar stock deal that benefited no one but the manipulators was considered heroic, and where "he who has the most toys when he dies wins" had taken on near religious connotations rather than being understood for the sick joke it really was—in a world like that, guys like Gannon got lost and forgotten. True heroes, who hated war and had experienced its horrors and sacrifices firsthand, were debased by the pretenders, the fantasy warriors, the clowns who put on camouflage fatigues to cover up their inadequacies and played weekend war games with guns that shot paint pellets. Wars where losing meant having to buy the beer. Christ!

Rafferty reached for a cigarette, then remembered he had quit months ago. He thought about the phone call and knew what Gannon was going to do. Despite the futility, he understood. He drifted slowly back to sleep thinking that it would be nice if the good guys could win one once in a while.

10

As Bill Rafferty drifted slowly back to sleep in his Manhattan apartment, 4,600 miles away, in the heart of Moscow, the morning sun was already glistening off the windows of the headquarters of the GRU. As the Main Directorate of Intelligence of the Soviet General Staff, the GRU (Glavnoye Razvedyvatelnoye Upravleniye) is a secret and powerful organization whose methods of operation are virtually identical to those of the KGB, including the use of Soviet embassies and consulates around the world as cover for its officers, but its mission is entirely different. Tasked with protecting the Soviet Union from external enemies, as opposed to the KGB's focus on preventing the collapse of the country from within, the GRU's operations range from stealing technology from the West to controlling battalions of special-purpose forces, known as Spetsnaz, for use in armed reconnaissance and sabotage behind enemy lines in times of war or as covert operators in peacetime.

The KGB is the largest intelligence-gathering and internal-security organization in the history of the world. In addition to thousands of full-fledged KGB officers, its ranks are swelled by millions of volunteers that form a massive network of informants infesting every level of Soviet life.

The GRU has no volunteers. Its officers are selected from the elite of the Soviet military, and in general they are better educated, more professional, and more dedicated than the highly politicized KGB. Free from involvement in assassinations and other "black" operations, they have no responsibility for safeguarding party loyalty, suppressing the people, guarding the borders, or operating the prison camps. Consequently GRU officers consider themselves the professional and moral superiors of their KGB opposites.

Unlike the KGB, whose headquarters are purposely located on a crowded square in the center of Moscow as a constant reminder of its watchful presence, the location, even the very existence, of the GRU headquarters is virtually unknown. Surrounded by an airfield and highly restricted buildings that house aircraft factories, the Institute of Cosmic Biology, and a rocket assembly plant, its compound is the most secure site in the city of Moscow. The airfield is restricted to GRU use for receiving and transporting its latest acquisitions of foreign technology. It is not unusual for a cargo plane to arrive in the middle of the night and unload stolen military hardware or a mainframe computer at a storage warehouse from which it will be transshipped to a remote testing and evaluation site. Or to defense specialists for analysis and eventual adaptation for use with existing Soviet weapons systems.

The GRU's headquarters building within the compound, a nine-story extended rectangle called "the Aquarium," is surrounded by fortresslike walls. Every inch of the facility is under constant surveillance by closed-circuit television; at night attack dogs prowl the perimeter, while during the day an equally ferocious group of GRU retirees living in an apartment complex adjoining the headquarters report any unknown faces to security guards. Admission is gained only after passing through three highly sophisticated security checkpoints, and restrictions are such that not even the General Secretary of the Soviet Union can bring a car into the GRU complex, nor can those who work there bring in a briefcase or so much as a pen.

A fierce rivalry and often open hostility exist between the

KGB and the GRU. As a result all overseas *rezident*s of each service have personnel specifically assigned to spy on the activities of the other, and to occasionally conduct covert missions to purposely foil each other's operations in attempts to prove its rival incompetent and usurp their claim to specific arenas of intelligence gathering. On a broader scale both services assign officers to infiltrate the other's organization, and those officers may spend their entire careers as long-term moles for their mother service. The fierce and relentless competition assures that the quality of work is maintained, and the incessant power struggle and jockeying for favored position suits the Party well—one organization keeping the other in check, a guarantee that neither will have a monopoly on espionage and intelligence gathering, thus eliminating the threat of a conspiracy to deceive the Politburo and upset the delicate balance of internal power.

General Vladimir Petrovich Antonov, deputy chief of the General Staff of the Soviet Armed Forces and head of the GRU, knew and understood the machinations of the KGB well. He started his day as he always did and sat at the circular green-baize conference table at one end of his spacious office on the seventh floor of the Aquarium. He scanned the stack of cables that had come in overnight from the Army Intelligence Directorates, Groups of Forces, and Fleet Intelligence. The traffic from the *rezident*s and the GRU Illegals always received his undivided attention, particularly those from the United States. The cable he now held in his hands caused him to grunt and nod his head with satisfaction and vindication. Sent from the GRU *rezident* in New York City on a special back channel free of the KGB's ubiquitous scrutiny, the message confirmed what he had begun to suspect months ago.

Antonov looked up to see his second-in-command, Colonel General Yuri Denisovich Volovich, enter his office and sit opposite him, then went back to reading the cable. Volovich squinted against the bright morning sun streaming through the windows and waited silently until General Antonov had finished.

"It seems that Comrade Malik is up to his old tricks again," Antonov said as he set the cable aside. "It is not easy to mistake his handiwork."

Volovich nodded in agreement. "Our *resident* in New York cannot be certain it is Malik, but he is conducting his own investigation into the incident. Unfortunately the KGB has denied him access to the driver of the limousine."

"It's him," General Antonov said. "And despite the denials from our KGB comrades, he is not operating without support and official sanction. My problem, Yuri Denisovich, is how high does that support reach? Where does his power lie?"

"The chairman of the KGB is still insisting that Malik is a rogue, completely out of control, responding to no one's orders but his own."

"Chebrikov is a liar," Antonov said. "The KGB *resident* in New York would not act of his own volition. No. He is a Line 'N' man and he is doing as Comrade Chebrikov instructs."

"Do you think it is possible Malik is still in New York?"

"The men assigned to locate him believe he is using one of the KGB's safe houses in the city, but so far they have been unsuccessful in locating him. He has slipped through our fingers before. Let us hope it does not happen again."

"If he already has, this may be of some help," Volovich said. He handed him the cable that had brought him to Antonov's office. "If our Paris *resident* is correct, Malik may be on his way to France."

Antonov took the cable, his eyes moving quickly over the message. "Who is Egon Zimmerman?"

"A terrorist, a West German national, and a member of the Red Army Faction. He was the one with Malik in East Germany four months ago, and he has been working closely with him ever since. They were reportedly seen together in

Nicaragua last month, and according to this cable, he is now in Paris."

"Do we have him under surveillance?"

"No. We have not yet found him."

Antonov stared thoughtfully out a window and drummed his fingers on the top of the conference table. "I want all of our people in Paris alerted to this Zimmerman's presence. Find him and interrogate him. If he does not lead us directly to Malik, he can perhaps at least shed some light on his plans and his timetable."

"Has the General Secretary been advised of the incident in New York?" Volovich asked.

Antonov shook his head. "The Comrade General Secretary wants to be informed of results, not speculation. Find Malik, and we will have something to tell him."

Antonov got up from his chair as Volovich left the office. He paced the length of the room, his thoughts on the delicate situation in which the General Secretary had placed him. He was firmly on Gorbachev's side, but would he, in the end, be on the winning side? He had seen power struggles before, and the signs were unmistakable. Thinly veiled attacks on the General Secretary's policies were becoming bolder, allegiances were shifting, loyalties were unknown. The rumblings had been there for over a year, and the resistance had intensified and become overt opposition from the Party conservatives and the Kremlin old guard. Now the decisive struggle was beginning in earnest. Many of the high-ranking bureaucrats saw the new policies of *glasnost* and *perestroika* as a threat to their power and privileges and were not about to give up without a fight. The intrigues and power plays within the Central Committee were growing, and there were those who had broken away from the Party Presidium and formed an anti-Gorbachev faction, accusing the General Secretary of only paying lip service to Marxist–Leninist ideology while secretly coveting the bourgeois way of life, of being poisoned by Western influences and not seeing consumerism for the philistine psychology that it was.

* * *

Most of the Kremlin's old guard hypocritically relished the life of the privileged class that came with their power. Predatory and paranoid, they wanted the game to continue as before. They believed that the Soviet Union could not feel entirely secure until all other nations felt entirely insecure. Gorbachev and his supporters believed that the Great Game had to end; it was simply too dangerous to play by the old rules in an age of nuclear weapons. They were a one-dimensional world power, a midget with one giant arm, their superpower status based solely on their military. Economic restructuring was his clarion call; deprive the West of an enemy with a foreign policy of less confrontation and build an economy that would provide the people with more than the basic necessities of life. There lay the road to true power and strength and the eventual triumph of the socialist cause.

The General Secretary knew that sheer power and influence and patronage were what counted, not simply policy. He had moved swiftly and expertly to consolidate his power base. He had purged many who opposed him and diluted the influence of the old guard, but he had not yet succeeded in dominating the Party. Even some of his new appointees to the ruling Politburo, the KGB chief in particular, Antonov thought, could not be counted on for full support. The new KGB chief, an orthodox ideologist and guardian of Communist conformity, saw only a loss of power and control for the KGB in the new policy of openness and left no doubt about his views on the contamination of Soviet youth by Western ideas and his contempt for dissidents and reactionary theological concepts.

Gorbachev's attempts to reorganize the military, a strategy Antonov had helped plan, had been done with a political purpose, to get the military out of politics, and in doing so, lessen their power. But it had left Gorbachev with enemies on the General Staff, powerful members of the Defense Council and the military establishment who saw his planned reductions of weapons systems and conventional forces as a plot to emasculate them and force large numbers of senior officers into retirement.

But his most dangerous enemies were the remaining old-line ideologues, who, like their predecessors, had decided the succession of power in the Soviet Union since the Revolution. In a calculated move to debilitate them, the Minister of Defense, formerly second only to the head of the Party in real power over the military, was relegated to just one of ten equals on the Supreme High Command.

And each of those demoted or purged had their own supporters in the Politburo, the Secretariat, the Central Committee, and the Party. Still, Gorbachev was gaining ground, but his opposition was also gaining strength, and outside of Moscow, among the Party hierarchy in the fifteen republics that make up the Soviet Union, his policies were viewed with skepticism and fear. To Antonov's way of thinking, this was where his real weakness lay. And he believed that the KGB was fomenting unrest in many of the distant republics —using Armenian sectarianism and nationalism in the Baltic States as stalking horses while encouraging unrest in the Eastern Bloc countries—in an effort to undermine Gorbachev's gains in the Kremlin, destroy his reputation as a reformer, and provide his enemies with examples of the folly of his policies.

But Antonov knew that all of the General Secretary's gains, his efforts to eviscerate his opposition and consolidate his power, would mean nothing, the intricate power plays and intrigues would pale to insignificance, if Nikolai Malik succeeded with his suspected objective. With or without proof of KGB complicity in his actions, his success alone would set off a brutal power struggle that would rock the very foundations of the Kremlin and bring an end to the Gorbachev era. Antonov's loyalty to the General Secretary was without reservations; they had known and liked each other since meeting during their university days. It was a friendship and mutual respect that had grown and deepened over the years, but unless he could find and stop Nikolai Malik, he would be powerless to prevent his friend's inevitable demise.

11

The midtown Manhattan skyline rises dramatically above the trees just outside Central Park, a perimeter of great buildings, massive facades of limestone and brick face, shouldered together along the avenue as far as the eye can see—a towering backdrop to the fragile, peaceful setting. The park was one of the few places Gannon had enjoyed on the rare occasions he had accompanied Kate to the city, and all morning he had been haunted by painful memories, terrible, palpable, bittersweet memories that seemed to transport him back in time to the days they had spent there: to a picnic on the lawn at Bethesda Fountain and boating on the lake and long autumn walks down wooded paths dappled with sunlight and shade, much as they were now. He paused as he crossed the Bow Bridge at the south end of the lake and stared into the glassy water that mirrored the willows on the bank and a delicate cast-iron gazebo on the far shore; he was beginning to realize that accepting Kate's death, as difficult as it had been, was not as hard as living with it.

Kate had said that the park was a place she could come to and be a child again: to run, fly a kite, fall in love (puppy love, she had quickly added as Gannon raised an eyebrow in mock concern), or, on beautiful autumn days such as this one, to cut classes and lie on her back in the cool grass of the Sheep Meadow and make animals out of the clouds. So

many of the things they had done together were flitting in
and out of his conscious thoughts that he tried to find solace
in them, in the time, however short, he had been given with
her, to treasure the moments they had shared. But the loss
was too great, the hurt too deep and too new.

He had started his search at sunrise, entering the park just
below the Metropolitan Museum of Art, and had crisscrossed its breadth to Central Park West and back to Fifth
Avenue. He had worked his way down to Sixty-sixth Street
by midmorning and followed the network of footpaths and
trails through the wooded hills of the Ramble and around
the Lake and Conservatory Pond. He had questioned every
homeless park dweller willing to talk to him, which, as it
had turned out, despite their numbers, were few and far
between. Some scowled and walked away, not wanting to be
disturbed, while others, lost in their own tormented world,
simply stared blankly, as though he was speaking in a language that was foreign to them.

One man, dressed in a carnival of assorted clothes, none
of which fit or had been washed in months, had raised Gannon's hopes. He had seen it all. "Yeah. I don't miss nothin'
goes on around here. People look at me, think I don't know
jack shit, but I see everything. Fuckin' 'a.' " Shortly into the
conversation, Gannon left disappointed. The man was lying,
getting the type of car and the time of night wrong and
placing the scene on the west side of the park.

A dapper-looking man, wearing a Brooks Brothers suit
and a snappy bow tie, sat on a stone bench before a statue.
As Gannon drew closer he saw that the man's hands were
moving constantly over his thighs, his trousers were worn to
a sheen above the knee. "Got to get some paperwork done,"
he repeated over and over in a glassy-eyed litany, his words
in rhythm with the movement of his hands. Gannon passed
him by and followed a path that led him to Fifth Avenue,
where he headed south along the chest-high sandstone wall
that bordered the park. As he neared the bookstands near
the Grand Army Plaza, a bum with a dog that needed medi-

cal attention, according to the sign around the dog's neck, struck a nerve, and Gannon gave the man five dollars. He returned a few minutes later with a soft pretzel for the dog and his owner and one for himself to stave off a gnawing hunger. The man had slept on Central Park West on Sunday night, but he'd ask around and if he heard anything he'd let him know. Gannon gave him his telephone number at the Carlyle.

Gannon continued past the statue of General Sherman, a stand of horsedrawn carriages, and again entered the park, now from Central Park South, and walked along a path that bordered the Pond. A tall, lanky man with a full beard caught his attention. He was carrying a huge, overstuffed tote bag, and his baggy pants were too long, their frayed edges dragging on the ground as he walked over to a bench and sat facing the Pond. One hand was deep in a pocket of an old army field jacket; the other scratched and pulled at the ratty beard. Pinned to the chest of the field jacket were three military decorations: a Vietnam Service Medal, a Silver Star, and a Purple Heart.

"Smell that?" the bum said in a loud, gruff voice as Gannon stopped in front of the bench.

Gannon nodded. There was a faint foul odor carried on the breeze coming off the Pond.

"That's shit," the bum said. "And it ain't just from the dogs. Place is like a giant latrine for every bum and loser in the city. And I ain't no loser, if that's what you're thinkin'. I was okay before the 'Nam. Till they sold us out. You got a few bucks?"

"I might." Gannon was about to say something else, but the bum rambled on.

"See that statue up there? General Sherman? Know what he did? I'll tell you what he did. Maniac torched everything in his fuckin' path, just like they made me do in the 'Nam. Fucker marched through Virginia, burned it to the ground."

"Georgia," Gannon said.

"What?"

"You're talking about Sherman's march through Georgia."

"Georgia. Virginia. One of them moron redneck states," he muttered, hawking up a white liquid blob that congealed when he spat it on the pavement. "Anyway, same shit we did in the 'Nam, only we used napalm."

"What outfit were you with?" Gannon asked, deciding to let him talk about the war if it calmed him down enough to question him.

"Green Berets," the bum said. He stared at Gannon with his best I've-been-there-and-back look. "Spent two years at Ben Ho with the Special Tactics Group. Assassinations and recon mostly. I could tell you stories . . . chill your blood."

Gannon stiffened. His eyes turned cold. "That's where you got the medals?"

"Damn straight."

Gannon propped a foot on the bench and leaned in close. "You'd think if you spent two years at a place you'd know how to pronounce it. It's Bien Hoa, not Ben Ho."

"I didn't have time to learn the language, man. I was too busy killin' slopes."

"Well, your story's got another hole in it. I spent twenty-three years in Special Forces and never heard of a Special Tactics Group."

Gannon tempered his response but, not about to let the man off scot-free, reached over and tore the medals from the bum's jacket and threw them out into the Pond.

"What the hell you think you're doin'? I'll take you apart like a cheap watch. I'll knock your dick in the dirt. And don't you think I can't do it, I got a tenth-degree black—"

"Shut up!" Gannon leaned in even closer, his face only inches away from the bum. The man's breath reeked of putrid wine and decaying teeth.

"I've got no use for people who steal a dead man's glory," Gannon said. "I had friends who died for those medals, and so do a lot of other guys. I strongly suggest you change your bullshit routine before you run into a vet who isn't in the mood to let you slide."

The bum drew back; his street smarts told him that the man leaning over him was in no mood to hear any more of his stories.

"Hey, we do what we gotta do, whatever works, ya know? No offense meant." Then, without skipping a beat, he added, "Anyway, you got a few bucks?"

Gannon shook his head in disgust but reached into his pocket and tossed three one-dollar bills in the bum's lap. He saw no point in questioning a self-admitted liar and continued along the path bordering the Pond.

A niche dweller like Nipper Denton, an organism at one with its ecosystem, could spot a tourist two blocks away—the way they walked was usually a dead giveaway. They scanned their surroundings as though they were on another planet, seeing what New Yorkers no longer bothered to see. He had witnessed the exchange between Gannon and the bum he knew as Rambo. At first he thought Gannon might be a cop and considered disappearing into the park, but after a few minutes of observing him, he dismissed it as unlikely that he was a cop or a local. And when he saw Gannon drop the money in Rambo's lap, he decided to play out his hand; the new message on his sign hadn't changed his luck, and the fifty cents he had scrounged out of coin-return slots in telephone booths was all he had to show for a morning's work.

His rheumy, bloodshot eyes followed Gannon as he walked along the path, heading toward his bench.

"Rambo been telling you how he won the war?" Nipper asked as Gannon approached.

"Rambo?"

Nipper jerked a thumb toward the bum Gannon had just talked to.

"Good name for him," Gannon said.

"Why'd you throw his medals away?"

Gannon shook his head, dismissing the question. "Mind if I talk to you for a few minutes?"

"I'm not goin' anywhere."

"Were you around this area late Sunday night?"

"Might have been."

"There was a traffic accident at Fifth Avenue and Sixty-ninth Street about four in the morning. Did you see it?"

"Maybe."

Gannon stared hard at what had once been a handsome face, now gaunt and discolored by old scars and scabs about to become new scars.

"What's your name?"

"Nipper. Nipper Denton." His nose dribbled and he wiped it with a crusty sleeve.

"Do me a favor, Nipper. Don't fuck with me. I've had a long morning. If you can help me, I'll give you what I can."

Nipper nodded half of an apology. "I saw a lot more than a traffic accident."

"What did you see?"

"Before the two cars smacked into each other, one of them, this big gray limousine, pulls into the curb not too far from the bench I was sleepin' on, and the back door flies open and this guy in the back throws this woman out of the car. At first I thought she was just drunk or somethin' and fell when she was gettin'—"

"You're sure there was someone in the car besides the driver?"

"The driver didn't get out of the car, so unless he had arms like an orangutan, there's no way he reached into the back of that limo and threw that woman out. And besides, when he pulled out and crashed into the other guy, someone got out of the backseat."

"Did you see him, the man who got out of the back?"

"Yeah. Not good though. It was dark. He was too far away."

"Can you remember anything about him?"

Nipper thought for a moment, then: "All I saw was that

he was tall, well built, had light hair, maybe blond, and he was wearin' a dark raincoat."

"Nothing else?"

"He said something to the driver, I didn't hear what, shook his finger at him sort of, then crossed the sidewalk and took the wall like it wasn't there and ran into the park. Moved fast, like he was in shape. That's it. Then the cops came."

"Why didn't you tell them what you saw?"

"I don't go lookin' for trouble. Why are you askin' all the questions?"

"The woman who was thrown out of the car was my wife. One of the men you saw, or both of them, murdered her."

"Oh," was all Nipper could think to say.

"Thanks, Nipper. You've been a great help," Gannon said, and extended his hand.

Nipper hesitated, then after wiping his own hand on his trousers, shook it tentatively, as though he felt the gesture was going to be withdrawn at the last moment. Except for the random beatings and attempts to rob him, it was the first time anyone had physically touched him in months. He smiled at Gannon and revealed a broken upper incisor, a souvenir from his last beating.

Gannon gave him one hundred dollars. Nipper stared at the five twenties in disbelief.

"Jesus! Thanks! Hey, ya know I think he hurt his head, the guy in the backseat," Nipper said, remembering something he hadn't realized he had seen. "I think he was holding his head when he got out of the car. Like this." Nipper placed the palm of his hand over his forehead.

"Was he bleeding?"

"Couldn't tell. Hey, where ya from?" Nipper brushed at the tufts of shaggy, greasy hair that curled over his ears and around the collar of one of his shirts. "Not from around here, huh?"

"North Carolina." Gannon searched Nipper's eyes and

got the feeling he wanted more than the money. Conversation maybe.

"Nice state, North Carolina. Too hot in the summer though."

"How'd you like to have some lunch, Nipper?" Gannon asked, then gestured toward a pair of Converse high-top sneakers that were disintegrating around Nipper's feet. "Then we'll buy you some new shoes."

Nipper looked at the money clutched tightly in his hand.

"My treat," Gannon reassured him.

"Or after lunch you could just give me the money for the shoes and I could buy them."

"I think if I did that, you might just spend it on something else. What do you think?"

"I think you might be right," Nipper said, "but it was worth a try." He broke into a hearty laugh that ended in a violent fit of coughing.

"Come on," Gannon said. "We'll get something to eat."

"You mean a real sit-down meal? Inside?"

Gannon smiled and nodded.

"Not too many places gonna let me in."

"You pick the place. We'll get in."

Nipper hitched up his trousers, tucked his sign and padded blanket under his arm, and followed his benefactor along the path that led through a pedestrian tunnel under the East Drive and on toward the Armory. He told Gannon about his life in the streets, talking almost nonstop. He paused to light a cigarette butt he had picked up earlier that morning and noticed that Gannon's attention was focused on the tunnel they had just exited. His whole demeanor had changed; he seemed tense and angry.

"Somethin' wrong?" he asked Gannon.

"Tell you what, Nipper. I want you to sit here on one of these benches and wait for me. I won't be long."

"Sure. If you don't come back, it's okay."

"I'll be back."

This was the third time Gannon had seen the man in the

tweed sport coat and gray slacks. He had chalked the second sighting up to coincidence, someone out for a walk. But the man had given himself away when Nipper paused to light his cigarette; he had stepped quickly off the path and pretended to admire a small statue just as Gannon looked in his direction.

Gannon continued toward the complex of brick buildings that had once served as the New York State Armory and was now the headquarters for the city's Department of Parks and Recreation. He cut down a narrow lane and headed for a cluster of garages and utility sheds behind the main building. He glanced quickly behind him before he ducked into a passageway between two of the sheds and waited.

The sound of footsteps hitting the pavement at a steady pace stopped, then started again, slower, more cautious. They grew fainter, then louder as the man backtracked and headed toward where Gannon waited.

The man caught a glimpse of Gannon out of the corner of his eye, but too late to avoid the arm that swept out and grabbed him by the hair and pulled him into the passageway, where he was slammed against a brick wall, pinned there with a forearm jammed in his throat.

"Talk to me," Gannon said, slowly applying pressure.

"Back off, Gannon," the man rasped.

"After you tell me why you're following me."

"I'm a cop."

"I don't think so. Let's see your shield."

"I don't carry it when I'm undercover."

"Bullshit. Who are you?" He pressed harder, slowly cutting off the man's air supply.

"Knock it off, Gannon." With a swift, practiced move the man broke free and spun away.

As Gannon moved to grab him the man drew a 9mm pistol from a holster in the small of his back, pointed it at Gannon, and backed out of reach.

Gannon stopped in his tracks and stared hard into the

man's eyes. If he was going to shoot, he would have done so immediately.

"You might kill me with that, but you're not going to scare me." Gannon circled slowly to his left and maintained eye contact with his opponent, who was nervously backing out of the passageway. The barrel of the pistol followed Gannon's every move.

"You can either shoot me or you can put that away. But if you keep pointing it at me, I'm going to take it away from you and shove it so far up your ass it'll take a team of proctologists to get it out."

"You're in over your head here, Gannon. Go home," the man with the pistol said as he continued to back out of the passageway.

"Hey!" Nipper Denton shouted from behind.

The man with the pistol looked for only an instant, but it was all the time Gannon needed to close the distance and disarm him and break his thumb in the process. A short, hard blow to the lower stomach put the man on his knees.

"Whoever you are, stay out of my way," Gannon warned as he left the passageway.

The man groaned and fell onto his side.

"Jesus," Nipper said, "hangin' around with you could be hazardous to my health." He looked back toward the man on the ground. "Nice jacket, think he'd miss it?"

Gannon took Nipper by the arm and led him away. He discreetly tossed the pistol into the Pond as they walked back toward Central Park South. "I thought I told you to wait back there for me."

"I saw that guy take off after you. My mother didn't raise any fools; I still got a meal and new sneakers comin'."

"You're a good man, Nipper Denton."

"Spread it around, will ya?"

Gannon put his arm around Nipper's shoulders, much to Nipper's surprise.

"What would you have done if that guy had reacted faster?"

"Died?" Nipper said.

12

Sergei Alipov left the Soviet Mission on East Sixty-seventh Street at 9:00 A.M. and spent the next two hours "dry-cleaning" himself of the FBI counterintelligence surveillance team that was assigned to follow his every move.

He spent the first hour on a circuitous route that took him in the opposite direction of his intended destination. At the garment district he turned into a narrow street lined with workshops and warehouses and jammed with young men pushing racks of clothes on hand trucks. He timed his next move perfectly. Horns blared and drivers shouted epithets that questioned his family's lineage as he squeezed past a truck that completely blocked the street immediately after he passed. He glanced into his rearview mirror and saw a dark blue sedan with two men in it. They had driven up onto the sidewalk in an attempt to get through, only to be hemmed in by another truck that backed out of a warehouse and added to the traffic jam. Alipov knew there were more to be ferreted out and evaded, and he continued the cat-and-mouse game he had learned to enjoy.

Expert at detecting and avoiding surveillance, his senses were attuned to spot even the most subtle signs. Every location had its own rhythm of activity that even the most experienced surveillant could inadvertently violate—a reaction against the normal flow of movement that caused visual incongruities that stood out against a composite of normal patterns and eventually betrayed a surveillance effort. Alipov never failed to spot them. He prided himself on his ability to lose his "tail" and continue with his business, when less experienced men would break off a meeting or the servicing of a drop at the first hint of surveillance.

The second hour of dry-cleaning involved a more elaborate plan, which Alipov, before leaving the mission, had carefully orchestrated and gone over with four of his most experienced KGB officers. He assigned them to separate relay points along the surveillance detection route he had planned and drove past each of them three times. He had worked out the route on a timing sheet so the men at the relay locations knew approximately when Alipov would drive by, and after passing each man's location he contacted them on their small hand-held portable radios. If anyone was following him, the men would report the color and make of the car and its occupants, or if necessary, after instructions from Alipov, use their own cars to impede the progress of the surveillants. When done properly it always worked. The surveillance team had only two choices: follow him through all of his repetitive evasive maneuvers and be spotted by the relays or fall back and lose him. Either way, Alipov won in the end.

By the time he crossed the Brooklyn Bridge he was free of surveillance, but he still drove past an apartment house on Ocean Avenue where he had stationed a lookout. With the final all clear, he parked six blocks away from the Brighton Beach safe house and went through the intricate procedures to flush out anyone who might have spotted him and was following on foot.

Once a decaying urban enclave, the Brighton Beach section of Brooklyn had been rejuvenated in recent years by an influx of Soviet emigrés. Entire blocks that had been boarded up were now crowded with Russian delicatessens, discos, shops, and supper clubs. On summer nights, when he was feeling particularly homesick, Alipov occasionally came to sit on the boardwalk and drink kvass—a brew made from fermented black bread—and listen to the minstrels play their balalaikas and sing of the Motherland. But love of all things Russian was not the only reason Alipov came to Brighton Beach. The thriving emigré community was fertile ground for KGB support facilities. It provided ample opportunities for recruitment operations and was a natural place for Illegals to disappear into the immigrant population.

The "Russian Mafia," a gang of criminals that operated in the community, were a natural ally for Alipov. They specialized in fraud, extortion, and counterfeiting, and preyed on other Russian immigrants who were easily intimidated because of cultural unfamiliarity and language barriers. The criminal element acted as "spotters" and notified Alipov of any disenchanted patriots and those who were in need of money. Both were a potential source of recruits for agents and assets who provided safe houses and other support for his operations. He had an impressive list of well-educated emigrés who, either voluntarily or through coercion, had become agents in place and sleeper agents, some of them now holding sensitive jobs in the government and defense-related research firms. A few had even acquired high-level security clearances.

Alipov walked around the block three times before ducking into an alley where he entered the rear of a grocery on Brighton Beach Avenue. He climbed the steps to the second-floor apartment that served as one of his safe houses. He knocked twice, then twice again, and opened the door to see Nikolai Malik sitting in an easy chair reading *The New York Times.* A tray of breakfast dishes, brought up by the woman who owned the grocery, sat on a nearby table. The food had not been touched.

"Sergei Grigorevich," Malik said, addressing him in a familiar way with no respect for Alipov's rank. Although he put down his paper, he did not bother to rise from the chair.

"You are late, Comrade," Malik said as he glanced at his watch.

"I am cautious, something you are not. And it is Comrade *General,* Colonel Malik."

Malik grinned and two-fingered a cigarette out of a pack in his shirt pocket—one of his practiced Americanisms he enjoyed showing off.

"When are you leaving the city?" Alipov asked.

"Shortly. I have some unfinished business with our Nicaraguan friends."

"That is not your only unfinished business?"

"Ah, yes. I thought that might be the purpose for this meeting."

"Kirilenko has said nothing to the police or anyone else, but I cannot guarantee our GRU comrades will not find a way to interrogate him and use his wife and children in Moscow as leverage."

"Fuck the GRU."

"No, Nikolai Petrovich. Fuck you! You have put our entire operation in great danger by bringing us unwanted attention."

Malik's gaze hardened. His dark eyes threatened for a brief moment. "I am your entire operation." He got up from the chair in a way that caused Alipov to take a step back. Malik flashed another contemptuous grin. "Besides, it will pass. No one other than yourself and Kirilenko knows I am here."

"And how much does he know? He has eyes and ears, and there have been times when you have not been the most circumspect operative."

Malik shrugged. "What does it matter? He will talk to no one."

"I want to be assured of that," Alipov said. "But I will not jeopardize any of my officers to clean up your mess. The CIA and FBI will be watching them closely. I have not sent Kirilenko back to Moscow or held him under house arrest, which as you know is the usual procedure when one of the mission staff is involved in an incident with the police, and that in itself will alert the GRU."

"I will take care of it, *Comrade.*"

Alipov bristled at his insolence. "See that you do. I have taken the position that the incident was a CIA provocation and sent Kirilenko back to work where you can get to him. He is on duty today; you will find him at the United Nations. And please," Alipov added emphatically, "do nothing on Soviet or United Nations property and try to at least give the appearance that it was something other than what it is."

"I said I will take care of it."

"Without delay. The GRU *rezident* at the mission is due back tomorrow. And there is one other thing," Alipov said. "There was an incident at the police station when we picked up Kirilenko. A man, I believe the husband of the woman who was murdered, attacked Kirilenko. If he gets to him before you do, we could very well have another problem on our hands."

Malik smiled; it was a smile without humor. "A grieving husband is the least of my concerns."

Alipov studied the hard, emotionless face that stared defiantly back at him. "Did you rape and murder that woman?"

"Is that what Kirilenko told you?"

"No. He said only that he did not do it."

"Do I look like a man who needs to force women to have sex with him? I am what the American women call a hunk."

Alipov shook his head and looked away. He was becoming uncomfortable in Malik's presence, a feeling he experienced on each of the few occasions he had come face-to-face with him.

"You cannot use any of the forged passports and documents that have been previously issued to you," Alipov said. "The GRU may have a list of your cover identities by now. I have brought new documents for you to use in getting out of the country in the event they learn of your presence here . . . if they do not already suspect that you are in the city," he added with enough invective to leave no doubt in Malik's mind what he meant.

"I will take care of my own needs. Your documents would give me no more assurance than those I already have."

Alipov went to the door and paused as he opened it. "If it were not for your father's friends and your operational successes, Colonel Malik, there are those of us who would prefer to see you in a labor camp where you would cease to be an embarrassment and disgrace to your superiors and the Committee for State Security."

"If pigs had wings," Malik said, and slammed the door in Alipov's face.

13

Bill Rafferty entered the small coffee shop around the corner from the Nineteenth Precinct station house to find Gannon already there. The elderly waitress behind the counter caught his eye and held up the coffeepot. Rafferty nodded and slid into the booth with Gannon.

"What's so important you couldn't tell me on the phone?"

Gannon waited until the waitress who brought the coffee left. "There was someone else in the limousine. He ran into the park before the cops arrived on the scene."

"Get a description?"

"Partial. Tall, probably blond, wearing a dark raincoat. Might have a minor head injury from the accident."

"That's not a hell of a lot to go on," Rafferty said. "And there's nothing I can do with it anyway. Like I told you before, whoever the other guy is, you can bet he's got diplomatic immunity, and even if he doesn't, what have you got? The driver sure as shit isn't going to testify against him, we can't even subpoena him. Can the person who told you they saw this guy get out of the limo that night positively identify him?"

"Maybe."

"Maybe? Maybe doesn't cut it. Who's your witness?"

"A guy who lives in the park."

"A bum?"

"Yeah."

"Jesus. Smells like a distillery, right? Sometimes can't remember what day it is or exactly where he was at any given time or maybe his full name?"

"I get the point," Gannon said. "I'm not asking you to go chasing after shadows, but if I can find out who this guy is, can you at least make sure he's got diplomatic immunity before you write off my wife's murder?"

"Hey, Gannon. I'm on your side. But I wouldn't be doing you any favors by bullshitting you on what your chances are of seeing this guy brought to justice. And what are you going to do if you find him and he does have full diplomatic immunity?" Rafferty raised his hand. "Never mind, don't answer that."

"That reminds me," Gannon said. "Did you have a tail on me?"

"No. Why?"

"Someone does."

"What happened?"

"I spotted him in the park and called him on it."

"Who was he?"

"Didn't say. He's American. And if he's not one of yours, then he's probably CIA or FBI."

Rafferty leaned forward in the booth, hunched over his coffee. "Look, Gannon, we didn't have this part of the conversation, okay?"

Gannon nodded in agreement.

"There's a lot of strange things going on with this case. And some of them point to our Federal Father. A friend of mine is with our Police Intelligence Unit and he told me the local CIA office got hyperactive when they found out about your wife's murder and the Soviets sent Kirilenko back to work as though nothing had happened. Normally they would have had his ass on the first Aeroflot flight back to Moscow."

"What are you suggesting?"

"I don't know. Like I said, it's the inconsistencies. And if Washington's involved in this, you're messing around with the wrong people. They don't have to play by cop rules, you know. They'll take you out if you get in their way, and they'll do it with impunity."

"They're not going to scare me off."

Rafferty sipped his coffee and carefully considered what he was about to say. "Something else my friend turned up."

Gannon leaned forward in anticipation.

"The night your wife was murdered, the Emergency Services people who went over the area around the crime scene found three Puerto Rican kids, dead, in a pedestrian tunnel inside the park, not more than a hundred yards from where the accident occurred. The bodies were still warm. Medical examiner estimates the time of death around the same time as the accident."

"What does that have to do with Kate's murder?"

"These kids were each shot twice in the eye socket at close range, .22 caliber. There were a lot of bums sleeping in the immediate area, yet none of them heard the shots. That tell you anything?"

"Silencer," Gannon said.

"Yeah. And the way they were shot says a pro did it. Not your normal Upper East Side response to an attempted mugging. Again, inconsistencies. So, just for the hell of it, let's say it was the guy who got out of the backseat of the limo. I don't know too many diplomats who pack silenced weapons or would have the balls to take on three muggers with switchblades even if they did have a weapon. You beginning to get a picture of what you might be dealing with here?"

"I appreciate your concern," Gannon said, "but I'm not backing away from this. I can't. I just can't let it go that easy."

"I understand that. I just want you to know what you're up against; I don't want to see you end up dead or in prison."

"I'll watch my step."

"You do that," Rafferty said. "And when you leave here you might want to go down to the United Nations. The Soviet drivers work in pairs. They stay with their cars while the diplomats are inside. They're usually in the underground garage or parked in the circle in front of the Secretariat building. Sometimes one of them leaves the UN grounds to get coffee or go shopping while the other one stays with the car."

"Thanks," Gannon said, "I owe you."

"Forget where you got it."

"Got what?"

"How long you been with Delta Force?"

"Since the begin—" Gannon caught himself and cast a questioning look at Rafferty, who smiled and winked.

"Hey, I'm a detective."

"We have a saying in Special Forces when people ask us about our classified missions," Gannon said as he got out of the booth.

"What's that?"

"If I tell you, I've got to kill you."

"How come I knew it would be something like that."

Gannon clasped Rafferty's hand. "I know you went out of your way for me, and I'm grateful for your help."

"Be careful, it's a jungle out there."

"I'd feel a lot more at home if it was," Gannon said, and threw Rafferty a choppy salute as he went out the door and disappeared into the rush of pedestrians.

14

Towering thirty-nine stories above the United Nations Plaza and the East River, the glass-and-steel structure of the Secretariat building sparkled in the midafternoon sun. Just outside the main entrance Viktor Kirilenko stood leaning against the fender of a black sedan parked at the curb of the circular drive. He was still overwhelmed by his good fortune. He had not been sent back to Moscow in disgrace as he had feared, in fact he had not been punished at all, a turn of events that puzzled him in light of what had happened. But General Alipov had been understanding and not pressed him when he denied having any knowledge of how the woman had died; he was grateful for that, not wanting to be caught between the wrath of his direct superiors and the vicious threats made by the man he knew only as "the Comrade Colonel."

Graphic images of what the colonel had done, vignettes that both terrified and disturbed Kirilenko, were still fresh in his mind. He wished now that his morbid curiosity had not drawn him to watch in the rearview mirror, but the brutality had been both hypnotically fascinating and repulsive at the same time. He had never seen anyone beaten and raped. The beautiful woman's screams and pleas for mercy were twice directed at him. She had begged him to intercede. But the colonel finally silenced her and continued to violate her in ways Kirilenko had never imagined possible. The man was the essence of evil, Kirilenko thought. He had frightened him more than anyone he had ever met, and he hoped he never had the misfortune of seeing him again and that the horrid images of that night would soon go away and allow him to sleep without being awakened in the middle of the night soaked with perspiration and shaking uncontrollably.

The General Assembly was in session and the two trade delegation officers Kirilenko had been assigned to drive would not be back until late afternoon. Today he had enough money left, after having sent most of his meager salary home to his family, to treat himself to a good meal— something he never got at the mission's Glen Cove estate, where he lived. He left the car in the custody of his partner and walked past the security guards and out through the drive-in gate. He headed up First Avenue, past the array of flags in front of the General Assembly building, where he crossed against the traffic and continued up East Forty-sixth Street to the corner of Second Avenue. The scent of Chinese cooking made him smile as he entered the restaurant and took a table overlooking the sidewalk. It was his favorite food, a taste acquired since coming to the United States, and he would enjoy it thoroughly; he had good reason to celebrate.

Jack Gannon had been watching Kirilenko for the past two hours. He had followed him from the moment he left the United Nations, staying well back for fear that he would be spotted and recognized from the incident at the police station. When a waiter approached Kirilenko and held his attention, Gannon fell in behind an elderly couple, entered the restaurant, and took a table in a corner near the door where Kirilenko would have to turn completely around to see him. He peered over the top of his unfolded newspaper, watching Kirilenko's hand lift and set down a cup of green tea.

A group of Japanese tourists, fresh from a tour of the

United Nations, cameras dangling from their necks and
laden with tote bags stuffed with souvenirs, came in the door
and momentarily blocked Gannon's field of vision. After
what seemed an interminable amount of time and discussion, they decided on a table and took their seats.

Gannon looked up to see that Kirilenko was gone. He
anxiously scanned the room and saw him go into a hall at
the rear of the restaurant. A sign on the wall said, "To Rest
Rooms." Gannon settled back in his chair and kept one eye
on the doorway and the hall leading off it. The area was
busy with waiters coming in and out of the kitchen and
patrons entering and exiting a rear door. Although it was
difficult to see the hallway clearly at all times, Gannon
opted against moving to another table closer to the back of
the restaurant. He did not want to be forced into acting
before he was ready. He planned to confront Kirilenko after
he left the restaurant. It would be easy to pull him into one
of the narrow alleyways along the street.

Outside the restaurant, parked at the curb across the
street, a surveillance team from the CIA's Counterterrorist
Group waited in a dark gray sedan. The man in the passenger seat sat up with a sudden start.

"That's him!" he said to his partner.

"You sure?" The man at the wheel craned his neck to see.

"Going in the rear door."

"I don't see him."

"He's inside now. It's Malik, I'm sure of it. I've been
studying the bastard's photograph all morning."

"We'll take him when he comes out," the driver said.
"He's not going to go down easy, and I don't want any
gunplay in a crowded restaurant."

"Call it in. I want another team here for backup. If we
lose him, Driscoll will have us guarding empty warehouses
in Greenland."

"The closest backup's over in Brooklyn, checking out safe
houses. We're on our own."

The two men got quickly out of the car. They stayed on the opposite side of the street and took up positions where they had a clear view of both the front and rear doors to the restaurant.

A waiter poured Gannon a cup of tea and handed him a menu, from which he absently ordered something by its designated number. He glanced at his watch and began to feel uneasy. His view of the hallway was now obscured by a small party of businessmen who had come through the rear door. Near the center of the dining room two of the Japanese tourists excused themselves from their table and headed for the rest rooms.

Gannon got up and walked slowly toward the back of the restaurant, wondering if Kirilenko had returned to a different table. As he neared the opposite end a commotion broke out. The two Japanese tourists rushed out of the hallway, obviously frightened, shouting hysterically in rapid-fire Japanese to their friends and the clientele at large.

Gannon angled his way past the waiters at the entrance to the kitchen and nearly knocked down another man making his way to a table. Sprinting down the hallway to the men's room, he threw open the door. A pair of shoes, cocked at an odd angle, edged out of a stall. The stall door was cracked open, and Gannon looked inside. Kirilenko sat sprawled on the toilet, his head tilted upward, his bullet-punctured eyes staring blankly at the ceiling as bright red rivulets of blood streamed from the sockets.

Gannon ran back to the dining room. The entire table of Japanese were now chattering and gesturing wildly to the manager. Gannon caught something in his peripheral vision —someone running outside in the street. He pushed his way through the excited crowd of diners and threw open the rear door to the sidewalk.

Two men, pistols in hand, dodged and weaved their way through the one-way traffic, their attention on someone farther down the block. Gannon looked in their direction and caught a glimpse of a man ducking into an alley. He was tall, blond, and wearing a black raincoat.

Gannon gave chase and followed the two men ahead of him. Halfway down the block they turned into the alley. Gaining on them, Gannon rounded the corner and immediately dived to the ground as two silenced shots ricocheted off the building only inches from his head. He rose to a crouch behind a trash container and peered around at the two men lying motionless farther up the alley. The tall blond man turned to face him; they locked eyes for a brief moment, long enough for Gannon to see the small discolored lump on his forehead, and then he was gone, disappearing around the corner of another building.

Gannon stayed low and scurried to where the two men lay dead from head wounds. He picked up one of their automatic pistols, then decided against it and threw it away. Up and moving, he ran down the narrow passage between two buildings where the man had gone. He saw him, fifty yards ahead, exiting the passageway onto First Avenue. With smooth, powerful strides, Gannon began to close the distance.

Malik darted across the avenue, repeatedly glancing over his shoulder. The third man had surprised him. He had spotted the two men in the gray sedan on his way into the restaurant and had planned to deal with them when he had finished with Kirilenko. But where had the third man come from? Perhaps a plainclothes cop who had happened onto the scene. He slowed to a brisk walk and blended with the tourists crowding the sidewalk in front of United Nations Plaza as he headed for the delegates' entrance to the General Assembly building.

Gannon was running flat out as he reached the street. He hurtled a stack of crates being unloaded from a van and dashed out into First Avenue with an abandonment born of desperation. Cars swerved and tires squealed as startled motorists leaned on their horns and braked frantically. Traffic came to an abrupt halt. An irate taxi driver, his head out the

window, cursed Gannon as he scrambled over the hood of
his car and jumped down onto the sidewalk in front of the
visitors' entrance to the United Nations, directly into the
midst of a group of schoolchildren exiting a tour bus that
was parked at the curb. Momentarily losing sight of the man
he was chasing, he stopped to search the crowd of people on
the sidewalk ahead of him. He looked in the opposite direction, then back, finally spotting the blond hair and the
shoulders of the black raincoat above the crowd as the man
stopped at a security gate.

Malik walked calmly up to the security guard at the delegates' entrance and flashed his forged identification. The
guard nodded and stood aside as Malik continued on toward
the General Assembly building. Again looking back over his
shoulder, he saw that the third man was still with him. He
picked up his pace and followed the curved elevated
rampway leading to the entrance of the building.

Gannon sprinted the distance to the gate, quick-cutting
his way through the pedestrian traffic. Directly in front of
him, he saw the security guard alert to his approach.

The guard stepped out of his glass booth and placed himself squarely in the center of the opening in the wrought-
iron fence, his eyes fixed on Gannon, who gave no indication
of stopping.

As Gannon reached the gate the security guard grabbed
him by the arm to slow him down, but Gannon spun away,
intent on the door he saw the blond man approaching.

"That man killed my wife," he shouted as he shook off
the guard. "He's a murderer."

The guard pressed the button on a small remote pager
kept in his pocket, then reached for the .38 Special he carried out of sight on his hip. He drew and cocked the weapon
and took aim at Gannon's back.

"Halt!" the guard shouted in a high-pitched voice that
revealed his anxiety about having to draw his weapon for
the first time and the fear that he might have to use it.

Gannon broke stride. He slowed down at the sound of the

guard's shouted command and the sight of two more armed guards ahead of him, who burst out of a door at the top of the entrance ramp, weapons in hand. The futility of his actions hit him, and he stopped running. In the distance, at the top of the ramp, he saw the tall blond man pull open a door and pause before entering the building; he thought he saw him smile just before he stepped inside.

Gannon turned and walked slowly back toward the uniformed guard at the gate, his hands at his side, spread open in a gesture of surrender. The guard slowly, gratefully, lowered and holstered his weapon.

"That man just killed three people," Gannon said.

"I don't know anything about that," the guard said. "But this entrance is for delegates and official UN personnel only. Get on the other side of the gate or I'll have you arrested."

"Arrest *him,* goddamnit!" Gannon could see that the guard's only concern was getting what he considered to be a possible madman back outside the perimeter security fence, and his better judgment made him move in that direction.

The uniformed guard waved an all clear to the two men who had come out of the General Assembly building. They disappeared inside as quickly as they had appeared.

"There are two men lying dead in an alley a few blocks from here and another one in a restaurant," Gannon said. "And that son of a bitch killed them. At least call the goddamn police."

"Just calm down, mister."

"How did he get past you and I didn't?"

"He's got a pass."

"He's a diplomat? What's his name?"

"I didn't check the name. Just looked at the picture. Now get away from the gate or I will call the police, but not about the other guy."

Gannon remembered Rafferty's admonitions and saw no point in pressing the issue. He looked back in frustration to where Malik had disappeared, then walked slowly away from the delegates' entrance and crossed to the other side of

First Avenue. He returned to the small parklike setting directly across from the drive-in entrance to the Secretariat building and sat on a bench, resuming his vigil from the same vantage point where he had watched Kirilenko.

15

Twenty-five minutes after Gannon walked away from the delegates' entrance to the United Nations, a report of the incident, along with the preliminary details of the deaths of Kirilenko and the two CTG officers, had reached CIA headquarters in Langley, Virginia. Ten minutes later another report arrived: Malik had been found . . . and lost.

The United Nations, considered under the law as international territory, was off limits to the FBI but not to the CIA, whose Foreign Resources section ran operations there ranging from simple intelligence gathering to false-flag recruitments. The FR officer trawling the delegates' lounge when Nikolai Malik entered had immediately recognized him. He tried, without success, to eavesdrop on his conversation with a Nicaraguan diplomat, then left the lounge for no more than a few minutes to call the local office. He returned to find Malik gone. With the help of three other FR officers, he conducted an exhaustive search of the building and the garage, but Malik was nowhere to be found. A garage attendant told him that two Soviet-owned vehicles had left within the past few minutes, none carrying a passenger matching the description of the man they were looking for. But then he couldn't see inside the trunks of the cars, and hiding someone in the trunk of one car, with another car leaving at the same time as a decoy, was a ploy the Soviets occasionally used to secret someone out of the building.

"There's no doubt it was Malik," Tom Driscoll told the Deputy Director for Operations. "The security guard at the gate confirmed it from the photo we showed him."

David Wilson shook his head in exasperation. "That slimy son of a bitch! And I see Gannon damn near botched the operation before we even got a chance at Malik. I thought you said you had him under surveillance and under control."

"As I told you earlier, he's a loose cannon. We'll just have to increase the pressure."

"Two of our men dead," Wilson said in disgust as he looked at the report on his desk. "First one with a broken thumb. Now this. How did he break his thumb anyhow?"

"Gannon did it for him," Driscoll said. "The man was new, his first field assignment. When Gannon ambushed him, he panicked and drew his weapon."

"I don't want any more interference from that cowboy. Medal of Honor or not, make sure he gets the message that things are going to get nasty, fast, if he persists."

"He was only a threat as long as Kirilenko was alive to lead him to Malik. Without that he's reached a dead end. He's got nowhere to go but home."

"See to it that he does just that," Wilson said. "If he doesn't listen to reason, I want him pulled in and put on ice for a while. Put the arm on the Police Intelligence Unit, they owe us a few. If he's still in the city tomorrow and goes anywhere near the Soviet Mission or the UN, see if they can make his life miserable. Arrest him as a suspect in the murder of Kirilenko. Give him something else to occupy his mind."

"I don't want to come down too hard on him, Dave," Driscoll said. "He's trouble, but he's not doing anything you or I wouldn't do in the same situation."

"Then turn the heat up in increments. Give him a chance

to back off of his own volition," Wilson said, his tone softening. "But I want him out of the equation."

"I'll take care of it."

The Peace Park, as it was designated by a bronze plaque bolted to a small fence, was no more than a narrow slip of an island planted with trees and shrubs in the center of an extended sidewalk across the street from the United Nations. Park benches lined a white marble wall, part of which bore the inscription "They shall beat their swords into plowshares, and their spears into pruning hooks; nation shall not lift up sword against nation, neither shall they learn war any more."

Dream on, Isaiah, Gannon thought as he looked away after reading the inscription. He had been watching the main entrance to the General Assembly building for over an hour, his intellect telling him that it was foolish to expect the man he was after to simply walk out as if nothing had happened, but his emotions would not let him give up.

A car swung into the curb directly in front of the bench he was sitting on, partially blocking his view across the street.

"Get in," Bill Rafferty called out from behind the wheel.

"I can't leave yet. The man who murdered Kate could still be in that building."

"Use your head, Gannon, there's a dozen ways out of there. Get in!" Rafferty demanded. "You'll leave with me now or in about five minutes you'll leave under arrest and wearing handcuffs."

Gannon got up and crossed to the car. "I didn't kill Kirilenko."

"I know that, and they know that," Rafferty said. "But I told you these people don't play by the rules, and the game's about to start."

"You know about the two guys who bought it in the alley?"

"Yeah, I know about them."

"I think they were CIA," Gannon said.

"They were."

"Well, if they aren't after the guy for Kate's murder, what do they want with him?"

"They've got their own agenda, Gannon, and they don't consult me. Someone once described their profession as a wilderness of mirrors. I've found it's best just to stay out of their way. Now, let's go."

"If I leave now, I don't know if I can pick up his trail again."

"He's gone, for Christ's sake!" Rafferty saw the fatigue in Gannon's face; he had seen it before, in men so distraught and tired that it drastically affected their judgment. Acting irrationally was the next step in the debilitating process.

"Look, Gannon, my head's on the block. This isn't my precinct and I've got no business being down here, certainly not to warn you that you're about to be busted for disturbing the peace, loitering, or any other bullshit charge they can pull you in on. And the word is, if you're still hanging around tomorrow, you become the principal suspect in a homicide. Now get the fuck in the car."

Gannon got in and Rafferty pulled quickly out into the stream of traffic. As he put on his turn signal to turn onto a cross street heading west, he looked in his rearview mirror and saw two detectives in an unmarked car pull into the space he had just left.

"How'd you know where to find me?"

"It's where I'd be if I were you," Rafferty said. "You've got to go home, Gannon. There's nothing more you can do here except hurt yourself."

"Go home and do what? Forget it? We've already been through that."

"Go home and regroup. Think it through; find another approach to getting this guy if that's what you have to do. But if you stay around here and start harassing the Soviets, the Feds are going to be on you like white on rice."

Gannon slumped down in the seat. He felt tired, physically and emotionally drained. "You're right," he said, his voice cracking with exhaustion. "I know you're right; I just can't let go."

"Just go home," Rafferty said. "If I can find out anything, and I mean anything, about this sick son of a bitch, I'll let you know immediately. But believe me, Gannon, it's over for you here in the city. The Feds are calling in markers with the department to get you out of their hair."

"I need a name to go with the face," Gannon said.

"I'll see what I can do."

"I've never done anything like this in my life, you know, gone off half cocked. I'm a firm believer in having a good operational plan."

"Then put one together. Your background suggests you might be able to tap a network of your own for a little help."

"Maybe," Gannon said, the strength and spirit gone from his voice. "Drop me at the Carlyle, will you? Kate's mother's arranged for a private service tomorrow. I'll leave when it's over."

"Where's the funeral being held?" Rafferty asked.

"No funeral. Just a prayer service in the Presbyterian church on Madison Avenue down from the hotel. Kate hated funerals; she wanted to be cremated."

Rafferty made a mental note to stop by and pay his respects.

Gannon felt depleted, a hollow shell. He couldn't stop thinking about Kate or what would physically remain of her, an urn full of ashes. He laid his head back on the seat and closed his eyes; it was all he could do to keep the tears from flowing uncontrollably.

"It isn't over, Kate," he said, his voice barely audible. "I promise you, honey, it isn't over."

16

Alain Casson had spent the better part of the day touring the narrow, quiet streets of Greenwich Village with his friends. It was the last day of his week-long vacation in New York City. Tomorrow night he would be back in Paris and the following morning back behind his desk at the bank. He was thoroughly bored. He had seen enough quaint curio and antique shops, galleries, open-air art displays, and craft shops to last him a lifetime. The attempt to evoke the atmosphere of Montmartre and St. Germain des Prés failed on all counts as far as he was concerned. And besides, he hadn't come to the Big Apple to be reminded of Paris.

His friends, still in the company of the two women they had met over lunch, opted for an evening at an Off-Broadway theater and a late-night tour of the clubs and coffee houses. Casson declined the invitation to join them. He had had his fill of culture for one day and felt uncomfortable as the odd man out. With his friends gone, and a rendezvous point agreed on for early the next morning, he walked through Washington Square Park, fending off the entreaties of street hustlers and drug dealers, and a wild-eyed vagrant whom he believed to be some kind of religious zealot. At the central water fountain he joined a group of students from nearby New York University who had stopped to listen to an impromptu twilight concert by a trio of folk singers of

questionable talent. A scattering of raggedly dressed and
mostly unscrubbed middle-aged hippie types, left over from
a previous generation, drifted in and sat cross-legged on the
sidewalk, gazing wistfully as they sang and swayed to the
decades-old songs that Casson suspected had once been
their anthems.

With the addition of a growing number of concurrent
performances, the area around the fountain was taking on a
circus atmosphere: A leather-clad duo of ersatz cowboys
cracked whips and lassoed each other, while a noisy demonstration of disco roller skating by young blacks with huge
radios balanced on their shoulders competed with the folk
singers. A unicyclist caught Casson's attention. The man
was in desperate need of instruction; if not for the helmet
and kneepads he wore, his repeated tumbles to the pavement
would have resulted in serious injury. Casson soon left,
walking west from Washington Square into the heart of the
Village, where he wandered along the Londonesque jumble
of little streets and browsed in small shops with names like
Serendipity and As You Like It.

He was hungry, having eaten only a small portion of the
poorly prepared quiche he had ordered for lunch at a sidewalk café. When he entered an overdecorated nook of a
restaurant on a quiet street, his senses were again assaulted
by another failed attempt at Parisian bistro ambiance. Bare
brick walls were adorned with ugly still lifes of flowers and
tablescapes, and the tiny dining room, crammed full of what
could best be described as insubstantial stick furniture, had
far more plants than customers. The murky lighting caused
him to bang his shins twice as he followed an overly solici-
tous waiter to a table in an even darker corner. The meal
turned out to be commensurate with the decor, and the
price was something Casson preferred to forget.

When he left the restaurant he began following the directions his friend in Paris had given him. As he turned onto
Christopher Street it was soon apparent that he was headed
in the right direction. Men, casually walking arm in arm in

the cool night air, some with their hands in each other's back pockets, appeared from apartment buildings and small clubs and bars.

A lone stroller, a young man, attractive enough, Casson thought, slowed his pace and smiled warmly as he approached from the opposite direction. Casson made no response. He felt awkward, unsure of what to do. It was his first venture into the gay world. If you don't try it, his friend in Paris had told him, you will never be sure. No one knows you in New York, it is the perfect place for your initial tryst. The sound of music and laughter carried out into the street from a dimly lit nightclub. Casson gathered his courage, and after a cursory appraisal by a well-muscled man blocking the doorway, he entered a large room hung with a forest of ferns and crowded to the point of anonymity.

He ordered a drink at the bar, and as his eyes grew accustomed to the lighting, he saw that the dance floor was jammed with men in every imaginable type of embrace. The throbbing disco beat encouraged the most sensuous of movements and Casson stared openly, slowly becoming somewhat more comfortable with his surroundings as well as the feelings that stirred inside him. But not comfortable enough to handle the advances from a man standing elbow-to-elbow with him at the bar; he ignored him, more out of nervousness than the fact that he thought he was singularly unattractive. The man who made the second approach fared no better, being rejected with an urgent shake of the head when he asked Casson if he wanted to dance.

The third man who approached, Casson found intriguing as well as exotically attractive. They were approximately the same height and he looked vaguely familiar, until Casson realized that it was the strong resemblance they bore to each other that accounted for the déjà vu.

"We could be brothers," Casson said.

"Yes," Nikolai Malik said. "You are smaller-boned and your features are more refined, but there is a certain resemblance." A resemblance that had caused Malik to follow him when he came out of the restaurant, ending a search that had begun when he left the United Nations.

"You are an American, from New York?" Casson said.

"Yes. My name is Nick," Malik said. "And your name is?"

"Alain. I am French. A Parisian, actually." Casson found himself almost shouting above the music, which had increased in volume.

"I have spent a great deal of time in Paris," Malik said. He switched from English to French with a smoothness and fluency that both impressed and relaxed his listener.

"It is my last night in New York," Casson said.

"Then perhaps we should not spend it here." Malik flashed a charming smile and winked.

He was pleased with his stroke of good luck; the man would have a passport, and the photograph and physical statistics would favor him enough to pass any superficial examination by immigration officials. He had three current passports of his own, but Alipov's concern was valid. All of his pseudonyms and the passport numbers could be retrieved from a computer at the Center in Moscow, and there was no guarantee that GRU moles could not gain access to them.

"What would you suggest?" Casson said. His voice betrayed his uneasiness.

"My apartment is not far from here. It is much quieter and far more comfortable." Malik gestured with his head toward the door.

Casson hesitated, then shrugged and followed Malik outside. It was now or never, he thought, and never would not answer the questions or assuage the secret desires that had plagued him for the past two years.

"I should tell you that I am inexperienced," he said. "The truth is, it is my first time."

"How intriguing," Malik said. "Then the introductory course is in order."

"You're not rough, are you?

"Gentle as a lamb."

Casson forced a faint smile as Malik put an arm around his shoulder and led him into a alley.

"A shortcut to my apartment," Malik said in response to Casson's tensing as they entered the dark narrow corridor between two buildings.

Malik glanced back toward the street as they moved farther into the deep shadows.

"This is a dead end," Casson said, noticing that they were headed toward a chain-link fence blocking the other end of the alley.

"So it is," Malik said, taking a step back and placing himself directly behind Casson. Quickly, expertly, he gripped his unsuspecting victim with his powerful arms and, with a vicious twisting action, snapped his neck before he could cry out.

Casson went limp in his arms, and Malik lowered him slowly to the ground, propping him in a sitting position against a trash container where he could not be seen from the street. He took off his black raincoat and exchanged it for the light gray silk-and-cotton one Casson was wearing. He then rifled the dead man's pockets and took his wallet and passport. Again checking the street, he conducted a more complete search and stripped Casson of anything that could immediately provide the police with his identity: an airline ticket, hotel-room key, restaurant receipts, and a wristwatch bearing his initials.

Malik exited the alley and paused momentarily on the sidewalk, adjusting his new raincoat; he liked the silken feel of the fabric. Smiling to himself, he walked back to the gay bar he had just left.

17

The only light in the ranch-style house on Cottonwood Avenue in Fayetteville, North Carolina, came from the television screen in the den. The cozy wood-paneled room was filled with sounds and images of Kate Gannon, laughing, clowning, posing, grinning mischievously as she held up a trout that dwarfed the one her husband had caught. For Gannon they were moments outside of time now that only increased the pain of loss rather than providing the solace he sought. His eyes red and puffy, his face lined with fatigue and covered with a two-day growth of beard, he pointed the remote control at the video recorder and played back a scene where he had captured Kate crawling out of their tent on the shore of a Maine lake, her hair a mess, her face full of sleep; she flicked him the bird in protest as she ran and dived into the cold, clear water.

Videotapes were stacked on a table next to where he sat, and empty beer cans from three twelve-packs of Coors littered the floor near his feet. When the tape ended he stared blankly at the snowy static, finally getting up and ejecting it, only to insert another and remove a fourth twelve-pack from the refrigerator before returning on unsteady legs to sit heavily in the chair. He popped the top on another beer as a tropical beach at sunset appeared on the screen—an R and R leave in Hawaii in 1970, the first time he had seen Kate since their brief honeymoon the previous year. Magnificent in a scant bikini, she swam to shore and walked out of the surf.

Gannon pressed the freeze-frame button and smiled to himself at the fond memories of the week they had spent together. A week he had desperately needed after eleven months of harrowing over-the-fence missions into Laos and North Vietnam, where he had seen three close friends die horrible deaths. The frequency of their suicidal reconnaissance missions had increased drastically following the Tet Offensive and so had the casualties, reaching a killed-in-action rate of 80 percent in the previous six months. He had never been a man who loved violence, but he was at home with it. Lately it had begun to seem meaningless, with no end or goal in sight, and Kate, nonjudgmental despite her deep-felt opposition to the war, had understood and helped him gain some perspective before he returned for his fifth and final combat tour.

His gaze shifted from the television to the coffee table and the black cloisonné vase containing Kate's ashes, then to the 12-gauge shotgun propped against the arm of the chair. Twice, during the small hours of the morning, he had placed the cold, shiny barrel in his mouth, and twice something other than the fear of death had kept him from pulling the trigger. "A man with outward courage dares to die; a man with inward courage dares to live," he remembered reading in one of Kate's Oriental philosophy books. He was struggling to find that inner courage.

He had returned home to a house full of memories and Kate's things, returned to face a life without her. It had been the last and most difficult stage in accepting the permanence and finality of her absence. He had spent most of the night in her closet, taking a bottle of Jack Daniel's and the telephone in with him. Her scent was strongest there, particularly on the dark-green silk blouse she had worn recently. He had closed the door behind him and sat on the floor and held the blouse in his arms, being careful not to soil it with

tears. It was her favorite blouse. There, in the darkness, he
called his four closest friends, men he had fought beside and
with whom he had faced death and life and shared his hopes
and dreams. Kate had been his anchor all these years, now
they were all he had left.

Despite the intended purpose of the calls, he was unable
to tell them about Kate's death. Until the last call, to Scott
Lyon in Las Vegas. They had rambled on about old times
and old friends who never came home. Swapped funny stories, some funny only now that time and distance had
dimmed the fear and terror that had surrounded them. Remember the night we sang to Kate on the terrace of the
Oriental Hotel? Lyon had said. It was your honeymoon,
right? You lucky bastard, that's one gorgeous, terrific lady.
Tell her I'm looking forward to seeing her at the next re-
union. Yes, Gannon assured him, he would give Kate his
best. Hey, remember the day before your wedding, when we
all went for that boat ride down that river in Bangkok, kind
of a floating picnic, and Monaghan, drunker than shit, fell in
and Kate thought we were going to let him drown, we kept
throwing food and beer cans at him every time he came up
for air? She was ready to go in after him if we hadn't pulled
him out when we did. Monaghan's worshiped her ever since,
like Androcles and the lion.

Kate's dead! Gannon had finally brought himself to say it.
He blurted it out to Lyon and then hung up and took the
telephone off the hook when it began ringing incessantly.

Kate's dusky laugh rose above the background noise of
the rowdy crowd at the Special Forces Association picnic
held a few months ago in Fayetteville, the last pictures he
had taken of her. Gannon turned up the volume to hear the
animated conversation she was having with the wife of a
longtime friend with whom he had gone through Special
Forces training. He didn't hear the two young men who
entered the house and now stood in the doorway of the den;
nor did he see them until they came between him and the

television screen. Through hazy vision he finally recognized them as Delta Force troopers from his old squadron.

"Hey, Boss," one of them said. "The colonel sent us to bring you over to his house. A buddy of yours from Las Vegas called, thought it might be best if you were with friends for a while."

"I'm okay," Gannon said. "Just need some time."

The young man's eyes surveyed the room and came to rest on the shotgun propped against the chair.

"Sorry, Boss. Colonel said don't come back without you."

One of the young men turned off the television and the VCR while the other took Gannon's arm and slung it around his shoulders, grasping the wrist tightly while placing his other arm around his waist as he pulled him out of the chair.

Gannon offered no resistance; his feet dragged across the floor as he was half carried out of the house.

The body of Alain Casson was found at six o'clock in the morning by a sanitation worker. Casson's friends, worried when he didn't show up at the hotel restaurant for breakfast, had called the police, and by late afternoon the John Doe in the morgue, who had been found in a Greenwich Village alley, had a name. On learning that Casson had had his passport with him and that it was now missing, the Police Intelligence Unit sent his name and description to Interpol to be added to the list of stolen passports provided to customs and immigration officials around the world.

"Malik went through British immigration at London's Heathrow airport this morning," Tom Driscoll told the Deputy Director for Operations. "He was using the passport of a French tourist murdered in New York the other night."

"They've got him?" Wilson said.

"No such luck. Interpol was slow in getting the information out and the Brits didn't get the alert until he was long gone. But the man who checked him through tentatively identified Malik from a photo one of our people from the London station showed him."

"Any line on where he's headed?"

"Nothing. MI6 says they'll let us know if he turns up."

18

The Marais Quarter of Paris, despite the sandblasted cleanliness of urban renaissance, still evokes the Paris of another era. Twenty years ago its magnificent buildings, with gables and turrets and steep slate roofs, had deteriorated almost beyond recognition; a third of its houses lacked even running water. Today it is an elite residential enclave, one of Paris' most patrician addresses. Located on the Right Bank of the Seine, removed from the grand boulevards and extravagant esplanades of the postcard image of Paris, even the light is different. Soft off-white and ocher gently illuminate the architecture of centuries past on slivers of streets hemmed in by brooding medieval houses recently transformed into luxury town houses and co-op apartments. Hundreds of carriage-trade galleries, boutiques, designer showrooms, sidewalk bazaars, and quaint cafés line the cobbled walkways through the ancient neighborhood that now caters to its new, affluent residents leading quietly expensive lives.

From the fifth floor of a scaffolding-draped building in the midst of refurbishment, three men looked down on the mid-morning strollers on a tree-lined square just off the Rue des Francs Bourgeois. In the center of the square a pretty girl sat at the edge of a fountain watching a young mime apply makeup in preparation for his noontime performance aimed at the Gallic preppies who converged on the area for lunch. On a far corner an artist set up his easel as a woman with plump arms and eyes of heartbreaking sadness came out of a bakery, her shopping basket brimming with loaves of bread and pastries. A priest swept the sidewalk in front of his church with a crooked straw broom; he greeted the sad-eyed woman as she turned and disappeared through an arched entrance to an alleyway that led to a maze of courtyards, gardens, and cloisters.

Inside the fifth-floor apartment Sam Pavlik and Mike Duggan watched the activity below with trained professional eyes. The third man in the unfurnished and recently painted living room of the apartment, Steve Markum, adjusted the telephoto lens on his video camera, changing the focal length to take in as much of the square as possible. Pavlik and Duggan, positioned at an adjacent window, used lenses of a dramatically different nature. Duggan's spotter scope magnified the tables of a sidewalk café directly across the street from the apartment, while Pavlik's sniper rifle, equipped with a telescopic sight, rested on a cloth "shot" bag filled with Styrofoam popcorn that positioned the weapon at the proper angle on the floor before the partially open floor-to-ceiling window that overlooked the square.

Markum watched in fascination as Pavlik and Duggan prepared for their lethal task with cool, practiced precision. The civilian clothes they wore did little to soften their military bearing; though only in their early thirties, their hard, intense eyes were those of seasoned professionals, and their quiet manner did nothing to encourage idle conversation. All Markum knew about them was their names and that they were both Green Berets, members of Omega Group, a top-secret team formed within Delta Force and patterned after the Israeli "Wrath of God" units that had hunted down and killed the terrorists responsible for the Olympic massacre of Israeli athletes. The Omega Group was similarly tasked with tracking down and assassinating terrorists responsible for deaths of American citizens.

PAYBACK 125

The end result of a decision made at the highest levels of government—to take the war on terrorism to the terrorists—Omega had been operating with devastating effectiveness for the past two years. No longer limited to broad-spectrum messages, like the raid on Libya, to simply deter those who sponsored and gave sanctuary to terrorists, the focus was now on the individuals and organizations who actually carried out the senseless slaughters and manipulated and brainwashed the disfranchised, the dispossessed, and the fanatics for their own political purposes. What Omega did was unheralded and done with surgical precision; they eliminated the mindless pathological degenerates who reveled in killing and escaped justice, often protected by Western governments who refused to extradite them for fear of reprisals.

The principle was sound: Destroy them before they destroy us and our way of life. And if it was a war on terrorism, then it would be fought as a war, where enemies were killed, not taken to court. The decision was firm. Nothing justified the indiscriminate killing of children and innocent civilians—not national liberation, not political grievances, not for the restoration of a homeland. Omega's missions were limited and carefully thought out: They selectively removed the most effective leaders and the most dangerous, murderous practitioners, disrupted their networks, demoralized their followers, and caused temporary leadership gaps. The principle had its roots in the controversial Phoenix Program in Vietnam—a program that after the war the North Vietnamese military leadership admitted was the most effective operation the United States had carried out, the thing they feared most. Selectively assassinating high-level military and political leaders in North and South Vietnam, the program at its zenith had virtually destroyed the Vietcong infrastructure and delivered crippling blows to the Communist war effort until left-wing political pressure at home brought it to a halt.

When Markum thought about it, Pavlik and Duggan, and what they did, scared him. It was his first assignment since

being transferred to the CIA's Counterterrorist Group a
week ago. Formerly part of the Company's Technical Services Division, his experience with the darker side of the
intelligence business was nonexistent, and he had viewed
with trepidation his orders to report to the CIA safe house
that Omega Group was using as a base of operations on the
outskirts of Paris.

"You enjoy what you do?" Markum asked Duggan after a
long silence.

"Sometimes," Duggan said as he continued to stare
through the spotter scope.

"I don't think I could do it."

"Your job is to take pictures," Duggan said coldly, without taking his eye from the scope. "So take pictures."

Markum returned to his video camera. He slowly turned
the focusing ring on the powerful telephoto lens and
brought the images below into even sharper focus. Satisfied
with the effect, he turned to look at the exotic rifle Pavlik
had positioned at the window. It was unlike any Markum
had ever seen, equipped with the latest in space-age technology. The butt plate and cheekpiece were fully adjustable and
provided the shooter with a custom fit, and inside the butt-
stock was an integrated miniature ballistic computer connected to a laser range finder mounted under the barrel. The
computer made minute corrections inside the telescopic
sight to compensate for range and weather: when the laser
pinpointed the target, the combination day/night scope was
automatically adjusted by the computer for perfect hits at
ranges up to fifteen hundred meters. Digital displays on the
scope screen told the sniper the distance to the target as well
as information about ambient humidity, wind drift and direction, and temperature—all factors that can alter the
speed and course of a bullet and affect first-shot accuracy,
possibly throwing the point of impact off enough to kill the
hostage rather than the hostage taker. With its integral
sound and flash suppressor, and its subsonic ammunition,
the weapon was virtually undetectable from a concealed po-

sition, making no sound that could be identified as a gun shot above normal street and traffic noise.

Deployed as a team of two men who could spell each other, the Omega Group snipers avoided the inherent problems of their demanding profession: problems of vision deterioration from looking through optical devices for extended periods of time, and physical discomfort, fatigue, and boredom from remaining motionless for long periods in which total concentration was required.

Duggan, taking his eye from the spotter scope for a short break, watched a small traffic jam in the narrow street that circled the fountain. The driver of a battered Fiat, leaving no doubt as to how it got that way, attempted a U-turn against the flow of traffic. He used complicated hand signals to order a produce truck and van into a series of minuscule geometric maneuvers that only worsened the situation and brought traffic to a complete standstill until he gave up and continued in the direction he was originally headed.

"Goddamn Frogs are the worst drivers I've ever seen," Duggan said. "They wouldn't last five minutes on the L.A. Freeway before some crazy blew them away."

"What time is it?" Pavlik asked. He was stretched out in a prone position behind the sniper rifle, a lightweight foam pad between him and the hardwood floor. He cross-checked the minute adjustments to windage and elevation that the miniature computer in the stock of the weapon had automatically made as he changed his point of aim by no more than a few yards.

"Ten o'clock," Duggan replied. "If our information's right, he should be along any minute."

Paris is a city of cafés, with virtually two on every corner and a few on the street in between, but with lunchtime two hours away, the professional café sitters were the only patrons at the sidewalk tables across the street from the apartment house. Three men carried on a heated discussion as they sat hunched over glasses of wine and small cups of *l'express,* a black foamy liquid served with a sugar cube that they dipped in the potent coffee and ate. A couple looked deeply into each other's eyes, while a man, sitting declaratively alone, looked into his cup. Another man smoked, munched, and sipped in sullen silence, totally immersed in the rhythms of time and place as he watched the interlocking mini-dramas unfolding in the square.

Duggan was looking through the spotter scope, amused by a dog who was obviously a regular at the café. The old mutt wandered among the customers, butting their legs with his head, demanding food scraps. Judging from the dog's healthy condition, Duggan guessed he was either well liked or feared by those who responded to his persistent nudges. A short, dark-haired man, out of sync with his surroundings, came into Duggan's field of vision. The man had a thin, heavily pockmarked face, his hair was combed to perfection, and his expensive double-breasted gabardine suit was well tailored. He paused at the fountain to survey the area, then continued across the cobbled street and sat at a table overlooking the square.

"Come to Papa," Duggan said. The remark got Pavlik's immediate attention. "There he is—the fifteen-hundred-dollar suit with the ten-cent face."

Markum put his eye to the video camera lens and watched the man who had caused the atmosphere in the apartment to crackle with tension.

"Who is he?" Markum asked. He had been told none of the details of the Omega operation, just that he was to capture it on film.

"Egon Zimmerman," Pavlik said, his right eye now pressed against the eyecup on the telescopic sight. "We've been tracking this bastard for eight months . . . now we've got him." His voice was an icy monotone.

"What did he do?"

"He's a scumbag," Pavlik answered without looking up from the scope.

Markum didn't press the issue and returned to peer through the camera lens. He was suddenly gripped by the realization that he was looking at a man who was about to die.

"Just tell me when you want me to start filming."

"Now," Duggan said.

Egon Zimmerman fastidiously adjusted his suit coat, then picked up a newspaper from the table. He snapped it open and neatly folded it as he glanced casually about the square and the half-empty café. Two young couples, who had arrived just as he did, sat nearby, and a few more customers drifted in; one was an elderly woman whose poodle sat in her lap and snarled at the resident mutt, who paid it no attention. Zimmerman's gaze returned to the paper, shifting occasionally back to the people around him. He again tugged at a lapel on his coat and smoothed out a wrinkle.

Unlike most terrorists, Zimmerman had no deep-seated political convictions or philosophies; the only reason the ugly little fucker became a terrorist, Pavlik had said earlier that day, was so he could get laid. A virulent psychopath who had become involved with the Red Army Faction through friends with whom he had lived in a Frankfurt commune, he had carried out a series of vicious attacks on German industrialists and politicians and their families, then disappeared into the terrorist underground, where he stayed until fourteen months later when he reemerged with a vengeance. He had made the Omega "wanted" list after two extremely monstrous, bloody bombings in West Germany. The first had killed twenty-six American grade-school children on a bus leaving Bitburg Air Base for a school outing; the second had killed thirty-two American servicemen and dependents in the PX at the Rhine-Main base. On both occasions he had left a letter near the sight of the blast to take personal credit for the bombings. Arrested two days after the Rhine-Main attack by the Amsterdam police, he was released on a questionable technicality that saved the timid Dutch government from having to deal with his friends. Again going underground, he finally surfaced in East Germany six months ago, eventually turning up in Paris, where his trail had been picked up by an electronic surveillance team from the Army's Intelligence Support Activity who had been monitoring the telephones of Action Direct, a French terrorist organization. An intercepted phone call had tipped them to the café Zimmerman used as a meeting place.

Pavlik stared through the telescopic sight with no more emotion than if he were about to kill a rabid animal, which was an analogy he had often used. He centered the cross hairs directly between Zimmerman's eyes just as the fastidious terrorist ran a hand through his hair.

"Don't worry about your hair, asshole," Pavlik muttered. "I'm gonna put a permanent part in it for you in about six seconds."

As Pavlik slowly increased pressure on the trigger a man entered his sight picture and obscured his target. The scalloped edge of the blue-and-white awning that extended out over the café dining area hid the man's face as he stood talking to Zimmerman.

"Who the hell is that?" Pavlik said, and released the pressure on the trigger.

"Never saw him before," Duggan said as he watched Nikolai Malik sit down and take a chair that placed him between Zimmerman and the men in the apartment.

Markum observed the two men through the camera lens. "They seem to know each other."

Pavlik picked up a small hand-held radio and pressed the transmit button.

"We've got an unsub," he said into the radio, using the Omega vernacular for an unknown subject. "Just joined the target."

There was a brief hesitation from the man in the communications room at the safe house on the outskirts of the city, then the radio came to life.

"Get him on film and continue the mission," came the reply.

Pavlik pressed the transmit button briefly to acknowledge the command.

"I don't have a shot until that guy moves," Pavlik said, his eye back on the scope.

"We'll wait him out," Duggan said. "If they leave together, we'll take him when they get up."

A gap-toothed waiter wearing a traditional white shirt with black bow tie and vest approached Zimmerman's table and took Malik's order for a glass of wine. Shortly after the waiter left Malik stopped talking in mid-sentence. His eyes locked onto a man getting off a motorcycle that had pulled into the curb farther up the sidewalk.

Zimmerman turned to see what had caught Malik's attention as a black Mercedes with smoked windows crept slowly into the square, circled the fountain, and drove past the café before it stopped in front of the bakery across the street.

The man getting off the motorcycle unzipped the jacket of his leather riding suit as he walked toward the café. To the casual observer it was an innocuous scene—a man stopped at the café for lunch, opening his warm leather jacket to relax and cool off. But the way the man's hand remained poised at his waist made Malik recognize it for what it was.

Slowly, imperceptibly, Malik slipped his hand inside the open raincoat he wore and gripped the butt of the 9mm pistol resting in the inside-the-belt holster just to the left of his belt buckle. His eyes swept the café; he hadn't missed the black Mercedes, but parked across the square as it was, he didn't consider it an immediate threat. He glanced over his shoulder and spotted a second man. He had gotten out of the Mercedes and was approaching from the opposite direction.

The man from the motorcycle made eye contact with his accomplice, who nodded and continued toward Zimmerman's table. Malik saw the signal and reacted instantly. He jumped to his feet and pulled Zimmerman up with him, holding him in front of him as a shield. He fired twice at the man from the motorcycle and killed him instantly as the rounds impacted in his head and neck.

Malik quickly turned to face the man behind him. His powerful arm still held the frantic Zimmerman as a shield as he fired again, a split second after his startled target fired a sustained burst from a mini-Uzi. The flurry of rounds from the deadly submachine gun tore into Zimmerman, killing him and a couple sitting at an adjacent table. The man with the Uzi dropped to his knees from Malik's well-placed shots, then, in a final reflexive action, fired wildly across the square before falling facedown on the sidewalk.

The café and the surrounding area were in chaos. People screamed and dived under tables; others ran across the square in blind panic. The old woman with the poodle lay dead; the dog whimpered and shook at her side. Sprawled across the lip of the fountain, the young mime's white makeup was streaked with blood from a bullet hole in his forehead.

From across the square an engine roared and tires howled as the black Mercedes tore away from the curb and skidded around the fountain toward the café. Malik stepped onto the sidewalk and fired into the windshield as the big car sped by and out of sight as it turned onto a narrow street leading away from the square.

The three men in the fifth-floor apartment had watched, stunned, as the scene rapidly unfolded. Markum had filmed it all as he watched through the camera lens.

"Shit!" Pavlik said. "Where's the tall blond guy? I lost him."

"He ran down an alley," Duggan said.

Pavlik grabbed the radio. "We've got a situation here," he said. "The unsub just took out two gunslingers. Zimmerman's dead."

"Clear out," was the order that came back.

Pavlik turned to Duggan and Markum. "Pack up. We're outta here."

19

Pavlik's debriefing report and Markum's videotape were transmitted via satellite link to Delta Force headquarters at Fort Bragg, North Carolina, within two hours of the carnage at the Paris café. The windowless briefing room inside the operations center at the Ranch was set up to show the tape to the Delta Force officers and men who had been called in to see it after an initial viewing by the commanding officer and his immediate staff.

Lieutenant Colonel Tom Halstead, the operations officer, was about to close the door to the briefing room when Gannon appeared in the doorway.

"Hey, Jack," Halstead said, clapping him on the back. "How's it goin', buddy?"

"A little better each day," Gannon said. He forced a smile for his friend.

Colonel Bill Mize, Delta's commanding officer, crossed the room to greet him. "Thought you were going to stay at the house, Jack, take a few more days off."

"And do what, knock back a twelve-pack every few hours? No. If I don't get back to work, I'm going to lose it completely," Gannon said. "I'm ashamed of myself, Bill. Kate would have been ashamed of me if she could have seen me the last three days."

Mize put a fraternal arm around Gannon's shoulders.

"You're pulling out of it. That's what counts." He led him farther into the briefing room and added, "Come on, sit in on this one."

"What do you have?"

"Somebody stepped all over Omega's Paris mission. We've got it on tape."

Gannon took a seat at the large conference table that filled the center of the room as Mize gave the signal to roll the tape. Halstead closed the door and turned off the lights. A video projector came on, illuminating the large rear projection screen at the back of the raised briefing platform.

Egon Zimmerman's image appeared on the screen in a close-up shot, then the camera lens backed off and took in most of the café and part of the square. Gannon recognized the terrorist immediately from the Omega mission-planning sessions. He watched as a tall man in a light gray raincoat approached the table; the camera angle obscured his head behind the café awning. As the man sat down Gannon leaned forward in his chair, his eyes hard on the profile of the blond-haired man. As Nikolai Malik turned to look out over the square, his full face toward the camera, Gannon bolted from his seat and moved closer to the screen.

"Stop it!" he shouted. "Stop the tape!"

The tape stopped on a frame with a distant shot of Malik's face.

"What is it, Jack?" Mize asked.

"Can you zoom in on that frame?" Gannon said, his body rigid, his eyes glaring at the image on the screen.

The projectionist hit a few buttons on the control console and a grainy, extreme close-up of Malik filled the screen.

"You know him, Jack?" Mize asked.

"That's him," Gannon said. "That's the guy who killed Kate."

"You sure?" Mize said. He got up and went to Gannon's side.

"Positive. I got a good look at him in an alley in New York and right before he ran into the UN. Who is he?"

"That's what we've been trying to find out," Mize said. "I looked at the tape when it first came in and checked our files, then I faxed a blowup of him out to CIA, DIA, FBI, State, NSA, DOE, everybody with a data bank on known terrorists. Nothing. Nada. Nobody can match the face with a name."

"What about doing a run on descriptions of Zimmerman's associates?" Gannon said. "Look for any intersects?"

"We already tried that. Same story," Halstead said. He got up from the conference table and handed Gannon a printout of the negative responses they had received.

"Watch the rest of the tape," Mize said. "Then tell me what you think."

"An attempted snatch," Gannon said moments later. "The two guys he blew away were trying to grab him, not kill him. They could have taken him out before he had time to react, if that was the plan. You notice the trunk of the Mercedes was popped as it drove by. That's where they were going to put him."

Mize nodded in agreement. "My thoughts exactly."

"Did you get a make on the two shooters?"

"The Company's Paris station identified the one on the motorcycle as a low-level GRU officer from the Soviet Embassy in Paris."

"GRU?" Gannon said. "Not KGB?"

"Gets curiouser and curiouser, doesn't it?" Mize said.

"That's not a GRU-type operation."

"No it isn't," Mize said. "And I've got a serious problem with the across-the-board negative responses we got back. This mystery man travels in elite terrorist circles, draws heat from the GRU, and handles himself like a pro, and nobody knows anything about him, like he was born yesterday. You know the odds against that? Remember where all our information on Zimmerman came from?"

"The Company," Gannon said. "They had an in-depth bio on him."

"Right," Mize said. "But it took them only twenty minutes to get back to us today when we sent them the other guy's photo. When's the last time we got an answer that fast from them on anything?"

"Whenever they have the information we're requesting and don't want to give it to us," Gannon said. "They've got to know who he is. He killed two of their people in New York who were chasing him after he killed the driver who was with him the night Kate was murdered."

"One of the intel reports in Zimmerman's bio had an interesting entry under 'suspected connections.' "

"I remember," Gannon said. "They had reason to believe he had KGB connections . . . to an Illegal no one's been able to identify."

"Now," Mize said. "I'll show you something that's enough to puke a buzzard off a gut wagon." He gestured to the projectionist and said, "Start the tape where the camera pans the people at the café after the unsub showed up."

The tranquil scene at the Parisian square again came on the screen and again erupted into the violent, bloody exchange.

"Okay," Mize called out. "Stop it there and blow it up."

The aftermath of the gun battle was on the screen; the tape was stopped at the point where Malik had dropped Zimmerman to the ground. The scene included the couple sitting at an adjacent table who had been gunned down by the blast from the mini-Uzi. They now lay on the ground near Zimmerman. As the projectionist enlarged the still frame the faces of the couple were clearly visible.

Mize stepped up on the briefing platform, took a telescopic pointer from the podium, and moved close to the screen.

"One of our intelligence analysts recognized the girl," Mize said. "She was Army, an undercover operative for the Intelligence Support Activity until last year when she resigned her commission. Guess where she went to work?"

Mize said, pausing for effect. "The Company's Counterterrorist Group, that's where."

"What was she doing there?" Gannon said. "CTG knew
about the Omega operation, their man was behind the camera. Why would they put someone that close to the target?"

"I don't think she knew anything about Omega's mission," Mize said. "The Company's so goddamn turf conscious and compartmented that not only don't they tell the
rest of the intelligence community what they're doing, they
don't even tell their own people when their operations over-
lap. They're uncomfortable when the left hand knows what
the right hand's doing."

Mize moved in closer to the screen and placed the tip of
the pointer on the girl's shoulder bag lying at her side; the
top flap had fallen open. "Blow this section up," he called
out again.

"Look closely at the shoulder bag," Mize said to Gannon.
"What do you see?"

Gannon stared for a moment, then: "A pistol grip. Looks
like the H&K we use; fires tranquilizer darts."

"That's exactly what it is," Mize said. "Same thing with
the guy lying next to her." He used the pointer again. "You
can see part of the grip in a shoulder holster where his
jacket's hanging open."

Mize stepped down from the platform and signaled for
the projector to be shut off and the lights to be switched on.

"There were two cars parked just up the street on the
same side as the café. One of them's probably theirs," Mize
said. "So what do we have? Two rival factions trying to grab
the same guy. Not kill him, but snatch him. And the fact
that one of them is the GRU, and the guy they're after is in
all probability a KGB Illegal, really muddies the water. The
man obviously has access to some pretty valuable information . . . to both sides."

"How do you want to proceed?" Gannon asked.

"I don't," Mize said. "Our operation's over. Zimmerman's dead. That was the objective. The rest is somebody else's business."

"And mine," Gannon said.

Mize raised a hand to silence Gannon, then turned to the officers and men in the briefing room to dismiss them. When they had all filed out of the room, he turned to Gannon.

"I know what you have in mind," he said. "And I'll do whatever I can to help you, unofficially, and so will the rest of your buddies. But I can't get Delta overtly involved in a personal vendetta no matter how much I'd like to."

"I understand," Gannon said. "I wouldn't ask you to. But I'd like an eight-by-ten blowup of the blond guy's face."

"You got it."

"And I'll need a leave of absence, open-ended."

"For health reasons?" Mize said with a smile.

"For health reasons."

He moved in close to Gannon and spoke softly. "Remember Dan Pitzer?"

"Yeah. He was with Delta for six or seven years."

"Well, after he retired, he went to work for the Company . . . CTG," Mize said. "He's here at Bragg for a few weeks, some coordinating work with the Joint Special Operations Command. I stopped by to see him after I looked at the tape. He's a good friend, wouldn't bullshit me. I asked him if he had any idea why CTG was trying to snatch a probable KGB Illegal. He swore he knew nothing about the operation, and he's in a position to know if there was one."

"It's obvious there is," Gannon said.

"Right. Which tells you that it's pretty goddamn highly classified if it's compartmented enough to exclude Pitzer; he's one of their top intelligence analysts."

"I want that guy, Bill," Gannon said. "And I'm going after him. I don't give a shit whose throat I have to step on."

"I'm not trying to talk you out of anything, Jack. Just keep in mind that you're going up against a couple of real heavyweights."

"I'll keep it in mind."

"Anything else I can do for you now?" Mize said as the two men left the briefing room.

"I'd like an hour or so alone in the computer room, then I'll be on my way."

20

The CIA's Special Operations computer system consists of only a few terminals located in a cipher-locked room and is completely separate from all other Agency data bases. Access to the SO data base is severely restricted, with multilevels of security requiring specific code-word access for individual operations. Anyone interrogating the system, trying to break in without the proper code words and using invalid commands, will encounter the computer's security safeguards and be denied access, setting off a series of alarms resulting in the automatic tracing of the person trying to gain entrance. Various outside intelligence agencies and military intelligence units, including DIA, FBI, NSA, and the Army's Delta Force, have subject-specific access to the SO data base, but only for intelligence information pertinent to their ongoing joint operations with the Agency.

The call that came in over the secure line from Delta Force headquarters at first drew no attention. Not until the caller began to ask the Special Operations computer for information exceeding his clearance level. After three "invalid command" responses, the caller was disconnected, only to call back two more times, unsuccessfully attempting to gain entry through another path, his objective being the systems photo data base and the CTG's current operations files.

Tom Driscoll had been alerted and informed that the

source of the call was Delta Force headquarters; the nature of the system interrogation left no doubt in his mind who was behind it . . . and why.

"It's Gannon," Tom Driscoll told the DDO. "Our surveillance team reported that he returned to work today."

"Which means he identified Malik on the Omega tape," Dave Wilson said. "And he now has a photo of him."

"We tried to keep the tape out of Delta's hands," Driscoll said, "but in all the confusion we didn't find out that Malik was on it until it was too late. We couldn't make an issue out of it without drawing a lot of unwanted attention to our operation."

"Gannon's like a bad penny," Wilson said. "If I remember correctly, you assured me he would cease to be a problem after Kirilenko was taken out of the picture."

"The photo of Malik won't do him any good," Driscoll said. "Outside of the Soviets, we're the only ones who know who Malik is and what he's involved in."

"What the hell were your people doing at that café, in the middle of the Omega operation?"

"They didn't know anything about it. Neither did I. CTG's part was minor, just to get it on film," Driscoll said. "Our intel section set it up with Delta. I wasn't briefed. That Omega team's been looking for Zimmerman for six months. We gave them the bio on him before we found out he was connected with Malik. Anyway, when I learned that Malik was using a French passport, and that Zimmerman was in Paris, I put him under surveillance on the off chance that he would lead us to Malik. As it turned out, I was right."

"And we lost two more people."

"There was no way to anticipate the GRU action," Driscoll said without apology. "We almost had him."

"Do you have any idea why Malik went to see Zimmerman?"

"I've got an opinion."

"Let's hear it."

"I think he went there to kill him," Driscoll said. "Zimmerman's the only one who was with him in East Germany, from the beginning of this mess. He knew too much, maybe enough that if we, or the GRU, got our hands on him, he could bring Malik and a few others down with him."

"Why wasn't Zimmerman picked up before?"

"He just surfaced. He was our alternate target at the café. We were going to grab him if Malik didn't show. Malik was feeling the heat from us, and the GRU, and knew Zimmerman was a weak link. I think he made the decision to go the rest of the way alone."

"Which makes him all the more dangerous and difficult to find."

"That's why I want to conduct the rest of this operation from the field," Driscoll said. "Where I'm in a position to react faster."

"Whatever it takes," Wilson said. "But I want results. I want Malik, and I don't want any more interference from Gannon."

The DDO's secretary tapped on the door, stepped into the office to hand Driscoll a message, and left.

"Gannon's withdrawn every cent he has in the bank . . . twenty-three thousand four hundred dollars," Driscoll said, a concerned look on his face. "Converted it all to traveler's checks. And he called a friend, asked him to stay at his house for an indefinite period."

"He's going operational," Wilson said. "This is getting out of hand, Tom. No more assurances of what he can or can't do, I want him stopped. Reel him in and put him on ice. Now!"

Driscoll's face tinted with embarrassment as he handed Wilson the message. "Three of his Delta Force buddies jammed up our surveillance team while Gannon broke away. They have no idea where he is or where he's going."

General Vladimir Antonov's voice thundered off the walls of his office at GRU headquarters. His fist slammed onto the top of the green-baize conference table. A carafe of water and eight crystal glasses crashed to the floor.

"You were to abduct him!" Antonov shouted at the major standing before him. "Not attempt to kill him."

"My men did not fire first, Comrade General," the major said. He remained at rigid attention, his eyes straight ahead. "They had no choice but to defend themselves."

"According to the report I received, they panicked when he began shooting and left without even attempting to complete their mission," Antonov said. "You killed one and lost the other. Now there is no doubt in Malik's mind that we are after him. You didn't even think to leave someone behind to follow him."

The major remained silent, perspiration beaded on his forehead.

"Get out!" Antonov bellowed.

Colonel General Yuri Volovich, Antonov's second-in-command, entered the office as the major hurried out into the hallway.

"Incompetent fools," Antonov grumbled as Volovich sat down opposite him. "With Zimmerman dead, we no longer have a direct link to Malik."

"I have reason to believe that the KGB warned Malik that Zimmerman was known to us," Volovich said. "If the major's men hadn't unintentionally killed him, Malik would have."

"The man has nine lives," Antonov said. "And an uncanny ability to anticipate and counter our every move."

"He is only human. He will make a mistake, and then we will have him."

"Soon, Yuri Denisovich," Antonov said. "We'd better have him soon."

"I have a list of safe houses outside of Paris that Zimmerman has been known to use," Volovich said. "It is possible Malik will go to one of them."

Antonov looked up at the large framed photograph of Gorbachev on the wall opposite the portrait of Lenin. "The

General Secretary is in need of more than possibilities. His enemies are beginning to circle; they have caught the scent of blood."

"I have instructed our Paris *rezident* to place all of the locations under surveillance. It is somewhere to start."

"And if he has already left the country?"

"I still believe his ultimate destination is Nicaragua," Volovich said. "That is where his support base is, I am certain of it."

Antonov nodded in agreement. "Then I will inform the General Secretary that that is where we will concentrate our efforts."

21

Low-lying clouds scudded across a dreary, slate-gray sky, shrouding the rolling hills and meadows of the northern Virginia countryside in a cold autumn mist. Four miles west of the town of Middleburg, the gentleman's farm, with a nineteenth-century stone farmhouse and barn set in the middle of eighty acres of lush green pastures and hardwood forest, looked much the same as it did 170 years ago, thanks to the efforts of its owner, retired Army Lieutenant General Maxwell Taylor Stanton. Meticulous in his efforts to preserve the period appearance of the farm, General Max, as he was affectionately known by the men who had served under him, had had the telephone and power lines placed underground and the macadam drive put in by the previous owner torn up and replaced with gravel.

He found great pleasure and peace of mind in walking the wooded trails around his property, and after Jack Gannon's call that morning, disturbed and saddened by the news of Kate's death, he had taken a light lunch his housekeeper had prepared for him and, despite the damp cold, had spent most of the afternoon following well-worn footpaths through the October woods with Bubba, his golden retriever, at his side. There was little about the trim, vigorous, and distinguished-looking old war-horse that suggested his

sixty-four years as he kept a strong, steady pace on a narrow
trail that led up a rise and through a stand of cedars.

His thirty-five-year army career began when he was parachuted behind German lines as a nineteen-year-old second
lieutenant with the newly formed OSS Jedburgh Teams, and
it drew to a close with a two-year tenure as Deputy Director
of the CIA followed by an equal amount of time as Director
of the Defense Intelligence Agency. The years in between
were spent mostly in special operations units, with a stint as
a CIA case officer running agents into Eastern Europe during the cold war and an assignment as a Defense attaché to
the Soviet Union, where, while stationed at the Moscow
Embassy, he was at the same time the de facto CIA station
chief. Few military careers were as distinguished or demanding, yet he had found time to continue his civilian education:
he had earned a doctorate in Russian studies and become
fluent in the language. Immensely courteous and cordial, yet
tense and alert, his rifle-barrel eyes, a cool blue-black, gave
no sign of emotion, yet told anyone with an ounce of sense
to beware. An aide had once instructed a newly assigned
staff officer, "Don't mistake kindness and decency for weakness; he's a good man, but fuck with him and he'll bury you
so fast you won't know where the dirt came from." It was a
fair and accurate appraisal.

His friendship with Gannon went back twenty years,
when, as a colonel and chief of the Special Operations
Group in Vietnam, he had put him in for the Medal of
Honor and given him a direct commission from staff sergeant to captain. He had known Kate almost as long, being
the best man at their wedding, and his relationship with
Gannon was such that, with no family of his own, Gannon
had listed him in his service record as "next of kin," after
Kate, to be contacted in the event of an emergency.

As he reached the top of the rise and walked along the
crest, his thoughts returned to a late-night call eleven years
ago, when he was director of the Defense Intelligence
Agency: Kate, in her sixth month of a difficult pregnancy

(her first and last, owing to medical complications), had been rushed to the army hospital at Fort Bragg. He had arranged for an Air Force jet based in England to bring Gannon home from a joint training exercise the fledgling Delta Force was conducting with the British SAS, and he had spent the night at the hospital with him, where they kept a prayerful vigil while Kate, after losing the baby, fought for her life. And now someone had taken that life from her, violently, senselessly, and he knew, with the loss of his own wife to cancer two years ago, some of what Gannon must be going through.

A wind came up and swayed the white birches that lined the footpath. It rattled the slender branches and sent a flurry of tiny red and gold leaves fluttering to the path at his feet. The mist changed to a drizzle and dripped heavily on the forest floor as he glanced at his watch, then faced into the wind and turned up the collar of his parka as he headed back toward the house. The sound of a car on the gravel driveway could be heard as he skirted the pond behind the house, and Bubba sprinted in the direction of the intrusive sound, his warning bark at full volume. General Max saw Gannon get out of his car and kneel to pet the dog, then, at the sight of his former commanding officer, rise and snap a casual salute.

The two men embraced in silence and, with arms draped over each other's shoulders, walked toward the house.

"I share your loss, Jack. Kate was a wonderful woman," General Max said with genuine warmth. "We have to believe she's in a better place."

"I wish I could be there with her."

"Someday you will be."

In the study off the center hallway General Max saw that his handyman had started a cheerful blaze in the fireplace that drove the chill from his bones and brought a warm glow to the room. He poured Gannon a scotch, and one for himself, and they sat in leather wing chairs facing the fire.

Raising his glass in a toast, he said, "To Kate."

"To Kate," Gannon echoed, and tossed down the contents of the glass.

"You said you needed my help," General Max said. "You know I'll do whatever I can."

Gannon told him everything that had happened from the time he arrived in New York City until his attempts to gain entry to the CIA's Special Operations data base. General Max listened silently, missing nothing. No one had ever been able to anticipate the reactions of this judiciously distant, cautious, guarded man. He was a person who kept himself to himself, but when he spoke it was with a firm grasp of the problem at hand and, more often than not, with a workable solution. And once he had given his word, he would never go back on it. He had been a man of action in a difficult world and was also a gambler of sorts, self-assured to the edge of recklessness but never crossing the line. Experience had taught him that once in the game, you had to accept that sometimes failure came with the play, but you never walked off the field. Gannon shared many of the same qualities, which was part of the reason their friendship had lasted and grown.

"And I thought, with your connections in the intelligence community, you might be able to find out who he is and how I can get to him," Gannon concluded, and handed him a print of the full-face photograph of Malik.

General Max studied the harsh-looking face before setting the photograph aside.

"The few close friends I had at the Agency retired about the same time I did," he said. "And if what you're after is that closely held, the people I know over there now are going to stonewall me."

General Max stared into the fire and slowly sipped his scotch, then glanced again at the photograph and turned back to Gannon.

"You said the two men this man killed in Paris were GRU?"

"According to the Omega debriefing report."

"And they were trying to abduct him?"

"That's what it looked like."

General Max nodded slowly, then, in a measured response, said, "There's one possibility. I'll give it a try tomorrow. In the meantime, you're my house guest, and we have a lot of catching up to do."

He poured them both another drink and raised his glass again. "To old times and old friends . . . and to those who never came home."

22

Brussels' Grand Place, bordered on all four sides by rare steep-roofed buildings dating back to the twelfth century, is one of the most striking public squares in all of Europe. An aura of soft amber, rich with age, glowed from the ancient structures as the late morning sun cast its golden light on their ornate facades. Nikolai Malik, heedless of the architectural beauty around him, strode through the crowded square, weaving his way through sidewalks crammed with café tables and past flower sellers with carts that brimmed with an infinite variety of blossoms. He passed beneath the brightly colored flags of Brussels' provinces that flew from the Maison de Roi and turned sharply down a narrow cobbled alley. He followed the alley until he emerged onto a small crooked street that paralleled the west side of the square.

At a shop window he feigned interest in a display of antique porcelain and checked the street in both directions before he continued on. After walking three more blocks he doubled back and made sudden stops and changes of direction. Certain he was not under surveillance, he continued directly to his destination.

The sign above the door of the small bar at 42 Rue Marche au Charbon read "La Renaissance," but in Belgium, as well as in select circles around the world, it was known by another name—Bar Simba. So named when the Katanga Brewery closed and left it as the only watering hole outside of Africa where former Congo mercenaries could drink Simba-Tembo beer and recall their exploits in the short-lived Republic of Katanga.

Slanted rays of sunlight streamed through the leaded windows, helping to illuminate the heavily paneled, dimly lit room, its walls hung with campaign and battle maps, yellowed and cracked with age, and other esoteric memorabilia from mostly long-forgotten wars and conflicts. As the headquarters of the Brussels branch of the French Foreign Legion Association, and the Force Publique Association that had once maintained order in Belgium's equatorial African colonies, it was a gathering place for a unique breed of men. Because of its reputation it attracted mercenaries, real and imagined, from every corner of the world—some to roleplay and posture, recounting hair-raising feats and extraordinary acts of heroism from battles fought only in their dreams, while others, their manner and bearing answering any questions about their authenticity, left messages for friends and comrades-in-arms with whom they had lost contact. Veterans from World War I to the Falklands came to drink, sing songs, and swap war stories, and the wall behind the bar was decorated with cap badges, unit patches, and airborne wings, all amounting to an impressive display of elite unit insignia donated by regular customers and clientele who had stopped to pay homage while passing through Brussels.

The man Malik was looking for sat in the shadows at a corner table at the far end of the room. With his waxed handlebar mustache, ruddy, freckled complexion, and bulging eyes, Jean-Louis Lecard was not difficult to spot. Nor was he difficult to find. Being a creature of habit, he drank and conducted business at the corner table every day from 10:00 A.M. until midnight. A master forger, he specialized in passports, birth certificates, and other documents of identification, sometimes creating elaborately backstopped legends

needed to convince authorities and enlistment officers that
you were someone other than who you really were. French
by birthright, Lecard claimed no nationality and did not
subscribe to the politics of any nation or organization. Unconcerned with whom he dealt, as long as they could pay his
price, he did not ask questions.

Business had been slow for Lecard; even his most lucrative customers from the international terrorist community
had slacked off. They were lying low after a particularly
bloody six-month rampage. The terrorists preferred to operate in spasms of violence, one spectacular feat following another, quickly and violently, before the authorities could recover from the initial shock and react with heightened
security measures. Attacks were stopped once the security
apparatus shifted into full motion. Having made their point
and grabbed the public's attention, dominating headlines
around the world for a period of time, there was no need to
expose themselves further. Security would eventually be
downgraded and normal routines would return, then it
would be time to strike again. Lecard merely had to bide his
time through the slack periods, knowing it was inevitable
that his valuable services would again be required by those
needing to temporarily disappear from the face of the earth.
In the meantime there were the old customers, like the one
who had just come through the door.

Malik had used Lecard before, when he had wanted even
the false identities of people he had personally recruited for
specific missions kept from his KGB superiors. He saw Lecard's eyes follow him from the entrance across to the bar
without so much as a blink of recognition, then the small,
wiry man rose and left by the rear door. Malik ordered a
beer, drank it slowly, and left by the front door ten minutes
later.

The window of the tiny curio shop on a side street two
blocks from the bar was piled high with pawned jewelry and
antiques of questionable validity. A bell tinkled as Malik

opened the door and stepped inside. Lecard appeared from behind a curtain strung across a doorway that led to a cluttered and dusty back room. He beckoned with a toss of his head and held the curtain aside as Malik crossed the shop and followed him into his office workshop.

"There have been people asking questions about you, my friend," Lecard said. He squinted against the smoke that curled into his eyes from a cigarette dangling out of a corner of his mouth. "The wrong kinds of people."

"When?"

"Just this morning."

"Anyone I know?"

"Countrymen of yours. They didn't identify themselves, but they offered to pay well for any information. Unusual for your people."

"And your prices have gone up accordingly," Malik said with contempt.

"Business is business," Lecard said with a Gallic shrug. "What can I do for you?"

"Three passports," Malik said, and handed him an equal number of snapshots. "Nationality doesn't matter as long as the spoken language is English, French, Spanish, or German."

Lecard took the snapshots and placed them on his desk. He removed an array of stamps and seals and three blank passports from a drawer.

"United States, Austria, and Great Britain," he said as he carried them over to his workbench. "Adequate, yes?"

"Yes," Malik answered, and wrote down three names that fit the nationalities and handed them to Lecard. He was getting an uneasy feeling about the nervous look in the forger's eyes. A sixth sense, one that he had learned to listen to through hard experiences, told him that something wasn't quite right.

Lecard, perched on a stool at his workbench, went about his work. He affixed the snapshots in the passports and applied the seals and stamps of exit and entry from various countries. An inch-long ash hung precariously from the tip of his cigarette and finally dropped onto one of the pages of the passport on which he was working.

"Authenticity." Lecard grinned as he brushed the ash away.

Malik's eyes swept the room. They searched each darkened corner and came to rest on the door to a storage room near the rear entrance to the shop. The door was cracked open a few inches. As Lecard worked Malik moved slowly and positioned himself off to the side of the door. Lecard glanced anxiously over his shoulder, turning back to his work when Malik looked in his direction.

Malik withdrew the silenced 9mm pistol he had used at the Paris café. Just as it cleared the shoulder holster the storage-room door flew open, hit him in the chest, and knocked him off balance.

A short, burly man lunged at him, but Malik quickly regained his balance. He adroitly sidestepped and tripped the charging man and fired two rounds into the back of his head as he landed facedown on the floor. A pool of blood formed and spread as the man's skull was shattered by the hollow-point bullets.

Out of the corner of his eye Malik detected the movement of another figure from within the storeroom. He spun around and dropped into a crouch and fired just as the man burst through the doorway swinging a leaded truncheon in a wide arc that missed Malik's head by only a few inches. Two rounds impacted in the man's chest, both tearing into his heart. He was dead before he hit the floor with a loud thud.

Lecard sat motionless on the stool at the workbench, his eyes wide with terror.

"They threatened to kill me," he pleaded.

"Are there others?"

"Two more," Lecard said, his hand trembling as he pointed to the rear door. "In a car in the alley."

"You called them when you left the bar?"

Lecard nodded. "They swore they only wanted to talk to you."

"Finish your work," Malik said coldly.

Lecard hunched over the workbench with one eye on Malik, cringing with his slightest move. He put the finishing touches on his forgeries and handed them over. Malik checked that the passports were in order while Lecard remained seated on the stool, resigned to his fate. It came with swift precision. The two rounds that penetrated his eye socket knocked him off the stool and blew apart the back of his head.

Malik moved to the rear wall and peered from the corner of a dusty window. A dark blue Audi sedan with two men in the front seat was parked a short distance down the alley, its occupants unaware of the carnage inside the shop. Methodically checking the workbench to make certain Lecard had not left behind any deathbed clues to his new identities, he left by the front door and circled the block. He entered the alley behind the shop and approached the Audi from the rear. The windows were down, and the attention of the two men was directed at the rear door of the shop. Coming abreast of the car, without so much as a word, he leaned into the window on the passenger side and fired two rounds into the head of each man, then continued walking casually to the end of the alley, where he hailed a taxi.

23

Of the five hundred-plus Soviet diplomats and employees of Soviet agencies in Washington, at least a third of them are GRU officers whose primary purpose is to gather military and scientific intelligence information through conventional tradecraft methods as well as to recruit Americans willing to commit treason for money. It is the task of the FBI counter-intelligence teams to prevent them from achieving their goals. The clandestine game is played on the home team's turf, throughout the Washington area: Capitol Hill, George-town, the cocktail bars and restaurants of Virginia and Maryland's rural countryside, any area not designated as off limits to the Soviets.

The GRU are good at what they do, managing to stay out of the public eye, and with the exceptions of their Illegals, follow the rules and provide a constant challenge to the FBI surveillance teams. If caught, the worst that can happen is being declared persona non grata by the State Department and sent back to the Soviet Union, shortly to be replaced by a new player in the never-ending game. In most cases, when there are no ulterior motives involving political one-upman-ship, expulsions for spying are unpublicized. With the United States conducting identical operations out of its Moscow embassy, publicity would simply result in the ex-pulsions of Americans from the Soviet Union in retaliation and lead to a disruption of normal diplomatic relations. The game is a mirror image of relations between the two superpowers, harassing each other on a daily basis while privately working toward maintaining and gradually improving the status quo.

Over three thousand of the FBI's nine thousand agents are involved in counterintelligence operations. The Washington field office alone has twenty counterintelligence squads—designated CI-1 through CI-20. The squads, each containing thirty agents, keep tabs not only on the Soviets but track the movements of diplomats from the Eastern Bloc nations and the People's Republic of China as well. On occasions, when situations require it, diplomats from other nations, friend and foe alike, are subjected to the same scrutiny but on a smaller scale. CI-6, known in the Bureau as the "GRU Busters," are assigned to the GRU officers that operate out of the Soviet Embassy under diplomatic cover as opposed to the more overt GRU officers working out of the Soviet Military Office as defense attachés, who are the responsibility of CI-3.

It was two members of the CI-6 squad that sat in a car near the Soviet Embassy complex, known as "Mount Alto," watching the two-story-high electronically operated entrance gate. Every time the agents thought about the location of the new embassy compound, and they tried not to think about it, it rankled them. It was a bureaucratic blunder, the great intelligence giveaway. Situated at 350 feet above sea level on the second highest point in Washington, the location gives the Soviets an unobstructed view of the White House, Pentagon, State Department, and CIA headquarters. Laser-based sound-surveillance systems trained on the windows of these buildings are capable of picking up vibrations from within, transmitting back conversations to Soviet listening devices.

Perched high above the electronic clutter of the city, and in sight of microwave relay towers, the Soviets have the capability to intercept communications ranging from long-distance and local telephone conversations to facsimile and data transmissions. Computer technology allows them to designate specific "high yield" telephone numbers and automatically listen in and record conversations. Key words that occur in those conversations (such as missile, Stealth, Trident, NSA, or CIA), denoting subjects and areas of interest targeted by the GRU, are programmed into the software and, upon being recognized by the computer, trigger the automatic recorders. Other, more mundane conversations often pay equally high dividends of another sort: intercepted personal calls from military and government officials with access to classified information can reveal disgruntled employees or those with marital and financial problems, indicating who might be in a vindictive frame of mind or in need of money and companionship, and therefore receptive to recruitment as Soviet agents. The stakes are high; the stolen technology saves the Soviet Union hundreds of millions of dollars in research and development costs, and the efforts of the skilled GRU officers are relentless and often ingenious. Their success rate is impressive considering the parameters of the game and the sophistication and determination of the forces allied against them.

The CI-6 agents watching the entrance to the Soviet compound knew by name every GRU officer who operated out of the embassy, even though they had never met nor spoken to any of them. Their faces, studied from photographs and constant surveillance, and their personal habits and histories, gleaned from Bureau files, were known by heart. Some of them—those who had earned respect for their operational capabilities and the degree of challenge they presented—had been given nicknames by the CI-6 agents. The man whose car was approaching the Soviet-compound gate was one of those.

"Old Smoothie's" dark green Volvo sedan pulled out onto Tunlow Road, then turned onto Wisconsin Avenue and headed into the heart of the city. The CI-6 agents fell in behind, purposely following too close. The red-white-and-

blue diplomatic license plates prefixed with the letters *FC*
identified it as a Soviet-owned vehicle, one driven exclusively by the man now at the wheel.

As the senior GRU officer and *rezident,* Old Smoothie,
General Anatoli Alessevich Belchenko, was on his fifth tour
at the Washington embassy. A seasoned professional who
operated under diplomatic cover as a cultural affairs officer,
he had the distinction of never having had one of his operations or agents compromised, and he was responsible for
some of the most important intelligence coups to come out
of the United States. No longer personally recruiting and
controlling individual agents or servicing dead drops (the
nuts and bolts of the intelligence game), Belchenko now
planned and orchestrated all GRU operations in the Washington area, a position that did not keep him under surveillance on a daily basis; rather, he appeared on the CI-6
agents' rotation schedule every few weeks.

Belchenko specialized in "honey pot" operations—the use
of beautiful women to form liaisons and carry on as many
affairs as possible with State Department officials, White
House and Pentagon staffers, congressional aides (especially
those working for senators and representatives on the intelligence and military oversight committees)—and he was not
surprised that this type of operation had not diminished in
its effectiveness, despite the deadly menace of AIDS that
loomed darkly in the background. His take from these operations had actually increased, confirming what he had always believed, that love and lust were powerful emotions
that held sway over even the threat of a slow, painful death.
One current operation in particular brought a smile to his
face: a beautiful and sexy Englishwoman, recruited in London and brought to Washington, was now sleeping with a
senior Defense Department official with access to top-secret
information. She was one of fifteen such honey-pot operations under his control but was proving to be the most valuable; her conquest felt the need to boast of his high-level
position and impress her with his knowledge of top-secret

projects while they made love, which, Belchenko was grateful for, was as often as four nights a week, with occasional matinees when he could get away.

As Belchenko rolled to a stop at the intersection of Wisconsin Avenue and K Street, he was well aware that he was under surveillance. He had spotted the FBI car shortly after leaving the embassy complex. He had no need to take any precautions; his purpose and destination had nothing to do with clandestine activities. He was simply on his way to one of the many legal areas of intelligence gathering available to even the general public. The openness of the American society had always amazed him; much of what is tightly guarded in the Soviet Union is readily available in the United States to anyone who knows where to look. He could even remember picking up valuable intelligence information while attending open congressional hearings, when blustering and unthinking politicians had inadvertently let slip highly classified information.

He left his car two blocks from the Convention Center and noticed that the FBI had either broken off their surveillance or had chosen not to follow him into the building once it had been established as his destination. He chalked it up to a show of presence, to remind him that he hadn't been forgotten, rather than a serious surveillance effort. He entered the massive structure on the Eighth Street level, which opened onto a sprawling exhibition hall crowded with people, display booths, and representatives of companies gathered for the Electronics and Micro-Computer Trade Show. He walked casually down the aisles and paused briefly at each booth to study the fascinating array of sophisticated equipment, then stopped and joined a small group watching a demonstration of a powerful information storage device known as a CD ROM, capable of storing as much as one quarter of a million printed pages of information on a single five-and-one-quarter-inch disk.

He felt, rather than saw, someone brush past him and glanced over his shoulder.

"Excuse me," a tall, distinguished-looking man with a military bearing said.

"Of course," Belchenko replied pleasantly as their eyes made split-second contact.

Belchenko looked after the retreating figure, dressed in a dark business suit. Even with only a momentary glimpse, he had recognized General Max and refrained from staring after him as he continued on his way to the end of the aisle and disappeared around the corner. The last time he had seen his old adversary, ten years ago, he was head of the Defense Intelligence Agency and was wearing the uniform of a lieutenant general of the United States Army.

Anyone who had seen the seemingly innocuous contact would have thought nothing of it, would not even have noticed anything out of the ordinary. People throughout the exhibition hall were jammed together, standing shoulder-to-shoulder at many of the display booths. To untrained eyes it was an occurrence in keeping with the rhythm and bustle of a crowded place.

Belchenko returned his attention to the demonstration he had been watching, and he waited until the instructor finished. He then continued walking up and down the rows of exhibits for another half hour before he left the Convention Center. Once outside he put his hand in the pocket of his overcoat and felt the slip of paper that had not been there when he entered the building.

Neither Belchenko nor General Max had spotted the man who now went to the bank of pay telephones near the exit and dialed a number for the direct line the Deputy Director for Operations had set up exclusively for those working on the mission called Operation Viper—the hunt for Nikolai Malik. Although the CIA's charter prohibited them from conducting operations inside the United States, the all-out manhunt for Malik was another case where the Director of the CIA, with the President's stamp of approval, deemed that the current crisis precluded any restrictions on their

activities. With the knowledge of the GRU attempts to abduct Malik, the DDO had assigned surveillance teams to
watch all high-level GRU officers.

"You'll never guess who just made a 'brush contact' with
Belchenko," the man said to the operations officer who answered the phone.

"I'm not in the mood for twenty questions," came the
terse reply.

"Maxwell Stanton," the caller said.

"Lieutenant General Maxwell Taylor Stanton." The voice
was tinged with disbelief. "The former head of the DIA?"

"The very same," the caller said.

"Stay on him, and put another team on Belchenko."

"Already done. My partner's got him covered."

"Don't lose him."

"Not a chance," the caller said. He immediately hung up
the phone and hurried out the door to join his partner.

24

The two sections of the polished black-granite wall are each 250 feet long. The east wall points directly at the Washington Monument, the west at the Lincoln Memorial. They converge at an obtuse angle ten feet below the meadow into which they are embedded. It is the most visited monument in our nation's capital, ten thousand visitors a week, a place of remembrance where people come to mourn and reflect, a place of catharsis and consolation where some find the solace of final reconciliation. Called a black gash of shame, a tombstone, and a ditch of disgrace by its detractors, the Vietnam Veterans Memorial, inscribed with 58,022 names, is the only national monument in the world to individually honor every man who died in the service of his country in a given war. On the far side of the memorial site, across a grassy meadow on a small rise, stands a bronze statue of three "grunts" dressed in fatigues and carrying automatic weapons; they face toward the wall as if their weary eyes are scanning for their own names. The statue is a concession to those who disapproved of "the Wall" and demanded a more conventional figurative sculpture. And along with the Wall it also serves as a haunting reminder that the posturing of politicians can swing the national fist into the collective stomachs of a generation, taking the best of them from us.

Families, loved ones, and former comrades-in-arms of the

dead come to the memorial to cry and to leave mementos: flowers, dog tags, unit insignia, photographs, a can of beer, and letters ("We didn't mean to leave you behind, but we had to get out of there"). They talk in hushed tones as at no other monument. It is a procession with liturgical overtones: the visitors move slowly, reverently, talking less and less, then fall silent as they read the names of the first man killed, in July 1959, an advisor watching a movie in Saigon, and the last to die, in May 1975, during the rescue of the freighter *Mayaguez.*

The Wall is a touchstone for the veterans of the Vietnam War, a place where they can come to feel the presence of their fallen buddies and to pay to each other the tribute denied to them elsewhere. The reflective black granite is dark, dreamy, and redemptive, a threshold where the living confront the dead and come to terms with the past. There is an overwhelming sense of union, and time spent there is not ordinary time. Nor is it an ordinary place—it is a sanctum, both beautiful and terrible, where a hand reaches out, touches the Wall, and traces a name with a finger in a tactile prayer. When facing the highly reflective surface you can see yourself clearly among the names. When it rains the names seem to disappear.

General Max stood before a panel near the vertex of the walls, his eyes fixed on a name a few lines from the top—the name of his only child, his son Matthew, killed in action at Phu Bai in April of 1966. Lost in his memories, he did not notice the reflection of the figure that stopped and stood beside him.

Belchenko's eyes scanned the panel and found the name upon which General Max's attention was focused.

"A relative?"

"My son," General Max said, snapping abruptly out of his reverie.

"Ah, yes. I remember now."

General Max turned to face Belchenko. The GRU general looked much the same as he had when they had first met, a few silver hairs highlighted the temples of the handsome Slavic face, but he was tall and erect and looked every inch the professional soldier despite the civilian clothes he wore. General Max reached out to shake his hand and said, "It's good to see you again, my friend. You look well."

"I owe it all to clean socialist living," Belchenko said with a grin.

A few "professional" veterans, those who for one reason or another still had not put their lives back together, stopped nearby. Unkempt and dressed in pieces of uniforms —ragged field jackets covered with military insignia and decorations, and "boonie" hats festooned with badges and buttons—they stared blankly at the Wall, occasionally looking around as if to see if there was anyone who wanted to hear their stories. General Max glanced in their direction and noticed incongruities in the array of decorations and unit insignia three of them wore, an indication that much of what they were wearing wasn't earned, and that their stories, if told, would be fabricated from what they had read or heard and not from what they had experienced.

General Max gestured toward the Constitution Gardens pool and the Washington Monument towering in the distance. "Let's walk."

The two men left the memorial site and crossed the meadow to the path around the free-form-shaped reflecting pool. Their relationship, which went back to General Max's tour as a defense attaché in Moscow, was unique. As the Soviet Armed Forces liaison to the U.S. Army, Belchenko had been General Max's Soviet counterpart. Both colonels at the time, their duties brought them together in an official capacity and in the insular world of diplomatic social functions. Shortly after General Max's arrival in Moscow, they had met at a reception given by the Hungarian ambassador, the beginning of a feeling-out process that soon convinced them that they were both too circumspect to let slip classified information, nor would either of them ever entertain the idea of crossing over to the other side. Their relationship, based on mutual respect, was cordial and correct, but a wary friendship soon developed out of shared experiences and common interests. General Max never completely gave up hope of recruiting Belchenko, and when he cropped up again, at the Soviet Embassy in Washington during General Max's stints with the CIA and DIA, an assignment that was decidedly not a coincidence, the arm's-length friendly relationship was continued on an official basis.

An incident that happened the year before General Max left the Defense Intelligence Agency found them working together for a purpose neither could have anticipated. They had, with the approval of the highest councils of both their governments, secretly conducted a "white flag" operation requiring the cooperation of the two military intelligence services to defuse a volatile situation created by a militaristic splinter group in South America that could have resulted in destabilizing the entire region—an outcome that would have benefited neither country at the time.

As the two men walked Belchenko glanced reflexively over his shoulder and studied the ground in front of him.

"The FBI's people terminated your surveillance when you entered the Convention Center," General Max said.

"It is not them I'm concerned with," Belchenko said. "My KGB brothers spend more time watching me than your government does."

General Max was familiar with the practices of the KGB's KR section, an internal security force that wiretaps, bugs, and conducts surveillance on Soviet overseas personnel to make certain they have not become double agents.

"Our meeting has a plausible explanation," General Max offered. "Two old adversaries, still playing the game, looking for an edge."

Belchenko grunted. "I must admit, I did not expect to see you again, Maxwell, certainly not under such curious circumstances. I know you can no longer harbor any hope of recruiting me, so I must assume you have finally seen the error of your ways and have decided to be embraced by the great Russian bear." He flashed a smile, then added, "But, please, say it isn't so. I am an old man, ready for retirement, you must leave me some illusions."

"Your illusions are safe, Anatoli Alessevich," General Max said. "I'm here to ask for your help with a delicate matter."

Belchenko's eyes narrowed. "I had heard that you were now comfortably retired, a gentleman farmer."

"I am."

"Then this is not an official request?"

"Unofficial and very personal."

"How did you know where to find me?" Belchenko asked.

"I remembered that technology trade shows always held a fascination for you."

General Max took the photograph of Malik from the inside pocket of his overcoat and handed it to Belchenko without saying a word.

The GRU general stared at the image but said nothing. The look on his face told General Max that he knew who the man was . . . and a lot more.

"Who is he?"

Belchenko remained silent and handed the photograph back as they walked along the path around the reflecting pool.

"Let me tell you what he's done," General Max said. "About a week ago that man raped and murdered the wife of a close personal friend. You and I both know there will be no justice from within the system."

"A personal vendetta?" Belchenko said. "That's unlike you, Maxwell, very unprofessional."

"An accounting," General Max replied. "We can both remember when only the players were targets and behavior such as this wasn't tolerated. And on the rare occasions when it did happen, the people responsible were dealt with swiftly and harshly."

Belchenko nodded in agreement. "Times change."

"I'm asking you as a friend and fellow human being—this

man cannot be allowed to rape and murder with impunity under the guise of intelligence operations."

Belchenko didn't respond. He stopped to look back toward the memorial; his eyes suggested he was wrestling with a weighty decision. He was a principled man, a true professional soldier, who loved his country, and his family, and had lived his life in the belief that politics and the necessities of his chosen profession did not preclude honesty and decency.

"He is not GRU," he finally said. "We would have quickly disposed of him with the rest of the trash. He is KGB, and this is not the first time he has committed such a crime. We have reason to believe there have been at least four other victims."

"If he's not GRU, why are your people trying to abduct him?" General Max asked.

Belchenko smiled. "For the same reason your CIA is." The cagey general saw from the look in General Max's eyes that he did not know why Malik was being sought by both sides. "But how did you know about our interest in this man?"

General Max told him about the Paris incident, but left out the Omega team's mission, and how Gannon had recognized him as the man he chased in New York.

"I'd like his name and anything else you can tell me about him."

Belchenko looked away again, then nodded to himself. He made his decision and turned back to General Max.

"We have helped each other in the past, Maxwell, so in deference to that, and for my own personal reasons, I will tell you all that I can, but not all that I know."

"Fair enough."

"His name is Nikolai Malik," he said with disdain. "He is a KGB Illegal and a very dangerous man."

"Why are your people looking for him?"

Belchenko hesitated, then: "There is a faction within our government, the hard-line Bolsheviks, who are not happy with the direction in which the General Secretary is taking our nation. They feel he is going too far, too fast. He has made many powerful enemies, especially among the KGB."

"We have conservatives in our own government who feel the same way about the concessions we've made," General Max said.

"But they are not plotting to overthrow your government."

"That's not how we solve our problems," General Max said. "But if you know the KGB is behind it, surely Gorbachev has the power to weed out those responsible."

"It is not that simple, my friend. The opposition is strong and widespread, and they are conducting a clever and insidious clandestine campaign. Nikolai Malik holds the key to their success, but the KGB is denying him, they are saying he is a rogue, a loose cannon over whom they no longer exercise any control. They are lying, but the General Secretary is not in a position to move against them at this time. Too many whose support he needs are waiting to see which way the wind blows. And if Malik is not found and stopped, the General Secretary's days are numbered, as you Americans put it."

General Max was familiar with the pervasive influence and awesome power of the KGB. Their paramilitary arm alone—the Border Guards Directorate—had more than half a million armed men, better trained and better equipped than most of the Red Army. They gave the KGB the strength to control not only their own citizens but the military and the Party as well. Though formed to serve the Party and the State, they were more inclined to serve only themselves, and their huge numbers and secret ways had created the illusions that they were everywhere, even when they weren't. But the Central Committee and the Politburo, with the help of the military and the GRU, had ways of keeping them in check, and General Max found it difficult to believe what Belchenko was telling him.

"One KGB Illegal has it within his power to cause Gorbachev's downfall?" he said.

"An oversimplification, but more or less correct."

"And somewhere in what you're not telling me is the reason you want this Malik alive and not dead."

"As I said, Maxwell. I will tell you what I can."

"If you were conducting the search for him, where would you look?"

Belchenko smiled. "Perhaps Nicaragua. The General Secretary has angered many of those who have grown accustomed to our aid to keep their failing revolutions alive. It is expensive enough to prop up those whose economies are in shambles, let alone those who are fighting a protracted war against local anti-Communist insurgencies. Gorbachev has focused on breathing new life into our own economy through his policy of *perestroika*. Consequently he has put the leaders of Cuba, Nicaragua, and Vietnam and others on notice that we can no longer afford to send them billions of dollars in military aid, they have got to do some restructuring of their own. Nicaragua is deeply resentful of what they consider a betrayal, and there is reason to suspect that they, along with Cuba, have thrown their lot in with the anti-Gorbachev faction and the KGB."

General Max listened patiently to the lecture. He knew that it was Belchenko's indirect way of answering his questions.

"I'm aware of the reduction in aid, it's the only thing that brought the Sandinistas to the peace table with the Contras. It's also the reason they've expanded their narcotics smuggling and distribution efforts to include drug-processing labs and marijuana cultivation. But how does this all tie in to Malik?"

"Our GRU *rezident* in Managua has learned that Malik, with the support of the Nicaraguan Ministry of the Interior and the KGB, has been secretly assembling and training an elite terrorist force comprised of recruits from many nations."

Having kept in touch through the "old boy" network of ex-intelligence officers, General Max was also aware of the increased presence of terrorist groups in Nicaragua. Recent reports had confirmed the presence of PLO, IRA, Basque ETA, and Italian Red Brigade terrorists, some even holding Sandinista army rank. It was nothing new, simply an extension of the Sandinistas' ties to the international terrorist community, which had supported and helped finance their revolution since it was founded in the early 1960s. In the seventies, while General Max was still at DIA, he had received confirmed intelligence information that PLO-trained Sandinistas took part in several terrorist operations in the Middle East, including an attempt to overthrow the government of Jordan's King Hussein.

"We suspect he's using the terrorist training camp as a base of operations," Belchenko added.

"Why haven't your people acted on the information?"

"It's a remote, mobile jungle camp, always constructed under heavy, triple canopy where our satellites cannot easily detect it," Belchenko said. "And they don't stay in one location for extended periods. On the two occasions when we have pinpointed the location of the camp, Malik's KGB friends learned of our efforts and warned them before we could mount an operation."

"What is it you fear most from Malik, an assassination attempt on Gorbachev?"

"If it were that, we would simply have killed him," Belchenko said, then looked away as he was about to continue, but stopped himself.

"That's the part you can't tell me about?"

"I would not have told you as much as I have were it not for the fact that if your friend, or your government, is successful in finding and stopping Malik, it will serve our purpose as well as yours."

"Our purpose?" General Max said. "How would it benefit us?"

Belchenko waved off the question.

General Max patted the GRU general on the shoulder. "You've given me more than I had any right to expect, Anatoli Allessevich. I'm grateful."

"Your friend will be going after Malik?"

"Yes."

"Alone?" Belchenko said, arching an eyebrow.

"Probably."

"Whatever action he decides to take, tell him to be careful, Maxwell. It is a very high-stakes game he is getting into. And Malik is exceptionally capable and very ruthless."

"I'll tell him."

General Max crossed Constitution Avenue to the small side street where he had parked his car. His call to Gannon completed, he decided to visit an old friend in Arlington before returning to his farm. As he inserted the key in the car door, he saw two men dressed in dark three-piece suits approach from across the street. They were young, trim and fit, full of purpose, and, from the way they carried themselves, armed. General Max pegged them as Secret Service agents.

The taller of the two flashed his Treasury Department identification and confirmed General Max's assessment. "General Stanton, I've been instructed to ask you to come with us."

"Do you mind telling me where?" General Max said.

The taller man repeated his exact instructions. "The White House, sir. The President would like to see you."

General Max followed the two agents to their car and climbed into the backseat. An ironic smile spread slowly across his face; he was more than a little chagrined at not having spotted whoever had had him under surveillance.

Gannon accelerated out of the entrance ramp and merged into the flow of traffic on Route 66, heading east toward Dulles International Airport. He went over in his mind all of the things General Max had told him and smiled at his request—"Don't tell me what you're going to do or how you're going to do it; the less I know the better."

Gannon reached over the front passenger seat and unzipped one of the outside pockets of his black nylon carry-on bag. He removed the photograph of Malik and held it in place on the hub of the steering wheel. "Nikolai Malik," he said aloud, and stared at the image as he drove. He burned the hard, unyielding features into his memory. Again he said the name out loud: "Nikolai Malik!"

His thoughts went back to the over-the-fence missions he had run in Vietnam. Top-secret missions, where he had been given photographs of North Vietnamese Army political cadre and high-ranking military officers. Inserted inside North Vietnam and Laos, sometimes his small four-man team would spend weeks deep behind enemy lines before locating their target. They were "black" operations, assassinations, shoot-on-sight missions planned and orchestrated by the CIA and carried out by the Special Operations Group. And now there was another photograph, and he was on his way to another jungle. If you stay around long enough, he thought, everything comes full circle.

Mentally sorting through possible plans of action as he drove, one plan continued to reassert itself over the others and he settled on it, his gut instincts telling him it was the right approach. What General Max had said about Kate not being Malik's first victim kept forcing its way back into his conscious mind, interrupting his thoughts. "But she'll be your last innocent victim, Malik," he vowed. "I swear to God, she'll be your last."

He felt in control now. He had a name to go with the face, and a probable base of operations, and a network of uniquely qualified friends to draw on. He pressed down on the accelerator and sped toward the airport and his flight to Miami.

25

The Secret Service agents brought General Max into the White House through the underground tunnel leading from the Treasury Building, a precaution taken to avoid drawing attention to his being summoned by the President. They escorted him down the West Wing basement corridor, past the White House Mess, to a heavy oak door with a small brass plaque that read "Situation Room." The taller of the two agents rang the buzzer and stepped back. The door opened almost immediately, and General Max stood face-to-face with an old colleague. Robert Burton, Director of the Central Intelligence Agency, had been head of Clandestine Services when General Max was Deputy Director. They had had a good working relationship for the two years they had served together.

The DCI's broad Irish face flashed a disarming smile as he extended his hand. "Losing your touch, Max," he said with a wink, and nodded toward the Secret Service agents flanking the door.

"Looks that way."

General Max glanced about the cramped, somber room designed for close-quarter crisis management. No larger than eighteen by twelve feet, most of the space was taken up by a teak conference table. Three of the walls were covered with rich, dark walnut panels that concealed an assortment of high-tech electronic equipment that included built-in video monitors, telecommunications terminals, and the remote controls for the equipment used to project and manipulate images on the large screen behind a curtain that was drawn across the fourth wall.

It was not the first time General Max had been in the White House Situation Room; he had been there on a number of occasions as CIA Deputy Director and DIA chief, to brief the National Security Council, and on two occasions since his retirement, again, as the country's foremost specialist in unconventional warfare, to brief the NSC on matters concerning the use of special operations forces. It was, however, his first visit since the new President, whom he had never met. He was accustomed to seeing the conference table, and the chairs lining the walls, filled with people as they usually were when the full National Security Council met, but there were only four people in attendance now, their suit coats off, collars and ties loosened, and shirt sleeves rolled up in what was obviously an intense working session.

Burton gestured toward the President, who was seated at the head of the table. "Mr. President, I don't believe you know General Maxwell Stanton."

"Only by reputation." The President rose from his plush leather chair to shake General Max's hand. He turned to introduce the others at the table. "My national security advisor, Bill Clinton," he said, and indicated the pudgy, nervous academic who was seated to his immediate right. "And Dave Wilson, the Agency's Deputy Director for Operations. And of course you know my DCI, Bob Burton."

General Max completed the cursory handshakes and gave Wilson a friendly pat on the arm in recognition of the time when the DDO, then a young case officer in the CIA's Moscow station, had worked for him. He then took the chair offered by the President and sat to his left, halfway down the table.

"Two of your former colleagues who are present in this

room have assured me that you are a direct and forthright man who has no equivocations about his duty to his country," the President said. "Your distinguished military record alone confirms that, so I'll get right to the point. What was the purpose of your clandestine meeting with General Belchenko?"

"Strictly a personal matter, Mr. President."

"A personal matter?" the national security advisor interrupted. He leaned forward, his baby-blue eyes too large and bland to turn into the hard, penetrating stare he had hoped for. "What *personal matter* could a former Deputy Director of the CIA possibly have with a GRU general?" His high-pitched voice rose to a nasal whine that General Max thought he was not alone in finding irritating. It was a voice that seemed tailor-made for the pudgy, sullen face.

"One of little or no significance to anyone in this room, I would imagine," General Max said.

The President raised a cautioning hand at Clinton, who was about to launch into a tirade. He turned his calm gray eyes on General Max.

"An old war-horse like you knew the minute the Secret Service approached you that this was no invitation for a casual chat. Succinctly put, it's a most urgent matter of national security, and whatever is discussed at this meeting has the highest possible security classification attached to it. Do we understand each other, General?"

"Yes, Mr. President," General Max answered stiffly.

"Good, then let's cut to the chase." The President nodded toward Burton, then said, "The DCI tells me that you are close friends with a man by the name of Jack Gannon, and that he has reasons to believe your meeting with Belchenko was on behalf of this man to learn the identity and where-abouts of a KGB Illegal by the name of Nikolai Malik. Is that true?"

"Yes, it is," General Max said. He had no intention of withholding information from the President.

"And what did you learn?"

"That there is a strong possibility that Malik is in Nicaragua at a secret terrorist training camp set up by the KGB."

Dave Wilson, the DDO, spoke up. "That squares with my Foreign Resources people, who spotted him talking to a member of the Nicaraguan Foreign Ministry in the UN delegates' lounge, and the information we got from French intelligence that the terrorist Zimmerman, who was killed in Paris, had an airline ticket to Managua in his coat pocket."

The President nodded and resumed questioning General Max. "And you passed this information on to your friend Gannon?"

"I did," General Max replied.

"And he is going to Nicaragua to find Malik to avenge the murder of his wife?"

"I don't know that to be a fact, but I would feel safe in assuming that is the case."

"And the fact that this Gannon is ADM trained is purely coincidental, I suppose," Clinton broke in, his eyes flashing as he held up Gannon's service record and jabbed a finger at the section on specialized training. "Well, for my tastes, there are too many coincidences involving this Gannon's entry into the equation, and I'm not buying any of it."

General Max stared at the national security advisor in genuine confusion. The connection between avenging Kate Gannon's death and Gannon's training in the use of Atomic Demolition Munitions while a Green Beret completely escaped him. But it did sound an internal alarm that alerted him to the fact that there was far more at stake than he had imagined.

The President shook his head slowly, his eyes fixed on Clinton. "If you don't mind, Bill, I'd like to continue without any further interruptions."

The national security advisor crossed his arms, leaned back, and settled into what looked like the posture of a sulking child.

"Gannon didn't confide his plans to you?" the President asked General Max, who was still running possible scenarios through his mind that could explain Clinton's puzzling, seemingly unconnected statement.

"No, he did not, and I didn't ask." Out of the corner of his eye he saw a small smile spread slowly over the DCI's face. Ever the spook, Burton thought.

The President took a long, thoughtful pause, then said, "In light of my national security advisor's untimely outburst, I think it advisable at this point that you be briefed on the situation we're dealing with."

The President glanced around the table. The DCI and the DDO both nodded in agreement. Clinton's face expressed his disapproval, but after a stern look from the President, he reluctantly made it unanimous.

"For reasons you will immediately understand, General Stanton, there are only a handful of men who know what I'm about to tell you. Your expertise and experience, along with your knowledge of your friend Gannon, might be of considerable help. So I would appreciate your full cooperation."

"I'll do what I can, sir."

The President paused for a long moment and then began. "You are of course aware of the scandal that rocked the previous administration involving a 'secret army,' for lack of a better term, made up of high-ranking officers in the CIA, Department of Defense, the National Security Council, and White House staff?"

"I'm familiar with most of what happened," General Max said, and poured himself a glass of ice water from the carafe in front of him. Through the old-boy network, before the story had broken in the press, he had heard rumors about the secret cabal at the Pentagon and the CIA and about the subsequent investigations that led to secret courts-martial and forced retirements that had ended a number of once-promising careers.

The President continued, "My predecessor in this office was more often than not ill advised and manipulated by a group of men who turned every international confrontation into a pecker contest. In effect, certain members of the National Security Council and the White House staff had assumed an operational role with off-line links to the CIA. They were running their own unauthorized covert operations, aided and abetted by elements of the Army's Special Operations Division who were virtually out of control."

"It was my understanding that all of that was quietly put to bed during the Iran–Contra hearings," General Max said.

"It was. At least the part that became public knowledge. But what the press latched onto and what the rumor mills circulated only scratched the surface. Those paranoid maniacs had decided that they alone knew what was best for the country, indeed for the entire Western world. And acted on it. And I was handed the legacy of cleaning up the worst of the mess."

The President paused, as though reliving the unpleasant revelations that had startled him on the day he took office. "When I took over ten months ago I received a briefing from the previous DCI that shook me to the core."

"It would shake this entire country and all our allies to the very core if it ever became known," the national security advisor chimed in.

The President turned to the DCI and said, "Bob, if you'll fill in the General."

Burton cleared his throat and sat forward in his chair, resting his arms on the table. "The operation in question started about six months before the former President left office. Some of his staff and advisors and most of the 'secret army' they controlled were literally up in arms about the concessions made to the Soviets through the disarmament treaties and in the spirit of détente. They considered anyone an imbecile who believed the Soviets had given up spreading their brand of communism merely to settle for protecting the Motherland and improving their economy. They were from the spend-them-to-death school of thought and had a profound distrust of the Soviets and considered it folly to give them a breather to deal with their social unrest and a ruinous economy. As far as they were concerned, the sheer destructive power of nuclear weapons, and not treaties and defensive systems, was a cheap and deadly way to keep the peace.

"But what riled them most was our bargaining away our European-based intermediate-range missiles in the face of the enormous improvements the Soviets had made in conventional arms and in their increased capability for short-warning attack against our NATO allies. They wanted to make certain that this country didn't leave NATO bare-assed naked against a conventional ground attack by the Soviets. They wanted something in place that would disrupt and stall a Soviet invasion, delay their advances until we could bring our Rapid Deployment Forces into play."

Burton paused and raised a meaningful eyebrow at General Max. "The decision was made to 'seed' a number of Saydums in Eastern Europe," he said, pronouncing the acronym SADM, which stood for Special Atomic Demolition Munitions. "They were deployed at strategic points along known invasion routes and left in place to be remotely detonated by satellite signal in time of war. Their thinking was, if they didn't do it now, the weapons would be lost through negotiations, and if they weren't in our inventory at the nuclear storage sites at the time they were to be accounted for, it would appear that we had complied with the treaty."

General Max stared in disbelief. He was more than familiar with the miniature nuclear weapons known as SADMs. He had written the training manual on methods of their deployment and use by Special Forces units. Light enough, at less than forty pounds, to be man-portable, they were designed as tactical weapons, intended for use in demolishing bridges, mountain passes, dams, railroad beds, airport runways, and missile launch sites, with the added effect, through radioactive fallout, of denying access to a considerable area around ground zero for periods ranging from months to years, depending on placement of the weapon and atmospheric conditions at the time of the blast.

He recalled a top-secret plan under consideration during the last years of the Vietnam War. SADMs were proposed as a method of denying the use of the Ho Chi Minh Trail to the North Vietnamese Army by deploying them at Mu Gia Pass, the main supply artery and choke point where the Trail entered Laos and snaked its way through the mountainous jungle to the south. The mission plan was to parachute an ADM-trained Special Forces team from the Special Operations Group into Laos, deploy the weapon, set the timers for a twenty-four-hour delay, and extract the team once they had reached a predesignated extraction site. Jack Gannon was to have been the team leader on the mission. General Max had argued against using the weapon and had prevailed only after a protracted, and at times heated, debate.

General Max glanced at the President. The Chief Executive's face was expressionless, but the telling dark circles beneath his eyes underlined the seriousness of the present situation. General Max's mind raced ahead; the pieces of the puzzle began to fall into horrifying place. "How many weapons were seeded?" he asked.

"Six," Burton said. "All fourth-generation models—4.5 kilotons each."

General Max was taken aback by the last statement. The weight-to-yield ration had improved significantly since he had retired. The nine-thousand-pound, ten-kiloton bomb carried by the B-29 *Enola Gay* and dropped on Hiroshima required nine hundred pounds of weight per kiloton yield. With miniaturization and other technological advances, the ratio had been reduced to less than thirty pounds per kiloton while he was DIA chief and was now down to just over seven pounds.

"Who deployed them?" he asked.

"Special Forces teams stationed at Bad Tolz, West Germany. They were parachuted into East Germany on six separate missions during December of 1988."

"Goddamn Green Beret cowboys," Clinton muttered, loud enough for all to hear.

General Max shot a withering glance at the national security advisor. He had instantly disliked the man, having seen his type before—a think-tank academic with no hands-on experience who had never put his ass on the line in his life. In his younger days, he thought, under different circumstances, he would have backhanded the arrogant, pencil-necked little shit off his chair. In light of his present position and status, he settled for a stern rebuke.

"For your information, Clinton, no one in the military gets up in the morning and decides he'll start a war. Those decisions are made in this room, by people like you. We don't make policy, we carry it out, regardless of how stupid or inane."

The forcefulness of General Max's words, and the deadly look in his cold blue eyes, instantly quieted the national security advisor. An equally sharp look from the President stopped the confrontation before it escalated.

"Are the weapons still in place?" General Max asked.

"I ordered them removed within two days of learning they had been deployed," the President said.

"We sent in some of our paramilitary people," the DCI added. "We pulled five of them out."

"And the sixth?" General Max said. He dreaded the answer he had already figured out.

"One of the Special Forces teams was lost . . . along with the weapon," Burton said. "They were dropped off course. We sent in three recovery teams, but came up empty. About a week later, through our agents in East Germany, we were able to piece together what had happened. The body of the team leader was found at the bottom of a ravine beneath a railroad trestle, apparently run over by a train. Two of his teammates drowned, and their bodies were washed up on a riverbed. And the fourth man, the one carrying the 'item,' " Burton said, using the euphemism for the SADM, "was killed on impact upon landing in a tree."

"And the Saydum?" General Max prompted the DCI.

"An East German Army patrol found it and turned it over to their commanding officer. It eventually ended up in the hands of the commander of the Group of Soviet Forces Germany, who entrusted it to the care of the GRU's Spetsnaz troops at their secret training facility at Fürstenburg in East Germany until he received further orders from Moscow."

"And you believe Nikolai Malik now has the weapon?" General Max said. The analogy that came to mind was letting a chain saw fall into the hands of a termite.

"All indicators point in that direction," Burton said. "Once we learned what had happened, we activated every agent and asset we had in East Germany to pinpoint the Saydum's location. Six months ago, within days of our learning it was being kept under heavy guard in a warehouse at the Spetsnaz base, Malik got hold of it before our recovery team could mount an operation to get in there and snatch it. From what we've been able to learn, Malik and three of his East German terrorist buddies posed as high-ranking GRU officers and drove a van onto the base and presented phony orders to transport the weapon to Moscow. By the time the ruse was discovered, the Saydum and Malik were long gone. Our people picked up his trail and followed it as far as Rostock, where we believe the Saydum was loaded onto a freighter. . . . That's where we lost track of it."

General Max stared at the far wall for a few moments, then said, "Since they found the bodies of the team leader and the man carrying the Saydum, that means they got both sets of numbers necessary to open the combination lock and arm the weapon."

Burton nodded, again cursing their bad luck. In order to arm the weapon the lock-secure cover had to be removed. For security purposes the combination to the lock was not known to any one man on the team. It was given to two men, the team leader and the man carrying the weapon.

Each had a set of three numbers that when combined would unlock the cover and provide access to the arming chamber Had both sets of numbers not been found, the PAL safety device, built into the SADM's lock-secure cover, was equipped with a limited-try feature that permanently locked the weapon after three failed attempts at entering the combination. The Permissive-Action-Link safety device would have rendered the SADM inoperable and useless, preventing it from being armed—any attempt to dismantle it would have activated internal denial devices that would have set off a conventional shaped charge, completely destroying the weapon and anyone within fifty yards of it in a non-nuclear explosion.

"How many people know the weapon is missing?" General Max asked the DCI.

"Besides the Soviets, most of the National Security Council, those of us in this room, the head of my Counterterrorist Group, and three of his people who led the recovery team we initially sent into East Germany," Burton said. "Everyone else involved in the hunt for Malik has no idea why we want him."

"How many of the European Theater commanders knew about the six weapons that were deployed?"

"Only three," Burton said. "And they were told that all of the weapons were recovered. Our agent net in East Germany was told that the team had lost highly classified satellite communications equipment. They had no reason to suspect differently, since the item was sealed in its jump container and, according to our sources, the East Germans didn't have time to figure out what they had before the Soviets took it from them and clamped a lid on the whole matter once they had the Saydum tucked away."

"And we've taken every precaution to ensure that the fact that one of our nuclear weapons is missing doesn't leak to the press or the public," the national security advisor said. "If even a hint of this got out, the panic that would ensue in this country and Europe could bring down governments," he added pointedly.

"Did Belchenko say anything about the Saydum or allude to it in any way?" the President asked.

"Yes. He alluded to it. And with what I've learned in this room, his sense of urgency about finding Malik is fully understandable," General Max said. "The GRU believes that Malik is under the control of an anti-Gorbachev faction in the KGB and that whatever he has planned is intended to cause Gorbachev's downfall."

"That's the reading we got," the President said. "At first we believed they intended to use the Saydum to embarrass us by exploding it in one of the NATO countries, make it look like an accident at one of our storage sites, or a weapon we had lost to terrorists through a lapse in security, and then reap the political benefits from the international repercussions. At the very least it would have given the antinuclear groups the added impetus they need to succeed in getting all nuclear weapons out of Western Europe and Great Britain."

"But since they're accomplishing their goals through diplomatic negotiations, they no longer stand to benefit from an action as desperate and dangerous as that," the national security advisor added. "We believe that's why the anti-Gorbachev faction stepped in. They saw an opportunity to discredit his policies, especially his openness with the West."

"It's a win-win situation for them," Burton said. "If Malik detonates that weapon and the KGB tie it to us, it makes Gorbachev look like a fool for trusting us to live up to the disarmament treaties. But even if they're exposed as the culprits, the anti-Gorbachev faction still benefits from the adverse effects the Soviets' diplomatic efforts would suffer because of it. They'd be international pariahs again, the hard-liners would be back in control, and Gorbachev and his reforms would fall by the wayside."

"And aside from the geopolitical ramifications is the specter of thousands of innocent people being killed," the Presi-

dent said. "So you can understand why we don't want this
friend of yours, Gannon, killing Malik. He's the only direct
link we have to the weapon. If he's out of the picture, we
lose track of the Saydum."

General Max sat silently for a few moments. "Have you
received any threats or ultimatums concerning the
weapon?"

"None," the President said. "The Soviets have never even
admitted to having it."

"Do you have any idea of a timetable for Malik's mission?" He directed the question at the DCI.

"Nothing concrete," Burton said. "But time's running out
on him, so he's got to act soon. Gorbachev obviously knows
or suspects what Malik has in mind or the GRU wouldn't be
out in force to stop him. And Malik knows by now that
they're onto him, so the longer he waits, the better the
chance they'll grab him."

"Mexico," General Max said.

"What about Mexico?" the President asked.

"If he's taken the Saydum to Nicaragua, Mexico is the
most likely target."

"Why?" the President asked.

"One of the Soviet–Cuban strategic goals is to cause and
support a major revolution in Mexico," General Max said.
"If that weapon is detonated in Mexico City, the effects
would be monstrous—tens of thousands killed outright,
thousands more from radioactive fallout, and with very few
of their buildings made of steel-reinforced concrete, the blast
damage would level every structure for three square miles.
But the result that would appeal most to the KGB would be
the five million or so refugees who would flood this country.
The effect on our economy alone would be disastrous, not to
mention the number of agents they could infiltrate with the
refugees and the political mileage they'd get from claiming
we've introduced nuclear weapons into Central America."

"It's a scenario we've seriously considered," the DCI
said.

"Who would believe we'd introduce nuclear weapons into Central America?" Clinton said. "It's illogical. Preposterous."

"Logic has nothing to do with it," General Max said. "It would be a powerful emotional issue backed up by the fact that one of our weapons did indeed detonate in Mexico City. The media would never believe us and neither would most of the world."

"Let's get back to the matter at hand," the President said, noticeably disturbed by the thought of a worst-case scenario. "Are you certain," he said to General Max, "that Gannon knows nothing about the Saydum?"

"Yes. His only purpose in going after Malik is retribution for what he did to his wife."

The President reached across the table and picked up Gannon's service record and skimmed the contents. "Gannon's got to be found and stopped before he gets to Malik. What do you suggest?"

"Finding him is one thing, stopping him is another matter altogether," General Max said. "I only know that his point of departure was Dulles airport, but it shouldn't be any problem to find out where he went from there. He'll be traveling under his own name."

"And if his destination is Nicaragua," Clinton said, "then he'll eventually turn up in Managua."

General Max smiled at the national security advisor's naiveté. "He's not about to enter Nicaragua posing as a tourist. Any American who shows up there is automatically suspect. They'd pull him off the streets within twenty-four hours."

"Then he'll probably go through Costa Rica or Honduras," Burton said. "We can stake out the airports in San José and Tegucigalpa. If he manages to get past us, he's still got to get equipment and weapons if he's going into the boonies after Malik. And his chances of accomplishing that without our people finding out about it are nonexistent."

General Max shook his head. "He won't surface in San

José or Tegucigalpa, or anywhere else you have a heavy presence and might spot him. He knows you don't want him to get to Malik. He doesn't know why, but he knows you'll try to stop him. Be advised, gentlemen, you're dealing with a clever, resourceful man with extraordinary skills he can apply with devastating results. He's also the best damn recon man I've ever known. So, believe me, he's not going to do anything you'd expect him to do."

"Then what will he do?" the President asked. "You were once his commanding officer, you know him, what would you do in his position?"

"He won't trust anyone he doesn't know," General Max said. "He'll go to his SOA buddies."

"SOA?" the President said.

"Special Operations Association," General Max said. "It's a fraternal organization for those who served in combat in Southeast Asia with SOG," he added, pronouncing as a word the three-letter acronym for the Special Operations Group.

"What good would that do him?" Clinton asked.

"They're a unique group of men with interesting backgrounds and even more interesting occupations in every corner of the world," General Max said, smiling with inward pride at the fond memories of his time in command of SOG.

"From the time SOG was formed in 1964 until it was deactivated in 1972," he continued, "its reconnaissance teams ran some of the most daring and dangerous missions of the war. Most of the men were pulled from Army Special Forces units, but there were a few Navy SEAL and Marine Corps Force Recon troops involved too. Out of a total of roughly thirty-six hundred Americans who ran over-the-fence missions during that nine-year period, only three hundred and fifteen are still alive. Less than a ten percent survival rate, gentlemen. Consequently, they're a tightly knit group who take care of their own. If I were Gannon, I'd look for one of my old buddies, someone who's run covert ops into Nicaragua at one time or another and knows the area, and I'd tap into any current sources he might have."

Dave Wilson, the DDO, nodded knowingly. "We've had a number of ex-SOG personnel working for us at different times as contract employees. Mostly paramilitary work."

The President put Gannon's service record back on the table. "What about letting Gannon go after Malik?" the President said. He directed the question to Burton. "Don't interfere with him."

"Recruit him to work with us?" the DCI said.

"If we can get to him, yes. If not, let him go after Malik for his own reasons. Let him lead us to him if he can," the President said. "He's certainly qualified for the mission, and he's familiar with the Saydum, he'd recognize it on sight and know what to do with it. We can keep track of him and step in at the right moment."

"And if he's caught, he's deniable," Burton said, with a quick glance at his DDO.

Wilson nodded his approval. "We limit our exposure, and if he screws up, the press will eat up his story—a distraught and grieving husband bent on revenge, with no provable connection to us."

"What makes you think he has any chance of succeeding? You've sent four paramilitary teams into Nicaragua in the last year trying to locate that terrorist camp," the national security advisor said. "And according to your reports, you never heard from any of them again except for two Miskito Indian guides from the last team who straggled back across the Honduran border half dead. If memory serves, they claimed they found the camp but were ambushed and shot to hell by well-trained troops that definitely weren't run-of-the-mill Sandinista soldiers."

"He can't do any worse," the DCI said. "And we can't keep pushing our luck. If any of our people are caught and tied to us, the anti-Contra clique on the Hill will be all over us."

"And we can't openly hunt for the weapon without the

distinct possibility that the press and Congress will get wind of it and start digging," the President said. "And the last thing we need is this whole sordid mess about the Saydum seedings getting out. Even though its roots are in the past Administration, I'll end up bearing the brunt of it." He turned to General Max. "Well, General Stanton, what about it? Can your boy Gannon get to him?"

"There are no guarantees," General Max said. "But I can tell you this much—Gannon doesn't know the meaning of the word *quit*. He'll get into Nicaragua, and if Malik's there, he won't come back until he finds him." He paused again, smiling at a flash of memory from a particularly hairy mission Gannon had run in Vietnam, then added, "There's only one way to stop Gannon and that's to kill him, and as a lot of highly trained people have found out, that's easier said than done."

"Then it's settled," the President said. "If we find him before he goes into Nicaragua, we'll recruit him. But either way, we let Gannon take the point."

26

Jim Boos sat staring at a fat cross-eyed cat and laughing into his beer. The huge white cat was perched contentedly on the crude plank bar; his ample stomach sagged over the edge, his insouciant, comical yellow eyes surveyed his kingdom— a one-room run-down shack of a bar and restaurant in a back alley of Montego Bay, Jamaica, called Daniels. The windows and front door of the crowded, noisy room were open to the humid evening air, and a large dog lay just outside the front stoop keeping a baleful eye on the cat with the hope that an occasional scrap, or the cat, would be tossed his way. A loud, pulsating reggae beat, a soulful synthesis of African, Caribbean, and Black American music, reverberated off the flimsy walls; its earthy, sensuous melody and lyrics, born of the Rastafarian movement, a lesson in Jamaican attitudes and feelings for those who took the time to listen carefully.

The oilcloth-covered tables were full without a tourist in sight. Daniels was a place the locals frequented; and the surly, brooding Rastamen, some with colorful berets set at jaunty angles on their sun-reddened shoulder-length hair, matted and twisted into dreadlocks, were not inclined to welcome outsiders or to make those who accidentally wandered in feel the least bit comfortable. A bluish-white cloud of smoke, heavy with the sweet, pungent smell of *ganja,* floated among the ceiling rafters and drifted slowly out into the alley.

A pretty young Jamaican girl brought a steaming bowl of goat stew to Jim Boos's table.

"Made fresh this very afternoon, Captain Jim," she said with a friendly smile.

Boos tasted the local delicacy and nodded his approval, to the girl's pleasure.

Seated with his back to the wall, a habit from the old days, his eyes scanned the crowded room from the corner table. His past was subtly evident in his manner and presence. Tall, broad-shouldered, narrow-waisted, with long, knotted muscles, he had been a warrior, a former Navy SEAL with four combat tours in Vietnam. He had lived in a world of action and danger for most of his adult life. But now he found himself content, even happy sometimes, living life at ten knots under sail. A boyishly handsome face, framed in short-cropped sandy-blond hair, belied his forty-three years and was offset by a slightly crooked nose and an uneven, engaging smile. His eyes were expressive and intense, and though he appeared easygoing, there was a vaguely disquieting edge to him—a hint of unpredictability, of still flirting with the brink.

His eyes abruptly stopped scanning the room when a familiar figure approached his table, a black nylon carry-on bag slung over one shoulder.

"Look at that cat," Boos said. "Is that the fattest, dumbest-looking goddamn cat you ever saw or what?" His greeting to Gannon would have led anyone listening to think it had been two hours rather than two years since he had seen his old friend.

"What in the name of God are you eating?" Gannon said, his gaze fixed on the semicongealed bowl of stew as he sat down.

"Whatever didn't make it across the road this morning," Boos quipped. "Where you at, Jack?" he said, his voice purposely heavy with the regional patois of his Louisiana Cajun background.

"If I take too many deep breaths in here," Gannon said, glancing at the cloud of marijuana smoke that clung to the ceiling, "in about five minutes I probably won't know where the hell I am."

"Cheapest high in town," Boos said. "How'd you find this place?"

"I asked some guy at the Yacht Club dinghy dock where I could find you. He suggested I didn't come unarmed."

"It's okay if you're with me." He gestured to the pretty waitress to bring Gannon a beer.

The conversation lapsed, as it often does when two men with a shared history feel no need for extraneous talk in each other's presence. Gannon surveyed the room and sipped his beer. He took note of some of the scariest-looking characters he had seen in a long while. His thoughts returned to when he had first met Boos, in Vietnam in 1967 at the Special Operations Group, Command and Control North compound outside of Da Nang. Boos and three other SEAL from the nearby euphemistically named Naval Advisory Detachment were to blow up a bridge deep inside North Vietnam. Gannon's Special Forces recon team, in a combined operation, was to lead the SEAL to the target area and provide security for the mission. After repeated U.S. air strikes had knocked out the bridge, located on a major trail leading to the North Vietnamese Army's supply routes to the south, the NVA had reconstructed it under three feet of water a few miles downstream. Invisible to the American reconnaissance planes from the air, it again served the purpose of allowing the enemy truck convoys to ford the broad, muddy river. Gannon's team had discovered it on a previous mission and four members of the elite SEAL team had been called in to apply their special skills in underwater demolitions.

The mission had initially gone well. The combined eight-man team had reached the target area without incident, the

SEAL had set the pressure charges to blow the next time a truck attempted to cross the bridge, and the team began the long trek back to a safe area where helicopters could be brought in for their extraction from behind enemy lines. As night fell Gannon spotted lights coming up trails on both sides of the river—flashlights flickering in the dense jungle growth. There seemed to be no end to them. The team had inadvertently walked into the middle of a battalion of North Vietnamese troops heading south. Six hundred men against eight was not Gannon's idea of good odds, although Boos had optimistically looked at it as an opportunity to drastically up his personal body count. But as team leader, Gannon had led the men back into the water to hide among the exposed mangrove roots along the bank.

The enemy battalion had chosen the immediate area as a bivouac for the night, and Gannon and his men, afraid of moving from their places of concealment, spent the next ten hours in water up to their necks. At dawn, after the NVA troops moved out, Gannon and his team continued on to the preselected extraction site. They ran into a squad of NVA stragglers, killing them with little trouble, but drawing the attention of the entire enemy battalion just ahead. They had run for their lives, calling in air strikes and helicopter gunships from the extraction site, until at last a helicopter was able to slip into the clearing after a series of napalm strikes. Gannon recalled the appearance of the team when, safely back at the compound, they had stripped to shower; to a man, their wrinkled skin resembled albino prunes from the extended period of time they had spent in the water.

There had been two other combined top-secret missions with Boos and his SEAL, both infiltrations from submarines off the coast of North Vietnam: the first a raid to destroy a surface-to-air missile-storage site south of Hanoi, the second a prisoner-snatch operation when they had crept into an NVA staging area and captured a colonel—it was that mission for which Gannon was awarded the Medal of Honor. He had refused to leave the beach for the scheduled rendezvous with the submarine waiting offshore until he had accounted for all of his men. His heroic efforts resulted in the rescue of three critically wounded members of his team despite an onslaught of enemy troops intent on saving their captured commanding officer. Bleeding profusely and in great pain from multiple wounds, Gannon had returned three times, under heavy fire, each time carrying one of his men to the beach and loading him into the rubber boat before going back for the next man. Boos had provided covering fire for him on the first rescue, before being wounded himself and knocked unconscious from a grenade blast.

After Gannon left Vietnam he and Boos lost touch for a few years but renewed their friendship after the war when both became members of counterterrorist teams—Boos with the Navy's SEAL Team Six and Gannon with Delta Force, where, as fate would have it, they were again involved in a number of joint operations. Boos, who retired from the service five years earlier than Gannon, had opted to spend as much of what remained of his life at sea, his first and, as Gannon had often suspected, only love. But they had made it a point to get together whenever possible at the Special Operations Association reunions, and failing that, an occasional letter or telephone call just to touch base.

"How's Carole?" Gannon asked, remembering that Boos and his wife were not on the best of terms the last time he had seen him.

"Fuck her," Boos said flatly. "Never trust anything that bleeds for a week out of every month and lives."

Gannon chuckled. "I take it that means it's over."

Boos shrugged and flashed a playful grin. "Rumor has it she was trampled to death during a balloon drop at a mall opening . . . bitch lived to shop." Taking a long drink from his mug of beer, he said, "You're the only guy I know with a wife worth a shit. Is Kate with you?"

Boos immediately detected the change in Gannon's mood. "Something wrong?"

He listened quietly, his face a solemn mask, as Gannon

told him what had happened to Kate and how the man who did it had escaped unpunished. When Gannon finished Boos sat silently for a few moments, slowly shaking his head.

"Those striped-pants State Department pussies," he spat out. "They're in the middle of a love feast with that Commie fuck with a wine stain on his head so they don't want anybody rockin' the goddamn boat." He reached across the table and placed a hand on Gannon's shoulder. "I'm sorry, Jack. I'm really sorry. I loved Kate. She had a way of making me feel I was worth something to somebody."

Both men fell silent again and nursed their beers. Boos stared off into the distance, the unsettling news of Kate's death evident in his subdued expression.

"In your last letter you said you got a job on a yacht, a sailboat," Gannon finally said.

"I'm the H.M.W.I.I.C.," Boos said, in an attempt to lighten the mood.

"The what?"

"The Head Motherfucker What Is in Charge," Boos said. "I'm the captain."

"Is it a charter boat?" Gannon asked.

"No way," Boos said. "She's the sweetest thing God ever put under sail. Her owner hired me last year—best job I ever had. I've probably died and gone to heaven and don't know it."

"What kind of work schedule do you have?"

"The owner has two boats, the *Mi Gaea,* a motor yacht he keeps at Antibes on the French Riviera, and the *Cheetah,* the sailboat he keeps here in the Caribbean. He spends his summers on the *Mi Gaea* and winters on the *Cheetah.* He's sort of in between right now. I've got a little over two weeks to myself before he's due."

"What do you do during the summer months?" Gannon asked.

"The thousand and one things that have to be done to keep the *Cheetah* in top condition, and the owner sends regional vice presidents of his corporations down for complimentary cruises. Sort of perks for doing a good job."

"What does the owner do?"

"He owns things. Lot of things."

Gannon sipped his beer and stared into the mug. "You have nothing on for the next ten days?"

"Nothing pressing, why?"

"I found out that the son of a bitch who killed Kate is in Nicaragua . . . at some sort of secret terrorist training camp he set up for the KGB."

"Yeah. I've heard rumors about that place. Nobody's been able to pin it down." Boos held Gannon's gaze, then added, "You know Walt Shumate? One of your Green Beanie SOG types, ran recon with Command and Control Central and Project Delta?"

"Yeah, he's a good friend."

"Well, he's running some kind of special ops for the Company across the Honduran border into Nicaragua. Might be able to help you out."

"Can't chance it," Gannon said. "I'd trust Walt with my life, but like I told you, for some reason the spooks don't want me getting anywhere near Malik. I don't want to put Walt in the middle if he's under contract to them."

"If they wanted you out of the way bad enough, they'd just kill you," Boos said. "It's not like it matters to them."

"Maybe if I get too close, they will."

Boos ordered another beer and propped the back of his chair against the wall. He leveled a knowing gaze at Gannon. "Okay, pardner, out with it. What you got in mind?"

"Can you get me into Nicaragua . . . without anyone knowing about it?"

Boos grinned. "Hell, I can do that in a New York minute. What part of the coast are we talking about?"

"Caribbean side. Best guess is north of the Rio San Juan area and the mountains near the Costa Rican border, but they keep moving the camp."

Boos thought for a moment and pictured his navigation

charts in his mind. "That would mean inserting you south of the Bluefields–El Bluff area. Maybe around Monkey Point."

"Are any of your old contacts still in-country?" Gannon asked. He recalled from their conversations at the SOA reunions that Boos, for a short time after he retired from the Navy, had done some contract work for the CIA—highly specialized agent insertions and extractions into and out of high-risk areas, including Nicaragua.

Boos hesitated, then nodded in response. "One . . . that I can trust. Remember Tony Santana?"

"Sandman Santana?" Gannon said. A vivid image came to mind of the Navy SEAL, who, when with the infamous Phoenix Program, was considered to have been the deadliest assassin and "black" operator of the entire Vietnam War era. The nickname "Sandman" was more than appropriate: Santana put people to sleep—permanently.

"Yep," Boos said. "The very same."

"I thought he was dead, never made it back from one of his kill-on-sight operations into Laos."

"Nope. Alive and well and roaming the mountains of Nicaragua. Last time I talked to him he was working the area you're talking about."

"For the Company?"

"Occasionally, but mostly for personal reasons. He was born in Managua, came to the States when he was six or seven. Still has relatives in Nicaragua. After 'Nam he was with a SEAL detachment at the spook base on Tiger Island off Honduras, running covert ops into Nicaragua. He retired as a master chief about seven years ago and went under contract with the Company on an off-and-on basis. Not so much for the money. He just hates the Sandinistas as much as he hated Somosa. He's one of the true believers, wants his country free without getting ripped off and stomped on by some clique of power-hungry psychopaths. Actually, I think it's just that he's not happy unless someone's trying to kill him. You know the type."

Gannon nodded. "Are you in contact with him?"

Boos again hesitated, then: "Yeah. We've got a sort of informal schedule of communications. Every odd-numbered day from 2100 hours until 2110 he listens on a prearranged frequency on the single sideband . . . in case I've got anything for him, or vice versa."

"Were you running covert ops with him in Nicaragua?" Gannon asked.

"No, he runs a twelve-man team he trained himself," Boos said. "But before I hired on as captain of the *Cheetah*, I was running a coastal freighter in and out of Panama, San Andrés Island, and Miami, trading mostly in tropical hardwoods. I got to know the Nicaraguan coast on the Caribbean side like the back of my hand, so every once in a while some of my old spook buddies asked me to drop off some live cargo to rendezvous with the Sandman."

"How'd you do it?" Gannon asked.

"We'd put the guy in a wet suit, gloves, boots, the whole works, and drop him off in an old wooden fishing boat . . . five, six miles offshore. He'd run the boat up on the reef about a mile from shore where it would break up, then he'd crawl across the reef and the coral heads and swim the rest of the way to the beach. Pieces of the boat would wash up on shore later, but a busted-up fishing boat in that area is run-of-the-mill stuff."

"I'll need you to bring me back out once I find Malik," Gannon said. "That present any problems?"

"Depends on how long it takes you to get to the guy," Boos said. "I could anchor in any one of a number of secluded coves in that area, hang around for a few days. The Nicaraguans don't patrol their Caribbean coast as heavily as they do the Pacific side, and a pleasure yacht doesn't draw much heat from them. Besides, their radar sucks, we can probably slip in and out without anyone even knowing it."

"What about your boss?" Gannon asked. "You putting your job on the line?"

"He's a cool head. We got this agreement—as long as I do

nothing illegal, no drugs, arms smuggling, shit like that, he's got no problem. He knows about my past affiliation with the Company. If I do any special stuff for them on my own time using the *Cheetah,* he doesn't want to know about it. He'll deny me if I'm nailed. So I guess it's sort of a tacit consent to put my ass on the line if I want to."

"What kind of ops is Santana running?" Gannon asked.

"He was originally sent into Nicaragua under deep cover, part of the CIA's 'pathfinder' operations. Looks and talks like a native. In the beginning he was secretly marking routes, setting up safe houses, landing zones, and support mechanisms in case the U.S. Embassy in Managua ended up in the same situation as the one in Iran—or if we had to invade the assholes for some other reason. He entered the country illegally, using a false passport that ID'ed him as a Bolivian, dropped from sight, then eventually joined up with a Contra element and formed his own special operations team."

"Will he help?"

"I got markers to call in on the Sandman till the next century," Boos said. "He'll help if he can."

Gannon tensed at the sight of a Rastaman, his bulging muscles threatening to tear his tie-dyed T-shirt apart at the seams as he approached the corner table, turned a chair around, straddled it, and sat down facing Boos. Gannon relaxed as the expression on Boos's face indicated the huge black man was a friend.

"What's up, Joseph?" Boos asked.

Joseph gestured to Gannon. "Your friend . . . he has two men waiting for him at the end of the alley," he said, the upward lilt of the Caribbean in his voice.

Boos looked to Gannon, who said, "I came alone."

Joseph eyeballed Gannon. "My friend tells me they followed you from the dock."

"Spooks?" Boos said.

Gannon nodded. "Probably."

"That's what my friend thinks," Joseph said. "He knows one of them, from Kingston. The other one he's never seen."

"Can you and a couple of your boys sort of detain them when we leave?" Boos asked.

Joseph smiled broadly. "Consider it done. My compliments." He signaled to three of his friends, each as menacing-looking as he was, and they left the crowded, smoky room. Joseph paused in the doorway and called back to Boos, "Cool runnings, Captain Jim."

Boos snapped off a brief salute.

"Those bastards never quit," Gannon said. "What the hell is it with them and that goddamn Russian?"

"We'll shake them," Boos said confidently as he got up from the table. "Let's go."

Gannon and Boos left by the front door. Boos tossed a piece of bread to the dog and leaned down to pet his head.

As they entered the alley and headed in the direction of the harbor, Gannon saw headlights flash on at the opposite end of the alley. An engine started, then stopped as three large black men stood in front of the car. Joseph stuck his head in the driver's-side window.

Tom Driscoll was at the wheel. "Get the hell out of the way!" he ordered Joseph, who simply smiled.

"Seems my friends don't want you following them," Joseph said calmly.

Driscoll reached inside his windbreaker to his shoulder holster but thought better of it as the CIA's Jamaican chief of station, seated beside him, nudged him. All three of Joseph's friends at the front of the car had pulled MAC-10 submachine guns from beneath their shirts. They jacked rounds into the chambers and aimed at the windshield.

"You're interfering with official government business," the CIA station chief tried.

"And whose government might that be, mon?" Joseph said.

Driscoll stepped from the car and called out to the two figures approaching the opposite end of the alley.

"Gannon! Hey, Gannon, I only want to talk. Give me a few minutes."

Gannon and Boos disappeared around the far corner.

"You stay here with us for a while," Joseph said. He reached into his pocket and pulled out a flat tin, pried it open, and removed a tightly rolled joint. "Ganja," he said with another of his broad smiles, "it will help you relax. Go on, mon, try it." Both men waved off the invitation. Driscoll slammed the steering wheel with the palms of his hands in anger.

"I think I know the man with Gannon," the station chief said just above a whisper. "I've seen him around. We'll check it out as soon as these clowns leave."

The narrow, winding alley opened on to St. James Street, where Gannon and Boos moved quickly past the carnival of sights, sounds, and smells of the marketplace and across the square to Harbor Street into the center of Montego Bay with its old sugar-port ambiance. The dock area was busy with fishermen unloading their catch and burly stevedores handling fruit, produce, and other local goods for shipment to foreign ports. Gannon and Boos weaved their way through the dock workers and watched over their shoulders as they continued on toward the dinghy dock. A final backward glance as they stepped into the small rubber boat revealed that Joseph had done his job well. No one had followed them.

27

The last of the evening light faded as the *Cheetah*'s rubber dinghy skimmed across the surface of the translucent patch-work–blue-green waters of Montego Bay. The sea contrasted with the darker greens of the hills and rugged mountains rising dramatically along the shore—a seascape of breathtaking beauty with a sculpted coastline trimmed with white-sand beaches. For Gannon the brief ride across the bay in the inflatable rubber boat brought back flash memories of insertions into North Vietnam more than twenty years ago, but they were quickly driven from his conscious thoughts as the elegant yacht came into view.

Two hundred yards from shore, the *Cheetah*, her nine-story mast rising majestically above all the other yachts in the harbor, looked fast even at anchor. A sixty-five-foot aluminum racing sloop, a converted maxi-racer, small for her class but designed for optimum speed and to contend with the most stringent nautical conditions, she had won more than her share of silver.

In the past three years she had undergone a massive two-year refitting and rebuilding at a cost in excess of one million dollars—with no corners cut and no details overlooked in assuring that she retained her original incomparable sailing characteristics and finesse while being transformed into a true luxury yacht.

Her stainless-steel-rod rigging and aluminum boom complemented modern performance sails, ensuring long life and speeds in excess of ten knots. At first glance her uniqueness was readily apparent only to the aficionado, such had been the painstaking efforts to retain her classic lines. On closer inspection, however, her innovative design and construction became evident. A high-tech, state-of-the-art Lewmar Hydraulic Commander winch and sail-handling system, supplemented by a Navtec mast-control system, made her safe enough to be sailed by two people. A Mercedes-Benz diesel engine provided her auxiliary power, with electric power coming from a 12-kw generator that, among other things, provided the below-deck areas with individually zoned air-conditioning.

As the dinghy came alongside Gannon climbed up the swim ladder onto the deck while Boos secured the line. On board, the two men sat in what used to be the crew work cockpit, now the entertainment cockpit, with cushioned bench seats flanking a varnished teak table.

"Beautiful boat," Gannon said, taking it all in.

"You'll never see another one like her," Boos said proudly. "She's a one-off."

Gannon's attention was drawn to the starboard side, just forward of the cockpit. Someone was coming up the swim ladder.

"You expecting anyone?" Gannon asked.

"It's Maria," Boos said. "She goes for a swim every evening."

Gannon watched as a slim young woman of medium height, probably in her late twenties, ascended the ladder. Her smooth, flawless olive-toned skin glistened with beads of seawater as she stepped on deck and cast a calm, assessing glance directly at Gannon—her dark Spanish eyes sparkling with the reflection of the lights from shore. With the deck shower's flexible hose, she rinsed herself off with fresh water and tilted her head back to let the water stream through silken shoulder-length sable-brown hair and down over her high-cut bikini.

Gannon was captivated by her haunting classic beauty. She had a subtle erotic appeal, a poised self-assurance, and yet there was a vulnerable, gamine quality about her.

"For someone who's sworn off women," Gannon said softly, "you seem to have done all right for yourself."

"It's not like that," Boos said. "The boss hired her; she's a first-class sailor. I'm the captain, she's the mate. Strictly business. Her choice, not mine," he added with a wistful smile.

"She's one of the most beautiful women I've ever seen," Gannon said.

"Oh yeah, she's that and a lot more," Boos said. "Got one hell of an interesting background too. Word of caution though, old buddy—don't piss her off, she's got a mean streak a mile wide."

Maria finished washing off the saltwater residue, and after toweling off pulled on an oversized white T-shirt that fell to mid-thigh and clung to her lithe, shapely body. Emblazoned across the shirt, front and back, in bold blue letters were the words WINCH APE. She stepped down into the cockpit, sat next to Boos, and stared at Gannon.

"Jack Gannon, Maria Padrón," Boos said in the way of an introduction.

Gannon offered his hand. Maria gave it a quick, perfunctory shake, taking in the prominent scar on the side of his neck.

"Take off your shoes," Maria said, casting a disapproving glance at Gannon's running shoes.

"Why?" Gannon asked.

"They'll scuff up the deck. You won't need them while you're on board." Her expression clouded and changed to one of caution as she noticed Gannon's black-nylon carryall. Her gaze shifted back to Gannon, her intelligent dark-brown eyes penetrating. "Have you sailed before?"

"No," Gannon said as he removed his running shoes and

socks. On closer inspection, his initial impressions of Maria were confirmed. Despite the hint of vulnerability in the exotically beautiful woman sitting across from him, he detected a tough, tensile quality that lurked just beneath the surface, a solid, eerie self-esteem found in the very strong that seemed completely out of place. Yet there was no role-playing or posturing. She was what she appeared to be, Gannon thought. A bruised angel with a will of granite and a formidable spirit. An intriguing paradox.

"We have some of those patches you stick behind your ear if you get seasick," Boos told Gannon in an attempt to contain Maria's mounting ire until he could talk with her alone. "They really work. Some people have a reaction to them—dizziness, blurred vision, brief psychotic episodes, stuff like that—but it goes away in a few hours. No big thing."

"No," Maria said. "No big thing. After all, how much damage can a psychopath do in two hours . . . on a boat . . . in the middle of the ocean?" There was a brief mischievous twinkle in her eyes that was gone as quickly as it had appeared.

"I think I'll be all right," Gannon said.

"Why don't you go below and stow your gear?" Boos said to Gannon. "Take the guest stateroom just forward of the main salon."

Gannon nodded to Maria and disappeared down the companionway with his nylon carryall.

With Gannon out of earshot, Maria stared hard at Boos. "Who's he?"

"An old friend."

"And . . . ?" Maria prompted.

"We'll be making an offshore passage," Boos said tentatively. "If you agree, of course."

"Where?"

"Caribbean coast of Nicaragua."

Maria shook her head and smiled indulgently. "You incorrigible Coon Ass. Your friend Gannon has trouble written all over him. I told you I didn't want any part of your CIA business."

"It's not for the Company," Boos said. "Word of honor."

"Then let's hear the rest," Maria said.

Boos filled her in on Gannon's wife and his hope of linking him up with Santana in pursuit of Malik, finishing with, "I owe him . . . and he's a good friend. So was Kate."

"We just made a two-week passage from St. Barts," Maria protested, "and the deal was we'd lie around and relax until the boss got here."

"We're talking nine days max," Boos said. "Sailing straight through, we can be there late afternoon of the third day, contact Santana, drop off Gannon that night, give him two, three days to take care of business, and be back in plenty of time to hook up with the boss."

"What if your friend doesn't find the Russian in three days?"

"That's all the time I can give him. He's aware of that."

"Sail straight through?" Maria said. "Your friend Gannon can't stand watch, that means the two of us doing four on and four off."

"Only on the way down," Boos assured her. "Like I said, he's my friend."

"And you owe him," Maria said resignedly. "Okay, Boos, but you owe *me* for this one."

"Anytime. Just name it."

"Count on it," Maria said. "Anyway, I sort of like him," she admitted after a brief silence. "His eyes didn't roam all over my body when he talked to me."

"I always knew there was something strange about 'him," Boos said with a broad grin.

Gannon stowed the contents of his carryall in an overhead compartment in the guest stateroom, separating his rucksack, load-bearing harness, web gear, jungle boots, ammunition pouches, canteens, a combat knife, and camouflage fatigues from the few civilian clothes he had brought. He pulled on a pair of swim trunks and T-shirt and paused to admire his surroundings. The guest stateroom's appointments were impressive: beautifully decorated in teakwood with leather trim, there was a full-sized double berth swathed in a fur blanket, a vanity, and ample overhead storage space. Secured on a shelf at the foot of the bed was an audio/video entertainment center with a monitor, video recorder, and tape deck.

The main salon, however, was as elegant as anything Gannon had ever seen on land or on sea. Expensive silk oriental rugs on the teak deck and fine art on the bulkhead. A bar, complete with fine crystal, its cabinets fronted with smoked Lexan. The entire salon was paneled in warm hand-rubbed teak and fitted with wraparound cushioned seating of butter-soft pale-green leather. An intricately designed adjustable dining and gaming table and the bar counter were finished in exquisitely burled olive ash. Soft music played through a surround-sound system of eighteen speakers, the likes of which Gannon had never heard.

He decided to have a quick look around the rest of the below-deck area. There was a galley equipped with every imaginable modern convenience, including a four-burner stove, oven, and refrigerator. He continued down the starboard side and paused to look at the navigation and control station just aft of the main salon. Everything about it was ultramodern, from the systems-monitoring display panels to the precision instrumentation and communications console. There was even a full-size chart table and a custom-made leather Recaro seat.

Looking aft, beyond the navigation area, he could see into the master stateroom: it was even more spacious, elegant, and luxurious than the guest stateroom; again, paneled with teak and trimmed in leather, with a fur-covered queen-sized berth, a well-stocked private bar, and an even more elaborate audio/visual entertainment center. He returned to the main salon and went forward, through the guest head, which contained a vanity, shower, and electric water closet, and entered the self-contained crew quarters, outfitted with three bunks.

A sharp wolf whistle from behind startled him as he was about to go back on deck. He spun around and was greeted by the impertinent stare of a yellow-nape Amazon parrot standing on a wrought-iron perch secured to the deck.

"Whatcha doin'?" the parrot promptly said.

The forward hatch to the crew's quarters—formerly the sail-handling hatch before the refitting—was directly overhead and open. Gannon looked up to see Boos on deck, laughing.

"Cute, huh? That's Clyde. Doesn't like anybody but Maria. Moron bites me every time I get near him; take your finger off if he gets the chance," he said. "If he wasn't Maria's bird, I'd stick the loud-mouthed son of a bitch in the microwave."

In the distance Gannon heard Maria's voice. "You do and it'll be your last act in this life."

The brilliant green bird with the bright yellow neck cocked his head and one-eyed Boos, who was still staring down through the open hatch. "Coon Ass," Clyde said, followed by a raucous, squawking laugh. "Coon Ass," he repeated.

"Fuck you," Boos said to Clyde.

Gannon walked over to the parrot's perch and cautiously extended his hand. Clyde climbed onto it and sat on his wrist, squawking a cheery "Hello."

Gannon stroked the bird's chest feathers and said, "Good boy, Clyde."

"Bird's got no class," Boos grumbled, then said to Gannon, "We need you on deck—time to get under way before your spook buddies get the scent."

Maria appeared at the open hatch. "I'll take him," she said, and reached down through the hatch to get Clyde and move him to the custom-designed perch just aft of the entertainment cockpit he occupied, weather permitting, while they were under way.

Gannon pulled himself up through the hatch and onto the deck. He looked slightly bewildered as to what he could do to help.

"You can help me strike the awning," Maria told him.

"Should I use a left hook or an overhand right?" Gannon said with a grin, not quite sure what she meant.

"Untie the small lines, here," she demonstrated, "and roll it up tightly as you go along. I'll take the other side."

Gannon followed her lead and, under Maria's direction, helped take down the awning. They stuffed it into a long canvas bag and tossed it into the open forward hatch to be stored in the forepeak. Gannon then went back to the steering cockpit at the stern of the boat and helped Boos with the halyard as they hoisted the dinghy's outboard motor on board and clamped it to the rail. Next came the dinghy, which was deflated and stored in the forepeak with the awning.

Maria took her position at the wheel in the steering cockpit. She raised the anchor with the remote button on a panel before her and started the engine with the push of another button on the same panel. Boos had removed the sail cover and used the electric-powered hydraulic winch to raise the mainsail by simply pressing yet another button.

Gannon sat on the padded wraparound bench seat in the steering cockpit as the *Cheetah* motored slowly out of the harbor under a brilliant canopy of stars. The music he had heard below could now be heard through two speakers built into the base of the bench seat—Maria had turned up the volume and changed the selection to a tape of the Miami Sound Machine.

Boos sat in the entertainment cockpit, where Clyde rested contentedly on his perch. When he thought no one was watching he handed Clyde a peanut, one of his favorite treats. Clyde took the peace offering and gripped it tightly with one foot, then, with lightning-quick reflexes, nipped Boos on the finger.

"Ungrateful little shit," Boos mumbled. Maria, who had

seen the whole thing, laughed. Boos moved away from the parrot and stretched out on the padded seat. He propped a pillow under his head to catch a short nap before it was time to relieve Maria at the helm; he was fast asleep in a matter of minutes.

Gannon shifted his position on the bench seat. He propped up his feet and leaned against the railing on the starboard side. He stared out at the darkening sea and relaxed in the cool ocean breeze and the rhythm of the gentle swells. His thoughts returned to Kate and how she had often talked fondly about her days as a young girl, sailing off Martha's Vineyard, and of how she had tried to convince him to take up the sport. *Well, I'm sailing now, Kate,* he said to himself. *And you were right. It is beautiful, and it is peaceful . . . and I miss you, terribly.*

"I'm sorry about your wife," Maria said, as though she had been reading his thoughts. "Jim told me what happened." She stared straight ahead, and after a long silence, spoke again. "In awhile only the most pleasant memories will be left, though sometimes they're the most painful." Her voice seemed distant, as though recalling some long-forgotten pain of her own. "But at other times they give you the most comfort." She fell silent again and glanced at the digital readouts on the instrument panel and at the compass as she returned her full attention to the task of keeping the *Cheetah* on course.

Tom Driscoll and the CIA's Jamaican chief of station walked slowly along the dock near the Montego Bay Yacht Club. The *Cheetah* was well out of sight, but they already had most of the information they needed. CIA headquarters had extensive files on Jim Boos as far back as his affiliation with SOG while a Navy SEAL.

"I knew I'd seen him before," the station chief said. "His bio's in our inactive files in my office. He did a few contract jobs for my predecessor."

Tom Driscoll looked out across the bay, his thoughts on Gannon and his need to keep track of his movements.

"We know where they're headed," Driscoll said. "And if I'm right, Boos will try and insert him on the Caribbean side."

"You're talking about roughly three hundred miles of coastline," the station chief said.

"We'll have it narrowed down in time," Driscoll said. "The Director has pulled out all the stops on this one. I've got access to whatever I need to do the job."

28

General Vladimir Antonov pulled out of the parking area of his luxury apartment on Kutuzovsky Prospekt in the heart of Moscow and headed west, out of the city. He had left GRU headquarters at his usual time and changed into civilian clothes at his apartment. He dismissed his driver and bodyguard and drove his own personal car, avoiding the center traffic lane reserved for the government hierarchy—to which he was entitled—and moved slowly along with the rest of the evening traffic.

An early October snow had begun to fall. Wet and heavy, it momentarily stuck to the windshield and the road, then quickly melted. It was at least a two-hour drive to the General Secretary's dacha, as General Antonov knew from past visits, ample time to organize his thoughts and fine-tune the rudimentary operation he had formulated in his mind when he received the updated intelligence information on Malik. He turned up the collar of his overcoat against the ineffective car heater, lit a cigarette, and settled back in his seat. The gloomy slate-gray horizon and thick cloud cover that drifted in from the north drew his attention. The snowfall increased and a thin layer began to accumulate on the rooftops and elaborate spires and domes of the Kremlin—a heralding that another brutal Russian winter was slowly, inexorably closing its grip over the land.

* * *

Dressed casually in gray worsted slacks and a thick wool sweater, the General Secretary of the Soviet Union paced before a roaring blaze in the huge stone fireplace in the great room of his private estate in the countryside west of Moscow. What was commonly called a dacha, or country cottage, had long since lost its humble meaning when it came to the sprawling, elaborate, and luxurious estates the Soviet ruling class had built for themselves. Set among hundreds of acres of evergreen and birch forests, patrolled and guarded by specially selected bodyguards from the KGB's Ninth Directorate, the General Secretary's dacha in Usovo had the atmosphere of a comfortable hunting lodge as opposed to the more opulent homes of other government elite.

His thoughts as he paced the great room were on the special meeting he had called that morning of the inner quorum of the Defense Council. A few weeks ago there was only a suspicion of backsliding by his staunchest supporters, but now he was certain that they were quavering, on the brink of going over to the side of his opponents.

Fools, he thought as he sipped the fine cognac that had been a gift from the President of France. Orthodox automatons who spouted slogans from the past, dogma that had never worked and never would. They had branded his policies an anathema to the socialist cause. How could they possibly question the wisdom of the INF treaty—dismantling Soviet missiles that could strike only at the heart of Western Europe in exchange for American missiles that could easily and accurately strike anywhere in the Soviet Union. And his detractors who decried the reduction in conventional forces in Eastern Europe—still leaving them with overwhelming superiority—and the removal of Soviet troops from Afghanistan. With no way of stopping the *mujahedin* rebels from being supplied with Stinger antiaircraft missiles by the United States, they had lost their air cover, which in turn meant the dismal prospect of either escalating the war beyond international tolerance or settling in to fight a protracted war of attrition that would inevitably lead to unrest at 'home and the disruption of his economic and social restructuring programs. They had to be made to realize that continuing to waste Soviet lives, funds, and energy in foreign adventures was counterproductive; internal restructuring and retrenchment required external harmony. He still had a tentative hold on those whose support he most needed, but if the undermining by his KGB and Politburo enemies continued unabated, it would all soon slip from his grasp.

The thought of a nuclear weapon in the hands of one of the KGB's most capable Illegals was something he couldn't have anticipated. He could, however, anticipate the consequences if the madmen responsible for the plot against him succeeded. Chernobyl was never far from his conscious thoughts when he thought of Malik and the SADM. Chernobyl had given him a glimpse of the horrors of a nuclear war, a brief window opened to a future that must be avoided at all costs. The two trips he had made to the region were indelibly imprinted in his memory.

There had been the chilling, bleak landscape, deserted apartment complexes and villages, an entire collective farm frozen in time: neatly trimmed, small white farmhouses with clothes hung on lines never to be taken down, children's toys scattered about, left where they were at the moment of the hurried, frantic evacuation. Once well-tended gardens now to remain forever fallow and tractors and farm implements deserted in the fields—large tracts of land that could not be entered for generations. And then there were the unanswered questions: How many thousands would die terrible deaths from cancers caused by the accident? Will the river ever sustain life again, and if so will the fish be safe to eat? Perhaps, the scientists say, if the contaminated sediment is not disturbed by the current. All this caused by one terrifying incident, an accident, that was only a small fraction of the massive destruction that would result from an all-out nuclear war. Chernobyl had forced him to face the facts: nuclear weapons were no longer pure and logical, no longer the panacea for other weaknesses, and the idea of surviving through civil defense was nonsense. There were better, more intelligent ways to strengthen his country and promote socialism, and that strength would be found in the people and the economy, and a determined conventional military force that would discourage all but a lunatic from attacking the Soviet Union.

The General Secretary's troubled ruminations were interrupted by one of his housekeepers, who informed him that the main gate had telephoned to report that General Antonov had just entered the estate. While he waited Gorbachev refilled his own glass with the excellent French cognac and poured another for his old friend. How far they had come since their days together at the university, he thought as he walked over to the French doors that opened onto a broad stone terrace. He peered through the frosted glass and watched the snow-covered grounds. Headlights winked and approached in the distance through the forest.

The snowfall, now fine and granular, and driven by strong gusts of wind, accumulated at a rapid rate. General Antonov drove slowly along the slippery surface, up the long, curving drive that led through a forest of birches, their supple limbs bent to the ground—a few remaining golden autumn leaves clung tenaciously to the branches under the weight of the snowy mantle. Up ahead, through the trees, he could see the General Secretary's dacha ablaze with lights. On the circular drive he stopped at the front entrance and got out of the car, his footsteps crunching on the new-fallen snow.

The General Secretary waved away a bodyguard and opened the door himself. He embraced his old friend and escorted him into the warmth of the great room as Antónov removed his overcoat.

"It is good to see you, Vladimir Petrovich," Gorbachev said, a broad smile spreading over his somber face.

"It is good to see you, Comrade General Secretary," Antonov replied more formally. Despite their close personal relationship, he had stopped using the familiar form of address on the day Gorbachev had ascended to power, more out of respect than from any fear of admonishment for not doing so.

Gorbachev handed him the glass of cognac he had poured and raised his own glass in a toast.

"To the future," he said soberly, "if indeed we have one."

"To the future," Antonov repeated, and added, "a future toward which we have made some progress."

Gorbachev gestured to two facing overstuffed sofas in front of the fireplace and the two men sat opposite each other. Gorbachev placed his glass of cognac on the coffee table between them and said eagerly, "Tell me, what have you learned?"

"We have traced the route of the weapon," Antonov said. "The freighter that transported it from Rostock was unloaded at Rotterdam. Its cargo was then transferred to another freighter under KGB control, which set sail for Central America. However, we are not certain where the second freighter off-loaded its cargo; it stopped at two ports of call —in Cuba and Panama."

"Then you have not found the weapon?" the General Secretary said, his voice full of disappointment.

"No," General Antonov said. "But one of our agents in Managua has learned the location of the KGB's secret terrorist training camp in Nicaragua. There can be no doubt that the camp is the ultimate destination for Malik and the weapon. All reason dictates that the camp will be the staging area for whatever operation he has planned."

Gorbachev's face brightened. "Can you be certain that the weapon is at the camp?"

"We have reason to believe that Malik is on his way there, and when he arrives the weapon will be there," General Antonov said with conviction.

"Then what are your plans?" Gorbachev asked.

"Malik has surrounded himself with some of the best, most highly trained and dedicated terrorists in the world," Antonov said. "The size of the training cadre at the camp is estimated to be between fifteen and twenty men, and they are well armed. Our intelligence information estimates the trainees at the camp at perhaps another twenty or thirty men and women—"

"Then we must send our best to deal with them," the General Secretary interrupted.

"Yes," Antonov said. "The GRU has a company of Spetsnaz troops in Cuba. I would like your permission to personally take charge of the operation . . . to go to Cuba, select a twelve-man team, and brief them for their mission."

"Yes. Of course. You have my permission, Vladimir Petrovich," Gorbachev quickly replied. "But only twelve men?"

"Twelve Spetsnaz," Antonov said with pride. "This is the type of mission for which they constantly train. Mobilizing a larger force would only assure that word of the operation would inevitably reach your enemies. Do not worry," Antonov added confidently, "with the element of surprise on our side, the terrorists will be no match for them."

"I have learned to trust your judgment," Gorbachev said. "You do what you think is best."

"I have taken precautions to cover my absence and my destination," Antonov said. "I do not want our KGB friends alerted to my actions."

The General Secretary rose to his feet. Antonov stood and the two men walked from the great room to the entrance foyer, where Gorbachev again embraced his old friend.

"You must stop this madman," he told Antonov, the passion rising in his voice.

"I will, my friend," Antonov said, and opened the door to a cold gust of wind. "And then we can deal with those who would see you destroyed."

29

The early evening sun hung low on the horizon, bathing the Panamanian seaport of Colón in an orange-red glow. Raucous and earthy, the dock area was crowded with fishmongers, merchants, stevedores, hawkers, and hustlers. The harbor, accustomed to handling two billion dollars' worth of cargo annually, was busy with container ships, tankers, freighters, trawlers, and tugboats. The pungent smells of fish, saltwater, and diesel fuel, and the din of piercing blasts from ships' whistles, the grinding and clanking of machinery, the squawking of gulls, and the yelling of men at work overwhelmed the senses.

Located on the Caribbean side of the Panama Canal, Colón was a paradigm of a bawdy, steamy, decrepit, exotic seaport, an open invitation to adventure, intrigue, and danger as well as a gateway to the sea. Ships passing through the canal moved in and out of the harbor at all hours. The docks were crowded and busy around the clock. Merchant seamen from all over the world and American servicemen from the U.S. Southern Command roamed the streets and bars in the mean parts of town, most of them in search of women and entertainment. The women were a unique mixture of races; many owed their heritage to laborers brought from the West Indies to build the canal. Dressed in halters and hot pants, with bright smiles and impudent eyes, they plied their trade with the same practiced, vulgar charm common to hookers the world over.

The city itself was run-down and grimy. Unpainted and peeling buildings and houses lined narrow, ugly streets that reeked of urine and rotted fish. Brightly painted buses and old cars spewed clouds of blue exhaust into humid, fetid air, while music blared and neon signs beckoned from dingy bars where drunken brawls spilled out into streets filled with sinister, desperate men; and migrant workers, their eyes blank with hopelessness and misery, or feral with resentment, constantly watched for likely victims.

It was through this foul, decaying neighborhood that Nikolai Malik walked. His eyes missed nothing around him as he made his way to the docks. None of the potential muggers who watched his progress even considered making an attempt on him—there was something about the way he walked, one had said. No, another said, it's the eyes. None of them wanted any part of the tall blond man with the long, confident stride.

Malik continued along the harbor until he caught sight of the Soviet container ship *Sverdlev* berthed at one of the major cargo docks. Three other freighters of medium tonnage were being unloaded at adjacent docks, but the Soviet ship, Malik noticed, was preparing to get under way. The *Sverdlev*'s main function was not maritime trade, but under the subterfuge of a legitimate merchant ship, a base from which the KGB infiltrated agents, collected intelligence information, or transported technology stolen from the West as well as smuggled drugs and arms. Part of her cargo, the part Malik was interested in, had originated at the Baltic port of Rostock; the rest was transferred from another ship in Rotterdam. She ostensibly carried raisins from Afghanistan and machinery from East Germany, but what was concealed among these mundane products was worth millions—precisely sixty million dollars' worth of heroin, its origins in Lebanon's Bekáa Valley and the poppy fields of Afghanistan.

The drugs were one of the KGB's sources of hard Western currency, used to help support its operations around the globe. Thanks to Panama's banking laws—more secret and stringent than those of Switzerland—the tiny Central American country had become Latin America's busiest banking center, a haven for the illicit funds of the drugs-and-arms-smuggling crowd as well as the espionage community. But Malik's mind was not on the massive shipment of heroin either. That would be stored and later sent through the convoluted distribution network to the lucrative markets in the United States and Europe, the proceeds going into an account designated for the special operations of the KGB's Illegals Directorate. His only concern was the small forty-pound canister hidden inside one of the containers. The miniature nuclear weapon not even the captain of the *Sverdlev* knew he had transported across the ocean.

Malik knew his deadly, precious cargo had arrived. The *Sverdlev*'s decks revealed she had already taken on new containers for another destination. Teams of heavily muscled, sweaty stevedores were leaving the dock, making their way down narrow alleys to cafés and bars. A four-man cast-off crew, two men to a line, fore and aft, stood by the pilings. The gangplank that led to the forward deck was hauled aboard as the cast-off crew slipped the giant hawsers off the pilings and freed the huge ship from the dock. A bass-tone departure signal sounded, filling the humid air, followed by shrill, high-pitched sounds that gave warning of her departure to all the vessels in the immediate area. From the bowels of the ship came the muted rumble of the engines and the meshing of gears as the giant screws churned up the dark, oily water at the *Sverdlev*'s stern.

Malik left the harbor and followed a debris-littered alley to the Trans-World Marine Agency building located just one block from the docks. The squat three-story building was a huge warehouse. Part of the upper story was used as office space. Antonio Rodriquez was the de facto owner of what operated as a legitimate import/export firm but was in real-

ity a KGB proprietary company—a front for its narcotics
trafficking and weapons shipments to Central and South
American Marxist groups.

Malik entered the building by a small side-door. His footsteps echoed throughout the huge open-storage bays as he
walked to a back staircase that led to a balcony of offices
two stories above the main floor of the warehouse.

Rodriquez, dressed in a soiled, badly wrinkled white linen
suit and a shiny lavender silk shirt open at the collar, looked
up from his desk as Malik entered. He forced an unconvinc-
ing welcoming smile. Malik was not one of his favorite people.

"Good evening, Señor Malik," he said, getting up from
behind the desk and not bothering to extend a hand Malik
was never inclined to shake.

Malik reached across the desk and picked up the telephone, quickly dialing a number. There were a few moments
of silence until someone on the other end answered.

"Twenty minutes," was all Malik said into the receiver,
then hung up.

"The cargo from the *Sverdlev*," he said to Rodriquez.
"Where are the machine parts from East Germany stored?"

"Come, I will show you," Rodriquez answered nervously.
He hurried out of the office, eager to be rid of the man who
made him perspire more than the ever-present humidity. "I
have had the crates separated and placed in a private bay, as
you instructed," he said as he led the way down the narrow
open staircase.

Rodriquez led Malik to a section of the warehouse where
various containers were secured in padlocked bays enclosed
in chain-link fencing.

"Here are the containers you cabled me about," Rodriquez said, and handed Malik the key to the lock.

"Bring me a crowbar," Malik said.

Rodriquez smiled a toothy grin. "I thought you might be
in need of one," he said. "It is just inside the bay."

"Leave," Malik said. "I won't be needing you anymore."

"Yes, Señor Malik," Rodriquez said in his most obsequious tone. "It has been a pleasure seeing you again." There was no reply as he quick-stepped out of the private storage area.

Malik waited until the door was closed, then unlocked the chain-link gate to the bay and immediately checked the crates. He found the identifying mark he had placed on the one for which he had personally supervised the loading. He pried loose one end of the six-foot-square crate and reached inside, over a heavily padded piece of machinery. A smile spread slowly across his face as he felt the web straps of the jump container in which the SADM was still stored.

He then reached farther into the crate and, using both hands, hoisted the SADM from its hiding place. The olive drab jump container, padded with foam rubber and fitted with straps attached to a pack tray, allowed the weapon to be carried like a rucksack, which is what Malik did, slinging it over his shoulders as he left the bay.

When Nikolai Malik reached the side door to the warehouse, a Toyota Land Cruiser pulled sharply into the alley. The man at the wheel nodded to Malik, who opened the door, carefully placed the SADM in the back, and climbed into the vehicle.

Fourteen miles outside the city of Colón, at a deserted grass airstrip in the countryside, a twin-engine Cessna waited. Its engines coughed and turned over as the pilot saw the Toyota bounce across the grassy field.

Malik secured the SADM in the rear passenger compartment and went forward. He took the copilot's seat as the Cessna began its takeoff run down the bumpy, seldom-used strip. Once airborne, the aircraft gained altitude until it leveled off at five hundred feet and headed a few miles off the coast, where it slowly turned to a northerly heading.

"Our estimated time of arrival?" Malik asked.

"No more than two and one-half hours," the pilot answered.

Malik relaxed in his seat. He watched the darkening horizon and smiled to himself again, this time in anticipation. Nothing could stop him now, he thought. Nothing.

30

The twelve men, dressed in camouflage fatigues, olive drab bandannas tied around their heads, their faces streaked and blotted with green, brown, and black greasepaint, were virtually indistinguishable from their surroundings as they lay hidden in the tall grass and scrub brush overlooking a bend in the river. Tony Santana, his lean, wiry body tensed, his handsome face fixed in concentration, lifted the field glasses that hung from a strap around his neck and focused them on the point where he knew the boat would first appear. His men were spread out along the hillside in a modified line ambush watching for Santana's signal to open fire. Armed with shoulder-fired rocket launchers, grenade launchers, M-60 machine guns, and automatic assault rifles, they were equipped to take out their target with devastating proficiency.

Santana was proud of his men, all of whom he had personally trained and fought with for well over a year. Only two days ago they had blown up three Soviet-installed radars used by the Sandinistas to monitor Contra communications and detect resupply aircraft. And during the past few months he had led them on a string of highly successful ambushes and raids, from mining river ports to blowing up oil-storage facilities. They were as well conditioned, well trained, disciplined, and as experienced as any combat

226   *J. C. Pollock*

troops with whom he had ever served. The proof lay in the team's casualty rate—one man wounded in the past year, and he was now back in action.

Santana's official mission was to provide intelligence to the CIA on Sandinista weapons-supply routes and the shipments of Communist Bloc weapons arriving at the port of El Bluff. He kept track of the massive numbers of small arms, howitzers, armored vehicles, trucks, and helicopters that poured into the country—occasionally taking it upon himself to ambush the convoys transporting the equipment inland and any other targets of opportunity he deemed worthy of his attention. He and his team were expert at interdicting the Sandinista supply routes and sabotaging key industrial installations and other soft targets that disrupted the Nicaraguan economy. They took pride in the fact that they could operate independent of any outside aid.

Santana knew that this was the direction in which the Contra movement had to go—a leaner, self-sufficient guerrilla force comprised of hard-core, dedicated men. The Sandinistas' repressive programs and ruinous economy were uniting the people behind the Contras, providing an invaluable and effective intelligence and support network across the entire country. The Sandinistas were using the on-again, off-again cease-fires and peace talks to give the Contra opponents in Washington the opportunity to kill the reinstatement of any large-scale aid program, while they used their own troops to regain ground they had previously lost. But, ironically, the Marxist junta in Managua had done something they had not counted on—proved to the determined Contras that they could fight, and win, a guerrilla war without the assistance of the United States or anyone else.

Operating in small groups, such as Santana's, they could employ the classic guerrilla strategy: establish base camps in remote areas and limit their ambushes and raids to weaker, smaller Sandinista patrols and isolated outposts. Thus they forced the Sandinistas to dispatch even larger patrols, which could be easily detected and avoided or ambushed, using hit-and-run tactics that inflicted heavy casualties. By demonstrating their capabilities they were gaining even more popular support. The weapons and ammunition captured from the Sandinistas were all they needed to continue fighting. Santana had been doing just that for almost a year. Increased support from the local population provided food and other necessities for their continued existence. If organized and controlled properly, a nationwide Contra political organization could be formed, mobilizing even more of the citizens for Contra activity. Small-scale aid of crucial items from the CIA, such as demolitions equipment and Redeye missiles to use against the Soviet-supplied helicopters, could easily be provided without raising an eyebrow among the anti-Contra forces in Washington. It would work, Santana knew. It had worked in somewhat the same fashion for the Vietcong and other guerrilla armies throughout history, and he was determined to make it work here, in the land of his birth.

The hum of an outboard motor snapped Santana's thoughts back to his deadly task and he felt the rush of adrenaline begin to flow. He steadied his field glasses on the bend in the river, expecting to see another small supply boat heading upriver to a remote Sandinista outpost. The sound of the motor grew louder as the boat appeared around the bend, its bow plowing through the muddy water, a .30-caliber machine gun mounted on her deck.

Santana lowered the field glasses and shouldered a LAW —a one-shot, Light Anti-tank Weapon with an effective range of two hundred yards, it was essentially a mini-bazooka, just under three feet in length when extended, with a powerful 66mm rocket packed into a throwaway launcher and capable of penetrating twelve inches of armor. The weapon could demolish the boat with one well-placed hit.

Santana removed the rear cover and strap, extended the launcher, and released the safety. He peered through the open sights as the boat drew closer and used the range-estimation lines in the front sight to determine the distance

to his target. Then he aligned the lead crosses to ensure a hit
on the center of the boat. He aimed carefully, then slowly
applied pressure to the firing mechanism. His well-disciplined men patiently waited for his signal before opening
fire. The supply boat carried more soldiers than usual; its
sides bristled with the barrels of assault rifles. But they
would present no problems, they were sitting ducks. It
would all be over in a matter of seconds.

Suddenly a frown creased Santana's brow and he lowered
the LAW. He again trained the field glasses on the boat, this
time focusing on a man sitting cross-legged on the deck near
the stern. He stared in confusion and disbelief as the boat
came abreast of their position and continued upstream. The
men on his immediate flanks glanced impatiently in his direction, wondering why he had not opened fire on the easy,
vulnerable target. The boat would soon be out of the primary kill zone.

Santana made a minor adjustment in the focus of the field
glasses, his attention now riveted on the olive drab, canister-
shaped backpack the tall blond man held in his lap. He read
the military-style black stenciling on the front of the container: H-912. He looked away, then quickly back to make
certain his eyes were not deceiving him. No, it read H-912,
there was no doubt.

"I don't believe this shit!" he said in a low whisper. "I do
not believe this!" No sooner were the words out of his
mouth than the powerful throb of diesel engines could be
heard as a seventy-foot Sandinista river-patrol boat rounded
the bend; twin .50-caliber machine guns mounted on its forward deck added significantly to the firepower of the weapons of the troops crowded on board. The big boat roared
through the kill zone, escorting the much smaller supply
boat upriver, and to his horror, Santana clearly understood
why.

With both boats out of sight, he silently signaled his team
to regroup on the other side of the rise. The men had at first
been disappointed, then relieved that they had not hastily

opened fire and been caught in the open within range of the
river-patrol boat's twin .50s and assorted lethal firepower of
the troops on her deck.

Santana shook off questions about what had made him
hesitate before the patrol boat had come into view. He was
too stunned by what he had seen to be certain whether or
not it could possibly be. He had recognized some of the men
on board the supply boat and knew they were part of the
terrorist training cadre from the camp he was intent on finding, but he had never seen the tall blond man before.

The team rose to their feet and followed Santana down
the backside of the hill to a narrow valley, where they disappeared into the deep shadows of the jungle, each of the men
puzzled by the unusual silence and the strange look on their
leader's face.

31

The *Cheetah* had made a pleasant, fast passage from Jamaica to the Nicaraguan coast. Under full sail, with a poled-out headsail, the trade winds behind her most of the way, she had run with the wind. A following sea with small whitecaps and six- to eight-foot swells created surfing conditions where the boat was picked up to surge down a wave, increase her speed, then picked up again to surge once more. The wind had died down only twice, for a few hours, and Boos and Maria had used the auxiliary power, motoring at eight knots to keep them on schedule.

The navigation aids between Jamaica and Nicaragua were few and unreliable. With the loran navigation useless, Boos had relied on the *Cheetah*'s satellite navigation equipment, which gave him an exact position fix every few hours. Between fixes he used dead reckoning, computing his course and speed to determine where he was.

When the *Cheetah* approached the Cabo Gracias a Dios, the northernmost point on the Nicaraguan coast, with its low, swampy shoreline and no identifiable objects for reference points, Maria had rounded the cape and stayed at least four miles offshore, using the surface radar to determine the *Cheetah*'s distance from the coast between SatNav fixes. She proceeded south through the Miskito Channel and gave wide berth to the numerous off-lying cays and coral islets, their vegetation stripped clean by heavy seas and gales from previous storms. She had handled the boat through the dangerous waters with a professional ability that drew praise even from Boos.

It was hurricane season, and Boos, using the charts from the weather facsimile printer, had kept a careful watch, getting weather updates three times a day. His caution was well founded. A few years ago, working on a coastal freighter, a sudden gale had brought the seas up twenty feet and more just off the bow, and winds of Force 8 and 9 had howled around the bridge. He had heard distress messages from big ships farther north where it was blowing Force 11, creating great waves with overhanging crests, foamy patches blown in dense white streaks, and heavy, tumbling seas. Later, when it had ended, he had come across salvage operations on a vessel blown high on a reef; the storm had been a "true norther," and he wasn't eager to repeat the experience.

But their luck had held, it had been an uneventful passage. They had spotted an occasional freighter on the distant horizon and, the previous night, had come close to only one other boat. A luxury motor-sailor had passed a few hundred yards off their port side, but thanks to Maria's quick reactions, the *Cheetah* had gone undetected. Once certain that they were not on a collision course, Maria had cut the *Cheetah*'s running lights. In the darkness they had watched the elegant 120-footer, aglow with lights that sparkled in the dark sea. There was a party on board and couples danced on her aft deck. As the sounds of music and laughter had drifted out to them across the water, Maria had observed that the motor-sailor's radar antenna wasn't turning. That explained why the *Cheetah* had slipped by completely unnoticed.

It was early evening on the third day when the *Cheetah* dropped anchor in a sheltered, isolated cove at one of a small cluster of islands eight miles off the coast of Nicaragua, just south of the Bluefields–El Bluff area. Boos had chosen the anchorage for its seclusion and for the fact that it was only a two-hour sail to the area where he hoped to insert Gannon that night. No more than a few hundred yards wide, it was located on the only island around for miles that wasn't flat. The cove was surrounded by high limestone cliffs, and in the last glow of the setting sun, pelicans, nesting in the jagged cliffs, soared and dived for food into the shallow water near shore.

Maria, dressed in her WINCH APE T-shirt and shorts, tired from three straight days of four-hour catnaps, reclined in the entertainment cockpit, a pillow propped beneath her head. Clyde was perched on her stomach, making contented chirping noises as he tugged at the letters on the T-shirt. Gannon, wearing swim trunks, was stretched out on the padded circular bench seat in the steering cockpit, enjoying the natural beauty and the serenity of the place. His skin glowed with the deep reddish-bronze tan that fair sailing had provided. Boos was below at the chart table measuring distances with a pair of dividers and reviewing his notes on the area around Monkey Point, personal notes he had made on past trips that appeared on no nautical charts.

Maria raised her head slightly, cocking an ear, then sat up and put the parrot on her shoulder.

"Good boy," Clyde said. "Whatcha doin'?"

Using the binoculars stored in a small deck compartment forward of the cockpit, Maria studied a vessel on the horizon until it became clearly recognizable as a fishing boat.

"What is it?" Gannon called from the stern.

"Local fishermen, probably," she said. "If they come alongside and ask if we want to buy any fish, just tell them no." She took Clyde with her and disappeared down the companionway and into the crew's quarters.

Gannon watched the boat draw closer. She was an old thirty-foot wooden fishing boat with a forward pilothouse. Her grimy white hull was painted with faded orange, blue, and yellow stripes. Aft of the pilothouse, covered with hatch boards and canvas, was a fish hold where two dark-skinned fisherman in faded cutoff jeans and ratty T-shirts stood waving and smiling as the boat drew abreast of the *Cheetah*. The hollow, high-pitched sound of her diesel engine and sputtering exhaust reminded Gannon of a city bus.

The fishing boat cut back on her power and drifted alongside, holding thirty feet off the *Cheetah*'s starboard side. The two fishermen now held up a large grouper and a red snapper and called out in Spanish, asking Gannon if he wanted to buy any fresh fish.

"Not interested," Gannon called back, not quite sure if the men understood English.

There was something about the look of the two men that set Gannon on edge—again, the same sixth sense that had kept him alive in the jungles of Vietnam. The bulwarks that surrounded the deck were high, and Gannon thought he saw something move on the side closest to the *Cheetah*. His mind sorted quickly through his options, which were virtually nonexistent save the choice of diving overboard on the port side.

There was more movement behind the bulwarks. Suddenly a third man stood up, an Uzi submachine gun in his hands. Before Gannon could dive for cover he was startled by an elongated burst of automatic fire, clearly recognizable to him as coming from an M-16.

The rounds tore into the man with the Uzi and sent him reeling across the deck into the bulwarks on the opposite side of the fishing boat. A split second later the two men who had been holding the fish dropped them and reached down and grabbed AK-47 assault rifles from under the canvas. Two short, accurate bursts from the forward deck of the *Cheetah* cut them down before they could fire.

Gannon looked toward the bow of the boat, genuinely astonished to see Maria down on one knee just outside the forward hatch, an M-203 held snugly to her shoulder. Gannon was more than familiar with the weapon—an M-16 with a grenade launcher mounted beneath the barrel.

Boos scrambled up the companionway, a stainless-steel

12-gauge pump shotgun in each hand. He immediately tossed one of the weapons to Gannon and shouted:

"Five rounds, double aught buck, chamber empty, safety off!"

Gannon and Boos pumped shells into their weapons almost simultaneously. They crouched low and moved forward. Their eyes swept the deck of the fishing boat for targets.

Maria also scanned the deck of the fishing boat, then fired an HE round from the deadly grenade launcher at the pilothouse. The high-explosive 40mm grenade crashed through one of the windows and blasted out the port side. Shards of glass and a storm of wood splinters flew in all directions.

One man, a semiautomatic shotgun in his hands, was blown out onto the deck, his chest torn open. A second man could be seen just inside what remained of the pilothouse. He was slumped over the jagged and splintered bulkhead. Half of his head was missing.

Maria moved forward cautiously; her eyes swept the carnage on the fishing boat's decks. She reloaded the grenade launcher with the speed and proficiency of someone who had trained with the weapon and continued to watch for any signs of life. When the boat had drifted at least another fifty feet from the *Cheetah,* she fired a second HE round, this time into the area of the fishing boat's fuel tanks. The stricken vessel continued to drift away, flames engulfing her charred and shattered pilothouse and aft deck. When she was another hundred yards away, burning like a funeral pyre, she exploded into an orange-black ball of fire and broke in half. She sank out of sight within a matter of minutes.

Gannon stood beside Boos and stared at Maria with a somewhat disbelieving if open admiration. "She sort of takes repelling boarders to heart, doesn't she?" Gannon said.

"Did I tell you she was something special . . . or what?" Boos said, a broad grin on his boyish face. "What are your chances of ever meeting a women like her again? Beautiful enough to show off out on the town, sexy enough to take home and make mad, passionate love to, and when you're finished, intelligent enough to lie back, smoke a cigarette, and talk fuckin' weapons systems with you. Huh? I'm tellin' ya, Gannon, they don't make 'em like that anymore."

Maria swung gracefully down into the forward hatch and disappeared. She reappeared in the main companionway moments later, unarmed. She came back on deck with a very subdued and slightly stressed-out Clyde on her shoulder and returned to her seat in the entertainment cockpit.

"Think we should move?" Gannon said.

"No. This is an isolated area," Boos replied. "The only thing for miles around onshore are local Indians. Even if they heard the explosion and saw the smoke, they don't give a shit about anything that doesn't directly concern them."

Gannon gave his shotgun back to Boos, who took it below. He sat opposite Maria and stared at her quietly for a long moment, studying her. There was not the slightest sign of emotional tension or any trace of the "combat high" that followed a firefight. With the exception of an increased breathing rate and a harder look in her eyes, she was perfectly calm, as though nothing had happened, as though what had just transpired was an everyday occurrence.

"How did you know?" Gannon finally asked.

"The identification letters and numbers on the side of the boat," Maria said. "CTG-174 identified her as being out of Cartagena, Colombia. Pretty far from her normal fishing grounds, wouldn't you say?"

"I guess so," Gannon said. "What the hell did they want?"

"The boat," Maria said. "These waters are full of pirates . . . drug smugglers looking for boats to use or just low-life thieves looking for people to rob."

Gannon had heard stories of the resurgence of piracy in the past decade. In Southeast Asia especially, where thousands of refugees had been robbed, raped, beaten, and killed by pirates, and of the scores of ships that had disappeared in the waters off Singapore, West Africa, and the Mediterranean, usually at the rate of one a week. Luxury yachts were prime targets for narcotics traffickers. Hundreds sailing the Caribbean had vanished. No distress signals were ever heard, no evidence of shipwrecks, and no trace of the passengers or crew were ever found.

"If you suspected trouble," Gannon asked, "why didn't you alert us to it?"

Maria flashed a charming, radiant smile. "I wasn't sure," she said. "And besides, I thought I was capable of handling the situation."

"Can't argue with that," Gannon said, smiling back. "Where did you get the M-203?"

"The owner of the boat is a devout believer in the old adage that an ounce of prevention is worth a pound of cure," Maria said. "A few years ago some friends of his sailing in the Bahamas were attacked by pirates. They murdered everyone on board and stole the yacht. The DEA found it about six months later in the coastal waters off Florida, disguised with a new paint job. Some small-time drug runners were using it to transport cargoes of marijuana and hashish. They never found the bodies of the passengers or crew, just bloodstains."

Maria set Clyde on his perch and said, "Come with me. I want to show you something."

Gannon followed Maria down the companionway and forward to the crew's quarters. A cleverly designed elongated cabinet was built into the bulkhead, and when opened with the key Maria held, it folded down to reveal a gun cabinet with an assortment of automatic weapons that even Gannon found impressive. Neatly mounted on individually padded racks were two M-16s, the M-203 that Maria had used, two CAR-15s (the shorter version of the M-16 that Gannon had used almost exclusively in the Special Operations Group in Vietnam), an M-79 grenade launcher, an M-60 machine gun, and the two stainless-steel pump shotguns. Held in place with Velcro straps was a variety of hand grenades and 40mm grenades for the M-203 and M-79. On built-in shelves just below the gun racks were what Gannon estimated to be at least two thousand rounds of ammunition.

"Quite an arsenal," Gannon said. "Looks like your boss knows some interesting people."

"He just decided that what happened to his friends wasn't going to happen to him . . . or us. And if it did, we weren't going down easy."

"I'd say you're on the right track," Gannon said with a grin as Maria closed the compartment and locked it.

Like spies throughout history, military satellites live in the shadows, their technology, launches, and missions highly secret—the guardians of whatever peace exists in the world. The CIA's satellite-intelligence-collection capabilities fall into two main categories. The first, imaging techniques acting as surrogate eyes—taking photos from two hundred miles up, detecting heat sources with infrared devices, pinpointing metal with magnetic detectors, distinguishing between barely moving and stationary objects through the use of Doppler radar, and radar that can detect objects that are covered or hidden by darkness. And second, communications-intercept techniques that act as surrogate ears, eavesdropping on all manner of signals from the human voice to electronic radio waves.

Orbiting over the South Atlantic in the cold silence of space, the electromechanical eyes of the KH-13—the United States' most secret strategic reconnaissance satellite—recorded the images below in digital form. To complicate the Soviets' efforts to intercept its data, it relayed its real-time imagery up to another satellite, which in turn coded and down-linked the signal to the innocuously named Defense Communications, Electronics, Evaluation and Testing Activity, otherwise known as the CIA's Office of Imagery Analysis, located in a large, windowless, two-story concrete structure at Fort Belvoir, Virginia, just outside Washington, D.C.

The KH-13 was tasked with a variety of missions: monitoring military bases, missile test sites, naval maneuvers, radar installations, ships at sea, and terrorist camps. Its system capabilities were such that it used no film. Instead it recorded elements of a scene as digital electronic impulses that could be relayed almost instantaneously, making it possible for the viewer on the ground to see things as they were actually happening. Once the down-linked imagery was received it was decoded, digitally restored by computers, and its extraordinary high-resolution pictures then projected on screens and scrutinized by photointelligence specialists who could, using computerized lenses, zoom in on objects and details of particular interest that had been previously hidden from the human eye. The images could then be transferred to film or tape and digitally manipulated to highlight particular features or characteristics.

Operating at high orbit when not engaged in reconnaissance, the KH-13 had the added capability of dropping to a much lower altitude when close-look scrutiny of a particular area was required, a maneuver that could be accomplished within the time frame of an hour. On request from the Central Intelligence Agency for just such close-look scrutiny, the Air Force Satellite Control Facility at Sunnyvale, California—the place from which all U.S. military satellites are controlled and known as the Big Blue Cube to those who work there—had transmitted the necessary commands to the KH-13's navigation and attitude-control systems to change the ultrasecret satellite's orbit.

Moved from its previous moderately elliptical orbit of 144 by 186 miles and an inclination of 96.4 degrees, the commands it received had maneuvered it into a position that allowed it to circle the earth once every eighty-nine minutes. It passed over every spot on its ground track once in daylight and once at night during each twenty-four-hour period, permitting it to take close-up photos from as near as eighty miles away.

Infinitely maneuverable, with ultra-enhanced real-time imaging and space-shuttle-compatible refueling capability, the KH-13 was the ultimate imaging platform. It was able to change orbits over long periods, thereby altering its ground track by substantial margins, extend its coverage, and make it unpredictable to Soviet satellite trackers. Its ability to produce three-dimensional images of a 150-square-mile area and detect objects six inches in size from eighty miles away was unparalleled. Its astonishing close-up detail was sharp enough to distinguish the name on a mailbox on a country road, the headline of a newspaper being read by someone on a Berlin street corner, or actually follow the pucks during ice hockey games at outdoor rinks in Moscow.

Its current mission, however, was far less challenging. Some eighty miles above the Caribbean Sea the KH-13 went about its silent, eerie work with a mechanical detachment. Its lenses accurately recorded the coast of Nicaragua, nothing escaping its cold, blank stare.

32

The CIA safe house in the resort city of La Ceiba on the Caribbean coast of Honduras sits on a large corner lot two blocks from the beach. The eight-room Spanish-style villa, surrounded by a ten-foot-high wall, is patrolled around the clock by CIA paramilitary personnel armed with H&K submachine guns and satchels full of hand grenades. The grounds are implanted with infrared sensors, and because of the top-secret nature of the encryption and transmission equipment in the second-floor communications center, the entire villa is wired with explosives, to be triggered by remote control in the event the safe house is overrun.

As Tom Driscoll glanced at the satellite photos coming out of the facsimile machine direct from the Company's Office of Imagery Analysis at Fort Belvoir, Virginia, the operations room came to life. A smile of satisfaction slowly replaced the knitted brow and sullen expression that had been with Driscoll most of the day.

On a large cork board at one end of the operations room Driscoll pinned a set of enlarged satellite photos together sequentially, forming a mosaic of ten square miles of the Nicaraguan coastline that included the small offshore islands south of the Bluefields–El Bluff area. Beneath the first row of photos he pinned a second row of blowups of the KH-13's close-look shots that revealed the *Cheetah* and the secluded cove. He turned on a row of hooded spotlights on a track above the cork board and studied the photos.

Phil Travis, the CIA's station chief in Tegucigalpa, looked over Driscoll's shoulder as he paused at an extreme close-up of the *Cheetah*'s deck at the time of the pirate attack. The electro-optical resolution of the photos was so good that even the scar on Gannon's neck was faintly visible.

"That must be Gannon with the M-203," Travis said.

Driscoll, who was studying the aft deck, where Boos and Gannon stood, gave Travis a questioning look, then glanced at the forward deck and said, "Not unless he's grown a nice set of tits and a great ass in the last three days, it isn't."

Travis looked again, closer. "Oh, sorry. Then who's she?"

"Don't know," Driscoll said. He looked at the close-up of Maria with a viewing lens that magnified and clarified the photo even more. "Must be one of the crew."

"Whoever she is," Travis said, "it looks like she just put a round from the grenade launcher into the pilothouse of that fishing boat."

The fishing boat could clearly be seen at the moment of impact. Another series of photos, taken from a reverse angle as the satellite passed over, showed her breaking apart and about to sink.

Driscoll copied the identification numbers of the fishing boat and handed the slip of paper to an assistant. "Check this out," he said. "My guess is it's just some local small-time smugglers trying to grab themselves a yacht."

The assistant glanced at the photos. "Looks like they picked the wrong one."

Driscoll continued to study the mosaic of the ten-square-mile area, concentrating primarily on the coastal section between El Bluff and Monkey Point.

A junior Honduran naval officer standing beside Driscoll spoke for the first time after examining the photographs.

"I think he's going to try and go in here," the naval officer said, and indicated a stretch of coastline that extended south from Monkey Point. "He anchored in that cove to put himself within easy reach of an insertion point. And it can't be too close to El Bluff, the port is the alternate point of entry for the Warsaw Pact's seaborne military deliveries. It's too well patrolled, and there are large concentrations of Sandinista troops providing security for the new military air base nearby."

Another Honduran, the junior naval officer's direct superior, added, "I'm familiar with that area. There's a lot of uncharted reefs and coral heads just beneath the surface. It's unpatrolled, but for a good reason. Nobody in their right mind would try to take a boat of any size through those waters."

"Unless he'd done it before and knows what the charts don't show," Driscoll said.

"Boos might know the area," Travis said. "According to his file, he's made a number of drops for us around there in the past. We're still checking for any debriefing reports from his old operations. They might give us the exact drop-off points he's used before."

"That's where he'll do it," Driscoll said without doubt while pointing to the coastline just south of Monkey Point. "It's the place he's least likely to run into any Sandinista patrols on the water or on the beach."

Travis checked the time; it was just after 7:00 P.M. "Do you think they'll insert tonight?" he asked Driscoll.

"Probably. But Boos has got to have a contact on the ground," Driscoll said. "He's not going to drop Gannon off cold. If our luck holds, we'll find out who, when, and where when he tries to make radio contact with him."

In a high-security compound in a remote corner of the Soviet-built air base at San Antonio de los Baños on the island of Cuba is a company of Spetsnaz troops whose area of operations is Central and South America. A specially selected unit from Headquarters, Group of Soviet Forces Germany, their current assignment was extended training in a jungle environment and advanced training in guerrilla tactics.

The Soviet Union's Spetsnaz (Special Designation) units come under the direct command of the GRU–Soviet Military Intelligence. Made up of noncommissioned officers and junior field grade officers, they are the elite of the Soviet military, the only troops in the Soviet military structure that are encouraged to be innovative and operate with a high degree of independence. Their training consists of airborne operations, SCUBA diving, silent killing, assassination, infiltration and exfiltration into and out of enemy-held areas, demolitions, clandestine communications and operations, psychological warfare, and extensive training in hand-to-hand combat. Their missions include assassination and kidnapping of enemy political and military leaders, sabotage, espionage, reconnaissance, and various counterinsurgency operations. They are, without doubt, the most highly trained, effective, and dangerous troops in the Soviet military.

The Spetsnaz very existence is classified, and their forces are known by "cover" unit designations, depending on the military district in which they are stationed. In the Group of Soviet Forces Germany they are called *Reydoviki,* or "raiders." In the Siberian Military District they are known as *Okhotniki,* or "huntsmen." As a result of this subterfuge Spetsnaz from different districts may meet each other by chance and each believe the other belongs to a totally different organization—such is the extent of the secrecy surrounding their existence and function.

Captain Vasili Fomenko had just returned with his Spetsnaz team from a rough-terrain jump and a seven-day field-training exercise in the mountains. He ran across the compound and entered the company headquarters building, proceeding down the hallway on the double. His mind sorted through the possible reasons for the urgent summons from his commanding officer. At the entrance to the major's office he brushed at his camouflage fatigues and cleaned off, as best he could, ground-in layers of dust and grime from the week spent in the mountains.

The door to the major's office opened immediately on the first knock. The major nodded to Fomenko, then stepped aside and left the office. Fomenko, confused, stared after the retreating major, then directed his attention to the man with the overpowering presence who sat behind the major's desk.

A chill ran down his spine. It took all of Fomenko's will-power to keep from physically trembling. The civilian clothes the man wore did nothing to conceal his military bearing or prevent Fomenko from recognizing the chief of the GRU. Fomenko snapped to rigid attention and saluted smartly.

General Vladimir Antonov gestured to a chair set before the desk. "Sit down, Captain Fomenko."

Fomenko sat as ordered, removed his cap, and placed it in his lap. His mind again raced through possible scenarios— from an imminent declaration of war to a top-secret assignment for which he and his men had been specially selected. Whatever the reason, the captain knew it had to be something of a highly classified nature for the GRU chief himself to be here. General Antonov read through a file folder that Fomenko suspected was his personal service record.

Antonov was simply reviewing information he had had on file at GRU headquarters in Moscow. Fomenko's exemplary record and those of his team were familiar to him. Although the forty-five-year-old captain sitting before him had started his military career as a private, his skills were such that he had been chosen for a four-man Spetsnaz team secretly sent to Vietnam in 1972 to test the then-new SVD sniper rifle on U.S. forces operating across the borders into Laos and North Vietnam. The twelve-man team he now commanded had served with him in Afghanistan, running long-range insertions into *mujahedin*-held territory—specializing in assassinations of the rebels command structure and cross-border operations into Pakistan against commanders of the *mujahedin* base camps and staging areas. Fomenko and his team had performed with devastating effectiveness, one of the few success stories of Soviet operations in Afghanistan.

General Antonov looked up from Fomenko's service record and smiled. "I see you have been trained in the use of miniature nuclear weapons," he said. "Are you familiar with the American weapons of the same nature?"

"Just the exterior, Comrade General," Fomenko said. "And only in principle. We have had only photographs of their man-portable tactical nuclear weapons with which to conduct our studies."

"You would recognize an American weapon called the Saydum if you saw it?" Antonov asked. "And know how to handle and transport it safely?"

"Yes, Comrade General," Fomenko said, his curiosity aroused.

Antonov went on to explain in detail the mission to recover the SADM and of the GRU officer in Managua who had learned the location of the KGB's secret terrorist camp. Fomenko restrained himself from showing the surprise and excitement he felt as the details of his mission were revealed to him.

"And I want no confrontation that could prove embarrassing to us," Antonov concluded. "Your main objective is to secure and recover the Saydum and to kidnap Nikolai Malik. If conditions preclude taking him alive, kill him.

"Any Contra or Sandinista troops you inadvertently encounter are not to be engaged in combat. You will disperse your men and rendezvous at a prearranged location and continue with your primary mission. You will limit any offensive actions to the personnel at the terrorist camp. Is that clearly understood, Captain Fomenko?"

"Yes, Comrade General," Fomenko said. "Very clearly."

"You will have your men ready to embark at 1730 hours tomorrow. Your departure from here will be timed to assure your insertion into Nicaragua at last light."

"And the method of insertion, Comrade General?" Fomenko asked.

"High-Altitude–Low-Opening parachute drop," Antonov
said, aware that Fomenko and his team were expert i
HALO jumps. "You will be thoroughly briefed by one o
our experts for that area of operations who will select
suitable drop zone as close to the camp as possible."

"And who will provide security for the drop zone?
Fomenko asked, not relishing the thought of jumping int
the heart of guerrilla territory without someone on th
ground to secure the clearing in which they would be land
ing.

"The GRU *rezident* in Managua will personally see to th
proper security arrangements," Antonov said. "If there
nothing else, Comrade, I suggest you gather your men an
report to the briefing room."

"Yes, sir," Fomenko said. He rose and snapped to atten
tion, and after delivering a proper salute, turned on his hee
and rushed from the office. A mission, he thought as he ha
walked, half jogged down the hallway. Finally, after all th
months of monotonous training and garrison life. Finally,
mission with a purpose, and one that could see them a
decorated and promoted if successfully accomplished.

33

In the remote, mountainous jungle six miles southeast of Nicaragua's Punta Gorda River, Tony Santana was walking point as he and his team moved warily along a dark, narrow trail that was little more than an animal track. The light from a full moon filtered through the towering trees and dappled the ground. They had moved past the place they had chosen to stop and continued scouting the immediate area ahead before fishhooking back to the tiny clearing ten yards into the dense underbrush off the trail.

Santana had only to give a brief hand signal and six of his men immediately vanished into the brush to take up perimeter security positions. The remainder of the team settled beneath thick triple-canopy jungle that blocked out the moon and cast the clearing into almost total darkness. Without a word another of the men strung a wire antenna over a high branch as Santana set up the radio and tuned in the four-megacycle frequency. He glanced at his watch; it was three minutes after nine o'clock. He sat motionless and listened on the handset to the oscillating hum and static hiss on the single sideband frequency.

Jim Boos sat in the leather Recaro seat at the communications console aboard the *Cheetah*. Tuned to four megacycles on the single sideband radio, he keyed the microphone.

"Sandman, this is Coon Ass. Do you read? Over."

The hum and static on the frequency were immediatel broken with a clear response.

"Sandman here. Go," came the reply.

Boos gave a confident thumbs-up to Gannon, who wa standing off to the side.

"Request rendezvous," Boos said. "Can you accommo date tonight?"

"That's affirmative," Santana replied. "When an where?"

Boos, aware that they were talking in clear voices, with out scramblers, on a frequency that could be monitored b anyone for hundreds of miles around, kept his instruction cryptic. He knew Santana would understand the message.

"Coon Ass to Sandman," Boos repeated. "Remember th last insertion?"

"That's affirmative," Santana came back.

"Same time. Same place," Boos said. "Confirm."

"Confirmed," Santana said, and immediately got off th frequency.

Boos turned off the radio and flashed his boyish grin a Gannon. The tension in Gannon's face was gone, replace by a look of satisfaction and eager anticipation.

"Midnight," he told Gannon. "A little beach area si miles south of Monkey Point. It'll take us about two hour to get there from here."

"You going in with me?" Gannon said.

Boos grinned again. "You don't think for one goddam second I'm going to miss a chance to get back in harness Come on, Gannon, you know me better than that."

Gannon nodded. "Can't think of anyone I'd rather hav along."

"Somebody's got to watch after your Green Beanie ass, Boos said. "God knows you couldn't handle it by yourself.

Gannon simply smiled and left for his stateroom, wher he began sorting through his gear.

With the insertion set for midnight, Boos and Ganno

began the process of preparing for a mission into enemy
territory, a ritual both men had gone through dozens of
times in Vietnam. This time was no different. The jungle and
the enemy had different names, but the game, the rules, and
the stakes were still the same.

Twenty-five miles off the coast of Nicaragua, at an altitude of twenty thousand feet, the specially configured
Beechcraft King Air flew wide figure-eight patterns, covering large tracks of the Nicaraguan coastline and the Caribbean Sea.

Ostensibly, the King Air belonged to the Pan-American
Technical Services Company and was conducting electro-
magnetic and navigation surveys for the Honduran government. Its true function was as a CIA spy plane. Painted in
civilian colors and carrying no military crew, if shot down
or involved in a crash, it could be plausibly denied, despite
the sophisticated electronic equipment on board.

Hundreds of thousands of dollars' worth of state-of-the-
art communications and prototype electronic eavesdropping
equipment was mounted in the back of the plane, where
signal-intelligence technicians, known as "knob turners,"
monitored and operated the consoles. The composite antennas built into the fuselage of the aircraft were ultrasensitive,
capable of picking up ground-radio communications, high-
frequency radio signals, ship-to-shore, and citizens-band
transmissions while flying at altitudes in excess of twenty-
five thousand feet.

At times the "take" was so phenomenal that the knob
turners were able to pick up transmissions that disclosed
Sandinista troop movements and locations. With the information relayed, the Contras were able to take defensive
measures, set up devastating ambushes, or simply disappear
into the Nicaraguan jungle until they could mount their
own offensive. Also, as a result of the communications in-
tercepts, Sandinista cross-border raids into Honduras,
aimed at the Contra camps there, were often thwarted along

with the interdiction of weapons-supply routes from Nicaragua into neighboring El Salvador.

The short transmissions between Boos and Santana had not escaped the knob turner at the King Air's communications console. It was the type of transmission his superiors at the safe house in Honduras had told him to be alert for. With a flip of a toggle switch, the message, which had automatically been recorded, was relayed to the communications room at the CIA's safe house at La Ceiba.

Another message, from Havana to Managua, intercepted only fifteen minutes earlier, had puzzled the technician, but his gut instincts told him that due to its unusual coding and back-channel method of transmission, it was somehow related to whatever operation it was that had the local station chief's blood pressure up. He sent it along to La Ceiba for good measure.

Tom Driscoll took the printout handed him by the radio operator, who had rushed down from the second-floor communications room.

"Coon Ass?" Driscoll said.

"Boos's code name when he worked for us," Travis, the local CIA station chief explained. "He's a Louisiana Cajun."

"And Sandman?" Driscoll said. He stared blankly across the room, searching his memory. "That name rings a bell. Who's Sandman?"

Travis smiled grimly. "Tony 'Sandman' Santana," he told Driscoll.

"He's one of ours, isn't he?" Driscoll said.

"Yes and no."

"Well, which is it?" Driscoll said, the irritation evident in his voice.

"He's done a lot of work for us in the past. Former Navy SEAL, used to be under contract," Travis said. "When we had to cut back support and supplies to the Contras, he

more or less told us to fuck off. He's gone native. Runs his
own team by his own rules."

"Do you know where he's operating now?"

"No," Travis said. "According to the last report we had,
a little over a month ago, he was running most of his ops in
the San Juan River area along the border with Costa Rica.
But he moves around a lot, depending on the intelligence
information he gets on Sandinista activities from his network of local agents."

"Can you contact him?"

"He maintains communications with us," Travis said.
"But it's always on his terms. When he has something he
thinks we can use, or he needs something only we can supply, he contacts us on a special frequency we use for agents-
in-place. It's monitored twenty-four hours a day."

"What the hell is he?" Driscoll snapped. "A free-lance
rogue?"

"Worse," Travis said. "A patriot."

"Christ!" Driscoll said. "Were they able to get a fix on his
position when he transmitted?"

"He's too smart for that," Travis said. "He wouldn't stay
on long enough."

The radio operator who had brought the printout to Driscoll spoke up. "There's something else," he said as he
handed Driscoll the decoded message the King Air knob
turner had relayed along with Boos's message to Santana.
"This was sent from a GRU officer in Cuba to the GRU
rezident in Managua. They sent it on a back channel but
used a code one of our agents inside the Soviet Embassy
managed to get for us last month."

Driscoll read the message. The deep frown again furrowed his brow. "They want a special team to secure a drop
zone at last light tomorrow?" Driscoll studied the coordinates given for the drop zone, then handed them to Travis.
"Pinpoint this DZ for me.

"You said they used a back channel?" Driscoll said to the
radio operator.

"Yes, sir. That's what the King Air reported."

Travis gave the message to his chief of operations, who went to the large-scale map of Nicaragua on the opposite wall. In a matter of seconds he stuck a red pin in the sector the coordinates indicated. It was a small mountain valley fourteen miles north of Barra del Rio Maiz.

Driscoll studied the location. His face twisted into a puzzled expression that was slowly replaced with one of dawning realization.

"They've located the KGB's terrorist camp," he said to Travis. "I'd stake my reputation that they're sending in a Spetsnaz team to take it."

"That would explain the back channel to avoid the KGB intercepting the message," Travis said.

"Goddamn!" Driscoll said. "If we could get a message to this Santana, he could track the Soviets to the camp."

Travis shook his head. "There's no way to reach him. He doesn't monitor the frequency he uses to contact us." Travis thought for a moment, then said, "I could put one of our paramilitary teams into the area before the Soviets make the drop. Their message said the DZ must be secured by last light tomorrow; that's about seven, seven-fifteen. Plenty of time to have our people in place."

"No," Driscoll said adamantly. "That's all we need—personnel who can be tied directly to us ending up in a shootout with Soviet troops. And if Santana is in that area, we'll have people tripping all over each other. No, we'll have to stick with Boos and Gannon and hope that Santana can lead them to that camp before the Soviets get there."

"Any word from Langley on the debriefing reports from Boos's past operations?" he asked his assistant.

"Nothing yet, sir."

"Get back to them," Driscoll said. "Tell them the only one we're interested in is his last operation into Nicaragua, specifically the point of insertion and the time."

Driscoll then turned to the senior Honduran naval officer. "Get your people cranked up to get under way in two hours.

I want to be en route to the general area of operations before this thing gets out of hand. My people will install the necessary communications equipment on your boats."

"The intended destination?" the Honduran asked.

"For now," Driscoll said, "we'll head for the cove where the *Cheetah* is anchored. It probably won't be there by the time we arrive, but at least we'll be within striking distance."

"We will be ready when you are, Señor Driscoll," the Honduran said. He motioned with a quick snap of his head to his junior officer, and they both strutted from the room, looking for all the world like bantam roosters in search of a fight.

Travis pulled Driscoll aside, out of earshot of the others in the room. "Don't you think it's about time you told me what's so goddamned important about getting to that camp before the Spetsnaz troops and what the fuck the GRU is doing trying to kill off a bunch of KGB-sponsored terrorists? And, more to the point, why we should give a shit if they do?"

Driscoll stared blankly at the CIA station chief and said, "No."

A hunter's moon shimmered on the calm turquoise sea, softly illuminating the deck of the *Cheetah* as she settled into an easy rolling motion with the tidal rhythm. A tangible primeval aura engulfed the secluded cove as the ocean rose and fell in gentle swells against the base of the steep-to shore; bats squeaked and fluttered from the small caves that pockmarked the face of the limestone cliffs, their ominous sound echoing out across the water.

Gannon, dressed in camouflage fatigues, a black bandanna tied around his forehead, sat in the forward cockpit. The CAR-15 he had chosen as his personal weapon rested on the padded bench seat beside him, field-stripped, cleaned, and reassembled. He finished loading his magazines with ammunition and carefully placed them in the pouches attached to his web belt. He had cut away the upper seams of the pouches for easy access and placed the tops of the magazines facedown, directed outward, to explode away from his body if struck by an enemy round. Each of the five ammo pouches contained six twenty-round magazines, giving him a total of six hundred rounds plus the twenty-round magazine loaded in the weapon. In addition to the two canteens of fresh water hooked to the rear of his belt, another canteen cover was used to carry four hand grenades. His combat knife was positioned upside down on the left side of his chest in the sheath attached to his harness.

He took a roll of black tape from an outside pocket of his rucksack and began taping the swivels on the CAR-15's sling as well as all the metal clips, snap links, and buckles on his load-bearing equipment and rucksack. As he sat silently, meticulously applying the tape that would eliminate noise and glare, the soft sound of music drew his attention to the forward deck.

Maria, dressed in jeans and a sweatshirt against the cool breeze coming off the ocean, was on deck just outside the forward hatch. Unaware of Gannon's presence, she was dancing, slowly, sensuously, to a throbbing rock beat that flowed from the speakers in the crew's quarters below. Clyde, the parrot, was perched at the open hatch, his head bobbing and weaving comically off-tempo. Maria seemed to be in her own world, her body movements one with the music, her silken hair waving its own rhythm with the night wind. Gannon stared in appreciation until she turned in his direction and stopped upon seeing him in the forward cockpit.

"Sorry," Gannon said as Maria approached. "I didn't mean to intrude." After an awkward pause he added, "Kate . . . my wife. She loved to dance."

Maria stepped down into the cockpit, placed Clyde on his perch, and sat on the bench seat across from Gannon. She studied his face and how different he looked in the military clothing and gear. He seemed to belong in them. Even his eyes had changed—they were harder, more distant. She had seen the look before, known men like him all of her life.

She saw Boos sitting in the steering cockpit, arranging his gear. He was dressed identically to Gannon, with the exception of his camouflage fatigues bearing a tiger-stripe pattern as opposed to Gannon's woodland pattern. Boos, too, had chosen a CAR-15, but had also slung an M-79 grenade launcher over his shoulder along with a bandolier of 40mm rounds for the deadly weapon. He was so intent on preparing himself and his equipment for the mission, he took no notice of Maria or Gannon.

"Jim told me you were awarded the Medal of Honor in Vietnam," Maria said, her eyes again drawn to the prominent scar on Gannon's neck.

Gannon nodded, then redirected the conversation. "Where did you learn to handle weapons?" he asked.

Maria sat silently for a moment, as though deciding whether or not she wanted this near stranger to know any more than he had to about her personal life. Then, after fixing her deep brown eyes on him, a curious stare that Gannon returned, she made her decision.

"My father died in 1961, when I was about two months old," she said. "My mother died a few months later."

"Accidents?" Gannon said.

"My mother, yes," Maria said. "An automobile accident. My father was a leader of the anti-Castro movement—the Revolution Recuperation Movement. He was killed at Giron Beach during the Bay of Pigs invasion while he was commanding Assault Brigade 2506."

"You must be proud of him," Gannon said. "And not too pleased with the way the three-piece-suits in Washington sold him and his men out."

Maria avoided Gannon's gaze and said softly. "I never knew him, except through the eyes of his friends and my relatives. But yes, I am proud of what they tried to do. I still have relatives in Cuba . . . grandparents, cousins . . ."

Her voice trailed off. "We still don't know what's happened to them."

"You didn't answer my question," Gannon prodded gently. "Where did you learn to handle weapons?"

Maria hesitated, then: "After my mother died I was raised by my uncle and aunt. They were both involved in the Cuban liberation movement. My uncle worked for the CIA. He coordinated the training of the anti-Castro guerrilla fighters, set up the camps, acted as liaison between the CIA and the liberation leaders, and organized and occasionally led commando raids into Cuba from gunboats and mother ships stationed offshore.

"I spent most of my life, until I was seventeen, moving from one secret training base to another—the Bahamas, Florida Everglades, any number of places in the Caribbean. After hearing all the tales of my father's exploits, I started to show an interest in the training. To make a long story short, my aunt made sure I got a formal education, while my uncle took care of the guerrilla warfare schooling. There are very few small arms I can't handle," she added with more than a trace of pride.

"The Company never tried to recruit you?" Gannon said.

"Oh, they tried," Maria answered. Her voice took on an edge. "When I was in high school in Miami, when I was in college in New York. They finally got the message that I wasn't interested. I haven't heard from them since."

"You were born in the States?" Gannon asked.

"Miami. Little Havana."

"And Spanish is your first language?"

"Yes. Why?"

"It's just that there's no trace of an accent. You sound like the all-American girl."

"I worked on it," Maria said. There was an almost instantaneous change in her expression, as though she had decided she had given enough of herself away. Then a bit of her gamine quality surfaced. She winked, flashed a dazzling smile, and in an affected singsong Spanish accent said, "I kleen your house for a month. I chine your choose."

Gannon laughed and found himself smiling at the beautiful face before him. It was the first time he had sincerely smiled since learning of Kate's death.

"You're a charmer, Maria."

"So they tell me."

34

A sultry, husky-voiced singer, draped over the side of a piano, belted out a nearly unrecognizable rendition of "Sep-
tember Song," trying in vain to be heard above the din of
the crowded, smoke-filled dining room. The small restaurant off Managua's Avenue Bolívar, known for its excellent
steaks, was filled to near capacity with representatives of
Eastern Bloc governments and those few Nicaraguans fortunate enough to afford the outrageous prices, which limited
the local clientele to mid- and high-level government officials.

Seated at the opposite end of the room from the piano
player and the singer, as he had emphatically requested,
General Pavel Olenev, the KGB's *rezident* in Managua,
glanced repeatedly at the ample cleavage of his escort, provided for the evening by his dinner company and host, an
assistant to the Minister of the Interior, who was accompanied by an equally eager-to-please young woman.

The young lady with the ample cleavage removed something from her purse and, beneath the table, slipped it into
Olenev's hand. When the waiter brought the menus, Olenev,
seated with his back to the wall, spread open the oversized
menu and read the message he had just been handed.

Despite his galvanic reaction to what he read, his outward
composure remained unchanged. The message was from one

f his agents on the GRU *rezident*'s staff and required his
mmediate attention. General Olenev made his excuses,
eigning a bad headache and a loss of appetite, and thanked
is host for the dinner invitation and returned to the em-
assy, where he went directly to the communications room.

The KGB's terrorist training camp lay hidden two hundred yards from the banks of a tributary of Nicaragua's
Punta Gorda River. Expertly concealed beneath triple-can-
py trees, in a connecting series of small clearings hacked
rom near-impenetrable jungle, the cluster of detached shel-
ers blended so well into their surroundings that one could
valk within ten yards of the camp's perimeter and not know
t was there.

Most of the camp consisted of simple, open-sided struc-
ures with thatched roofs, some with crude bench seats and
ables used for classrooms; one served as a mess hall and
others were strung with jungle hammocks as sleeping quar-
ers. The only buildings completely enclosed were the com-
nunications and supply shacks and five individual huts for
he upper-echelon instructors. Constructed of logs and
hatch, the huts were as well camouflaged as the rest of the
camp.

The twenty-man training cadre that Nikolai Malik had
 assembled as course instructors were accomplished blooded
and infamous members of the international terrorist com-
nunity. They were among the top practitioners of their
nurderous trade, with almost an equal number of them be-
ng Palestinians, Cubans from Castro's DGI (Directorate of
General Intelligence), and members of a special unit of East
German State Security.

The in-camp students were limited to thirty at a time—six
ive-person teams, each from different nations. The present
lass, now more than halfway through their course of in-
truction, had teams from France, West Germany, Spain,
Ecuador, Northern Ireland, and Italy. The students had
been secreted into Nicaragua by various means—some by

Soviet freighter or fishing boat, others under false passport
aboard civilian airlines.

Malik believed in creating small teams of expert killers
not turning out large groups of half-trained zealots. He in
sisted on thoroughly realistic training. This included an ac
tual operation successfully conducted by each team befor
graduating. The grueling, demanding six-month course en
compassed extensive training in the use of small arms, as
sault weapons, submachine guns, demolitions—includin
bomb making and improvised explosives and detonators—
making and reading maps, planning operations, cryptogra
phy, photography, document forging, physical disguise, firs
aid, subversive techniques, guerrilla and urban warfare tac
tics, clandestine communications, including the jamming c
police radios and setting up of safe houses and secure mee
ing sites. The constant relocation of the camp was also pa
of the training.

Physical conditioning and practical skills were not over
looked. A punishing regime involved long marches ove
rough terrain, establishing base camps, mountain climbing
swimming, canoeing, handling motor- and sailboats, escap
and evasion, and hunting for one's own food. In addition,
particularly brutal course in resisting torture and interroga
tion in the event of capture was taught. The graduates Mali
sent out into the world were not the mindless religious c
political fanatics who hijacked aircraft or took over embas
sies, willingly giving up their lives for some nebulous caus
They were highly motivated and valued professionals—th
next generation of leaders of the international terrorist con
munity.

The occasional student who excelled and held promis
received additional instructions in conducting intelligence
gathering operations in their home countries for the KGI
as well as organizing terrorist networks. They were ofte
sent to Moscow for advanced weapons and technical train
ing with the KGB's notorious Department V assassinatio
and sabotage units. On the whole, Malik was pleased wit

the caliber of students that the program he had personally
devised and supervised was turning out, and he hoped to
expand the operation into other countries once he had
proven to his superiors that his methods were sound.

A Coleman lantern burned in the crude log-and-thatch
hut that was Malik's quarters when he was in camp. It was
isolated from the other structures, on the side of the camp
closest to the river. The glow of the lamp was barely visible
through the heavy black sackcloth that hung across the
openings cut into two of the walls. A rough-hewn log table
and bench took up the center of the small hut. The only
other creature comforts were a footlocker and a jungle hammock strung across one corner of the room.

Malik, dressed in jungle fatigues, turned up the flame on
the lantern and stared at the drab olive-green container on
the table. A wave of pure pleasure swept through him as he
unsnapped the nylon straps and the rubber cushioning pad
that allowed the SADM to be carried as a backpack. He
removed the top of the jump container, its aluminum honey-
combed base used to further cushion the weapon. Carefully
he pulled out the nylon bag that aided in removing the
SADM from the tight-fitting compartment. Undoing the
zipper around the large end of the weapon, he slipped off the
bag and laid the SADM on its side on the table.

The size of the SADM was deceptive in light of its tremendous destructive power. Greenish-gold, and only twelve
inches in diameter and eighteen inches in length, it resembled a large .45-caliber bullet. Malik had always marveled at
the simplicity of design and operation of the weapon. The
KGB, unlike the GRU, had managed to compromise and
bribe a former U.S. Army officer who had knowledge of the
weapon and the arming procedures—information that at the
time was considered only of mild interest, due to the lack of
possession of an actual weapon. But filed away in the top-
secret vaults at KGB headquarters, the information had
eventually come to serve a completely unexpected purpose.

The flat end of the SADM contained a combination lock

in the center of the lock-secure cover that permitted access to the internal arming mechanism. Metal ribs led out in a star pattern to locking lugs on the rim, which held the cover in place. At the lower right-hand side of the cover was the external arming switch, used when the SADM was to have a radio receiver attached to it so that it could be detonated by a remote signal. On the upper right-hand side of the lock-secure cover was a small—approximately four inches—half-moon-shaped observation window through which the Arm Well could be observed, determining if the explosive wave generator was in place, which in turn revealed whether the weapon had been armed.

From inside his shirt pocket Malik removed the slip of paper with the combination for the lock. He dialed in the numbers. Beads of perspiration formed on his forehead and ran down the side of his face. It was an uncommon reaction for him, but then it was the first time in his life he had worked with a 4.5-kiloton nuclear weapon. With the last click-stop of the combination lock, he slid the metal ribs away from the locking lugs on the rim and was about to remove the cover when he heard someone outside the hut.

Fritz Graber, an East German who served as chief instructor and Malik's operations officer on the occasion when he used some of the instructors on actual missions, called out, announcing his presence, as he knew Malik insisted on everyone's doing before entering his quarters.

"Nikolai?"

Malik, recognizing Graber's voice, quickly grabbed a poncho liner from the top of his footlocker and covered the weapon before telling Graber to enter.

Graber's eyes fell on the bulge under the poncho liner.

"So, this is the surprise you have been telling me about?" Graber said, his eyes still fixed on the table. "How much longer do you plan on keeping me in suspense?"

"We leave for Mexico City in two days," Malik said. "Then you will know. Has the team you have selected for the mission been thoroughly briefed and rehearsed in their assignments?"

"Yes," Graber said. "To the point of exhaustion. I have chosen the team from Italy. The woman with them is quite steady and reliable. I have made her the team leader."

"She shows great promise," Malik said, recalling the attractive young woman, for whom he had had other ideas had she failed the course. "She is intelligent enough to acknowledge her own fears, yet courageous enough to carry out her assignments despite them."

Graber remembered the reason for his visit and handed Malik a coded radio message. "This just came in for you."

Malik glanced at the identifiers at the top of the message and knew immediately it was from the KGB *rezident* in Managua. He took his codebook from the rucksack propped against his footlocker and deciphered the message, which had been sent using a one-time pad. A cruel smile appeared at the corners of his mouth as he turned to Graber.

"It seems my GRU comrades have discovered the location of our camp," he said. "They are sending in a team of Spetsnaz to eliminate us once and for all."

Graber tensed. "When?"

"Tomorrow at last light. They are parachuting into a drop zone only a few kilometers from here."

"Then we must move the camp immediately," Graber said.

"That would be too disruptive," Malik said calmly. "Our mission is planned for two days from now, and that is when it will be carried out. Moving the camp now would only cause an unacceptable delay."

"But . . . Spetsnaz," Graber said. "They are not to be taken lightly."

"It is only a twelve-man team, Fritz," Malik said. "Twelve men who will be parachuting into a drop zone for which we have the coordinates and the estimated time of arrival. A duck shoot, as the Americans say."

Graber nodded. He knew better than to argue with Malik,

but wanted more information. "It would seem the GRU in Managua would arrange a security team for the drop zone."

"Six men," Malik said, glancing at the message. "It will be an excellent training exercise for some of our students. You and four instructors of your choice will take two of the teams in training. That will give you fifteen men with which to eliminate the GRU team securing the drop zone, then ambush the Spetsnaz and kill them before they ever reach the ground."

Graber thought for a moment, then said, "I'll take the Irish, they have proven the best in the ambush exercises. And the team from Ecuador, they have excelled in patrolling in this terrain."

"Fine," Malik said. He again looked at the decoded message and gave Graber the coordinates of the drop zone. "Make certain your people are properly briefed and familiar with the terrain features. You have until tomorrow afternoon to prepare them."

"They will be ready," Graber said. He cast one last glance at the shape of the object under the poncho liner, then quickly left the hut.

Malik returned to his work. He uncovered the SADM and removed the lock-secure cover to reveal the interior of the weapon. He again marveled at the simplicity of its design. The interior arming face contained two wells, or slots into which fitted the explosive wave generator—the generator's size and configuration reminded Malik of a miniature travel iron. The Safe Well, which was green, was where the explosive wave generator was kept while the weapon was unarmed. Once the explosive wave generator was moved to the red Arm Well, and in contact with the electrical conductor, the weapon was ready to be activated.

Just below the openings for the two wells were the digital clock readouts for the timing mechanism—one readout for hours, the other for minutes—and immediately below them were the clock-setting knobs, which enabled the clocks to be set from zero hours to twenty-four hours and zero minutes to fifty-nine minutes. Below and just to the right of the clock readouts was the internal arming switch for manual detonation, which started the clock generators and, subsequently, the countdown. The arming switch had three positions: Arm—Safe—External Arm. The switch was now in the Safe position.

A simple process of placing the explosive wave generator into the Arm Well, setting the clocks for the desired length of time for detonation, moving the arming switch to Arm, thereby activating the clock generators and starting the countdown, then replacing the lock-secure cover were all that was necessary to ready the weapon for deployment.

Malik had reread the intelligence information gained from the compromised army officer regarding the actual sequence of reactions before the SADM exploded. It was again an uncomplicated, deadly effective chain of events. When the clocks reached zero an electrical current, transmitted through a circuit to the electrical conductor in the Arm Well, ignited the electrical ignition system and fired the shaped charge inside the explosive wave generator. This in turn caused conventional energy to be converted to electrical energy, which was then transmitted through circuits to detonators that set off conventional explosives that initially formed a convex burning wave, which in turn ignited plastic explosives that inverted the convex burning wave into a concave burning wave. The concave burning wave, simultaneously from all sides, reached the vacuum in which the nuclear mass was suspended. Increasing speed in the vacuum, it crushed the nuclear mass uniformly to one third its original size, further increasing the density of the U-235, which was surrounded by a beryllium shell, and in turn crushing the nemo initiator, which was designed upon being crushed to create a huge influx of electrons, causing nuclear fusion and a supercritical mass. The result: a nuclear explosion.

Malik smiled again at the thought of being entrusted with a mission that, if successful, would have such far-ranging repercussions—possibly changing the face of international relations for decades. Carefully replacing the lock-secure cover, he ran his hand over the smooth surface, caressing the weapon before he zipped it back into its nylon bag and returned it to the jump container. He carried the container across the room and placed it gently on the floor beside him before he climbed into his jungle hammock.

He removed his H&K MP5 9mm submachine gun from where it hung by its sling from a nail in the wall and placed it across his chest. He closed his eyes. He was tired, but sleep didn't come, only the night sounds of the jungle and thoughts of the endless details and meticulous planning needed over the next two days.

35

The *Cheetah* slipped silently through the calm sea, leaving a trail of phosphorescent plankton glowing in her foamy wake. She responded like a high-performance sports car to the slightest course correction as Boos expertly sailed her through the maze of small offshore cays. He spotted his first radar-conspicuous target, a large, prominent cay a mile from shore, then, minutes later, his second reference point, an ominous reminder of the vagaries of the sea: an old rusted wreck lay on its side high on a reef due east of his destination. Another half mile and the brilliant moonlight revealed a spur of the reef that marked the entrance to the narrow channel he was looking for.

The full moon and gentle seas were godsends, perfect conditions for navigating through the treacherous uncharted reefs and shoals to the hidden horseshoe-shaped bay where he was to rendezvous with Santana. It had been three years since Boos had used this insertion point, and there was always the possibility that new reefs and shoals had grown. The area was also known for strong, irregular, and unpredictable currents that often reversed themselves for no apparent reason, and numerous live coral heads lurked just beneath the surface. The situation demanded extreme caution and an experienced hand at the helm. Boos was up to the challenge, relaxed, with the calm self-assurance of a professional, but still intensely focused on the perilous task that lay ahead.

The *Cheetah*'s high-visibility factor under the full moon was of little concern in this remote section of coastline, an extremely hazardous area that was never patrolled and was avoided by all but the local fishermen, who knew it well. And once through the channel and inside the bay, the *Cheetah* would be virtually invisible to anyone on the seaward side of the reef.

The sea breaking over the jagged coral reef had been visible for several miles, and now, a few hundred yards from shore, the sound of the breakers informed Boos that he was closing on the narrow deep-water channel between the reef spur and the sandbar. He made a course correction that lined up the *Cheetah* to enter the channel at the proper angle. His eyes began their constant vigil, darting from the fathometer and the compass on the instrument cluster in the steering cockpit to landmarks onshore that told him he was not straying off course. They would use the dinghy for the actual insertion. Reinflated and outfitted with a silent-running electric motor before they had left the offshore cove, it bobbed and swayed in the *Cheetah*'s wake at the end of the towing line.

The *Cheetah* was completely dark. Maria and Gannon were on the bow, keeping watch for local natives night-fishing for turtles in small skiffs and dugout canoes . . . and any other obstructions in their path. Ahead, along the shore, bold promontories and high bluffs rose above the beach. Gannon studied the coastline with the passive night-vision scope Boos had provided. The steeply rising jungle-covered terrain and the inland summits in the background reminded him of the mountains in Laos, misty, mysterious, and full of menace.

He thought of something Joseph Conrad had written, about a shadow line, that nearly imperceptible demarcation between a way of life that is vanishing and another that is inexorably taking its place. He and Boos represented two of the fortunate few who had survived the Special Operations Group's missions in Vietnam and were now nearing the end of their time for great adventures. He accepted that that was as it should be—the torch being passed to the next generation, as it was with Delta Force. But at that very moment he could not help but feel that his past and present and future were one and that whatever he had left to give would be called upon on this mission. He suspected it was to be his swan song, and maybe Boos's, too, the last time they would ever go into battle, in the military sense of the word.

There had always been a part of him that missed the old days, the dancing on the edge, the camaraderie, the inexplicable triumphant feeling of facing death and living to tell of it, of challenging the gods. But just beyond the selective memories of the good times and the pride of beating Charlie at his own game, of daring, suicidal missions accomplished under impossible conditions, lurked the darker memories of the horrors and pain, the loss of friends who died too young, without purpose, for an ungrateful nation. Those were the memories that restored the crucial balance; reminded him that war was not a game, not a macho challenge of will and skill, not a right of passage, but a brutal, vicious conflict with a price to be paid, sacrifices to be made, and that the reason he was here off this lonely stretch of beach in a foreign land, once again to fight in the jungle, was the pain of loss of the one person who had meant the most to him. Death and revenge had brought him here, as the deaths of his friends, the need to exact a price for those who had died in his arms; had kept him going back to Vietnam again and again, not wanting to die himself, but not wanting to desert his buddies in a war that was growing more costly with each passing year.

Gannon's thoughts abruptly returned to the present as Maria shouted an alert to Boos, who steered clear of a large coral head just breaking the surface off the port side only to have to make another quick maneuver to avoid an even larger coral head that Gannon had sighted on the starboard

side. But their luck held again, and Boos's personally annotated charts had proven accurate. They had left the treacherous channel and entered the hidden bay. Boos turned the
boat into the wind. Maria furled in the headsail and let loose
the mainsail, spilling wind and slowing the boat to less than
one knot. Gannon operated the electric windlass, as he had
been previously instructed to do, and lowered the anchor.

With the *Cheetah* secured fifty yards off the small, palm-
fringed crescent of beach Boos remembered well, there was
no time to waste. It was almost midnight. Standing on the
bottom rung of the swim ladder, Boos took the rucksacks
and weapons that Gannon handed him from on deck and
put them in the dinghy, which he had pulled alongside the
boat.

"Let's do it," Boos said.

Gannon and Maria descended the swim ladder and
boarded the dinghy. Maria's task was to come back to the
Cheetah with the dinghy and stand anchor watch until Boos
and Gannon returned. Just in case there were any surprises
waiting onshore, she took the M-203 and a satchel that contained ten extra magazines of ammunition and six 40mm
rounds for the grenade launcher. Boos and Gannon slipped
into their rucksacks and slung their weapons across the tops
of their shoulders in preparation for the landing.

"Don't forget," Boos said to her, "monitor four megs on
the single sideband. I'll keep you posted on what we're into,
and if you run into any problems here, give us a holler. We'll
listen in for five minutes every two hours."

"You take care of yourself," she said. There was a tender-
ness in her voice and eyes as she gave Boos a brief hug. She
turned to Gannon. "You too." Then she added, "I hope you
get the son of a bitch."

Maria unclasped the swing hinge on the electric motor
and lowered the propeller shaft into the sea. She started the
engine, and the dinghy moved slowly but silently toward
shore. A few yards from the beach she skimmed over a tidal
pool brimming with minnows. She pulled the propeller shaft

out of the water and let her forward momentum and a small
swell carry the rubber craft up onto the beach. Transparent
sand crabs whirred into their holes as Gannon and Boos
jumped out and, without a word, shoved the dinghy back
out into the surf, where Maria came about and headed back
to the *Cheetah.*

Thirty or forty yards from the high-tide line, the ground
rose in a craggy 150-foot wall, and Gannon and Boos,
crouching low, immediately ran for cover. The short strip of
jungle directly behind them was the only level ground before
the terrain began its steep incline. It was quiet, except for
the rustling of palm leaves and the sound of a gently foam-
ing surf. Too quiet, Gannon thought as his eyes swept the
area around them.

Suddenly, without a sound, Gannon felt the presence of
someone beside him. His head snapped to his right and he
was staring into the face of a small bronze-skinned man,
who placed a hand on his shoulder, then motioned for him
to follow. Another man, so well camouflaged as to be invisible in the dense undergrowth, appeared at Boos's side and
motioned with his head in the same direction.

The two men guided Boos and Gannon to the base of the
rocky incline. With their eyes adapting to the increased
darkness of the jungle, they had both glimpsed other barely
visible figures posted at perimeter security posts around the
spot where the two men brought them to a halt with a hand
signal. Gannon was impressed with what he had seen so far;
Boos's friend had trained his team well. Though heavily
laden with equipment and weapons, they had slipped
through the dense jungle with an economy of movement,
strictly adhering to noise discipline.

Boos and Gannon surveyed their surroundings. Patches
of bright moonlight shone through breaks in the overhead
canopy and cast strange shadows that made identifying the
perimeter guards they had previously spotted impossible. A
slender, raw-boned man of medium height appeared out of

the darkness. His leathery skin had a few days' growth of
stubbly beard, and his cold, black eyes glistened like polished onyx. There was more of the Castilian than the Carib
in his high-bridged nose and well-defined chin. The small
smile he directed at Boos contrasted sharply with a deeply
suntanned face streaked with camouflage paint. He reached
out and clasped Boos's shoulders with both arms and drew
him close for a hug and a pat on the back.

"Good to see you, Coon Ass," Tony Santana said, his
voice a raspy whisper.

Boos placed both hands on the sides of Santana's head
and kissed him on the forehead. "Don't ever die, you sweet
motherfucker," he said, following with his own embrace.
The words had once been a ritual within the Special Operations Group, spoken with emotion and deep-felt meaning to
friends who were leaving on an operation. They still held the
same power for the two men who now separated and smiled
at each other.

Here was a man Boos knew to be among the best at what
he did, yet he was completely out of place anywhere but
running special operations. It had been the same in Vietnam. There wasn't anyone who wouldn't jump at the chance
to go on an operation with the Sandman, but everyone, except his closest friends, steered clear of him in any situation
that required the usual chickenshit military discipline and
regulations. He was a man who thrived on combat but did
not function well in garrison life. And had it not been for his
constant exemplary performance in combat, Boos believed
that the SEAL would have mustered him out after his first
Vietnam tour of duty. Now, seeing him here in another jungle, dressed in combat gear, Boos couldn't help feeling as
though he was in a time warp, transported back twenty
years to the Naval Advisory Detachment at Da Nang, with
the intervening years having never happened, with Charlie
still out there waiting and Santana ready to continue the
mission.

Santana's attention shifted to Gannon. He stared hard at

the face he had never seen. "Who's your friend?" he asked
Boos, his wary eyes never leaving Gannon.

"Jack Gannon, this is Tony Santana," Boos said.

Santana did not extend his hand; he simply nodded. "You
got history?"

"SOG, CCN," Gannon said, knowing precisely what
Santana meant.

Santana nodded again, acknowledging Gannon's credentials and all they implied in the way of expertise. He, too,
had run a few combined missions out of the Command and
Control North compound with the Special Operations
Group. He paused for a moment, placing the name with
something else he recalled, then said, "Gannon. Special
Forces. Medal of Honor."

"Yeah," Gannon said.

He extended his hand and Gannon shook it. "What do
you want?" Santana was nothing if not direct.

Boos answered the question, telling Santana the purpose
of the rendezvous. When he was finished Boos was confused
by the angry, impatient look on Santana's face.

"And you believe that shit," he said. "Goddamnit, Coon
Ass, you must be losing it in your old age."

"What are you talkin' about?" Boos said.

Santana turned to Gannon, his voice still just above a
whisper, but now hard and demanding.

"You deserve respect for the Medal, and whatever you did
to earn it," he said to Gannon. "But that doesn't give you
the right to insult my intelligence. I know why the fuck
you're here, and if you lie to me again, I'm out of here and
you can go back to wherever it is you came from. My guess
is Company headquarters."

"I don't understand," Gannon said, confused by
Santana's angry outburst.

"I think you do."

"Am I missing something here?" Boos said.

"Your friend's been lying to you," Santana said.

"Hold on, Tony. You're out of line. I've known Jack a lot

of years, we busted bush together. He doesn't lie, especially
not to me, and never about Kate."

"You're former SOG," Santana said to Gannon. "You've
got access to the old-boy network. You could have had one
of your buddies get you into this country any number of
ways. Why this way?"

"The friends I have who are in a position to help are
doing contract work for the Company," Gannon said. "For
some goddamn reason the Company doesn't want me getting anywhere near Malik. I didn't want to put my friends in
a difficult position."

What Gannon had said struck a chord, and Santana fell
silent, his dark eyes expressionless. Then: "Tell me what this
guy who killed your wife looks like."

"Tall . . . about six-two, blond hair, prominent cheekbones, Slavic features," Gannon said. "He's a Russian, a
KGB colonel."

"Are you ADM-trained?" Santana said. He had also been
one of the select few who had been through the Atomic
Demolitions-Munitions training course when on active duty
with the SEAL.

"Yeah. I went through the course in '67. What the hell
has that got to—"

"What does H-912 mean to you?"

Gannon stared at Santana, his mind searching for the
meaning of the vaguely familiar designation. Then he remembered. "H-912 is the designation for the Saydum jump
container."

"Right," Santana said. "And two days ago I saw a man
fitting the description you just gave me coming up the Punta
Gorda River with a jump container with H-912 stenciled on
it. Now, you still telling me you're here because this guy
murdered your wife?"

"That's exactly what I'm telling you," Gannon said.
"And what you just told me explains why the Company's
been trying to throw a net over me ever since Kate's death."

He went on to tell Santana about his problems with the CIA preceding his contacting Boos to get him into Nicaragua.

Santana's mood and tone changed. Gannon was telling the truth. "He's probably taken it to the camp," he told Gannon.

"The terrorist training camp?" Gannon said. "You know where it is?"

"The general area," Santana said. "We've been closing in on it for the past two weeks but haven't nailed it down."

"Have you got a radio that can get a coded message to the Company?" Gannon asked.

"Yeah," Santana said. "One of our radios is a satellite relay with burst transmission capabilities."

"Do you have a Company control officer?"

"That's what he likes to think he is."

"Can you contact him?"

"When I want to."

"Then do it," Gannon said. "Tell them we know what their situation is and we'll do what we can. And tell them to stay the hell out of our way while we're doing it."

Santana grinned. "Is that all, General?"

"Sorry," Gannon said. "It's your show. I just know what a cluster fuck those clowns can put together if they're not kept in check."

"You're all right, Gannon," Santana said with a laugh. "We'll contact them in the morning. Right now I want to put some distance between us and this place in case anyone saw you two insert."

Santana motioned to one of his men who was resting on one knee in the deep shadows. The man disappeared into the jungle to bring in the perimeter guards.

"We don't have any choppers to extract you here, Green Beanie," Santana said good-naturedly to Gannon. "You go out the same way you came in. Think you can still hump that ruck on your back?"

"I'll do my best to keep up," Gannon said with a grin.

With Santana's other eleven men gathered around, Gannon looked them over. They were all dressed in well-worn Special Forces–issue jungle camouflage fatigues, faded and frayed at the cuffs and at the edges of the trousers' bottoms, where they were bloused paratrooper fashion over the tops of their jungle boots. They had on mountain rucksacks and harnesses and web belts laden with ammunition pouches and canteens, and a few wore camouflage boonie hats with the brims cut down, while others had simply tied olive drab bandannas around their foreheads. Gannon looked at the individual faces streaked with expertly applied camouflage paint, and taking into consideration the obvious ethnic differences, was reminded of the fierce, highly dedicated Nungs and Montagnards he had served with in Vietnam.

The mountains and highlands of Nicaragua, part of the Central American *cordillera*, were similar in appearance to the central highlands of Vietnam. They extended south from Honduras almost to the Costa Rican border. To the east of the mountains lay the Caribbean lowlands, a broad swath of savannas, pine forests, swamps, and jungles covering the entire length of Nicaragua's Caribbean coast. The people along the coast were a diverse group: descendants of British pirates and planters, escaped slaves, West Indian laborers who had been brought in to work the plantations, and indigenous Miskito Indians and black Caribs. Four of Santana's men were Miskito Indians, with their typical high cheekbones, copper skin, and raven-black hair. Their villages had been ripped apart by the Sandinistas and the people relocated to keep them from rebel influence—an action that had had the reverse effect, sending many of the young Miskito men to fight with the Contras. The rest of the team was composed of a Creole black, a Rama Indian, with the remainder being Nicaraguan *campesinos,* one a former sergeant in Somoza's National Guard.

All of them, with the exception of the man with the M-60 machine gun who had an M-79 grenade launcher as a backup, carried Soviet-made AK-47 assault rifles as their primary weapons. Gannon took note of the ammunition belt for the M-60. It was coiled inside the man's rucksack, feeding over his shoulder and down to a C-ration can set between the flanges that fed the ammo into the weapon. The C-ration can assured a smooth, even feeding of the ammo, virtually eliminating the possibility of jamming. It was a technique that experienced recon men had used in Vietnam and left no doubt in Gannon's mind that the man had learned it from Santana.

One of the men carried the deadly effective Redeye shoulder-fired antiaircraft missiles for use against the Sandinistas' Soviet-supplied helicopters, and Gannon noticed that six others carried disposable LAW rocket launchers slung over their shoulders across the tops of their rucksacks. Another man carried an RPG-7—a rocket-propelled grenade launcher designed as a tank killer capable of penetrating eleven inches of steel, but with an even more devastating effect when used as an antipersonnel weapon. A short, powerfully built man carried a 60mm mortar; Santana and another man each had a silenced 9mm pistol secured in a shoulder holster. From the sag and bulges in most of their rucksacks, and the satchels carried at their sides, Gannon suspected they were well stocked with claymore mines and an ample supply of rockets, grenades, and ammunition for all of the weapons. He estimated that each man was lugging at least ninety pounds of equipment.

The extent of the team's professionalism and attention to detail was impressive. Even the butt stocks of their weapons were partly covered with old camouflage T-shirt material, and the barrels were wrapped with foliage. Unnatural silhouettes of rucksacks and head gear were broken up by branches and strips of camouflage cloth attached to shoulder and pack straps. And, as Gannon had done aboard the *Cheetah,* Santana and his men had covered all buckles, snap links, anything that could jingle or shine, with a layer of black tape. They were a hard-looking bunch, lean, tough, and seasoned, and the look in their eyes said they weren't exactly happy about having two unknowns tagging along.

When Santana gave the signal to move out the men slipped expertly through the dense jungle and up the steep incline, finding foot- and handholds by the light of the moon or by feel on the sections of the rocky wall cast in shadows. Despite their heavy burdens, they all moved well. The only sounds alien to the jungle night were an occasional scrape of a boot against a rock or the soft whisper of uniform cloth brushing against itself or a bush.

The climb was grueling, almost straight up for more than an hour before they reached the ridgeline and descended the other side. They used an entirely different set of muscles to keep their bodies under control on the almost equally steep descent. Gannon followed a strict physical training regime at Delta Force headquarters and was in excellent shape. Boos, removed from anything remotely resembling the top physical conditioning he had maintained as a SEAL, suffered the most. But his only complaint was an occasional groan and muttered curse.

Santana's team were all locals. Unlike the U.S. troops in Vietnam, who had needed extensive training to fight and survive a jungle war and acclimate to their environment, these men knew the jungle, its moods, its dangers, and how to move through it leaving barely a trace of their passing. They could wield a machete to make a shelter, find the yucca and breadfruit, and hunt the wild boars, turtles, iguanas, and turkeys. They were experts in silently stalking their prey. Santana had merely honed their inherent skills and directed their native talents into finding and killing the enemy without being killed themselves.

Gannon heard Boos breathing heavily and muttering behind him. "You okay?" Gannon whispered over his shoulder just as a patch of soft ground broke loose from under Boos's foot, almost causing him to lose his balance and fall.

"Shut up, Gannon," Boos wheezed. "I'm a SEAL, not some common goddamn ground pounder. We're a little more technically oriented."

"I understand," Gannon whispered. "Putting one foot in

front of the other without falling on your face isn't something that comes easy to you technical types."

"Fuck you."

Gannon stifled a laugh.

Twenty miles off the coast of Nicaragua, Tom Driscoll stood on the bridge of the converted one-hundred-foot radar-equipped Cam Craft Point cruise boat, one of the Honduran Navy's heavily armed patrol vessels used to attack guerrilla-controlled coastal areas. Armed with four .50-caliber machine guns, a 20mm cannon at the bow, and a combination 81mm mortar and .50-caliber machine-gun rig at the stern, the boat was a formidable adversary for any of the Nicaraguan patrol boats.

Driscoll raised his voice above the roar of the three Detroit Diesel engines, each capable of developing 470 horsepower. They were running at near full throttle, carrying the eighty-ton dreadnought through the night at a steady twenty-five knots.

Driscoll glanced at his watch. It was three-thirty in the morning.

"Where are we?" he asked the Honduran naval officer at the wheel.

"We are approaching the Miskito Cays off our starboard side," the captain said. He looked up from the radar scope and gestured to a group of tiny dots barely visible on the moonlit eastern horizon.

The Cam Craft was serving a dual role—as patrol vessel and as a mother ship. She carried extra fuel for the two twenty-seven-foot Piranhas that skimmed along as outriders, held back from their top speed of thirty-five knots to stay abreast of the slower Cam Craft. Each of these bone-jarring speedsters was powered by two 50-horsepower Johnson outboards, radar-equipped, and armed with a .50-caliber machine gun at the bow and an M-60 machine gun port and starboard. Their primary use was as pursuit craft against gunrunning boats or for inland waterway operations, where their shallow draft allowed them to cruise close to shore.

"How much longer?" Driscoll asked the officer at the helm.

"If the weather holds, we will reach the *Cheetah*'s last known location at approximately 1600 hours," the captain said.

Driscoll looked outside the pilothouse at the high-speed outriders skimming along on the surface, his thoughts on Malik and the SADM, and the possibilities of Gannon being able to find him before it was too late.

36

The jungle terrain was straight up and down. Steep mountain trails descended into narrow valleys surrounded by more near-perpendicular slopes. Extinct volcanoes, their peaks reclaimed by the jungle, jutted prominently on the moonlit horizon. The valleys, crisscrossed by animal trails and countless streams, some bridged only by narrow logs less than a foot in diameter, required a delicate balancing act by the column of men burdened with weapons and gear. Twice Santana led them across broad rivers, up to their chests in cool, muddy water, their weapons held high over their heads. And twice they had recrossed shallow streams and walked backward up a hill to throw off any Sandinista trackers. They had spent the last hour walking down the middle of an ankle-deep gravel-bottom stream, and now cut into the jungle again and climbed another steep hill.

There had been only two five-minute rest stops in the past five hours—to monitor the frequency on which Maria was instructed to contact them in the event of danger. Despite his excellent physical conditioning, Gannon was feeling the effects of the punishing forced march through the hot tropical night. At times the climb had been so steep that the boots of the man in front of him were at eye level. He reached deep inside for the necessary stamina to keep up with the steady pace Santana had set, a pace that his men were accustomed to on a daily basis.

Boos held his own, but just barely. He began to feel the pain, first between the shoulder blades, then in the lower back and sides. He shifted his load higher on his back and adjusted the straps on his shoulder harness. The relief was only temporary, but he pressed on, keeping pace, fighting the steep, slippery animal trails and the dense underbrush. His eyes, still alert despite the fatigue, constantly swept the dark green foliage and moonlit patches on his flanks for a glimpse of an uncamouflaged face or the glint of a gun barrel.

There was still no relief for Boos in the descent into the next valley. It took all of his strength and agility to keep from tumbling forward or sliding down the slick, muddy trail. The impulse to reach out and grab a vine for support was instinctively rejected—lessons learned from Vietnam, where two-inch thorns that caused blood poisoning would penetrate the palms of the careless and uninitiated. The lush green beauty held other dangers as well: wait-a-minute vines that entangled legs and equipment, neurotoxic snakes with venom that killed in minutes, and poisonous caterpillars and spiders.

Once they reached the valley floor the terrain again leveled out. Then Santana halted the column and sent one of his men ahead as he signaled the others to take cover. Gannon and Boos dropped into prone positions at the side of the narrow trail and watched; the sudden change in routine snapped them to full alert. The man who had disappeared into the jungle reappeared on the trail ahead and motioned for the column to continue. Gannon and Boos followed, more cautious and wary now, not certain what had precipitated the sudden halt. The reason became clear a few minutes later when the jungle ended at the banks of a broad, smooth-flowing river.

Four of Santana's men pulled two long dugout canoes from beneath a covering of palm leaves and underbrush.

The four men slid the canoes into the water. Inside were paddles and outboard motors equipped with special exhausts for silent running. The motors were quickly clamped to the sterns of the boats.

The native canoes, hewn from huge cedar logs, held seven men each and were much more stable than they had appeared at first glance. Fully loaded, the boats moved swiftly with the current. Mosquitoes filled the air like a fine mist. The damp, fetid fragrance of the jungle carried out over the water as howler monkeys, beginning their predawn patrols, roared their territorial complaints, drowning out the waking chatter of exotic birds and the squawks of parrots as the canoes passed beneath their roosts. Another troop of howlers answered from deep within the jungle. Bats, silhouetted against the night sky, flashed beneath the trees and across the bow of the boats, hunting for insects. The thin gray line of first light began to spread slowly over the horizon.

With a friendly smile, one of the Miskito Indians in the lead canoe silently handed Gannon a bottle of mosquito repellent. Gannon took it gratefully, applied it liberally on his exposed skin, and passed it back to Boos. The pitch-black jungle growth along the shoreline occasionally opened up into stretches of grassland, desolate in the faded-blue light of the now cloud-covered moon. Patches of fog drifted across a bend in the river a short distance ahead; it changed into phantomlike shapes as it reached the opposite shore and drifted through the trees. The night became still again, the only sound the low sputter of muffled exhaust from the outboard motors.

Boos and Gannon, like Santana and his men, sat close together at the gunwales, their weapons trained on alternating sides of the riverbanks. Gannon pointed to some shacks set back from shore and gave the man behind him a questioning look.

"*Amigos.* Friends. Helpers," the man whispered.

Gannon understood why. Nicaragua was flat broke, with an inflation rate accelerating like an ICBM. They exploited their own people while working hand in glove with the Colombian drug cartels to earn hard cash, using their diplomats to smuggle hundreds of millions of dollars' worth of narcotics into the United States. They were arrogant ideologues who assumed they were above the law. Their machinations and complete disdain for their people, Gannon believed, would make Augusto Sandino roll over in his grave if he knew how they had manipulated his beliefs and debased his name in the name of the people. He doubted that the Sandinistas would ever completely eradicate the Contra movement unless drastic changes were made that gave the people a sense of worth and hope for a better life.

The farther downstream the canoes traveled, the narrower the river became. Tops of trees on opposite banks intertwined almost two hundred feet overhead and formed a dense canopy that extinguished the moonlight and blocked out the stars. Trees draped with moss and lichen, supporting secondary growths of ferns and orchids, lined the shore. Overhanging limbs trailed braided vines into the water, and they brushed lightly across the men in the canoes.

Gannon was startled for a brief second as a turtle plopped off a log, followed by a bullfrog bat that skimmed the water, missed its prey, and swooped low over the canoe and back up into a tree whose decaying bark, used by the peasants to decorate their Christmas trees, cast an eerie blue-white glow along the edge of the forest. Boos was fascinated with what appeared to be hundreds of pin-dot lights flickering on and off just ahead. A few moments later they were surrounded by them—a dense swarm of fireflies that dispersed and regrouped after the canoes had passed.

The thin gray line on the horizon grew as the predawn light spread quickly across the eastern sky. The man steering the lead canoe slowed down. On reaching a spot where the river broadened at the confluence of two small feeder streams, he cut the motor. The man in the second canoe did the same. Four men in each canoe took up paddles and the journey continued at a slower pace.

The Miskito Indian who had given Gannon the insect repellent leaned back and whispered, *"Piris."*

"Piris?" Gannon said.

"It's short for *piricuaco*," Boos said, leaning forward. "It's what they call the Sandinistas. Roughly translated, it means 'rabid dog' or 'beggar dog.' There must be an outpost around here."

The two canoes moved closer to shore. No one paddled now; they drifted silently under overhanging branches. Onshore the jungle was quiet, now darker than the predawn sky. The sounds of cicadas and katydids rose to a deafening crescendo as Gannon and Boos followed the lead of the other men, bending over and lowering their silhouettes as they passed by a stretch of open grassland that reached to the river's edge.

A few hundred yards farther and the men began to paddle again. The dawn light was nearly upon them and the jungle seemed to soak up the early-morning mist. A low-lying fog shrouded the shoreline and scudding clouds obscured the mountain peaks. They were deep in the rain forest of southern Nicaragua, and as the fog dissipated and the clouds thinned out, the pinkish morning light began to spread over the serene beauty of the emerald landscape.

The Miskito Indian in the lead canoe swung the long, narrow craft into shore; the second canoe followed immediately. Santana and his men quickly disembarked. Gannon and Boos helped pull the boats out of the water and camouflage them in the dense underbrush. Santana took the point and led the column through a particularly dense section of jungle to a narrow, deeply rutted trail that switchbacked up the face of yet another mountain. Near the ridgeline Santana halted the column and signaled to Gannon, Boos, and his radioman to come forward. The four men knelt off to the side of the trail while the rest of the team took up defensive positions to secure the area.

"We'll give the Company boys a shout," Santana said as he removed a small satellite radio from the rucksack of his radioman. He set up and oriented the small circular antenna, then coupled it to the state-of-the-art radio, approximately the size of a dictionary. He then took a whisper microphone that fitted over his mouth like an oxygenmask, plugged the cable end into the radio, and began to record his message in clear text. ·

"Sandman to Nighthawk," he said, his voice inaudible beyond three feet of where he knelt. "Coon Ass and friend are with me. Aware of your delicate situation. We are in the process of trying to locate and recover your package. Stay out of area of operations until further notice. Will keep you advised."

Santana pressed a button on the radio to scramble the message. Then another button that burst transmitted it up to a satellite and back down to a ground station in Honduras. The transmission of the recorded message sounded much like a tape recorder being played back at extremely high speed for a split second.

Santana disassembled the radio and returned it to the radioman's rucksack. He again took the point and, in the growing light of the morning sun, continued on the trail at the same demanding pace he had set earlier.

"Stay out of the area of operations?" Phil Travis, the local station chief said to Driscoll. He was reading the message that had been relayed from the communication room at the embassy in Honduras to the bridge of the Cam Craft as it continued south off the coast of Nicaragua. "Who the hell do they think they are, telling us to stay out of their way?" he shouted above the roar of the diesel engines.

Driscoll chuckled and shook his head. "They're the same guys we would have sent in to do the job had we had the choice," he said. "We let them run with it. They're the best chance we have right now, probably the only chance."

"And what is 'the package' Santana's talking about?"

Travis said, more than a little put out that Driscoll had not yet confided in him on the purpose of the mission.

"You're not cleared for that information," Driscoll said. "If they're successful, you'll know soon enough. If they fail, the whole goddamn world will know."

37

Following cattle paths that laced the steep-sided hills, Santana led the team deeper into the jungle. He gave a wide berth to isolated farms and villages known to be patrolled by the Sandinistas. It was late in the afternoon, and the hazy orange sun slipped slowly behind the sharp edges of the mountains on the western horizon as he halted the team in heavy underbrush, just below a ridgeline that commanded the terrain around them. Seen from this vantage point, the surrounding wilderness had a breathtaking beauty. Slow-moving clouds drifted above the hills and the long, deep valleys that stretched for miles in a patchwork of fields and forests in infinite shades of green.

A rusted, burned-out Soviet-built reconnaissance vehicle, disabled by Santana's men months ago, sat at the edge of a distant clearing in the valley immediately below them. Dark green groves of coffee bushes overflowed with ripe red berries and crowded the slopes of the ridges on the far side of the valley, with banana trees scattered along the lower elevations, where a small cluster of scraggly cattle enclosed by a crude fence grazed a grassy meadow on the perimeter of one of the small, nameless villages hacked from the jungle by *campesinos*.

There were times when the local and migrant workers refused to work in what they considered a combat zone, and militiamen, government employees, and "volunteers" from the Sandinista Front's political apparatus had to harvest the coffee crop. Although few, if any, had military training, they carried weapons with them in the groves. They were little more than cannon fodder against Santana and his men, who harassed and ambushed them in successful efforts to further ruin a failing economy by disrupting a harvest that earned the Marxist government vital Western currency.

Temperature fluctuations were minimal, and the humidity in the valleys was oppressive. A steamy heat, heavy with the fetid odor of the jungle, carried up the side of the mountain and brought back a rush of memories to Gannon as he sat on the ground, his back propped against a tree. Boos dropped to his knees beside him, clearly exhausted from the long, hard trek, which had begun at midnight. Their clothing was soaked with perspiration and still damp from the frequent stream crossings. It chafed in all the wrong places. The ocean breezes that made conditions tolerable along the coastline did not penetrate the inland jungle. In addition to the intense radiant heat of the near-equatorial sun, the team had to deal with a high thermal load, unable to lose body heat through evaporation in the high humidity. Santana and his men were acclimatized, but Gannon and Boos were ready to drop.

The well-disciplined team sat in the shadows of trees, eating beans and rice, canned tuna, and sucking on pieces of sugarcane they had hacked from a deserted field earlier. Immediately after finishing the nourishing, if sparse, meal, they began to field-strip and meticulously clean their weapons; some used toothbrushes in the process.

"Great to be back in harness," Boos said with a wry smile. "Time and distance have a way of making us forget the unpleasant side of this shit, ya know?" He adjusted the straps on his harness and leaned back against a tree. "Christ, what I wouldn't give for a green hornet," he added, referring to the powerful amphetamine capsules the recon teams had been issued in Vietnam to keep them awake for days at a time while on missions.

"Where's your buddy taking us?" Gannon said. He looked to where Santana knelt on one knee, studying a map and talking with one of his men.

"He says we're in the general area of the camp now," Boos said. "That guy he's talking to, Tigrillo—means 'Little Tiger'—he knows this area better than anyone."

Gannon stared at the stolid mahogany face of the young man with Santana. He was leaning over the map spread out on the ground, his black, almond-shaped eyes, pure Indio and impenetrable, darting from the map to the terrain features across the valley.

"The Sandman says he's the best point man and night stalker he's ever worked with," Boos said. "He's never seen unless he wants to be."

Claudio, a twenty-four-year-old kid with a wispy beard and a three-inch scar on his cheek, approached Gannon and Boos and sat down beside them. He was a former *campesino* whose family had been run off their land by the Sandinistas. He had long black hair and lively intelligent eyes. He smiled and a gold-capped front tooth glistened. He was in the process of wolfing down a ration of rice and beans. From his rucksack he produced two bananas that he had picked along the way. He handed one to both Gannon and Boos. They were eagerly accepted.

"I could tell this was not your first time in the jungle," he said to Gannon and Boos. "You served in Vietnam with Santana."

Boos and Gannon nodded.

"Snake said you got the Medal of Honor," Claudio said to Gannon, repeating what his teammate had told him. Many of the Contras adopted pseudonyms such as Snake and Little Tiger to protect their families from retaliation if it became known that they were fighting against the Sandinistas.

"That was then," Gannon said, uncomfortable, as always,

when the subject of the Medal was brought up. "This is now."

Claudio grinned. "No, Señor Gannon. That is forever." He noticed that Boos and Gannon had finished their bananas and handed them each an orange, more of his booty picked along the route of march.

Snake, curious about the newcomers, came over and sat beside Claudio. With the exception of Santana, Snake was the oldest man on the team. He had been a Sandinista with the rank of lieutenant in the infamous Special Destiny Company—his mission to infiltrate the Contras and disrupt their infrastructure through assassination and sabotage. He had been trained in subversive techniques in Nicaragua by Argentine *montoneros* terrorists, but he had defected to the Contras before completing his first mission. Although distrusted by most of the Contra leaders, Santana immediately recognized his unusual abilities and recruited him for his team.

Small and wiry, with sharp features, Snake had hard eyes that were a strange golden color, sensitive to the sun and penetrating in the dark, which suggested to Gannon how he had earned his nickname. Gannon also noticed Snake's skin. Like Claudio's and the rest of the team, it bore the same telltale signs—signs of men who had been living in the jungle for extended periods. Their faces were blotched by fungus infections, their hands and forearms covered with scratches and welts from the fleas, chiggers, and mosquitoes that attacked them daily. Gannon saw himself, twenty years ago.

Gannon noticed Santana and Tigrillo rise and walk together along the military crest of the ridge. Santana talked and pointed in the direction of the dense jungle at the far end of the valley below. Tigrillo nodded, then disappeared into the underbrush.

Santana gave the signal to prepare to move out. The copper-orange glow of the setting sun disappeared as evening shadows lengthened across the floor of the valley. Clouds that threatened rain appeared in the east. The team descended the steep slope and moved along an animal track in a staggered column. They stayed inside the edge of the jungle as they passed an abandoned farm with a grove of ripe oranges. The country they were moving through now was contested, a combat zone, and slowly becoming uninhabited.

Claudio, walking immediately in front of Gannon, stopped dead in his tracks, almost causing Gannon to trip over him. With a lightning-quick strike of his machete, Claudio cut off the head of a deadly pit viper. Gannon glanced at the snake's still-writhing body as he stepped over it.

Three miles from where Santana's team skirted the abandoned farm, Malik's second-in-command, Fritz Graber, and the four other men he had handpicked, two Palestinians and two of his East German comrades, led the column of Irish and Ecuadorian terrorist trainees along a jungle trail. They were eager, Graber thought. Maybe too eager. The Irish whispered to each other as they moved through the thick underbrush. The five-man team from Ecuador maintained silence, their eyes alert for impending danger. They were far more professional and less cocky than their Irish counterparts. Graber stopped to check his map and the terrain features, then angled off onto a small animal trail that, according to the map, would lead them directly to the clearing the Spetsnaz team had chosen as a drop zone.

Tigrillo had heard the column approaching long before they were within his range of vision. He took cover at the side of the trail and waited until they had passed, then shadowed them from a distance. The team all wore olive drab fatigues and baseball-style hats, as opposed to Sandinista uniforms, and Tigrillo watched as their apparent leader, a tall, dark-haired Yanqui, brought them to a halt, then went forward with two other men, Arabs, Tigrillo guessed, and began scanning the perimeter of the clearing.

Tigrillo soon spotted the object of their search. Scattered

along the edge of the clearing he counted six men, all wearing Sandinista uniforms and armed with assault rifles. Their shoulder patches identified them as a special unit attached to the Ministry of the Interior. One man had a flashlight with a red filter clipped to his harness. They were all resting, unconcerned. They sat on the ground, their eyes on the sky.

Tigrillo's curiosity was further aroused as he watched the tall, dark-haired Yanqui and the Arabs return and point out the positions of the six men at the edge of the clearing to two other men, who seemed to be older and more comfortable with their weapons and equipment than the others. The five men, each carrying H&K MP5 submachine guns fitted with sound suppressors, moved swiftly into position. Within a matter of moments Tigrillo heard the barely audible bolt clatter from six individual bursts. The men at the edge of the clearing fell over dead.

Tigrillo watched in total confusion as the Yanqui leader and the other four men hid the bodies in the dense underbrush and returned to direct the ten men they obviously commanded into ambush positions around the clearing. Tigrillo shook his head in disbelief. Surely this ambush was not being set up for them? These men could not possibly expect the Sandman to lead his team across an open clearing with nothing but knee-high grass for cover? And who were these men? And who were the six Sandinistas they had killed and what were they doing here? No other Contra units were operating in the area. Of that he was certain. He continued to observe, counting a total of fifteen well-armed men. Five of them were Latinos, he was sure, and the other ten were definitely not. The leader and the two Arabs he had seen before, but couldn't remember where. Then it came to him: they had been on the supply boat that Santana had, for some reason he had never explained, chosen not to ambush.

Tigrillo silently withdrew from his position just behind two of the Latinos and moved away from the area. He headed quickly back to the trail on which he knew Santana was approaching with the rest of the team.

38

Santana suddenly stopped in mid-step. He stood stock-still, then dropped to one knee and halted the column behind him by raising his hand; his fist was tightly clenched at first, then his open hand rotated in a circling motion. Gannon, Boos, and the rest of the team immediately crouched low and disappeared into the underbrush on both sides of the trail. They took defensive positions in the dense cover, their weapons trained up ahead. Santana's attention was on the thick tangle of vines and underbrush near a bend in the trail. Tigrillo appeared out of the jungle and Santana relaxed. He signaled again, this time for everyone to gather around as Tigrillo reported what he had seen during his reconnaissance patrol.

"If we move quickly, we can set up our own ambush and take them out before they know what hit them," Santana said when Tigrillo had finished.

"No," Gannon said. "Let's move in close and see what they're up to. It sounds like they're securing a drop zone. Think about it," he said to Santana. "Nothing else makes any sense."

Santana stared at Gannon, then slowly nodded his head. "Travis, the station chief at Tegucigalpa," he said. "I'll bet that moron fuck is sending in some of his paramilitary people."

Gannon disagreed. "The six men Tigrillo saw the others kill were Sandinistas, probably sent to secure the DZ. They sure as hell aren't working for the Company."

"Then who?" Santana said.

"Maybe the GRU," Gannon said. He recalled what he had learned at the Delta Force headquarters briefing after the incident in Paris and what General Max had told him after his meeting with the GRU officer.

"They want Malik as badly as the Company does." He went on to explain what General Max had told him about the probability of the Soviets wanting to stop Malik for their own reasons, which now made sense in view of the SADM if the KGB and the GRU were involved in some sort of arcane power struggle.

"We'll try it your way," Santana said. "And if Tigrillo is right about recognizing three of them from the supply boat we saw the Russian on, then the probabilities are they're from the terrorist training camp and we can follow them right to it."

"Or we can snatch one of them," Boos said. "Make him tell us where the camp is."

"Whatever works," Santana said.

"Boos is right. We grab one of them," Gannon said. "Even if they are from the camp, if we tried to follow them, they could lead us right into a Sandinista outpost, or they may damn well have road guards out that we'd have to engage and give away our position."

"All right," Santana said, and got to his feet. "We'll see what they're up to and take a prisoner if the opportunity presents itself."

Santana took out a terrain map and Tigrillo indicated the location of the clearing. He scraped away the debris on the ground and drew a crude sketch of the approximate positions of the fifteen men he had seen. Santana diagramed the approach the team would take to the clearing, assigned each man an observation post, and selected a rendezvous point if they got separated.

The team came alive, expectant, ready for whatever it was
that lay ahead. Gannon felt the soreness and stiffness of the
arduous day leave his body as if by the touch of some magic
hand. His senses were heightened, his mind alert and focused. He was close now, he could feel it.

Tigrillo took the point. At first he moved quickly along a
narrow, rutted animal track. As they neared the clearing he
paused every ten yards to stop and listen before signaling the
team to continue. With the clearing in sight, the team dispersed to their assigned positions. They advanced cautiously
through the jungle to within twenty yards of the unsuspecting men set up in an L-shaped ambush in one corner of the
drop zone. Gannon and Boos stayed together and settled
into the brush directly behind the short end of the L. Gannon's eyes were fixed on the evening sky, waiting for what
he knew would be the inevitable blossoming of parachutes.

The last of the evening light was beginning to fade. From
an altitude of eight thousand feet the terrain below looked
like a solid blue-green mass of interwoven triple-canopy jungle. The drop-zone clearing was nowhere in sight. Vasili
Fomenko descended to earth at a speed in excess of 130
miles an hour. His body was in the tracking position—head
up, arms at his sides, his legs stretched out and spread
shoulder width apart—an airfoil configuration that gave
him forward momentum as he tracked thirty-five degrees
horizontal to the ground. The force of the rushing air tore at
his jump suit and stretched the exposed skin on his face.

The Soviet AN-30 reconnaissance aircraft, disguised as an
Aeroflot commercial airplane, had taken off from the Cuban
air base at San Antonio de los Baños and climbed to thirty
thousand feet. It had stayed within the commercial airline
corridors except for a slight detour to the release point for
the drop. Two miles off the coast of Nicaragua the twelve-
man Spetsnaz team, equipped with individual oxygen bail-
out bottles, exited the aircraft and began the exhilarating

free-fall part of the High-Altitude–Low-Opening parachute jump.

Fomenko, with the rest of his team stacked at intervals above him, tracked over two miles of open water. Upon reaching the coastline he began to scan the ground for reference points. He could clearly see the junction where the two rivers converged and the ridgelines that formed a V a few kilometers to the west, but not the clearing. His wrist altimeter confirmed that he was now twenty-five hundred feet from the ground. He changed his body position, pulling his arms forward and arching his back into a full spread-eagle— a maneuver that caused him to flare from the tracking position, stopped his forward momentum, and slowed his vertical rate of descent. He grabbed the D-ring on his harness, pulled his rip cord, and seconds later felt a powerful force jolt him upright as his canopy unraveled and filled with air. As he unsnapped his oxygen mask and shoved his goggles up onto his helmet, he took hold of the steering toggles and over his shoulder watched eleven other parachutes pop open in rapid succession.

Fifteen hundred feet from the ground, Fomenko breathed a sigh of relief. As he crossed over a series of low ridges, he spotted the clearing in a bowl-like, remote mountain valley surrounded by jungle-covered hills. The drop zone was approximately one hundred yards long and half again as wide, an easy target for experienced parachutists such as Fomenko and his men. Swinging gently beneath the risers, Fomenko's eyes searched and found the bright orange fluorescent panel, laid out in the shape of an arrow, indicating the direction of the wind.

As the twelve canopies approached the ridge Gannon recognized the jumpsuit camouflage pattern of the Soviet Spetsnaz units. Their oxygen masks hung off to one side of their helmets as, one after the other, they turned into the wind and began a controlled descent into the clearing. Gannon watched with a lump in his throat. It was every airborne soldier's nightmare, landing in a drop zone believed to be secure while an ambush awaited. Russians or not, it was no way for a soldier to die.

He watched as the leader pulled down on both steering toggles of the highly maneuverable ram-air parachute, almost stalling the canopy in preparation for a near-perfect stand-up landing. With his boots only inches from the ground, the quiet, peaceful evening erupted into ear-shattering bursts of automatic weapons fire. From among the unmistakable reports of AK-47s, Gannon picked out the distinctive sound of a Type-56 Chinese-made light machine gun.

The leader was riddled with bullets and crumpled to the ground. His men, startled by the sudden turn of events, hung helplessly below their canopies. The fire from the tree line tore into their bodies as they tried to defend themselves by unslinging the weapons strapped to their sides. But from above the clearing it was impossible to see muzzle flashes as the gunfire continued to crack in rapid bursts from within the dense jungle. Even if the men made it to the ground safely, Gannon realized, they were trapped in a large, open killing zone with nothing but knee-high grass for cover. Within thirty seconds from the time the ambush was sprung, twelve men died, eleven of them hanging limp in their harnesses as they collided with the ground.

As the fifteen-man ambush team withdrew from their positions and regrouped, Gannon watched the eight men who were obviously not Latins or Arabs. Malik was not among them. He heard the clearly recognizable sound of an Irish brogue when five of the men loudly congratulated each other on the slaughter of the Spetsnaz team. Gannon nudged Boos. One of the Irishmen left the others and walked toward the Sandinista soldiers' bodies, stacked like cordwood nearby. Boos nodded his understanding. A souvenir hunter.

Unaware that one of the team was lagging behind, the leader of the ambush formed the men into a column and in the pale evening light moved down a trail away from the clearing. Gannon noticed the awkward duck-walk peculiar to all Cuban-trained combat troops. They pivoted their entire bodies from side to side, their weapons ready to fire.

The lone Irishman knelt beside the dead bodies and tore the unit insignias off two of their uniforms. He stuffed them into a pocket of his fatigue jacket and set out on the trail to close the distance between him and his teammates. He got no more than a few steps before Gannon's arm swept out of a thicket of twisted vines and heavy brush. He cupped a hand over the Irishman's mouth and swiftly pulled him out of sight. The only sound had been the rustle of the brush, which had gone completely unnoticed by the retreating team, now nearly out of sight. The startled man ceased struggling when he felt the razor-sharp edge of cold steel on his neck.

"Make a sound and I'll slit your throat," Gannon whispered into his ear.

Boos forced the frightened man's mouth open and stuffed in a rag, which he secured with a bandanna tied around his head. With the prisoner's hands bound behind his back, Gannon marched him away from the clearing with the barrel of his CAR-15 planted firmly at the base of his skull.

39

Gannon shoved the Irishman to the ground as the team stopped at the base of a hill where the terrain was flat and covered with thick brush. A golden patchwork of maize and tobacco fields spread outward across a valley and halfway up the surrounding hills to the edge of the jungle. Directly across from them was the run-down farm of a *campesino* who was part of Santana's intelligence network.

Santana removed the binoculars from his rucksack and studied the scene around the farm. He watched for anything out of the ordinary, and in particular for the placement of a hoe with a broken handle by the fence gate near the barn—a signal that would warn him it was not safe to approach. The hoe was not in sight.

The *campesino* who worked the farm had once produced a substantial tobacco crop, only to have it confiscated by Sandinista officials, who issued him a ration card with which to draw food from a government-controlled storehouse that seldom provided the basic necessities without at least a few weeks wait. His tobacco was sent to the Soviet Union, along with sugarcane and coffee, to pay for weapons. Like most of the *campesinos,* he had been an easy recruit to the Contra cause.

Santana observed him in the failing light: he was tilling a small vegetable garden beside an unpainted, dilapidated shack that housed him and his family. The shack, made of scraps of wood and tin, was built on stilts for protection against the flash floods that came with the rainy season. Ragged, faded clothes hung from a line strung across one end of a rickety thatched-roof porch, while the man's wife lay in a hammock made of corn sacks that was stretched across the opposite end. She was watching two naked children play with a deflated ball in the dusty patch of ground in front of the shack. Pigs roamed the yard, where raw sewage ran in rivulets down the hill from the outhouse.

Behind him Santana heard and then saw the approach of the six men he had left behind to strip the dead Sandinistas and the Spetsnaz team of their weapons and equipment. The men were loaded down with assault rifles, ammunition pouches, silenced pistols, spring-blade knives, hand grenades, night-vision optics, and everything of military value the soldiers had carried, including their rucksacks and personal effects.

With the return of the six men, Santana left his place of concealment. He warily approached the farm along a hedgerow between two fields. Gannon followed, keeping the prisoner under close guard at his side, while Boos and the rest of the team stayed ten yards apart, their weapons covering all points of the compass as they crossed the open area. Three emaciated, mangy dogs ran from beneath the shack and stopped at the edge of the field, barking at the sight of the strangers. The *campesino* looked up from his work and, recognizing Santana, came to greet him. The dogs gathered around, jumping and twirling in hopes of getting a few scraps of food.

Despite his outward appearance, there was a quiet dignity in the scrawny *campesino*'s bearing. His trousers were torn and tattered, buttons were missing from his faded, almost threadbare shirt, but he held himself erect and looked directly into Santana's eyes as he spoke. His wife, dressed in a patched and stained shapeless shift, got out of the hammock and watched; she stood silently for a few minutes while her

husband talked to Santana and led him toward a long tobacco barn with slatted walls.

Her eyes were fixed on the Yanqui, who was bound and
gagged. As Santana led the team past the shack the naked
little girl stopped kicking the deflated ball and smiled at
Gannon, revealing the black edges of decaying teeth.

Gannon glanced at the silent mother's deformed feet, then
at her stoic expression.

"Piris," Snake said as he noticed Gannon's questioning
gaze. "They pulled out her toenails, then smashed her feet
with rifle butts. She told them nothing."

Once inside the tobacco barn, the *campesino* lighted two
kerosene lamps hanging from the rafters. He nodded to
Santana and silently left.

Santana grabbed the Irishman, pulled the gag from his
mouth, and dragged him by the scruff of his neck to an old
wooden chair, forcefully shoving him into a sitting position

"What's your name?" he asked the Irishman, who was
now collected enough to flash a cocky grin.

"Gallagher," he said. "And that's all the information
you'll be gettin' from me."

Santana struck him with a vicious backhanded blow that
brought tears to Gallagher's eyes and a trickle of blood from
the corner of his mouth. He still managed a confident smirk

"I want the location of the training camp your Russian
friends set up for you and your buddies."

Gallagher grinned and said nothing.

Santana drove a fist solidly into Gallagher's stomach, elic-
iting a loud grunt and sudden expulsion of air. The Irishman
gasped for breath, but again said nothing.

"Where's the camp?" Santana repeated as he delivered
another powerful blow. This time to the man's kidney.

Gallagher doubled up and groaned in pain, but still remained silent.

Gannon sat on his heels in a corner of the barn, studying
the Irishman's face. In his twenties, tall and handsome, with

deep blue eyes and a strong chin. A ladies' man, Gannon guessed.

Santana approached Gannon and squatted down beside him.

"This guy presents a problem, Gannon," Santana said in a low voice. "If I had a hand generator and the better part of a day, with a little electrical interrogation I could make him tell us everything he knows and then some. But this clown's smart enough to know he'll go unconscious from the beatings soon enough or get to the point where the pain doesn't make any difference. I've heard they teach them that shit at the camp."

Gannon continued to stare at Gallagher. The Irishman was grinning again, sure of himself, confident he could take whatever was coming next. Gannon's eyes hardened into a steady glare. The terrible image of Kate's battered, swollen face as she lay on the stainless-steel table in the morgue elevator kept superimposing itself over the face of the man in the chair.

"Strip him to his shorts," Gannon said coldly, and got slowly to his feet. "Then tie his hands and legs to the chair."

Santana ordered Snake and Claudio to strip and bind the Irishman securely to the chair. Gallagher's eyes were fixed on Gannon as he walked toward him.

"Gannon is it?" Gallagher said. "Then it's Irish you are. One of us."

Gannon's voice was deadly calm. "No," he said. "I'm an American. My grandparents came from County Monaghan, but they weren't cowardly sneaks and murderers like your lot."

"The 'troubles' weren't of our makin', Mr. Gannon. The cause is just," Gallagher said.

"The cause is an excuse for simpleminded psychopaths who enjoy killing innocent people in the name of the 'old sod,' " Gannon said. He remained silent for a moment, then added, "Are you familiar with the term O.B.E.?"

Gallagher shook his head. "Can't say that I am."

"It means 'Overtaken by Events,' " Gannon went on, his voice still flat, his eyes hard and penetrating. "It's a military term applied to intelligence information that will be useless after a certain period of time."

"You'll not be gettin' any information from me, Mr. Gannon, O.B.E. or not."

"Your pals are going to realize you're missing, if they haven't already," Gannon said. "They'll send a patrol back to the ambush site to look for you. They might even think you were hit by a stray round. But they're going to find that the Russians and the Sandinistas have been stripped of their gear, and they'll put two and two together and realize what's happened. So," Gannon said, looking at his watch, "in about another two hours the information concerning the location of your camp will be O.B.E. They'll relocate the minute the patrol gets back and reports what they've found."

"Two hours or two days, Mr. Gannon," Gallagher said. "The results will be the same. I have nothin' to tell ya."

Gannon's face smiled but his eyes didn't. The chilling effect was not lost on the Irishman. It caused his cocky grin to lose some of its believability.

"You a tough guy, Gallagher?" Gannon said.

"Tough enough."

Gannon smiled the nonsmile again and nodded. He turned and walked over to where Snake and Tigrillo were carrying the confiscated Russian and Sandinista weapons and equipment down through a trapdoor into a hidden storage room excavated from beneath the floor of the barn.

"Do you have any time fuse?" Gannon asked Snake, who quickly confirmed that he did. "And I'll need two nonelectric blasting caps, some army green tape, and an igniter for the fuse."

"No igniter," Snake said. "Broke."

"Then get me a handful of stick matches."

Snake nodded and disappeared into the subterranean cavern.

Gannon walked over to Santana and said, "Just stand back and let me do this without interruption."

The look on Gannon's face gave even Santana pause. "What do you have in mind?"

"We've all got a darkness inside us," Gannon said in an icy monotone. "I thought I'd buried mine for good after 'Nam."

Without any further explanation Gannon walked over and stood in front of Gallagher. Picking up the gag that had been used previously, he roughly forced open Gallagher's mouth and stuffed it inside. Snake arrived with the items Gannon had asked for and put them on the floor beside him, his curious golden eyes staring at Gannon's calm but menacing expression as he stood back to watch what the hard-looking Yanqui was up to.

Gannon cut a strip from the roll of army green tape and stretched it across Gallagher's mouth to hold the gag in place. From the spool of time fuse he cut off a two-foot length, which, along with one of the nonelectric blasting caps and three stick matches, he took to a wooden work-bench set against the far wall of the barn.

All eyes were on Gannon as he tapped a small amount of black powder from one end of the cut fuse and broke off two match heads, packing them inside the fuse. Crimping the other end of the fuse to the nonelectric blasting cap, he taped the cap to the three-inch-thick leg of the bench. With the third match he lighted the match heads inside the fuse, thereby providing enough concentrated heat to start the fuse without the use of an igniter. He stood back and watched the sweep hand on his watch. Exactly twenty seconds later the blasting cap exploded, blowing the thick leg off the workbench as though it were a twig.

He walked back over to Gallagher. "The fuse burns at the rate of one foot every ten seconds. Put it to memory. That little piece of information is going to become very important to you."

Gallagher stared at the shattered bench leg, signs of the brave front draining from his once-defiant Irish eyes.

Gannon began unraveling the spool of quarter-inch-thick time fuse. He wrapped it in evenly spaced coils, four to five inches apart, around Gallagher's body. He started at his right ankle, continued up around his thigh, around the back of the chair to his right wrist and arm, up and around his neck, and down his left arm and leg. At Gallagher's left ankle Gannon measured out another four feet of fuse, cut it from the spool, and crimped the other nonelectric blasting cap to the end. Dropping to one knee in front of the chair, he taped the blasting cap to the seat of the chair directly beneath the Irishman's genitals.

Gannon stood up and faced the man, whose full attention he now had. "There's eighteen feet of time fuse wrapped around your body. At a burn speed of ten seconds per foot, that gives you exactly three minutes from the time I light the fuse until you've got a serious problem on your hands."

A muffled, unintelligible protest came from Gallagher's mouth; his eyes were now terror-stricken.

"Believe me," Gannon said without emotion, "they will be the longest, most painful three minutes of your young life."

Pointing to Claudio, he added, "That man's the team medic. He'll stop your bleeding and I'll personally make sure you get to a hospital. The bottom line being, Mr. Gallagher, you will live a long, uneventful life looking like an Irish zebra without any balls and with a prosthesis between your legs that's good only for taking a piss."

Another muffled sound, this time longer in duration, came through the tape covering Gallagher's mouth. His face was red with rage, the veins in his head throbbing as he struggled to make his epithets understood.

Gannon got the terrain map from Santana and spread it out on the floor at Gallagher's feet. "It's your call, tough guy. I personally don't care one way or the other. I'll find your camp sooner or later. But for you, my Provo friend, it's now or never. Just nod your head when you're ready to give me what I want."

Gannon again dropped to one knee in front of the chair. He purposely prolonged the process of packing the match heads into the end of the fuse that began at Gallagher's right ankle. He struck a match, paused, then brought it close to the fuse. "Say when, tough guy."

The match heads inside the fuse flared and the powder ignited and burned. Gallagher's entire body stiffened and his back arched in a violent spastic motion that rocked the chair backward to the point where Gannon had to steady it to keep it from falling over. The green rubberized covering on the exterior of the fuse bubbled from the intense heat and a gray-white plume of smoke rose in a spiral. Gallagher's leg tightened and twitched in pain. The smell of smoke from the powder mixed with that of burning flesh. The fuse burned through all three layers of skin and partway into the underlying tissue as it worked its way around the shin and on toward the knee.

Gallagher's muffled screams shook his entire body. His eyes watered and his face was distorted from the strain of attempting to overcome the intense pain. Gannon was close enough to hear the Irishman gnash his teeth in an attempt to take his mind off the agony of his tortured flesh.

Snake's fear-filled eyes looked at Santana, who seemed mesmerized by what he was watching. Santana, while with the Phoenix Program, had seen any number of interrogations in the small isolated buildings to be found inside the Embassy House compounds in the provinces of South Vietnam. Some techniques had been more brutal and vicious, but he had never seen any with such prolonged, calculated torment or as diabolical and psychologically terrifying. The entire team was transfixed by the sheer horror on Gallagher's face, his eyes, wild, bloodshot, bulging. Even Boos, who was no stranger to field interrogations, winced at the muffled screams and the uncontrolled spasms that rattled Gallagher's body.

Gannon stood off to one side of the chair, his face impassive. He saw the first sign that Gallagher was losing the will to resist. The fuse had burned halfway up his right thigh when he made eye contact with Gannon. Gannon stepped in front of the chair. The spiral band of burned flesh was now spreading upward toward the groin, where it would then offer a brief respite as contact with Gallagher's body was broken until it burned down the length of fuse that ran behind the chair before continuing up his right arm.

Gallagher went limp as the burning fuse bypassed his body and worked its way around the back of the chair. One of the intended effects in having lengths of fuse burn away from the body, giving the victim relief, was that it made the thought of having it all begin again that much more horrible.

Gallagher nodded his head vigorously, his eyes pleading with Gannon. Gannon pretended not to understand. Gallagher's muffled shouts and thrashing increased as he felt the heat of the burning fuse approach his right wrist. Gannon pulled the knife from the scabbard on his harness and cut the fuse just as it was about to begin burning flesh again. It had been exactly forty-eight seconds since Gannon had lighted the fuse. To Gallagher it had been a lifetime, an experience he would never forget—the permanent spiral burn scars on his right leg serving as a constant reminder.

An atmosphere thick with the tension of every man's worst nightmare left the room as though driven out by a strong wind. Santana and each of his men seemed relieved that they had not had to see the outcome if the Irishman had not broken.

Gannon pulled the tape from Gallagher's mouth, the strong adhesive abrading a layer of skin as it came off. Gallagher spat out the gag, breathing in and exhaling huge gulps of air.

"You're an inhuman bloody bastard!" he shouted at Gannon, his voice cracking with hysteria.

Gannon didn't respond. He simply reached into his

pocket and pulled out three more stick matches, holding
them in front of Gallagher's face. Nothing needed to be said.

"All right," Gallagher said. "All right."

Gannon moved behind the chair and cut the ropes binding Gallagher's hands and feet. He picked up the map and,
saying nothing, put it in the now acquiescent Irishman's lap.

Gallagher studied the map for a few moments, then
pointed out the location of the camp.

Santana looked over Gannon's shoulder and smiled. "I
know the area. We can be there in less than an hour."

"Where do you post your perimeter security?" Gannon
asked.

Gallagher pointed out the various positions where the
guards were posted.

"Is Nikolai Malik at the camp?"

Gallagher's face expressed his surprise that Gannon knew
of the secretive KGB agent of whom he knew next to nothing. "Yes. He arrived three days ago."

"Where are his quarters?"

"He has a small hut on the west side of the camp, closest
to the river."

"What are his immediate plans?" Gannon asked.

Gallagher shrugged. "All I know is that one of the teams
in training is to provide support for a special mission he has
planned within the next two days. I know none of the details."

Gannon pulled Gallagher to his feet. "If you've lied to
me, I'll be back. And the next time there'll only be enough
fuse to allow me to get out of the way after I light it. Do I
make myself clear?"

Gallagher nodded his head vigorously, all signs of resis-
ance gone.

"Tie him up and put him down in the storage area until
we get back," Santana said.

A few moments later Snake and Claudio locked the trapdoor and pulled the tobacco drying racks back into place,

hiding any trace of the entrance to their secret cache . . . and their prisoner.

"Where did you learn that little trick?" Santana finally asked Gannon, seeing that his expression was once again relaxed.

"From a man who knew how to get exactly what he wanted when he wanted it," Gannon said. "He was the most malignant sociopath I'd ever met, but the best goddamn field interrogator in Vietnam, if not all of Southeast Asia. Never saw anyone hold out past the neck."

Boos looked at the map; his finger traced a route along the coastline. The camp lay only a few hundred yards from the banks of a tributary of the Punta Gorda River. The coastline of the Caribbean Sea was only four miles east of the camp.

"Set up your radio," he told Santana. "I want Maria to move the *Cheetah* down the coast to about here." He pointed to a cove almost due east of the terrorist training camp. "Once we hit that camp whoever else is in the area is going to come down on us in a hurry. I don't want to have to hump that Saydum back over the terrain we just crossed, not with half the fuckin' Sandinista Army on our asses."

"The Company's going to pick up your transmission," Santana warned.

"Considering the stakes, something tells me they've got assets in the area," Boos said. "The sooner we turn the weapon over to them, the happier I'll be. If they're listening in, I think I can give them enough to find us without giving our position away to the Sandinistas."

Maria Padrón sat in the *Cheetah*'s forward cockpit, the M-203 at her side and Clyde roosting on her shoulder, his head turned back into his wing. Her eyes moved slowly from the entrance to the hidden bay, along the shoreline and back in a near constant vigil. A light breeze had picked up but the seas were still calm and the night bright and crysta clear. The sudden increased volume of the static hiss from the radio, followed by Boos's voice, startled her from her thoughts and Clyde from his sleep.

"Winch Ape, this is Coon Ass. Do you copy?" His voice was loud and clear and could be heard on deck.

Maria quickly put Clyde on his perch, and grabbing the overhead support, she swung agilely down into the main salon and ran over to the navigation station. She grabbed the microphone and keyed it.

"I copy," she said. "What is your situation?"

"I want you to move the boat."

Maria stared blankly at the microphone. There was a prolonged silence.

"Acknowledge, Winch Ape," Boos came back.

"By myself?" Maria said.

"Yes, you can do it."

"How far?"

"Precisely twelve point five miles south of your present position. You'll have to motor all the way," Boos said, knowing it would be impossible for Maria to sail the boat at night by herself. "The water is deep enough if you stay equidistant between the reef and the shore." Boos paused for a moment, then added, "Do not under any circumstances attempt to go back through the channel we used to pass through the reef."

Maria's brow furrowed—that was the last thing she would attempt to do without Boos on board. "I might be a little crazy, Coon Ass, but I'm not stupid."

"Understood," Boos said. "Remember, exactly twelve point five miles and stay equidistant from the beach and the reef."

"I copy. Will motor twelve point five miles south from present position."

"Good luck," Boos said. "Out."

Maria studied the charts before going back on deck. She found where twelve and one half miles would place her on the coastline, a sheltered anchorage with the closest inhabited area of any size being San Juan del Norte, a small Nicaraguan port town at the mouth of the San Juan River that had once served as a haven for Henry Morgan, the seventeenth-century British pirate. It was eighteen miles farther south, with nothing but tiny isolated fishing villages in between.

"Whatcha doin'?" Clyde said as Maria came back on deck. "Good boy. Whatcha doin'?"

"Not now, Clyde," Maria said, and glanced about the *Cheetah*.

After returning in the dinghy from taking Gannon and Boos ashore, she had furled in the mainsail, made up the lines, and readied the boat for a quick departure. She went over in her mind the procedures and the timing necessary for what she was about to do, then set about doing it.

She went to the steering cockpit and pulled the dinghy in close to the boat, securing the line to keep it from getting tangled in the propeller. She started the engine and left it in the neutral position as she ran up to the bow and engaged the electric windlass, pulling the anchor chain in and the *Cheetah* forward to where it was directly over the anchor.

She stopped the electric windlass and ran back to the steering cockpit and put the engine in gear, with just enough throttle to take the *Cheetah* out over the anchor to free it. She then put the engine back in neutral, ran forward, and again engaged the electric windlass to haul the anchor up into the anchor chock.

Back in the steering cockpit, she put the *Cheetah* in gear and added power to keep the boat from being blown into shore as she steered it out of the bay and into the deep-water channel that ran between the reef and the beach. She briefly put the boat on autopilot and went forward once again, just to make certain the anchor was secure in the chock before returning to the helm and disengaging the autopilot.

The *Cheetah* cruised along at an easy six knots. Maria was thankful for the full moon as her eyes constantly moved from the palm trees onshore to the water breaking on the reef to the fathometer on the instrument cluster in the steering cockpit. She had memorized the prominent landmarks that would tell her when she had reached her destination and relaxed a little, hoping there were no hidden coral heads or other unpleasant surprises awaiting her along the unfamiliar route.

The Cam Craft and the two Piranhas were anchored in the secluded cove in which the *Cheetah* had hidden prior to contacting Santana. Driscoll and Travis had a chart spread open on the bridge. The captain of the Cam Craft stood beside them.

"He told her not to attempt to go back through the channel they took through the reef," Travis repeated. "There was no need to tell her that. Boos had to know we'd be monitoring any transmission and he's trying to tell us where he's moved the *Cheetah*."

The Honduran naval officer studied the chart, then put his finger on a section of the reef. "This is the only opening with water deep enough for a yacht that size to get inside the reef," he said confidently. Measuring off twelve and a half miles from the point where the deep-water channel wound its way through the reef, he pointed to a sheltered anchorage approximately eighteen miles north of San Juan del Norte. "This is where the *Cheetah* is going. I am certain of it."

"How long will it take us to reach it?" Driscoll asked.

"Only a little more than an hour," the captain said. "Maybe less."

"Then let's haul ass," Driscoll said.

The Cam Craft's diesels roared to life, followed shortly by the higher-pitched sounds of the outboards on the Piranhas. The three heavily armed patrol boats moved quickly out of the cove into the open sea and headed due south, no longer bothering to stay outside the range of Nicaragua's mostly ineffectual coastal radar as they sped along only six miles offshore.

40

_____

Tigrillo moved silently through the deep shadows, avoiding
the bright silver-green patches where moonlight shone
through the openings in the triple-canopy jungle. The scent
of rotting logs and earth hung heavy in the night air. Broad-
leaved plants brushed softly against his thighs as he carefully parted the tangled waist-high scrub and thick strands
of twisted vines that hung from every tree. The jungle was as
dense as any Tigrillo had ever stalked, slowing his progress
around the perimeter of the camp. Yet, despite the heavy
cover, he had crept close enough to kill three of the guards
instantly with a single shot angled upward from the base of
the skull with his silenced 9mm pistol.

He completed his reconnaissance of the perimeter nearest
to the river and began to work his way toward the far side of
the camp. A stiff breeze coming down off the hills rustled
the leaves and helped mask his movement. He crouched low
and froze in position at the crack of a twig, followed by the
sound of a man clearing his throat just ahead. He slowly
lowered his silhouette until he was kneeling in the thick
underbrush. A shadow moved in his direction; a man was
hitching up his pants, having just relieved himself. Tigrillo
lay directly in his path.

Rising slowly to his feet, Tigrillo stood behind the trunk
of a huge mahogany tree and waited for the man to come

abreast of his position. The sound of footsteps drew closer and Tigrillo held the silenced semiautomatic pistol at his side. The footsteps stopped, and after the sound of a zipper being pulled up, they started again. The man passed by unaware of Tigrillo's presence.

Stepping from behind the tree, Tigrillo placed the tip of the sound suppressor at the base of the man's skull and pulled the trigger. The only sound was the hammer dropping. The round in the chamber did not fire.

The startled man tried to spin around, but Tigrillo reacted instantly. He dropped the pistol and clamped one arm across the man's throat in a powerful choke hold that kept him from crying out. Tigrillo kicked him in the back of the knee, and as he stumbled backward he drove his shoulder into the back of the man's head and leapt off the ground. They both fell simultaneously, the man's back and Tigrillo's stomach hitting the ground at the same time. With Tigrillo's arm tight across the man's throat and under his chin, acting as the fulcrum, the force of his body weight and his leverage snapped the man's neck.

The brief struggle was heard by the perimeter guard Tigrillo had been stalking. He began firing blindly into the jungle. The rounds came nowhere near Tigrillo, but the damage had been done, the element of surprise was gone.

The frightened guard's tracer rounds streamed through the darkness, giving away his exact position. Tigrillo quickly unslung his AK-47 and killed the man before moving away from the area and back to where Santana and the rest of the team were set up for the attack on the camp.

Nikolai Malik rolled out of his hammock when the bursts of automatic-weapons fire shattered the silence of the jungle night. He was rattled for a brief moment, puzzled by the unexpected attack, then grabbed his submachine gun and ran to the window that looked toward the main part of the camp.

Santana had assigned positions around the perimeter. The first order of business was to take out the communications

shack the moment the assault began. With the premature
shots coming from the rear of the camp, Santana wasted no
time. He braced himself against a tree, shouldered a rocket-
propelled grenade launcher—a Soviet-made RPG-7—and
turned briefly to make certain no one was within range of
the back blast. He sighted in on the roof, alive with antennas, cocked the hammer at the rear of the trigger-housing
handgrip, and squeezed the trigger. The 85mm high-explosive rocket roared from the launcher with a loud whooshing
sound. It left a fiery tail behind as it streaked toward its
target. Impacting in the side of the communications shack,
the rocket first penetrated, then erupted into a powerful
flash of orange-white light that blew the structure apart,
leaving nothing but small fires of scattered thatch that had
once been part of the roof.

At the sound of Tigrillo's and the guard's automatic-
weapons fire and the explosion of the RPG, men dived out
of hammocks strung beneath open-sided shelters and
grabbed their weapons, running in all directions, seeking
cover from the unseen attackers. Never drilled for a defense
of the camp, they had no plan for a coordinated counterat-
tack.

Santana's men opened up, cutting down twelve of the
trainees and three instructors who had scrambled out of a
hut. Tigrillo, now at Santana's side, fired the LAW he was
carrying into another of the huts, blowing out two of the
walls and caving in the thatched roof. As Santana had
taught him, he then fired his AK-47 on full automatic in
crossing arcs, cutting down four more instructors as they
ran from the burning hut.

No longer in doubt about the force of the attack, Malik
left the window and quickly removed the SADM's lock
secure cover. He stared briefly at the interior arming mechanism, took a deep breath to steady himself, and made his
decision. If he was to be killed or captured, he was determined that his mission would not fail, though the plan
would be somewhat altered. He carefully removed the Ex

plosive Wave Generator from the Safe Well, placed it into
the Arm Well, and gently lowered it until the sensitive transducer plate on the base made contact with the Arm-Well
locking cams.

Outside, the camp and surrounding jungle had erupted
into a succession of powerful explosions from the LAWs and
grenade launchers that Santana's men were firing into the
camp structures and areas where some of the trainees had
taken cover. Bursts of automatic-weapons fire were now being returned as the remaining instructors rallied their men
into defensive positions and instilled a semblance of fire discipline. Santana reloaded his RPG-7, took deadly aim, and
the supply shack exploded into a fireball, setting off secondary explosions from crates of ammunition that sent towers
of flame shooting up into the jungle canopy.

Removed from the immediate area of the firefight, Malik
paused to stare at the clock-setting knobs on the SADM. He
wiped the perspiration from his forehead and, after another
deep breath, set the timers. There was a grim smile on his
face as he quickly, methodically put the lock-secure cover
back in place and gave the combination dial a spin before he
slipped the SADM back inside its nylon bag and into the
jump container, which he then reattached to its pack tray.
With an anxious look in the direction of the main part of the
camp, he grabbed his submachine gun, slipped the pack tray
over his shoulders, and moved to the back of the hut. The
sounds of the raging battle covered the noise of the three
powerful kicks he used to knock a large hole in the thatch
and wood rear wall. Once outside, he disappeared into the
jungle.

Snake and Claudio had taken three men down near the
tall grass by the river's edge to set up an ambush for any
reinforcements that might come from that direction. Gannon and Boos were positioned outside of Malik's hut. Their
plan was to rush the hut, using neither Boos's grenade
launcher nor firing any weapons until they located the
SADM.

"Ready?" Gannon said.

"Ready," Boos replied, standing off to one side of the door to Malik's hut.

Gannon raised his foot and kicked in the door, immediately diving inside and rolling into a kneeling position, his weapon ready to fire. Boos rushed in right behind him. One look at the hole in the rear wall and they knew Malik had escaped. Gannon motioned in the direction of the river, considering it the most likely avenue of escape.

Snake and Claudio and the three men they had taken with them to secure the approach from the river were set up in a point ambush—a tactic most effective in wooded jungle terrain when the attacking force is less than forty feet away from the killing zone. The five men were good at what they did. The element of surprise would allow them to seize and control the situation: deliver coordinated fire into the killing zone, isolate the attackers, and prevent escape or reinforcements. If the attacking forces became overwhelming, they were prepared for a coordinated withdrawal from the ambush site, using a visual and audio signaling system among themselves and then a walkie-talkie to establish a rendezvous point with Santana once the attack was over.

Snake was the first to hear the low, powerful throb of diesel engines coming up the river. Claudio, lying nearby, heard them too. He cast a knowing glance at Snake, who settled in behind his M-60 machine gun and made certain the ammunition coiled inside his pack had an unobstructed route to the gun. Two of the other men had set up claymore mines along the trail leading from the river to the camp to cover their withdrawal if necessary. They lay in position, the clacker detonators for the antipersonnel mines held in their hands. The third man, crouched beside Claudio, had preregistered the 60mm mortar along the most likely avenue of approach, laying the six rounds he had at his side.

* * *

Gannon and Boos heard the sound of the diesel engines too. They picked up their pace, afraid that Malik was headed for the patrol boat. Making no attempt to cover the noise of their advance, they ran through the thick jungle vegetation, swatting at overhanging branches and trailing vines. Then Boos caught sight of someone up ahead, moving swiftly in a zigzag motion but headed in the general direction of the river.

He ignored Gannon's warning to slow down and picked up his pace to a near flat-out sprint and began closing the distance. Bringing his CAR-15 up into firing position, he raked the area in front of him, firing off an entire magazine and reloading on the run. He was still gaining ground on the man ahead of him and could now clearly see that he was carrying a pack tray with a cylinder-shaped container strapped to it.

Malik, aware that with the SADM he could not outrun the man firing and advancing on him, ducked off the narrow trail and tucked his submachine gun into his shoulder. Moments later Boos appeared, charging with wild abandon through the thick brush. Malik fired two three-shot bursts and watched as Boos tumbled head over heels to the ground and lay motionless.

Malik jumped to his feet and continued running toward the river. The noise behind indicated someone else was still chasing him but was not close enough to make a target of him.

Gannon raced to where he had heard the shots, knowing by the sound that they had not been fired by a CAR-15 and fearing the worst. He saw Boos lying just ahead. He knelt at his side and cradled him in his arms. There were two holes where rounds had entered Boos's head just below the eye at an upward angle. His eyes were rolled back, with only the whites visible. The wet, sticky mess Gannon felt oozing onto his hands as he held his friend's head told him all he needed to know. The back of Boos's head was completely blown apart.

"You crazy coon-ass son of a bitch," he said, the tears welling in his eyes. "You crazy son of a bitch," he repeated, and rocked him in his arms. "I told you to slow down. Goddamnit!"

Gannon regained his composure by focusing on his reinforced hatred of Malik. He gently lowered Boos's head to the ground, then ran in the direction of the river, where he could hear the boat drawing closer and the sound of someone thrashing through the underbrush.

From behind him Gannon heard the tempo of the firefight at the camp increase. The staccato roar of machine guns and the chatter of assault rifles, mixed with the explosions of rockets and grenades, echoed off the nearby hills, carrying for miles down the river and out over the countryside. Gannon ran straight for the river, hoping to reach the shore before Malik, cut him off, and get a clear shot before he could reach the boat. And then he saw him.

Malik's pace had slowed considerably; he had tripped on an exposed root and twisted his ankle. With the injury and the added weight of the SADM, he was moving at little more than a jog. The jungle was thinning out as it approached the riverbank and Gannon saw a chance for a shot. He dropped to one knee, squeezed off a burst from his CAR-15, and saw Malik stumble and fall to the ground fifteen yards ahead.

Malik felt a wave of pain and dizziness sweep over him but he fought it off and crawled into a dense thicket. He made a cursory examination of his wound by probing the hole in his fatigue shirt with his finger. He was relieved to find that it was only a flesh wound, the bullet having passed through his upper arm and out the other side without hitting the bone. His eyes immediately swept the area where he had fallen, looking for the SADM pack tray. It lay only six feet away, but to get to it he would have to crawl into an open area. He could no longer hear the hurried advance of the man who had shot him and reasoned that whoever it was, was now approaching cautiously, closing in for the kill.

Gannon saw the SADM and again dropped to one knee. He scanned the shadows where the jungle thinned out near the river's edge. As he moved toward it a thundering noise caused him to dive back under cover. A huge seventy-foot Sandinista patrol boat roared past close to the bank, then backed off on its engines as it maneuvered into shore. The deck of the boat was crowded with troops. Gannon estimated the reinforcements at thirty or forty men, probably from the outpost five miles downriver that Santana had mentioned.

The volume of fire that broke loose on the riverbank, twenty yards away on Gannon's right flank, was deafening. Snake and Claudio had triggered their ambush. The seventy-foot patrol boat unleashed a devastating barrage of fire from the twin .50-caliber machine guns mounted on her bow and the pedestal-mounted .30-caliber machine gun on her starboard side. The dense jungle foliage was shredded by the continuous covering fire as the soldiers prepared to jump ashore.

Trees and scrub were torn up all around Gannon and rounds cracked overhead. He hugged the ground, unable to move from his prone position without being shot to pieces. He heard the hollow thump of a mortar round leaving its tube just off to his right, followed by a loud explosion and screams of pain as it landed amidships on the seventy-foot patrol boat, hurling half a dozen men off the deck and into the river. Another hollow thud and the boat was struck farther aft, blowing away a part of the stern and sending a storm of shrapnel into a squad of soldiers waiting to jump ashore.

The Sandinista barrage stopped long enough for Gannon to dash out into the small grassy area near the bank and pull the SADM pack tray back under cover at his side. His eyes swept the surrounding area for any sign of Malik. But nothing moved. He felt certain he had only wounded him, and judging from the way he had fallen, he suspected the round had struck him in the arm or the shoulder.

Malik had been applying a tourniquet to the flesh wound on his upper arm when Gannon had crawled out to get the SADM. He had looked up just in time to catch a brief glimpse of him as he disappeared back into the underbrush. Malik knew better than to give away his position by firing at a target that might already have moved. Instead, he began a slow, steady crawl to the river. The thought of the SADM now being in the hands of the Contras made him smile. Before they figured out what they had it would be far too late.

Gannon slipped the pack tray over his shoulder and began low-crawling in the direction he had seen Malik fall. He could hear the ambush off to his right reaching a crescendo. The Sandinistas resumed laying down covering fire with their deck guns as twenty or so men rushed ashore into the hail of fire the ambush team was directing toward them. More than half of them were cut down by Snake's M-60 as they ran and dived for cover in the scrub and tall grass.

A smaller boat, a Boston Whaler, carrying only a squad of men, appeared out of nowhere and pulled into shore. It immediately took a direct hit from the 60mm mortar that set the stern on fire. The man at the helm was blown into the river, and the troops that were not wounded or killed jumped into the water and swam to shore. The abandoned Boston Whaler continued to burn as the current began taking it back downriver.

More than 80 percent of the Sandinista troops on board the boats had been killed by the deadly attack. Snake and Claudio signaled to the rest of the ambush team and quickly withdrew to a second defensive position, using the radio to alert Santana to their situation and the strength of the Sandinista reinforcements. Santana had the camp under control. It was now a smoldering ruin with only a small pocket of resistance remaining. He told Claudio to withdraw back to the camp, where they could regroup.

Snake stayed behind as Claudio and the rest of the ambush team moved quickly away. The remaining Sandinistas were now organized and advancing slowly along the trail that led to the camp. Snake was more than familiar with the Russian-trained Cuban style of combat the Sandinistas had adopted. It took three ambushes to neutralize the large numbers of men and mortars they usually sent: the first a frontal attack, then another at the middle to take out the officers, and finally one to the rear to take out the heavy weapons.

At this moment Snake was concerned with only one man, and he spotted him ten yards in front of the column, leading the Sandinista troops along the trail. He was a Nicaraguan peasant, a dangerous man with knowledge of the jungle and of this specific area. To kill him was to slow down the enemy advance. Snake took aim when the peasant came into full view and cut him nearly in half with a prolonged burst from the M-60. The Sandinistas spotted his muzzle blasts and returned fire, but by the time they did Snake had already crawled off into the jungle and was headed back to join Claudio and the others.

Gannon rose to his knees behind a rotted deadfall. The rate of fire from the Sandinista patrol boat had died off now that the troops were ashore and in pursuit. He had watched them pass by on his right flank, knowing that they were headed directly into another of Claudio's and Snake's ambushes. A sudden movement ahead on his left flank materialized into the crippled boat that had caught fire. It was drifting back downstream, scraping and bumping along the shoreline. A column of thick gray smoke rose from her stern. In his peripheral vision Gannon saw a man silhouetted against the flames. It was Malik, and he was making a run for the boat as it passed his position.

Gannon got to his feet and gave chase. He closed to within twenty yards before Malik dived from the riverbank and landed on the bow of the boat just as it bumped against

the shore. Gannon tried desperately to reach the boat before
it drifted back out into midstream, but saw that he could not
possibly make it. He stopped running, dropped to a kneeling
position, and fired at Malik, whose body was half hidden by
the smoke from the fire. The rounds ricocheted off the steering cockpit. Malik ducked down, gave the engine full throttle, spun the boat around, and roared off down the river.

Gannon stopped on the bank and continued to fire, even
though the boat had reached a bend in the river, far out of
range of the CAR-15. Then Gannon saw a sudden flash
spread across the deck like a napalm strike. The fire reached
the fuel tank, causing a tremendous explosion that blew the
stern completely apart and sent the bow crashing into the
bank and the rest of the boat to the bottom of the river.

Gannon continued to watch the distant river bend to see
if Malik had somehow gotten off the boat before the explosion, but the darkness, the smoke and debris prevented him
from getting a clear view. The explosion had erupted with
such force and spread so quickly, he doubted anyone could
have survived it.

Using the walkie-talkie Santana had given him, Gannon
tried to raise someone on the radio. It was Claudio who
responded. He gave Gannon their position, but told him to
rejoin Santana as they continued their rearguard action.

Gannon, the SADM slung over one shoulder, made his
way back to the camp, to find it totally secure. Santana had
taken no prisoners. His men had killed all of the terrorists,
instructors, and trainees while suffering only one casualty to
the team—one of the *campesinos* had taken a round in the
leg, but it had been a clean wound and the man was ambula-
tory. Sporadic fire came from the trail leading down to the
river. Snake and Claudio and the three men with them had
the remaining Sandinistas pinned down, their numbers now
dwindled to four survivors, who were trying desperately to
get back to the patrol boat rather than continue pursuing
the Contras.

Snake waited patiently as he spotted the four men, crouching low and moving single file, heading for the river. They were within ten feet of a claymore mine. Having over-run the point where the mine was placed before it could be triggered, the Sandinistas were now unknowingly retreating back into the kill zone. Snake waited until the first two men were a few feet past the claymore, then he squeezed the detonator. All four men were blown into the air; two of them had the clothes torn from their bodies and arms and legs severed. When the smoke cleared, the last of the rein-forcements lay dead. Snake signaled to Claudio, who alerted the rest of the ambush team, and they returned to the camp-site.

Santana's men were scavenging what weapons and sup-plies they could from the bodies and debris scattered around the camp when Santana called to Gannon. "Where's Boos?"

"Dead," Gannon said. "Down near the river."

"The Russian?"

Gannon nodded.

"Did you get him?"

"I think he went up in flames when one of the boats exploded," Gannon said. "But I can't be sure."

Santana called two of his men over and told them to bring Boos's body back to the camp.

"But you got the Saydum," Santana said, staring at the container as Gannon lowered the pack tray to the ground.

"Yeah, but I need you to get whoever it is that's monitor-ing the four-megacycle frequency on the single sideband. There's something about this that's making me nervous."

"What's that?"

"Malik gave it up too easy," Gannon said. "He simply made a run for it, never tried to recover the weapon."

"So?"

"It doesn't make sense for him to back off without a fight, not unless . . ." Gannon quickly undid the straps on the pack tray and removed the SADM from its container and the nylon bag.

"Shine your light down here," he said to Santana, who unclipped the flashlight from his harness and aimed the beam at the small observation window for the Arm Well. Both men stared at each other, their eyes locked in a mutual expression of both horror and fear.

"The motherfucker's armed!" Santana said. He looked again to make certain his eyes and the shadows weren't playing tricks on him. The Explosive Wave Generator was in the Arm Well. The 4.5-kiloton nuclear weapon was indeed armed.

"The clocks?" Santana said. "What are the countdown clocks set for?"

"I have no way of knowing without removing the cover," Gannon said. "And I can't do that without the combination."

"Who has the combination?" Santana said.

"Malik had to have had it, but whoever has been tracking us down here has got to have it too."

Santana immediately set up the team radio, dialed in the frequency, and handed the handset to Gannon.

"Who's your control officer?" he asked Santana.

"Travis," Santana said. "The station chief in Honduras."

"What's his call sign?"

"Nighthawk," Santana replied.

"Get him on the hook, then give him to me."

"I suggest we evacuate the area first," Santana said.

"If my hunch is right, we may not have time," Gannon said.

Santana keyed the microphone. "Nighthawk, this is Sandman. Over."

The Piranhas, and the Cam Craft carrying Travis and Driscoll, were within fifteen minutes of where Maria had relocated the *Cheetah.* Santana's voice could barely be heard above the noise of the diesel engines as his transmission broke the static hiss on the frequency.

Travis immediately grabbed the microphone from the radio on the bridge of the Cam Craft and cranked up the volume control.

"Go, Sandman," he said.

"We've got an emergency situation here. I'm going to turn you over to the man Coon Ass brought in. Code name"—he paused and looked at Gannon—"code name 'Bird Dog,' " he said, using the call sign used by forward air controllers in Vietnam—men whose skill and extraordinary courage the reconnaissance teams often depended upon.

Gannon took the handset and keyed the mike. "Nighthawk, I need the combination for the item we have just recovered. I have reason to believe that disaster is imminent."

There was a long pause, then Travis replied, "Can not comply, Bird Dog. That information has the highest classification. Bring the item to us as quickly as possible and we will handle the emergency."

"I do not believe we have enough time," Gannon said. "I have to get a look at the clocks."

"Negative, Bird Dog," came the reply from Travis. "I repeat, I can not comply."

"Then patch me through to someone who can," Gannon shouted into the mike. "If not, I'll leave the item where it is and evacuate the area A.S.A.P. We're dealing with a borderline psychopath who's capable of anything. He would not abandon his mission this easily."

A middle-aged man stepped from behind Travis and took the microphone. It was the nuclear weapons specialist from the Department of Energy's Nuclear Emergency Search Team who had been taken on board the Cam Craft in Honduras.

"Sorry, Travis," he said. "It's my show from here on in." The NEST team commander man had the power and authority to usurp command in any situation involving a missing nuclear weapon and did just that.

"Bird Dog," the NEST man said. "Are you ready to copy?"

"Ready," Gannon came back immediately.

The NEST man read off the combination, then waited for Gannon to read it back to him. Gannon then set about dialing in the numbers and removing the cover from the SADM.

"Lock-secure cover removed," Gannon transmitted to the NEST man on the bridge of the Cam Craft, a nervous edge to his voice that came through on the other end.

"What do the clocks read?"

"Seven minutes, thirty-eight seconds and counting," Gannon said.

"Son of a bitch," Santana whispered as he looked over Gannon's shoulder.

"Are you prepared to disarm the item?" the NEST man asked.

"Yes," Gannon replied, "but we'll have to cut out the shorthand conversation because I'm a little rusty at this."

"Roger that," the NEST man said. "Proceed and inform me of each procedure as you prepare to do it."

Gannon was confident he remembered precisely how to disarm the weapon; it was a simple yet dangerous process. The clocks could not simply be reset to zero, stopping the countdown. The weapon had been designed to prevent anyone from doing that. Conventional explosives could be attached to the outside of the weapon to destroy it before the nuclear explosion, but they did not have the right conventional explosives at hand.

The process was to remove the Explosive Wave Generator from the Arm Well by giving it a half-turn to release the locking cams at the bottom and pulling it out of the well, replacing it in the safe well. The problem lay in the delicate technique of getting it out of the well, a problem Gannon was immediately reminded of when the NEST man's voice came over the radio.

"Before you remove the EWG from the Arm Well, you must lubricate the sides of the well," he said. "If you cause any friction while withdrawing it, it may cause the electric conductor at the top of the well to set off the EWG. Do you understand?"

Gannon was already in the process of using a can of gun oil to lubricate the Arm Well when the NEST man transmitted his warning. That done, he took the EWG by its handle and slowly began drawing it up out of the well. The clocks now read three minutes and seven seconds.

Halfway out, the EWG caught against the sides of the well. Gannon immediately stopped pulling and applied more oil to the sides. The EWG still didn't budge. He informed the NEST man on the Cam Craft. The clocks were now at two minutes and forty-three seconds.

"Slowly push it back down into the well and try again," the NEST man instructed Gannon.

Gannon did, and this time the EWG moved up past the point where it had previously snagged. Pausing to steady his hands, Gannon brought the EWG alongside the electric conductor, squirting a liberal dose of oil over the spot where the conductor would come in contact with the transducer plate on the base of the EWG. The Explosive Wave Generator cleared the conductor and came smoothly out of the Arm Well with exactly fifty-six seconds left on the clock.

"Wait until the clocks are completely wound down before you put the EWG in the Safe Well," the NEST man advised.

Gannon did, breathing a sigh of relief as a whirring and clicking sound came from the clock circuitry, transmitting a current to the electrical conductor at the top of the Arm Well. There was a brief spark at the tip of the conductor, but with nothing to carry the current forward, the sequence of events stopped. Gannon placed the Explosive Wave Generator into the Safe Well and replaced the lock-secure cover.

"Good work, Bird Dog." It was Driscoll's voice that came over the radio. "Now get the item to us as soon as possible. We are in the immediate area of Winch Ape and have support waiting once you reach the designated area."

"Let's get that goddamn thing out of here now," Santana said. "I won't feel comfortable until it's completely out of the realm of possibility of it falling into that asshole Ortega's hands."

Gannon put the SADM back into its container and shouldered the pack tray as Santana rounded up his men. They set out on the three-mile trek through dense jungle to the coastline. The camp they left behind was littered with bodies, its structures nothing but charred and smoldering piles of debris.

The two men who had dug a shallow grave and buried Boos showed Santana and Gannon where he lay at rest. With Boos having no family, Gannon had made the decision to bury him in the jungle, where he had always been at his best. He and Santana paused and stared at the fresh mound of earth covered over with leaves and twigs. They each said their silent good-byes before moving on.

At first Nikolai Malik thought he was dreaming, floating weightless in the night sky, then his senses began to return. He was floating faceup in the shallow water at the bank of the river. The sound of the explosion and the sensation of being thrown into the air were the last things he remembered. He began to take inventory, moving his extremities one at a time, finding that they all worked. There was a dull ache in his upper left arm, but he remembered that it was from the flesh wound he had received before jumping onto the boat.

He looked about and saw that his shoulders had come to rest on a small sandbar along the shore, and the rest of his body was floating. He pulled himself up onto dry land and sat for a moment, then was jolted back to his full senses at the thought of the SADM. He looked at his watch. The weapon should have exploded twenty minutes ago. He should be vaporized, nothing but ashes at the bottom of a crater a mile deep and twice as wide. He cursed his failure while wondering what had gone wrong. He tried to assuage the wave of anger and frustration that swept over him by telling himself that perhaps the clocks were faulty and the weapon would still detonate. But reason told him that it was more likely it had fallen into the hands of the Americans, not the Contras, and was now disarmed.

He got slowly to his feet and found that every muscle in his body ached as he shuffled away from the grassy bank and into the shadows of the brush. He heard a helicopter off in the distance, then the sound of three, possibly four, Nicaraguan patrol boats coming upriver, heading toward the camp. He didn't even turn to look as he began to make his way inland through the dense jungle. His mission was over. But there would be other missions. There were always other missions for men with his talents.

41

To everyone who served in combat in Vietnam the sound of a helicopter is one never to be forgotten or mistaken for anything else.

Gannon and Santana heard the familiar sound at the same time. They were halfway across a bright, moonlit clearing they were forced to use to avoid a swampy area. The sound of the helicopter was immediately followed by the crack of automatic-weapons fire a mile or so behind them, where Claudio and Snake and four other members of the team had set up an ambush to fight a rearguard action against the Sandinista reinforcements brought by the three patrol boats that had arrived as the team left the camp.

The rhythmic beat of the helicopter grew louder as it suddenly appeared over the crest of the hill at the south end of the grassy clearing. It was flying nap-of-the-earth and dropped even lower as it cleared the hill and headed for the seven men the pilot saw advancing in a staggered column.

Santana led the team at a dead run for the mangrove swamp on their right flank. The Soviet-made MI-8 Hip twin-turbine helicopter was primarily a troop carrier but was armed with a heavy machine gun and two missile pods carrying 57mm rockets. Its main weakness was its vulnerable fuel system. A weakness of which Gannon was well aware.

On its first pass the helicopter strafed the edge of the clearing. Its heavy machine gun ripped up the grassy turf and cut down two of Santana's men as they ran for cover. The rotor wash from its massive blades as it thundered low overhead flattened the knee-high grass when it pulled into a steep climb and banked into a turn to position itself for a second pass.

One of the men killed in the strafing run had been loading the team's Redeye missile launcher when he was gunned down. Gannon ran back into the clearing and grabbed the launcher. Standing in the open, he shouldered the weapon and took aim, holding his fire until the helicopter, which had turned for another pass, was close enough for him to see the outline of the pilot in the glow of the cockpit lights. Rounds from the aircraft's machine gun ripped into the ground around him. He waited until the last possible second, then squeezed the trigger and sent the surface-to-air missile streaking upward toward its target.

The helicopter had fired two 57mm rockets a split second before Gannon fired. They roared overhead, exploding far off target in the jungle behind him. The Redeye missile struck home, rupturing the fuel tanks and blowing the helicopter from the sky in a huge fireball. The crippled aircraft banked into a steep dive and crashed just below the ridge behind Gannon. A plume of black smoke, marking its point of impact, rose through the jungle canopy.

"Take off," Santana said to Gannon as he ran back into the mangrove thicket and retrieved the SADM pack tray. "My men are in some deep shit, I've got to go back and help them." The sounds of grenade blasts and increased automatic-weapons fire came from the camp.

"You've got only about a mile and a half to go to the cove where Boos had the boat moved," Santana said. "The trail at the end of the clearing will take you directly to it."

Gannon hesitated, looking back in the direction where Santana's men were engaged in the firefight.

Santana read his thoughts. "I can manage without you, Gannon. Just get that goddamn nuke out of this country."

Gannon shook Santana's hand. "Thanks for your help."

"No problem," Santana said. "I'll radio Travis that you're on your way. Now get the fuck out of here."

Swinging the SADM pack tray over one shoulder, Gannon took off at a dog trot along the edge of the clearing until he reached the trail and disappeared into the jungle.

Snake and Claudio and four of their teammates had their hands full even though the line ambush they had set up had worked well enough, killing the first twenty or so men who had entered the area. Positioned parallel to the enemy's route of march, the line ambush placed maximum firepower into the kill zone. The terrain was well suited to the tactic. Due to natural obstacles, the Sandinistas were forced to travel in close line-formations, making them vulnerable to attack on their flanks and disrupting their patrol formations. On the far side of the kill zone, where, once under attack, the enemy dived for cover, Snake had set up a line of claymore mines, and two men with grenade launchers were zeroed in on that area. The ambush team was approximately twenty-five yards from the kill zone, using aimed fire, which was far more effective in this situation than full rock 'n' roll.

But the reinforcements were greater than they had anticipated—at least two companies of crack troops from an elite Sandinista battalion trained in antiguerrilla warfare by Vietnamese and North Korean military advisors. Snake and Claudio and the others had settled into a well-rehearsed fire discipline. They fired three-round bursts at individual targets of opportunity barely visible in the pale moonlight that filtered through to the ambush site. Claudio had spotted three tan Cuban officer's uniforms among the olive green of the Sandinista ranks and had made it his personal goal to kill all three of them.

Heavy bursts of probing fire ripped through the jungle. No longer bunched together on the trail, the Sandinistas quickly got out of the kill zone. They moved effectively over the rough terrain and organized counterambush tactics while they returned as much suppressing fire as possible and maneuvered to outflank and surround the ambush team and form their own assault.

Claudio and Snake were on the verge of being overwhelmed. Enemy mortar rounds impacted too close for comfort, and a steady stream of automatic-weapons fire cracked through the brush overhead and thudded into trees. They both tossed smoke and tear-gas grenades to cover their withdrawal as their ambush team broke off contact with the Sandinistas and retreated to a preselected rallying point to be used as a secondary line of defense.

As he ran along the trail, bringing up the rear, Snake snapped open a canvas bag that was slung over his shoulder and rested at his hip. It was full of foot-poppers, deadly Soviet-made antipersonnel mines they had captured from the Sandinistas. Clay-red, with a hard plastic casing and a rubber gasket bearing numbers and Russian Cyrillic lettering, the OTK-10 pressure-detonated mine was no larger than a hockey puck, yet powerful enough to blow the foot or leg off the person who stepped on it and disable anyone else within a ten-yard radius of the explosion. Pausing every ten to fifteen yards, Snake quickly armed and placed them along the trail, covering them with leaves and debris from the jungle floor.

At the top of a steep rise that overlooked the trail, Snake stopped where the rest of the team was already positioned. Claudio had set up the 60mm mortar but had only three rounds left. Two claymores had been hidden just off the trail at the bottom of the rise, their detonating wires leading up to the team's position. There had been no panic on the part of the team, just fast, proficient actions. They had retreated from cover to cover until they reached the top of the rise. Their tactics were sound: a guerrilla force maximizes the number of enemy killed but never holds ground to the last man. Defensive actions are taken by dropping back to the next line of defense as soon as the enemy exerts overpowering force.

Snake heard the first of the foot-poppers explode and knew that the Sandinista advance would now be slowed down while the point man proceeded with more caution, searching for other mines. A voice came over the walkie-talkie Snake had clipped to his harness. It was Santana. He and the other team members were only a hundred yards behind them, on their way back to reinforce their position.

Gannon stopped running as he saw and heard the ocean through breaks in the thick jungle terrain. He caught a glimpse of the *Cheetah* gently rocking in the shimmering sea forty yards from shore. As he drew closer to the cove he saw the rubber dinghy pulled partway up onshore and caught a flicker of movement and what appeared to be a silhouetted figure in a thicket just in from the beach.

He crouched low, circled, and closed in from behind on the spot where he had seen the movement in the brush. The silhouette was no longer there. Hit with a sudden blow to his solar plexus that knocked him backward, he swung his CAR-15 into position to fire and found himself looking up at the face of Maria Padrón and the barrel of the M-203 pointed at his head. He released the pressure on the trigger and got to his feet.

"Sorry. Had to be sure who it was," Maria said as she lowered her weapon. "I heard Santana's radio call to the guy on the boat. I figured you'd be along soon, so I came ashore to wait." Maria looked about expectantly, her eyes searching the shadows around them. "Where's Jim?"

The look on Gannon's face gave her the answer she didn't want to hear. "Oh, no," Maria said. She started to speak again, but simply shook her head and turned away.

"It was quick," Gannon said. "He never felt a thing."

Maria made no reply as she stepped out of the jungle and onto the beach. Gannon followed, loading the SADM pack tray in the small rubber boat.

"What's that?" Maria asked.

"You don't want to know," Gannon said.

"I want to know," Maria demanded. "If it has anything to do with the reason Jim Boos died, I want to know."

"It's a man-portable nuclear weapon."

"Ours or theirs?"

"Ours."

"Where the hell did you get it?" Maria paused for a brief moment, then before Gannon could answer said, "Never mind, you're right. I don't want to know."

Gannon shoved the dinghy out into the surf and jumped aboard as Maria started the electric motor and headed for the *Cheetah*.

"What did you do with Jim's body?"

"We buried it in the jungle. It was—"

Maria raised her hand to stop any further explanation. "I didn't even get a chance to say good-bye," she said softly, more to herself than to Gannon.

Maria pulled the dinghy alongside the *Cheetah* and Gannon climbed the swim ladder, taking the SADM with him. After securing the dinghy Maria came aboard and paused to look at the SADM container. The thought of what it represented made her shudder involuntarily.

A sudden roar of powerful engines startled them both as two Piranha patrol boats entered the cove and sped past the *Cheetah*, port and starboard. One stopped and kept its bow pointed toward shore. The other made a tight showboat turn, spinning around to face the *Cheetah*, its .50-caliber machine gun manned and aimed at her deck. The Cam Craft stayed on station outside the reef, her powerful array of deck guns trained on the shoreline.

Cutting back on the power, the crew of the Piranha that faced the *Cheetah* tossed out fenders and came alongside. Two men Gannon judged to be Americans boarded the *Cheetah*; Gannon kept his CAR-15 pointed at them. Maria did the same with the M-203; the grenade launcher affixed to the barrel was loaded and ready to fire.

"Gannon," the taller man said, "I'm Tom Driscoll, CIA."

"I've seen you around," Gannon said. "Montego Bay wasn't it?"

Driscoll smiled sheepishly, then gestured to the man be side him. "This is Clayton Thomas, Department of Energy Nuclear Emergency Search Team. He's here to take charge of the item." Driscoll spotted the pack tray and SADM container on the deck and his eyes fixed on it.

"Not until I see some ID," Gannon said, fully aware o his tenuous situation. He and Maria didn't stand a chance against the men and weapons on board the Piranhas.

Both men flashed their identification cards and Thoma immediately went to the SADM. He opened the containe and gave it a complete inspection.

"Good work, Gannon," Thomas said as he handed th SADM over to Travis, who was waiting on the deck of th Piranha, then jumped back on board himself and again took possession of the weapon.

"Boos with you?" Travis called from the deck of the Pira nha.

"He's dead," Gannon said flatly.

"He was a good man," was all Travis said.

"You Travis?" Gannon asked.

Travis nodded.

"What's Santana's situation?" The sound of a heav firefight could be heard in the distance. Bursts from machine guns, grenades, and mortar rounds echoed out over the hill and down through the valleys to the coastline.

"It's about to dramatically improve," Travis said with grin.

Driscoll paused before going back aboard the Piranha. H locked eyes with Gannon. "You get your man, Gannon?"

Gannon shrugged. "I think so. The boat he was on blev up. Couldn't verify it."

"Too bad," Driscoll said. "The sick son of a bitch de served to die slowly and painfully." He looked at Maria

"These two boats are going to escort you out of Nicaraguan waters. You'll be in good hands."

"Do you need me on board?" Gannon asked Maria.

"There's no way I can get this back to Montego Bay alone."

"You know I don't know anything about sailing."

"I'll teach you what you need to know."

"Good luck," Driscoll called out as he boarded the Piranha. "Your country owes you a debt, Gannon, as I'm sure you're aware."

Gannon helped Maria bring the dinghy aboard and prepare the *Cheetah* for the passage back to Jamaica. They would motor until out of Nicaragua's territorial waters, with the Piranhas as outriders, then sail the rest of the way. The two Piranhas, their drafts shallow enough to allow them to skim over part of the reef, waited until Maria guided the *Cheetah* through the deep-water channel they had marked for her with buoys on their way in.

Clyde, intimidated by the strangers on board, had sat quietly on his perch until they were gone and the *Cheetah* was under way. Ruffling his feathers, he looked quizzically about the deck. He cocked an eye at Gannon, then at Maria. "Good boy, Coon Ass," he squawked. "Whatcha doin', Coon Ass?"

Maria tried to fight back the tears, then turned her head so Gannon couldn't see them stream down her face.

The pounding of rocket-propelled grenades punctuated the rolling crescendo of machine guns along with the chatter of automatic-weapons fire and explosions from grenade launchers. The sounds of the intense attack grew to deafening proportions as the main body of the Sandinista troops coordinated their assault on Santana's position.

The blast effects and shock waves from the Sandinista mortar rounds fired in rapid succession rippled the ground around Santana and his team as they lay atop a ridge that overlooked the small valley into which they had drawn the

Sandinista troops. Blast followed blast as the Sandinistas walked the mortar rounds up the slope toward the top of the ridge, zeroing in on and bracketing Santana's position. More than a hundred men were approaching from across the valley, heading for the ridge, with at least another hundred coming behind them. Santana was beginning to doubt Travis's word when the voice came over the radio.

It was the AC-130 Spectre gunship that Travis had called in from the CIA base in Honduras. "Sandman, this is Spooky," said the pilot of the gunship. "Turn on your strobe so I can get a fix on your position."

Santana put the small strobe light into the barrel of an M-79 grenade launcher to prevent any lateral reflections and pointed it upward.

"We're on top of the ridge north of the valley," Santana said. "The bad guys are all right where you want them."

The Spectre pilot spotted the strobe immediately. "Gotcha, Sandman. Keep your heads down. It's danger close."

From fifteen hundred feet up the pilot dumped a series of flares that lit up the valley with an unearthly glow. At least 150 Sandinista troops were caught out in the open. Once locked on target, the pilot unleashed the Spectre's awesome firepower. A constant barrage from the aircraft's computerized gun system, consisting of a 105mm howitzer, a 40mm cannon, two 20mm cannons, and four 7.62mm mini-guns capable of firing six thousand rounds per minute, devastated the valley floor, tearing up huge chunks of earth as well as bodies.

When the Spectre completed the first run, spreading its deadly fire over the entire open area, nothing moved on the valley floor. On its second pass the pilot directed his fire into the jungle at the far end of the valley, where the few remaining Sandinista troops had taken cover from the first pass. Again the ground erupted from the terrifying fusillade that streamed from the night sky. The leafy canopy was shredded; rocks, debris, and dismembered bodies were tossed into the air and bounced across the ground; huge trees were up-rooted as though they were mere seedlings. Within the span of seven minutes the Spectre's attacks had killed an esti-mated two hundred troops. The withering fire had been so accurate and so pervasive that the 150-square-yard valley once covered with waist-high grass now looked like newly mown lawn.

"That should do it, Sandman," the pilot said.

"And then some," Santana replied. "I owe you one."

"Travis said to tell you that you owe him three or four."

"Tell him not to press his luck," Santana said. "I'll be in touch. Out."

With that Santana and his team withdrew from the ridge, each man looking down into the smoking, moonlit valley and the carnage that the Spectre had left behind. Santana had lost two of his men and a close friend, but at least two hundred enemy troops had paid with their lives. It was a kill ratio that would have made even Boos happy, Santana thought, a sad smile at the corners of his mouth as he looked back in the direction where his friend lay buried in a shallow jungle grave.

"I'll miss you, you sweet motherfucker," he said just above a whisper.

42

Montego Bay Harbor sparkled beneath the last of a late afternoon sun, reflecting the shining brilliance of the Caribbean like a sea of diamonds. A soft breeze drifted in from the ocean. It gently fluttered the awning over the *Cheetah*'s entertainment cockpit, where Gannon sat watching the sun hang briefly above the distant mountains before it dropped slowly below the mainland horizon. The *Cheetah* had sailed into Montego Bay that morning and docked at the yacht club. Gannon, his black-nylon carryall sitting on the deck, was packed and ready to leave for the airport for his evening flight to Miami.

Maria had prepared a special meal and began handing the plates up through the galley pass-through. It was a Cuban menu of poached red snapper in a delicate sauce, with dishes of rice, black beans, and sweet fried plantains. Maria was as expert a cook as she was at whatever else she put her hand to.

"It's excellent, Maria," Gannon told her halfway through the meal, but they had little else to say to each other. Boos's absence was still tangible. The rough six-day passage back to Montego Bay had given them little time to think of anything except the tasks at hand. And now, anchored in the quiet harbor, each fell silent, privately reliving the times they had shared with a friend they had both admired and loved.

PAYBACK 343

Maria had been particularly upset when she had called the *Cheetah*'s owner and informed him of Boos's death. He had taken the news as hard as Maria and told her he would arrive within the week, his concern for her heightened upon hearing the pain and sorrow in her voice.

"The owner keeps a car here at the club," she said to Gannon after a long silence. "I'll drive you to the airport."

"I can take a cab," Gannon said. "Someone should stay with the boat."

"No," Maria said. "I want to." She had grown to like Gannon, felt closer to him, as people do when thrown together in difficult situations and are forced to depend on each other. On the return voyage she had seen some of his strength of character along with the gentleness and compassion that lay just beneath the surface of what at first had seemed an impenetrable warrior exterior. She had never heard a man speak so endearingly about his wife and their life together and how much he missed her. Once, while he had been sleeping on deck, she had heard him murmur Kate's name in a dream.

A few passersby strolled along the dock. One in particular stopped at the end of the *Cheetah*'s gangway and waved a brief hello.

"May I come aboard?" Tom Driscoll asked.

Maria nodded. She recognized him from the cove in Nicaragua.

Driscoll slipped off his Gucci loafers as he stepped on deck and came forward to the entertainment cockpit. He sat beside Maria, opposite Gannon.

"Would you like something to eat?" Maria offered.

"It all looks delicious," Driscoll said, "but I have a plane waiting for me. A glass of wine would be nice, though."

Maria poured him one as he leaned forward and spoke to Gannon in a conspiratorial tone.

"Nikolai Malik is still alive."

The words went through Gannon like a jolt of electricity. "Where is he?"

"One of our people in France on another assignment spotted him in Antibes," Driscoll said. "He's on a motor yacht, the *Jameel*, docked at the high-security area at the International Yacht Club, the guest of some high-powered Arab gunrunners who dabble in terrorism."

Maria's eyes widened at the mention of Antibes, but she remained silent.

"Where's Antibes?" Gannon asked.

"French Riviera, about ten miles west of Nice," Driscoll said. "I passed the information on to some friends of yours. They're sitting on him until you can get there."

Gannon's eyes grew distant, then he leaned over and clasped Driscoll's hand. "Thanks. I know how you people work. You didn't have to do this."

Driscoll smiled. "Malik is no longer of any immediate interest to us. We personally don't give a shit what happens to him. And you're wrong about how we work if you think we don't appreciate those who help us. We owe you."

Driscoll nodded to Maria, then got up and walked back to the gangway, pulling on his loafers. "By the way, Gannon. I wasn't here."

"Never saw you before in my life," Gannon said.

Maria, having contained herself until Driscoll was out of sight, grabbed Gannon by the arm, her voice full of excitement. "I know where Malik is . . . I mean I know the area and the boat. The owner of the *Cheetah* keeps his motor yacht, *Mi Gaea*, docked at the same place—the International Yacht Club d'Antibes. He has a slip there. I worked on the *Mi Gaea* before I came aboard the *Cheetah*."

"I've got to do this myself," Gannon said, shaking his head. "I appreciate the offer, but—"

"*Bullshit!*" Maria said. "That Russian son of a bitch killed Jim. I have almost as much at stake in this as you do now. And believe me, I'm not exaggerating when I tell you I can be an asset to you when we get there—as a matter of fact, before we get there."

Gannon saw the fire and determination in Maria's eyes,

"You're right," he said. "I've got no right to cut you out. But this isn't a game. Malik's a psychopath and a professional."

"I have a girlfriend, Sally Hooper," Maria said. "She's the chief stewardess on the *Mi Gaea*. She and a couple of her friends keep an apartment in Antibes as a home base."

"So?" Gannon said.

"The *Mi Gaea*'s in port. I can give her a call before we leave here," Maria said. "The *Jameel*'s slip is only four or five down from the *Mi Gaea*. You'd be surprised how much she can find out for us about who's on the *Jameel* and what's going on. The crews from all of the yachts based there know each other and get together socially when they're in port."

"Call her," Gannon said. "I've got a call of my own to make." He had spoken to General Max on the day he got back to Montego Bay, but with this new development he wanted to call him again and ask one more favor of him.

"I have a friend here who'll take care of Clyde and the boat," Maria said. "Give me ten minutes to make the arrangements and I'm ready to leave."

Gannon and Maria made use of the car the *Cheetah*'s owner kept at the yacht club. Gannon drove through the streets of Montego Bay en route to the airport. They stopped at Maria's request, and Gannon waited while she entered a Catholic church just off the main square.

"What was that all about?" Gannon asked as Maria returned to the car.

"I lit a candle for Jim," she said solemnly. "And one for you."

"Can't hurt," Gannon said, accelerating out of a hairpin turn as they passed through the congested part of town and onto the main road to the airport.

43

Backdropped by deep green forest, silvery olive trees, and white limestone hills, the French Riviera has few rivals for natural beauty and climate. From Monte Carlo to St. Tropez brilliant sunshine bathes seemingly endless stretches of beach on a magnificent coastline that ranges from sheltered inlets to great sweeping bays, some with flat, gentle shores, while others plunge steeply into the deep blue of the Mediterranean Sea.

The coast along the ancient town of Antibes is flat and open, with wide bays. It is a gentle coast, with the Cap d'Antibes Peninsula its only promontory. The town of Antibes, founded in the fourth century B.C. by the Greeks of Massilia, was originally named Antipolis—meaning opposite city—a name derived from its location across the water from Nice. When the Romans supplanted the Greeks it was renamed Latinum Antipolis and an arsenal and aqueduct were built, while sailors and fishermen settled along its shores. The barbarian invasions destroyed its prosperity and until the early fourth century A.D., when the first markets were established, it was a virtual ghost town. Upon realizing its military significance, the kings of France later made it a frontier post, reinforcing it as a stronghold against the dukes of Savoy, who controlled Nice.

Today all that remains of the old fortifications is Fort

Carré, a square blockhouse of a structure overlooking the entrance to the harbor and the seventeenth-century seafront ramparts. But the town of Antibes flourishes as a tourist mecca and as one of Europe's primary centers for the commercial production of flowers. A large marina, capable of holding up to six hundred boats, now replaces the old harbor, making the port of Antibes a major international yachting center. Lying just beyond the remnants of the seafront ramparts, the picturesque old-town section still maintains the charm and wistful air of ancient times, with its covered outdoor market, sunny squares, and maze of tiny side streets crammed with pricey boutiques, craft shops, and art galleries.

Separated from the crowded, busy main marina is the International Yacht Club d'Antibes. The club was built by the French Mafia and an Arab cartel as a high-security large-yacht basin. It provides berths for nineteen heavy-tonnage yachts and claims to be the most secure yacht harbor in the world. The cost of two million dollars for a thirty-year lease on a single berth makes it the exclusive domain of billionaires and multimillionaires to whom security considerations are a necessary part of their everyday lives.

Closed-circuit television cameras are positioned to cover every square inch of the half-mile-long quay and its facilities. Vapor lights come on and off automatically at dusk and dawn, and a twenty-four-hour security guard mans the only entrance to the quay, making it impossible for anyone to enter and roam the area undetected. The yacht basin was created by dumping thousands of tons of rocks to create a breakwater that slopes into the sea, forming a private peninsula. Behind the breakwater a fifteen-foot-high concrete seawall, with a walkway on top, extends the entire length of the yacht-club area to the harbor entrance. A modern *capitainerie* at the far end of the quay contains administration offices on the lower level, with the upper level being a circular glass-enclosed observation deck, serving to control the arrivals and departures of the member yachts and as the center where the console of security-camera monitors are located.

The dock area, as wide as a two-lane road, provides parking for the yacht owners' vehicles against the seawall directly across from their berths. Tourists are allowed to enter the area on foot and walk along the quay, which, during the height of the season, from May to October, ensures a near constant stream of admirers hopeful for a glimpse of the rich and famous. It is a practice that does little to violate the security of the area, considering that everyone entering must pass through the guarded entrance gate, and most of the yachts have their own private security forces, preventing anyone from coming on board.

The *Mi Gaea* was berthed midway down the quay. She was flanked on either side by two slightly larger yachts with modern high-performance hulls, sleek, streamlined decks, and smoked-glass windows. They, along with most of the luxury motor yachts moored at the exclusive berths, were new boats, built within the last five to seven years. Although all were in the twenty- to thirty-million-dollar price range, alongside the *Mi Gaea* they had all the ambiance of a string of Quality Court motels erected next to New York's Carlyle Hotel.

A classically eloquent yacht, the *Mi Gaea* was a 120-foot oceangoing vessel, designed and engineered for unmatched seagoing comfort and luxury. Built in Scotland in 1963, she had undergone a massive three-year rebuilding and redesign in 1984, with workmanship of incomparable quality and detail. In stark contrast to the fiberglass and space-age plastics look of the newer yachts, and their garish ultramodern interior decors, the *Mi Gaea* had an aura of elegance and a prestigious stature, evoking an era when the great yachts ruled the sea.

Her quality and elegance were visible at a glance, even to the uninitiated. Meticulously maintained, her exterior had a mirrorlike finish, with teak railings that glowed with the high gloss of multiple coats of varnish. Beveled-glass doors framed in teak led from the aft deck to the main salon—a genial, intimate room paneled with the rich, warm patina of solid teak and the golden gleam of a brass wet bar, evoking an Edwardian atmosphere of Old World gentility. As on the *Cheetah*, exquisite silk oriental carpets and fine art accented the gracious decor; but dominating the salon, from a paneled wall in the center of the room facing the aft deck and visible to passersby through the beveled-glass doors, was a stunning, priceless Renoir.

Just aft of the main salon, in a lavishly equipped office/study, finished in finely detailed raised paneled oak and complete with a fully computerized satellite communications system, Sally Hooper had taken the call from Maria on the land line. Maria had made repeated attempts to call Sally at her apartment in town before leaving the airport in Jamaica, finally reaching her aboard the *Mi Gaea* during her four-hour layover in London for the final leg of the flight to Nice.

Sally, a pretty, blue-eyed English girl with short-cut blond hair and an engaging personality, sat staring at the telephone after hanging up. It was five o'clock in the evening when she got up and left the office, a mischievous smile spreading slowly across her coquettish face.

It was a slow, restful time aboard the *Mi Gaea*. With the owner gone until the following spring, the crew was mostly concerned with maintenance and general upkeep. Steve Jacover, the *Mi Gaea*'s captain, his stern, handsome features framed with a mass of naturally curly reddish-brown hair, was on the aft deck having a drink when Sally rushed out from the main salon.

"Good news?" Jacover asked. His piercing blue eyes searched for a clue to the unusual exuberance prompted by the telephone call.

Sally shook her head and grinned, then continued onto the gangway, turning back to smile and wave. "I've always wanted to be a spy. I truly have."

"Whatever you're drinking, you'd better back off it a bit,"

Jacover called after her good-naturedly. He watched her cross the quay, climb on her motorcycle, and roar off in the direction of the yacht club's entrance gate.

Sally Hooper's departure had not gone unnoticed by Sam Pavlik, but her activities were of no interest to him; in fact, he had no idea who she was or of the role the *Mi Gaea* would eventually play in what was about to unfold. Pavlik's attention was riveted on the *Jameel,* a two-hundred-foot motor yacht six berths down from the *Mi Gaea.* Two garishly painted Mercedes-Benz limousines—one candy-apple purple, the other a bright off-green color that Pavlik referred to as camel-shit yellow—belonging to the *Jameel*'s owner were parked against the seawall across from the yacht. They flanked a small motor home with blacked-out windows that served as a security van for the *Jameel*'s four exterior guards, who patrolled the quay and the walkway atop the seawall in the immediate area of the yacht.

Nikolai Malik, the Arab owner of the yacht, and two of the owner's Arab companions were aboard the *Jameel.* From his vantage point, using a high-powered scope, Pavlik could look down on the boat deck where the four men sat around a table engaged in animated conversation. Malik was drinking a bottle of wine, while the Arabs abstained. Adjusting the scope, Pavlik scanned the decks for the three onboard security guards he had pegged as mercenaries, probably of West German origin. One stood on the aft deck guarding the entrance to the main salon, another was forward on the boat deck, and the third was out of sight, stationed inside the yacht. All, he had noted earlier, carried mini-Uzi submachine guns in shoulder holsters under loose-fitting jackets.

Mike Duggan sat eating a candy bar on a wooden crate behind Pavlik. They had staked out the *Jameel* for the past two days, and sandwich and snack wrappers and empty soda cans littered the dusty barren room. They had taken videotape of everyone boarding and leaving the yacht and made notes on the routines of the security guards on board and those assigned to the van on the quay.

The surveillance of Malik, on the rare occasions when he left the yacht, was carried out by another Delta Force Omega Team member—Staff Sergeant Dave Maurer—who had volunteered his services on learning that Malik was the man who had killed Gannon's wife. Pavlik and Duggan had grown close to Gannon when he was their squadron commander and felt a bond that all men have with those with whom they have faced death. But Maurer's respect and admiration for Gannon knew no bounds; Gannon had not only been Maurer's mentor, but as Maurer often said, "If I have a hero, it's Jack Gannon."

Maurer had rented a motorcycle, a common conveyance around the quay and the town, making it possible to stay close to the limousines without drawing attention to himself. But the habit pattern of Malik and his Arab friends when leaving the yacht was an uninteresting routine that involved nothing more than a quiet dinner at a restaurant in town or a visit to a local disco.

Their observation post was one of the many flaws the Delta Force men had immediately spotted in the yacht club's highly touted security arrangements. Adjoining the seawall near the entrance gate, actually an integral part incorporated into the seawall, was the rear wall of a deserted boatyard building. From a broken third-story window that overlooked the entire yacht-club area, Pavlik and Duggan could not only observe every activity but by simply crawling out of the window and lowering themselves to the rocky breakwater under the cover of darkness, they then had easy access to the walkway along the top of the private seawall.

The entrance to the deserted boatyard was outside the yacht club's security gate, fronting on the crowded quay along the public marina, and gaining access to it was a simple matter of climbing a section of its ten-foot chain-link fence, which was hidden from view by old machine parts and parked cars. Once inside the yard one had only to proceed to the floor above the huge two-story open bay, which had once been the work area, to the windows facing the Mediterranean and the yacht club.

Pavlik stifled a yawn, removed his eye from the scope for a few minutes, then went back to observing the *Jameel* and the quay. At this time of evening the tourist traffic strolling along the quay and admiring the yachts was at its peak—couples, arm in arm, dreaming childish what-if? dreams, enthralled by the wealth and opulence around them. A tall, broad-shouldered older man, walking alone, caught Pavlik's attention. He had a distinct military bearing and looked vaguely familiar.

"Hey, Mike," Pavlik called to Duggan. "Come here. Take a look at this guy."

Duggan came to the window and put his eye to the scope. After a few moments he said, "That's General Max!"

"I knew I'd seen him before," Pavlik said. "Christ, he's virtually the patron saint of Special Operations."

"If it wasn't for him," Duggan added, "Delta Force wouldn't exist. Is this a coincidence . . . or what?"

"Get a grip, Duggan," Pavlik said. "Considering what's going on here, it's no coincidence when someone like General Max appears on the scene. The man's a living legend."

Duggan continued to peer through the scope, following the casual pace of General Max as he approached the end of the *Mi Gaea*'s gangway and engaged Jacover in a brief conversation before being invited on board.

Picking up the small hand-held portable radio at his side, Pavlik keyed the microphone. "Hey, Maurer," he said. "A blonde with short-cut hair riding a maroon Harley-Davidson sportster passed by you a few minutes ago."

"I saw her," came Maurer's quick response, never one to miss a Harley or an attractive woman.

"Pick up on her and stay close," Pavlik came back. "There's something weird going on here."

"I'm on her," Maurer said. He was parked outside the yacht club's security gate at an opening in the ramparts that led to a public beach he had named "Titty City" due to the abundance of topless sunbathers. It was an observation post he had personally selected for the view. Starting the rented BMW motorcycle, he spun around and weaved his way along the crowded quay in the direction he had seen the Harley and the blonde go.

Sally Hooper made a left turn off the quay and drove through the old sea gate—a tunnel through the ancient ramparts—and onto Rue Aubernon in the old-town section of Antibes. She followed the narrow, crowded street for a short distance and pulled into the curb in front of Chez Harry's Shack, better known as Harry's Bar to those who frequented it on a regular basis. It was the crew bar, the unofficial gathering place for all those who worked on the big yachts, a place to drink, have a snack, and catch up on the latest gossip. As Sally extended the kickstand and slid gracefully off the Harley, she took no notice of the man on the silver BMW who passed by and parked farther up the street.

The evening crowd had already spilled out onto the sidewalk tables, and small groups of mostly Englishmen and other Brits filled the tables, the overwhelming majority wearing knit polo-style shirts with the names of the yachts on which they worked embroidered on the front. Sally's eyes roamed the crowded, noisy café as she smiled back at a few friends and would-be boyfriends.

Spotting Calvin Hardiment, a rugged-looking Englishman with a sporty mustache and a no-nonsense face, she approached his table at a corner inside the bar where he sat alone, putting the finishing touches on a pitcher of beer.

Hardiment was the engineer aboard the *Mi Gaea* and a former airborne-qualified Royal Marine who had served with the Special Boat Squadron and fought in the Falklands. His first love was the sea; his second, jumping out of airplanes. Having indulged the second for a ten-year military career, he was now thoroughly enjoying the first.

"Here to drive the lads wild?" he said to Sally with a friendly smile reserved for those he liked.

"I need some information," Sally said. "On the q.t."

"What sort of information?"

"Do you know anyone who works on board the *Jameel* and talks too much?"

"Sure," Calvin said. He pointed with his glass at a table out on the sidewalk. "See that lad with the greasy brown hair. Harry Bingham's his name. Ugly enough to turn a funeral up an alley."

Sally looked where he was pointing. "Oh, my God! I damn near have to beat him off with a club every time he gets near me."

"Grin and bear it," Calvin said with a wink. "He couldn't keep a secret if his life depended on it. Just passed on an interesting tidbit to me earlier."

"What was that?" Sally asked.

"The *Jameel*'s owner's son wipes his ass with washcloths. Different one every time. Consequently, the job of laundress aboard the *Jameel* isn't exactly a highly sought-after position."

"That's disgusting," Sally said, making a face.

"It's him that does it, love. Not me."

"Thanks, Calvin," Sally said. "You're a dear. Guess I'll have to bite my tongue and work whatever charms I have on Mr. Bingham."

"Your charms are considerable. I wouldn't worry about that," Calvin said, refilling his glass with the last of the beer. "Your immediate problem may lie in keeping him from biting you. Then there's the tetanus shots to consider. Nasty business."

Calvin watched Sally as she walked outside and bestowed a flirtatious smile on the rather unattractive young man. Bingham rose to offer her a chair and in his enthusiasm sent a bottle of wine to the sidewalk, where it smashed and splashed all over Sally's white deck shoes.

"I'm so sorry," Bingham said. "How clumsy of me." He

started to drop to his knees to wipe off her shoes with a
napkin.

Sally patted him on the shoulder. "It's quite all right,
Harry. They needed a bit of color." She sat at the table, and
what appeared to be another smile was really the manifesta-
tion of her gritting her teeth to keep her anger from boiling
over.

She looked back to see Calvin giving her the victory sign.

44

It was just past six o'clock in the evening when Gannon and
Maria drove into Antibes from the Nice airport. They
parked their rented car on a side street just off the Rue
Aubernon and walked the short distance to Harry's Bar
where Maria saw Sally seated at a sidewalk table. There was
a look of unqualified relief on Sally's face as she waved and
stood up and embraced her friend Maria. She had gleaned
all the information there was to be had from her companion
and was eagerly looking for a graceful way out.

Maria pulled Sally aside. "Doesn't that man you're talking with work on the *Jameel*?"

Sally nodded and smiled. "I suggest we find somewhere to
talk."

She turned back to Bingham and said, "Thank you for the
wine and the conversation, Harry. I must be going."

"I'll be in port for two more days," Harry said, a somewhat pleading look in his eyes.

"I'll remember that," Sally said, and excused herself. She
led Maria and Gannon down the street in the direction of
the marina.

Sally cast an appreciative glance at Gannon and smiled
Maria introduced them.

"You wanted information, deary, I got you information,"
Sally said as they walked out of earshot of the sorely disap-

ointed Bingham. "The interior layout of the *Jameel,* the guards' habits and posts, and which stateroom this Russian fellow is in."

"Did he say why the Russian is here?" Gannon asked.

"I don't think he knows."

As they reached the sea gate through the old ramparts, Sally led them left on to the Boulevard D'Aguillon, a narrow side street that ran parallel to the ramparts. The crowded street, closed to vehicular traffic in the evenings, was little more than a continuous row of outdoor cafés on one side; on the opposite side, along the ramparts, street vendors had set up stalls beneath colorfully striped umbrellas and awnings that displayed paintings, jewelry, questionable *objets d'art,* and knickknacks. It was the most popular section of the old town in the evenings and late into the night.

Maria and Gannon followed Sally to a café midway down the block. They took a table overlooking the constant stream of pedestrian traffic—mostly groups of young singles in search of each other, with occasional clinging couples oblivious to their surroundings.

Gannon's attention was drawn to an attractive French girl sitting at a corner table. A young man with a guitar sat with her, accompanying her as she began to sing a melancholy love song that brought a rush of painful memories back to Gannon. Kate, a student in France for a time, used to play the guitar and sing to him in French when they were alone. The song he was listening to now, which carried over into the adjoining cafés and stopped people in the street to listen, was one Kate had sung. Gannon closed his eyes for a terrible moment, caught hold of his emotions, then continued to stare at the girl, enthralled by the song and her beautiful, untrained natural voice. He continued to stare, lost in his memories, after the song had ended.

Dave Maurer had seen Gannon when he and Maria reached Harry's Bar and had followed on foot. Slipping into

an alleyway, he took the portable radio from inside his
jacket.

"The boss is here," he reported to Pavlik.

"Where is he?"

"He and some great-looking broad I think I'm in love
with met the blonde you put me on at Harry's Bar. They're
at one of those Frog cafés just inside the ramparts having a
drink."

"Keep 'em in sight," Pavlik said. "I'm on my way."

Pavlik hurried from the room overlooking the yacht club,
leaving Duggan in charge of the observation post.

"If Malik or any of the sand niggers make a move," he
told Duggan, "give me a holler."

The café was a brisk five-minute walk from the deserted
boatyard, and it took Pavlik only a few minutes more to find
Gannon on the busy, cluttered street. He took a seat next to
Sally as though he was expected, put his arm around her,
and kissed her cheek, much to Sally's surprise.

"Play along," Pavlik said with a charming smile. "I'm
with him." He nodded toward Gannon, who was surprised
to see one of his former squadron troopers sitting across
from him.

"Hello, Boss," Pavlik said, using the term of affection and
respect afforded to Delta Force commanders by their troops.
"Good to see you."

"What are you doing here?" Gannon said. He had not
realized that Driscoll had been referring to active-duty
Delta Force personnel when he stated that "friends" were
keeping an eye on Malik.

Pavlik made a slight motion with his head, indicating that
Gannon should look off to his left. Gannon did and saw
Maurer feigning interest in a painting at a stall across the
street. He made eye contact with Gannon but gave no visible sign of recognition. It was a practice followed by all
Delta Force personnel when working undercover; putting
two or three of them together in a public place alerted an

astute observer that these were not ordinary tourists. They looked too much like what they were.

Maria began to tell Sally what had happened to Jim Boos, but, as Gannon had requested, she did not mention anything about the SADM or the CIA's part in the mission into Nicaragua. With Sally and Maria involved in their own conversation, Pavlik leaned across the table, the music and crowd noise concealing his words from all but Gannon.

"You remember Duggan?" Pavlik asked.

"Of course," Gannon said, recalling the bull-like trooper who had been one of his best shooters, second only to Mauser.

"He's over at the observation post we set up at the yacht club."

Gannon shook his head emphatically. "I appreciate the effort," he said to Pavlik, "but I can't involve active-duty personnel in this."

Pavlik grinned. "Hey, Boss. We're on official leave. And besides, we all have false ID backstopped to the nth degree by your spook buddy Driscoll in the event anything goes wrong. And we got the unofficial word that the Ranch's position on this is what they don't know they can't prevent, and if push comes to shove, they can blame it on the Company. We never were just your troops, Boss. We're your friends."

Gannon smiled and slowly shook his head. "Sounds like you've got it all figured out."

"Most of it," Pavlik replied with a confident grin. "Except why General Max is here. He just boarded the yacht the blonde works on." He gestured to Sally.

Gannon nodded. "I called him in."

"Do I need to know why?"

"Not now," Gannon said.

Pavlik eyed Maria, then said, "What's she doing here?"

Maria overheard the question and bristled at all that it implied. "*She's* here to help," she said, answering for herself.

"Civilians, especially the female type, just screw things up, honey," Pavlik said. "No offense, but you can go powder your nose until this is over."

"She's in," Gannon said. "Malik killed a good friend of hers. And she's no amateur. Trust me on that."

Pavlik acquiesced immediately. "If you say so, Boss." Looking to Sally, he asked, "And her?"

"I've got information you need," Sally said.

Again leaning close to Gannon, Pavlik said, "Want to take a look-see from the observation post?"

"The man I'm after got a good look at me in New York," Gannon said. "I don't want him spotting me before we're ready to move."

"Not to worry, Boss," Pavlik said, getting up to lead the way. He looked back at Maria and Sally and added, "Come on, you can come too."

"Oh, golly gee," Maria said, her voice dripping with sarcasm. "We can? How neat. Can I hold your gun?"

Pavlik grimaced. A further evaluation after a long look into Maria's eyes told him he had made a hasty, erroneous snap judgment.

It was approaching dusk when Gannon peered through the high-powered scope in the third-floor window of the deserted boatyard. He felt a wave of hatred and loathing pass over him as Malik's hard Slavic face filled the lens. He was still at the table on the *Jameel*'s boat deck, laughing and drinking with his Arab companions.

Eleven of the club's nineteen berths were occupied. Moored stern-to, they were an impressive array of oceangoing vessels. One stood out above all the others: docked in the slip closest to the entrance was the *Jessica,* a two-hundred foot, three-masted topsail schooner, reminiscent of turn-of-the-century schooners. Under sail she was a breathtaking sight, capable of leaving even the most jaded yachtsman speechless. A few berths up from the *Mi Gaèa,* and almost as elegant, was the 186-foot motor yacht the *Belle France.*

few, especially those flanking the *Mi Gaea,* stood out more for their lack of style and elegance, despite their hefty price tags.

"Nice toys, huh?" Pavlik said as Gannon looked up from the scope and scanned the quay and the luxury yachts. "This is where the big boys come to play, Boss. The real heavy hitters."

"Yeah," Duggan said, gesturing toward the *Jameel.* "But look at what that rag head's done to that boat." He was referring to the striped awnings and other garish exterior decorations on the *Jameel.* "Who else could take a thirty-million-dollar yacht and turn it into a fuckin' double-wide trailer? Only thing missin' are Florida plates."

"Do yourself a favor, Duggan, and save yourself some embarrassment," Maria said with a friendly smile. "Don't ever take the foreign service exam."

"No?" Duggan played along. "Damn, and here I was considering bein' a career diplomat after I left the Army."

Gannon went back to the scope, concentrating on Malik and his companions.

"Easy shot, huh, Boss?" Maurer said, taking his sniper rifle from its case. "I could turn his head into road pizza from here. No sweat."

"I want him alive," Gannon said. "Nobody gets killed. We neutralize the people we have to, but nobody gets killed," he emphasized a second time.

"What if it's us or them?" Maurer asked.

"Only if your life is in danger," Gannon replied. "But I want this planned and carried out so everything possible is done to avoid that contingency."

Pavlik looked to Maurer and Duggan. They both nodded. "That calls for a different approach."

"Break down the security setup for me," Gannon said, still looking through the scope.

Gannon listened carefully, asking no questions until they had finished reporting what they had observed.

"The biggest obstacle is the three guards on board," Pavlik said. "One stays on the aft deck guarding the entrance to the main salon. One patrols the boat deck, watching for any approach by water, SCUBA divers, and like that. And one stays inside all the time. He's the only unknown. Hard to tell where he is at any given time."

"The one who has the night shift is lazy. He spends most of his time in the crew's entertainment lounge below decks watching videos," Sally Hooper said. "The lounge is forward, just below the main dining salon."

"Any electronic security?" Gannon asked.

"Yeah," Pavlik replied with a Cheshire-cat grin. "The key pad that activates and deactivates the internal alarm system is on the bulkhead on the aft deck, to the left of the doors leading into the main salon." Pavlik paused for effect, then continued. "Took me two days. I put the scope on them every time they punched in the code and got it a piece at a time." He held up a slip of paper with the code numbers for the security system on it.

"You get an 'atta boy' for that," Gannon said.

"They have another electronic surveillance system inside the yacht," Sally contributed again.

"What's it for?" Gannon asked.

"It seems the owner is a bit of a voyeur. He has audio bugs and infrared cameras hidden in all the staterooms. I should think that might present a problem if you want to take the Russian off the boat alive."

"Who monitors the system?" Gannon asked.

"The owner does," Sally said. "The video monitor and recorders are in the master stateroom."

Gannon thought for a moment, then said, "We'll have to deal with that if it comes up. The first order of business is how to get aboard the yacht in the first place without starting a gun battle. I take it they're all armed?"

"Mini-Uzis, every one of them," Pavlik said.

"How qualified are they?"

"They're efficient and in shape," Pavlik said. "Every indication is, they can handle themselves."

"They speak German to each other," Maurer, who was fluent in the language, added. "Good probability some of them are former GSG-9 men," he said, referring to the elite West German antiterrorist group.

"What's the routine for the guards at the security van?" Gannon asked.

"They work in shifts," Pavlik said. "Two of them stay locked inside while the other two patrol the immediate area, one on the walkway on top of the seawall, the other on the dock. When they rotate, two knocks on the van door, followed by a pause and one more knock gets the guys inside to open up. The windows are blacked out and they've got curtains pulled across them. They never look outside, just open up when their buddies knock. One possible problem. I don't know what's inside the van other than the two guys. Could be nothin', but you never know."

"What about the monitors for the outside surveillance cameras?"

"There's a bank of them in that glass observation deck on top of the *capitainerie*," Pavlik said. "You can see part of them if you put the scope on it."

Gannon did, then asked, "How many guards in the *capitainerie*?"

"Just one after midnight," Pavlik said.

"What about the guard in the booth at the entrance gate?"

"The guy who takes the graveyard shift's got an H&K squeeze-cocker .380 in an inside-the-belt holster. By the looks of him I'd say he's no problem. He works for the Yacht Club, not for the Arabs."

"On the way over here I saw another guy manning a pole barrier on the dock along the public marina," Gannon said. "What's his story?"

"He's an unarmed one-legged drunk who goes off duty around 10:00 P.M.," Pavlik said. "The only other variable is a harbor cop who drives around with a German shepherd in the car with him. The dog's afraid of his own shadow and the guard does a turnaround at the entrance to this area once he gets the wave-off from the guy in the booth. If he shows up while we're making our move, he won't be any problem. Maurer can bullshit his way out of anything. We'll have him take out the guy in the booth and replace him. In the event the cop with the dog gets wise, he can always neutralize him."

"What have you got in the way of equipment?" Gannon asked.

"We've all got nine-mike-mikes with hush puppies," Pavlik said, using a colloquialism for the silenced 9mm pistols they all carried in shoulder holsters. He handed Gannon the pistol and holster they had thought to bring along for him. "Just in case it all falls apart."

"As far as takin' people out without killing them," Pavlik continued, "we've got a couple of spring-loaded Syrettes with a fast-acting knockout drug; takes a couple of seconds if you stick them in the neck. We got a bunch of chloroform pads sealed in foil pouches . . . and our hands."

"All right," Gannon said. "Let's brainstorm it and come up with a plan."

They all gathered around, pulling up crates and whatever else was available to sit on. Maria sat cross-legged on the floor and said to Gannon, "I've got an idea for getting you on board the *Jameel* without any gunplay."

"Let's hear it," Gannon said.

"The crews from the different yachts are always paying social calls on each other. It's an everyday occurrence, nothing out of the ordinary."

They all sat and listened to Maria's plan, each adding suggestions and extemporaneously improvising on how to make it even better and coordinate it with the rest of the actions that would need to be taken. Dusk faded into night and the vapor lights came on as the deadly serious discussion continued unabated.

* * *

Steve Jacover, the captain of the *Mi Gaea,* could not believe his ears. The man who had identified himself as retired General Maxwell Taylor Stanton was on the bridge. He had rigged a highly sophisticated scrambler to the radio and was transmitting on a special frequency, speaking fluent Russian, rapid-fire, like a native. Jacover listened for a few moments. He recognized the language but understood none of it, and he stepped out of the pilothouse and leaned on the railing. Some things were better left unexplained, he decided. Besides, the general had the boss's blessing.

45

It was three-thirty in the morning when the Harley-Davidson roared up to the small space between the wall and the
entrance barrier to the International Yacht Club d'Antibes.
Sally slowed down just enough to wave a cheery hello to the
sleepy guard in the booth. It was her usual way of saving
him the trouble of raising the barrier, one he appreciated
more often than not. He took notice of Maria sitting on the
jump seat behind Sally. Maria smiled and waved. The guard
waved back, recalling that he hadn't seen the beautiful dark-
haired girl in the past year but remembering her well, as
everyone did who ever saw her.

The timing for their arrival had been carefully chosen:
midway through the graveyard shift, when the guards
would be most inattentive and weary of their monotonous
routines. The on-board yacht parties were over for the night
or had moved inside for more intimate activities. The quay
was deserted with the exception of the *Jameel*'s guards.
Sally gunned the Harley to a throaty howl and sped up the
quay, slowing as she approached the security van, where she
and Maria again waved and smiled, this time to the guard
on the wall and the one standing off to the side of the van.
Both men were thoroughly bored and returned the greetings
with wistful looks. Sally got the distinct feeling that she and
Maria were being mentally undressed as they drove by.

Pulling into a space at the seawall across from the *Mi Gaea,* they got off the Harley. Sally boarded the yacht while Maria, dressed in shorts and a *Mi Gaea* crew shirt, removed a bottle of champagne that was protruding from her shoulder bag and uncorked it. She giggled hysterically when the cork blew off and began walking unsteadily down the quay toward the *Jameel.* Stopping to take a long drink of the bubbly liquid, she giggled again, kicked off her shoes, and continued on her way, barefoot and swaying.

At the far end of the seawall, near the entrance to the quay, Gannon, Duggan, and Pavlik lowered themselves the short distance from the third-floor window of the boatyard to the jagged rocks of the breakwater. The walkway atop the seawall was only six feet above the top of the sloping breakwater, and the three men began making their way along the rocks on the seaward side of the wall. The security guard was approximately one hundred yards ahead. Gannon's only reservation about the plan was Maria's exposure to a considerable amount of danger for a period of time when she would have no immediate available backup. He cringed inwardly at the thought of her falling into Malik's hands, but there had been no other way, without killing the guards, to accomplish what he had in mind.

Maurer had exited the boatyard onto the quay along the public marina. He approached the pole barrier at the entrance to the yacht club and walked around it. Crossing to the half-glass-enclosed security booth, he stepped inside, much to the amazement of the guard. Before a word of protest could be said, Maurer hit the man with a powerful overhand right that knocked him cold. Propping him in a sitting position in a corner of the booth, out of sight of anyone passing by, he took a roll of tape from his jacket and bound and gagged the unconscious man. He took his position at the door to the booth, his pale gray eyes—a sniper's eyes—focused halfway up the quay, intent on the area around the *Jameel.*

The guard walking the seawall followed Maria's every

move, his rapt attention having nothing to do with security
Fifteen feet below him on the quay, leaning against the side
of a small concrete transformer house that jutted out from
the seawall near the van, the second guard was equally at
tentive to Maria's physical attributes.

Maria waved to him as her eyes alertly swept the area
flicking from the guard on the aft deck of the *Jameel*, whose
attention she had also drawn, to the man on the wall and
back to the one near the van. She began to sing to herself
moving her body sensuously to the self-made music.

Occasional power surges and fluctuations caused some of
the vapor lights to dim intermittently. The ones closest to
the *Jameel* were among those affected, possibly due to the
amount of power being drawn to keep the entire yacht
ablaze with lights. The dimmed vapor lights threw areas
into deep shadows, which provided Gannon and Pavlik with
an unexpected bonus. Reaching the point in the breakwater
close to where the guard was walking the seawall, Gannon
and Pavlik stopped, taking cover among the large jagged
rocks. Duggan continued walking. He hugged the wall as he
passed unnoticed beneath the guard, the sound of the gentle
surf masking any inadvertent noise. He was heading to
where the seawall made a sharp left and connected to the
building housing the *capitainerie*, a few hundred yards far
ther on.

Maria, still singing and swaying to her tuneless song, ap
proached the *Jameel*'s stern. Flashing her most seductive
smile, she stepped onto the end of the gangway and stopped

"Hi," she called out to the tall, stoic-looking man stand
ing before the doors that led into the *Jameel*'s main salon

The guard smiled but didn't reply.

"Permission to come aboard," Maria said. She purposely
slurred her words as she moved farther up the gangway, half
dancing, half walking. Soft music could now be heard com
ing over the outdoor speakers on the *Jameel*'s aft deck and
she moved provocatively to its rhythm.

"I'm sorry," the guard said in a stiff, formal tone, "you

must not come on board. It is forbidden." His English was heavy with a German accent. His eyes took in the *Mi Gaea* crew shirt and he relaxed a bit.

Maria continued up the gangway, one enticing step at a time, maintaining eye contact with the aft-deck guard. "Aren't you lonely?" she said, using her put-on singsong Spanish accent. "I am lonely, very lonely." She had now reached the top of the gangway. She held out the bottle. "Champagne?"

The guard glanced about, tempted not by the champagne but by the possibility of spending time with Maria when his shift ended. "Perhaps you could come back in the morning," the guard said.

"Oh, but I have to work in the morning," Maria said. "But tonight I can play." She held her breath as she stepped off the gangway and onto the aft deck. If the guard didn't insist she leave at this point, she knew she had crossed the first major hurdle.

Pavlik peered over the top of the seawall, and seeing that Maria had positioned herself so the aft-deck guard's view was obstructed, nodded to Gannon, giving him a thumbs-up.

Maria approached the guard, dancing and smiling. "Dance with me," she said, setting the champagne bottle on the outdoor dining table in the middle of the deck. "It is no fun to dance alone." The music changed to a romantic ballad, and Maria moved in closer, smiling and singing along with the song she knew well.

The guard lost some of his hesitancy as Maria stopped directly in front of him. She put her arms around his neck and pressed her body against his, still swaying with the music. The guard began to respond, placing his hands around Maria's waist.

The security guard on top of the seawall was no longer walking. He stood with his back to the breakwater. His attention had been on Maria, but she was no longer in sight. The *Jameel*'s upper deck extended out over the aft deck, forming a roof, and from the top of the seawall the angle of view prevented him from seeing the doors leading to the main salon, where Maria and the guard were standing.

Gannon and Pavlik again made eye contact. This time Gannon nodded and they both moved with lightning speed up onto the seawall.

The guard on the wall had his back to Gannon. He struck him a solid blow with the edge of his hand at the base of the neck and literally threw him off the wall down onto the rocks on the breakwater. Jumping down after him, Gannon began binding and gagging him with tape. He had moved so quickly that his exposure had been limited to less than five seconds.

Pavlik was crouched on top of the seawall, above the guard standing in the shadows next to the transformer house. He dropped directly onto the unsuspecting man, his solid 220 pounds driving him to the ground. The guard's head had hit the cement quay with such force that he was already unconscious, but Pavlik, using a sap, hit him again for good measure before he dragged him behind the van and began taping him.

What little scuffling noise Gannon and Pavlik had made was not heard on the aft deck of the *Jameel.* The music was still playing, and the guard's attention was elsewhere.

"Oh," Maria said as they swayed together to the music. "You have such strong hands. You take me home with you, I kleen your house for a month, I chine your choose."

The guard laughed. He wrapped his arms tighter around her, his body moving with her. Maria let one of her hands slip from the man's neck down to his chest. "And such hard muscles," she said, letting her hand drop lower, into the open top of her shoulder bag. Removing the spring-loaded Syrette, she brought her hand back up slowly, then, without a moment's hesitation, jammed the needle into the base of the man's neck.

The powerful drug's reaction was nearly instantaneous. The full weight of the guard's 190 pounds slumped in her arms, knocked her off balance, and sent them both to the deck. Rolling out from underneath the inert body, she heard the sound of footsteps approaching across the boat deck directly above her.

She cursed silently. The boat-deck guard usually stayed forward, near the wheelhouse; he must have heard her come aboard. Thinking quickly, she grabbed the champagne bottle and stepped into the shadows beneath the companionway leading to the upper deck.

"Klaus?" a man's voice called out as he came down the steps. He saw his friend lying on the deck and knelt at his side.

Maria stepped from beneath the companionway and swung the champagne bottle with all her strength. There was a loud thud as the bottle struck the man's head and knocked him unconscious. Despite the dead weight of the two large men, she managed to drag them off to the side of the deck, out of view of anyone who entered the main salon.

In the guard's booth at the entrance gate, Maurer saw a flash of headlights along the public quay. A car was moving slowly, and as it drew closer Maurer saw it was the port police car. The head of a dog, a German shepherd, was sticking out the open rear window.

The local cop drew to a stop at the barrier and got out of the car, stretching muscles that were cramped from a long night behind the wheel. He opened the rear door, snapped on the dog's leash, and let him out. The big-boned German shepherd immediately lifted his leg and sprayed a rear tire. When the security guard didn't come out to talk with him, as was his custom, the cop walked around the barrier toward the booth. Seeing it was empty, he approached with caution, his hand on the grip of his holstered pistol.

Maurer stood in the dark against the wall, a few yards from the booth. He had his silenced pistol cocked and ready, pointed at the dog as opposed to the cop. The cop looked inside the booth and into the angry eyes of the now wide-awake security guard, bound and gagged on the floor. He spun around at the sound of his dog's half hearted bark.

Maurer, having grown up with dogs, read the animal's intentions correctly. He was not about to attack, if he was indeed even trained to do so. Closing fast on the cop, Maurer, a firm believer in the simplest methods being the most effective (and inclined to use his fist in settling most disputes), caught the cop with a perfectly executed left hook, followed by an overhand right, dispatching the inept man before his weapon cleared his holster. The dog barked once, then whimpered, licked his master's face, and lay down beside him, resting his head on his chest.

Maurer secured the cop with the roll of tape, offered the dog a candy bar, which he eagerly accepted, then went back to watching the entrance and the quay. A few moments later the dog sat at his side, nudging his hand, looking for another treat, which Maurer gave him.

At the opposite end of the quay Duggan swung up onto the seawall and, crouching low, sprinted across to the door leading to the upper-level observation deck of the *capitainerie*. The door was unlocked. He slipped inside and moved along the hallway toward the control room. The room was dark with the exception of the bluish-white light from six video monitors set in a console with a telephone and a toggle switch that when activated sent a direct signal to the local police.

The man sitting at the monitors had his back to Duggan. Removing a chloroform pad from its foil pouch, Duggan silently crossed the room to where the guard sat flipping through a nudist magazine in the dim light. He cupped the hand with the pad over the man's face and held it in place until he felt the body go limp. From the windows facing the quay he flashed a small penlight twice in the direction of the security van.

Gannon and Pavlik saw the signal and moved around to the side entrance door to the van. Gannon pulled the silenced 9mm pistol from his shoulder holster and stood out of sight as Pavlik knocked twice, paused, then knocked again.

When the van door handle turned, releasing the lock, Pavlik grabbed the door and flung it all the way open. Gannon rushed in, knocking the sleepy, dazed man before him into the opposite side of the van. He immediately scanned the rear of the vehicle for the second man. Pavlik jumped inside, closed the door behind him, and quickly held a chloroform pad to the face of the stunned man Gannon had sent sprawling.

Gannon found the second guard half asleep, swinging out of the bottom level of a double-decker bunk bed at the back of the van. He knelt before him, clamped a one-handed vise-like grip on the man's throat, and jammed the silencer on the 9mm automatic into his mouth.

"Which stateroom is the Russian in?" Gannon asked, wanting to confirm the information Sally had given him.

The man, now wide awake, said nothing.

"We can do this easy or we can do it hard," Gannon said. He cocked the hammer on the automatic. "I don't want your boss. Just tell me where the Russian is and you'll all walk away from this clean."

The guard hesitated, then nodded. Gannon took the gun from his mouth.

"The main guest stateroom. All the way aft." Sally's information had checked out.

"Take care of him," Gannon said to Pavlik, who had already begun stripping off pieces of tape with which to gag the guard. "Then keep an eye on the dock and the other yachts for any sign of unusual activity."

As Gannon headed for the door Pavlik put a hand on his shoulder. "If you aren't off that Abdul's tub within ten minutes, Boss, I'm calling in Maurer and Duggan and we're coming after you."

"It won't take me that long," Gannon said as he stepped over the man who had opened the door and went back out onto the quay.

Maria saw him coming and glanced inside the *Jameel*'s main salon, making certain the interior guard had not made an unexpected appearance. Gannon crossed over the gangway and went directly to the keypad, punching in the code Pavlik had given him. The status light went from red to green, indicating that the internal alarm system was disarmed.

"Good work," he said to Maria, glancing at the man she had crowned with the champagne bottle. He handed her one of the foil pouches containing a chloroform pad and gestured to the man, who was now beginning to stir. "Hold it over his face for about thirty seconds, then get out of here . . . fast."

Gannon quietly opened the door to the main salon and entered, picturing in his mind the simple sketch Sally had drawn of the stairwell that led to the main guest stateroom. He found it just aft of the main salon and slowly descended the thickly carpeted stairs. To the left and right at the bottom of the stairs were two staterooms bearing brass plaques identifying them as port and starboard guest staterooms. The main guest stateroom lay directly ahead at the end of the passageway.

Reaching the door, Gannon listened for a few moments, then, hearing nothing, drew his pistol and slowly turned the doorknob until it clicked. He carefully opened the door a few inches and peered inside. It was dark, but the nightlights on the stairwell and in the hallway cast a glow into the room, revealing a queen-sized bed with a human shape beneath the covers. The rush of air from the air-conditioning system was the only sound to be heard.

Behind the bed were decorative smoked-glass panels, and as Gannon inched the door open a little farther, a thin, humorless smile spread slowly across his face.

The stateroom being directly beneath the aft deck, Malik had undoubtedly heard the disturbance caused by Maria. His age-old tactic of arranging pillows beneath the covers to make it appear he was sleeping would have worked had it not been for the glass panels at the head of the bed. In their murky reflection Gannon could see Malik's outline behind the door, a pistol in his hand. Waiting.

Drawing himself up, Gannon put every ounce of his considerable strength into driving the door open and slamming it into the body behind it. He repeated it again and again with devastating speed and force. He finally entered the room, but kept his shoulder to the door, effectively pinning Malik to the bulkhead behind it as he did.

Once inside, his own pistol cocked and ready, he pulled the door closed. Malik dropped forward like a felled tree, unconscious, his nose broken and his face bloodied from the repeated impact of the row of solid-brass clothes hooks on the back of the door.

Gannon threw a shoulder into him and caught him at the waist as he fell. He carried him from the room and down the passageway toward the stairs. A sharp *click* made him freeze in position. To his right he saw the door to the starboard guest stateroom open and a sleep-filled Arab face appear.

A single, sharp blow to the temple from the barrel of Gannon's pistol sent the man reeling back into the room, where he crumpled onto the end of the bed. Gannon paused, listening for any movement in the stateroom across the hall, but its occupant was obviously a heavy sleeper.

Ascending the stairwell with Malik draped over his shoulder, Gannon reached the main deck only to stare into the barrel of an Uzi submachine gun as he entered the main salon. No doubt the owner had summoned the interior guard when he viewed the attack on Malik on the monitor in the master stateroom. A short, stocky Arab with a neatly trimmed beard, dressed in silk robe and pajamas, stood beside the armed German guard.

"Drop your weapon," the guard ordered.

Gannon stood motionless, his pistol pointed at the Arab, Malik hanging limply over his shoulder.

"Drop your weapon!" the guard shouted.

Gannon motioned with his head toward the Arab, keeping his eyes locked on the guard for the first sign that he was ready to fire. "I can kill him before you get off a shot," he told the nervous guard.

"And you will die," the guard said.

The tension in the room was such that no one noticed nor heard the door leading from the aft deck to the main salon click open. Maria entered and stood behind the guard. She placed the barrel of a Walther PPK pistol at the base of his skull.

"And so will you," Maria said, this time without her affected Spanish accent.

The guard stiffened, afraid to look behind him for fear of giving Gannon an opening.

The Arab studied Gannon's face. "How many of my men did you kill?"

"None," Gannon replied. "They'll all have headaches in the morning, that's it."

"It seems we have reached an impasse," the Arab said with a weak grin.

"No impasse," Gannon said. "I only want the Russian. Have your man here put down his weapon and we'll leave. No one has to get hurt."

The Arab shrugged. "I care nothing for the Russian. They will send another with whom I can make the same deal." Looking to his security guard, he said, "Do as he says."

The guard reluctantly dropped the Uzi. Maria immediately brought the barrel of the Walther down on the back of his head, knocking him unconscious.

"We made a deal," the Arab protested indignantly.

"I can't have you sounding any alarms until we're out of the area," he told the now frightened and angry man. "But I can assure you better treatment than him," he added, gesturing to the guard lying on the thick carpet. He placed his pistol inside his belt and tossed Maria another chloroform pad, which she opened and applied with no struggle from the Arab, gently lowering him to the deck as he passed out.

Gannon dropped Malik onto a sofa while he bound and gagged the Arab and the guard. He looked up at Maria, who was keeping watch on the interior hallway and the aft deck.

"I thought I told you to leave."

"And if I had, do you think you would have walked away from this?"

Gannon didn't answer her directly. "How'd you get that Walther into the country?"

Maria smiled and winked. "The customs officer's attention was on my swooping neckline, not the contents of my bags."

Gannon chuckled. "Like I said, Maria. You're a real charmer."

Hoisting Malik back onto his shoulder in a fireman's carry, Gannon followed Maria out onto the aft deck and down the gangway, where they moved quickly toward the *Mi Gaea*.

Sally Hooper opened the door to the *Mi Gaea*'s main salon with an audible sigh. "Thank God! I've been having conniptions." Her eyes fell on the bloodstained face of the man slung over Gannon's shoulder and she winced.

"That's him?" she said to Gannon. "The Russian?"

"That's him," Gannon replied.

General Max came forward from the bridge with Jacover and smiled at the sight of Gannon and his quarry. He gave him a pat on the back as he carried Malik down the hallway to one of the staterooms where Calvin Hardiment, the engineer, waited, shotgun in hand. Hardiment had been told that the Russian had killed Jim Boos as well as Gannon's wife. Boos had been his friend.

"I'll take great personal pride in watching over this one," Hardiment said. "Don't you worry about a thing."

"I want him alive when we reach our destination," Gannon told the hard-eyed engineer.

"Oh, and it's alive he'll be, sir," Hardiment said. "And if

he should try to escape, I'll use only the force necessary to subdue him."

Throwing Malik on the bed, Gannon left the room. Hardiment sat in a lounge chair opposite the bed, the shotgun pointed at Malik's head.

Back on the aft deck, Gannon took the small hand-held radio from his jacket pocket.

"All clear," was all he said into it.

"See you back at the Ranch, Boss," came Pavlik's reply. "Take good care of our boy. Out."

Returning to the main salon, Gannon and General Max proceeded to the bridge. Jacover, following General Max's earlier instructions, had had the crew ready the yacht for an unscheduled departure.

"I'm taking you at your word, General," Jacover said as he started the *Mi Gaea*'s engines. "There'll be no gunplay. The owner takes a dim view of bullet holes in his yacht."

"You have my word, Captain."

Gannon stepped outside and leaned on the railing, looking out to sea as the *Mi Gaea* got under way. In his heart he knew what he was doing was right, but his gut feeling, his more primal instincts, wanted him to go below and tear Malik apart a piece at a time.

46

Twenty-five miles off the coast of San Remo, Italy, the morning sun peered over the horizon, casting a shimmering orange glow across the gently rolling Mediterranean Sea.

Steve Jacover sat in the captain's chair, his eyes moving in a constantly sweeping arc as he maintained the course and speed General Max had requested. For the past half hour he had been tracking a blip on the radar screen that would shortly intersect the *Mi Gaea*. Then he saw it. Grabbing the binoculars, he focused on the distant object approaching them from the southeast. At first he couldn't believe what he was looking at, then he turned to General Max, who stood just outside the pilothouse, his eyes fixed on the same spot on the horizon.

"Is that what we're waiting for?" Jacover asked.

"That looks like her," General Max said.

"General," Jacover said, the incredulity heavy in his voice, "that ship is flying a Soviet flag. And if I'm right, she's an intelligence-collection vessel."

"You're right."

"Then correct me if I'm wrong," Jacover said, "but isn't the man we're holding captive a Russian KGB agent?"

General Max nodded. "Right again."

"You don't think that might upset them a little if they find out," Jacover said. "I don't mean to be an alarmist,

General, but that vessel has guns that can blow us clean out of the water, not to mention the surface-to-surface missiles she's carrying."

General Max smiled and stepped inside the pilothouse. "That's the last thing she wants to do," he told Jacover. "You'll have to trust me on this one."

Jacover shook his head and went back to the binoculars, watching the Soviet BAL'ZAM-class intelligence-collection ship steadily approaching, her decks and superstructure brimming with radomes and assorted signal-collection antennas. At 360 feet from stem to stern, she dwarfed the *Mi Gaea*. After receiving a coded message from Moscow she had left her station in the Adriatic Sea off the coast of Dubrovnik and immediately sailed toward the secret rendezvous with the luxury yacht.

"There'll be no radio contact," General Max said. "She'll come alongside and hold about thirty feet off your port side. They'll send a tender over to pick up our passenger."

"Are they coming aboard?" Jacover asked.

"No," General Max said. "Just lower your swim ladder and we'll send Malik down to them."

Jacover smiled and again shook his head in disbelief. " wish my boss could be here to see this."

"As he told you, it's got his stamp of approval," General Max said, having personally contacted the *Mi Gaea*'s owner after Gannon's call from Jamaica.

"No disrespect, General," Jacover said, "but if he hadn' told me I was to cooperate fully, I wouldn't be doing this. can guarantee you that."

General Max patted Jacover on the shoulder, then wen below to where Gannon was sitting on the aft deck talkin with Maria and Sally. They had also seen the huge Sovie ship approaching.

"It's time," General Max said.

Gannon had avoided going below since carrying Mali aboard for fear of breaking his prayerful promise to Kate

Malik was sitting upright on the bed, his nose and ey

wollen, his face streaked with dried blood. Gannon again
elt the overpowering urge to send Hardiment from the
oom and have Malik to himself.

"Unfortunately, Mr. Gannon," Hardiment said, rising
nd handing Gannon the shotgun, "our Russian friend has
een behaving himself. Not so much as a peep from him."

Gannon gave the shotgun back to Hardiment, still afraid
f what he might do in a moment of blind hatred. He took
Malik by the arm and led him up to the main deck and
orward to where General Max waited at the swim ladder
hat had just been set in place.

Hardiment followed, still holding the shotgun, hoping
gainst hope that the man who had killed Jim Boos would
ive him a reason to blow his head off.

Malik's battered face was impassive until he saw the So-
iet ship approaching off the port side. His eyes widened and
is head snapped in the direction of Gannon, then to Gen-
ral Max. The anxiety and fear he was feeling were quite
vident in his expression.

"You can't be serious about this?" he said to General Max
nd Gannon.

"Oh, but we are," General Max said. "Deadly serious."

"I can be invaluable to your Central Intelligence
gency."

"You have nothing we want, Mr. Malik."

"You're a fool if you believe that," Malik said, his eyes
ow fixed on the Soviet ship as she came alongside and kept
ace with the *Mi Gaea*. A large inflatable rubber boat with
n outboard motor was being lowered over her side and four
rmed GRU officers stood by ready to descend.

Resigned to his fate, Malik turned to Gannon. "I know
his man by reputation," he said, referring to General Max,
but who are you? I've seen you before. Where?"

Gannon was still struggling with the violent urges just
eneath the surface, but managed to remain calm. He didn't
nswer.

"Who are you?" Malik shouted.

Gannon didn't reply. He stared coldly at Malik, then fixed his eyes on the rubber boat as it reached the *Mi Gaea*. One of the GRU officers on board took hold of the swim ladder and looked up at the men standing at the top.

Gannon grabbed Malik by the scruff of the neck and forced him toward the first step on the ladder. Malik resisted.

"Do it on your own or I'll throw your ass overboard and they can fish you out of the water."

Malik glared at Gannon as he descended and was pulled into the rubber boat, which immediately cast off.

General Max's attention was on the Soviet ship. A tall, heavily built man stood on the forward deck. He wore the uniform of a Soviet Army general and was staring directly at General Max.

It had been years since General Max had seen the man, then a young GRU colonel, who had been one of his adversaries while stationed in Moscow. But he had no problem in recognizing the head of Soviet Military Intelligence. Though dressed in civilian clothes, General Max drew himself to attention and saluted the chief of the GRU.

General Vladimir Petrovich Antonov smiled broadly, drew himself to an equally correct posture of rigid attention and returned the salute. He held it until General Max lowered his hand, then disappeared inside the ship.

As the rubber boat pulled away from the *Mi Gaea*, porpoising through the gentle swells, Malik braced himself and stood up in the bow, shouting above the sound of the outboard engine:

"Who are you?"

Gannon turned away, returning to the aft deck, where he sat listening to Malik's repeated shouts growing fainter. Then there was nothing at all—only the sight of the GRU officers dragging Malik aboard, retrieving the rubber boat, and the huge ship moving steadily away to become a dot on the horizon, taking the rage inside Gannon with her.

* * *

A car, sent by the CIA's station chief at the American Embassy in Paris, had picked up General Max upon the *Mi Gaea*'s return to Antibes. Gannon had accepted Jacover's friendly invitation to stay on board for a few days to rest up. He had spent most of the time sleeping and lounging in the warm October sun on the boat deck. The *Jameel* was no longer in port, and the gossip among the crews and the locals was that there had been an attempted robbery aboard, but it had been successfully repelled by the *Jameel*'s security guards even though the criminals had escaped.

Gannon's plane back to the United States left from Nice in an hour, and a taxi was waiting for him at the entrance to the yacht club. He was at the head of the gangway, his carryall slung over his shoulder, when Maria came out onto the aft deck and stood beside him.

"You still haven't told me why you consented to turning that animal back over to his own people," she said. "He'll probably get nothing more than a slap on the wrist for what he did—or a few years in a labor camp at worst."

Gannon looked out across the quay, then turned back to Maria. Malik had killed a friend she had loved, she had a right to know.

"Kate hated violence," Gannon said softly. "I had no right to kill him in her name. It would have demeaned everything she believed in."

"But how could you just let him walk away like that?" Maria said. "Jim Boos was your friend, too, and I can assure you, he wouldn't have shown that bastard an ounce of mercy if Malik had killed you."

Gannon saw the pain and disappointment in Maria's eyes. "I think, in the end, both Kate and Jim will be satisfied," he told her.

"Would you care to explain that?"

"Malik was running operations for a faction of the KGB that was trying to overthrow Gorbachev," he said. "That faction, including the KGB chief and most of his cronies, has been ousted. Malik, however, is a sort of special case. He exceeded acceptable limits. Both the KGB and the GRU reserve a special treatment for those who have violated their oaths and disgraced their service. They use them as an object lesson for others."

"What?" Maria said. "Cleaning latrines at their training school?"

Gannon smiled and shook his head. "No. General Max told me about a building inside the top-secret GRU compound in Moscow. There are bleachers set up to hold a few hundred officers. There's also a blast furnace inside that building, with a specially constructed conveyer belt feeding into it. The man who is to be the object lesson for the hundreds of present and future intelligence officers in attendance is strapped naked onto the belt and fed feet first into the furnace, an inch at a time. I've been told it is one of the most gruesome, painful deaths imaginable."

Maria said nothing at first, repulsed by the image that had formed in her mind, then a smile spread slowly across her face. "Jim would have liked that."

"Kate wouldn't," Gannon said. "But then I won't have a hand in it, will I?"

Maria embraced Gannon, kissing him on the cheek. "You take care of yourself."

"I'll do that," Gannon said. As he walked toward the taxi waiting at the entrance barrier, he heard Maria call out from the aft deck and turned to look back.

"Hey, Gannon! Maybe I'll stop at Fort Bragg and pay you a visit on my way back to Jamaica." With a broad wink and a stunning smile, she added, "I kleen your house for a month. I chine your choose."

Gannon laughed and waved as he climbed into the waiting taxi.

EPILOGUE

Lieutenant Bill Rafferty shoved a stack of files off to one side of his desk and propped his feet up on the edge. He rubbed his tired eyes, red and sore from the city grit, and glanced at his watch. It was six o'clock and he was again going to be late getting home. So what else is new? he thought as he arched his back and stretched his arms over his head. It had been a long and trying day.

Jack Gannon entered the Nineteenth Precinct station house and stopped at the tall desk. A sergeant shouted above a domestic argument the cops were trying to get under control and told Gannon that Rafferty was in his office in the detective squad room. Two of the detectives pecking away on typewriters looked up and nodded to Gannon as he stood at the entrance to the crowded, noisy room. They recognized him from three weeks ago when he had laid into the Soviets.

"You looking for the lieutenant?" one of the detectives asked.

"Yeah," Gannon said.

"Hey, Lou," the sergeant yelled, calling Rafferty by the diminutive used throughout the department for lieutenants. "You got company."

Rafferty opened his eyes and swung his feet off the desk as Gannon entered his office.

"Hey, Gannon. How you doin'?" His cop eyes made a quick appraisal. "Got yourself a nice tan. Been on vacation?"

"Sort of," Gannon said. "I'm on my way back to Fort Bragg from France. My connecting flight to Charlotte isn't until tomorrow morning. Thought I'd stop in and say hello."

"Glad you did," Rafferty said. "I've thought about you every now and then. It's good to see you're working it out. Little vacation time, trip to France never hurt, huh?"

"I thought I might treat you to a nice dinner," Gannon said. "You pick the restaurant."

"You're on," Rafferty said. "I know this great Italian restaurant over in Brooklyn, wiseguy place. Best pasta you ever ate. Let me give my wife a call and we're outta here."

Gannon watched the activity in the squad room as Rafferty made his call. The cage at the back of the room was filled to capacity with an assortment of unsavory types—one demanding to see his lawyer, another sitting in a corner, knees drawn up to his chest and shaking uncontrollably. A huge detective with massive hands nodded to Gannon; it was the one who had shoved the black kid back into the chair during the fight. Gannon smiled and nodded back.

"So," Rafferty said as he slipped on his overcoat and stepped out of the office. "How was France?"

"To tell you the truth," Gannon said, "I didn't see much of it. Mostly Antibes."

"Never heard of it," Rafferty said. "What's there?"

"An old friend of ours was there," Gannon said with a grin.

Rafferty stopped walking and held Gannon's gaze. "You got the son of a bitch, didn't you? You got the slime-ball."

Gannon nodded and smiled.

"Hey!" Rafferty shouted to the room at large, drawing the attention of everyone in it. "You guys remember the Gannon case? Well, the good guys finally won one."

"All right!" one of the detectives shouted, accompanied

by "Fuck them where they live" and a variety of other remarks that were followed by a few congratulatory pats on the back.

"I hope the bastard burns in hell," Rafferty said.

"That's more of an appropriate analogy than you might think," Gannon replied.

Rafferty put an arm around Gannon's shoulder and escorted him out of the room and down the hallway past the tall desk. "Feels good, huh? So tell me all about it."

"If I tell you, I've got to kill you," Gannon said with a grin.

Rafferty laughed. "Hey, fuck you, Gannon. I'm a squad commander in the NYPD. This is my fuckin' city, and I got the gun. Now I want to hear every last detail."

"You got it," Gannon said.

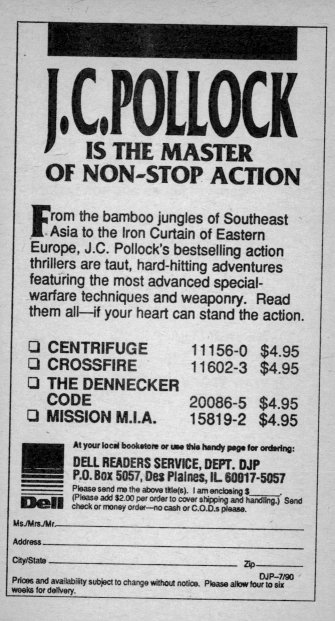